Milan Kundera was born in Czechoslovakia. He worked as a labourer, then as a jazz musician and finally ended up devoting himself to literature. For several years he was a professor at the Prague Institute for Advanced Cinematographic Studies, where his students were the creators of the Czech New Wave in film.

After the Russian invasion in 1968, he lost his post and saw all his books removed from the public libraries in his country. In 1975 he settled in France, and in 1979 the Czech government, responding to the publication of *The Book of Laughter and Forgetting* (1979; Penguin, 1982), revoked his Czech citizenship.

The Joke, his first novel, and his collection of stories, *Laughable Loves*, appeared in print in Prague before 1968. His other novels have not been allowed publication in his homeland. *Life is Elsewhere* won the Prix Médicis for the best foreign novel published in France in 1973, and *The Farewell Party* (1976) won a similar prize, the Premio Mondello, for the best foreign novel published in Italy in 1978. In 1981 he was awarded the American Prize 'Commonwealth Award' for all his work. His latest novel is *The Unbearable Lightness of Being* (1984). His most recent book is a work of non-fiction, *The Art of the Novel* (1988).

Kundera now lives in Paris as a French citizen. He writes in both Czech and French.

MILAN KUNDERA

THE JOKE

TRANSLATED FROM THE CZECH BY
MICHAEL HENRY HEIM

PENGUIN BOOKS

PENGUIN BOOKS

Published by the Penguin Group
27 Wrights Lane, London W8 5TZ, England
Viking Penguin Inc., 40 West 23rd Street, New York, New York 10010, USA
Penguin Books Australia Ltd, Ringwood, Victoria, Australia
Penguin Books Canada Ltd, 2801 John Street, Markham, Ontario, Canada L3R 1B4
Penguin Books (NZ) Ltd, 182–190 Wairau Road, Auckland 10, New Zealand

Penguin Books Ltd, Registered Offices: Harmondsworth, Middlesex, England

First published in Czechoslovakia under the title Zert 1967
Published in Penguin Books 1970
This English translation first published in the USA by Harper & Row, Publishers, Inc. 1982
First published in Great Britain by Faber & Faber Ltd 1983
Published in Penguin Books 1984
9 10

Made and printed in Great Britain by
Richard Clay Ltd, Bungay, Suffolk
Set in Century Schoolbook

AUTHOR'S PREFACE

When in 1980, during a television panel discussion devoted to my works, someone called *The Joke* "a major indictment of Stalinism," I was quick to interject, "Spare me your Stalinism, please. *The Joke* is a love story!"

I began writing it back in 1962, when I was thirty-three, and the spark that started me off was an event in a small Czech town: the arrest of a girl for stealing flowers from a cemetery and offering them to her lover as a gift. As I thought it over, a character took shape before my eyes, the character of Lucie, for whom sexuality and love are two completely different, irreconcilable things. Her story then came together in my mind with the story of a male character, the character of Ludvik, who concentrates all the hatred he has accumulated during his life in a single act of love. And that is *The Joke*: a melancholy duet about the schism between body and soul.

The plot of *The Joke* is itself a joke. And not only its plot. Its "philosophy" as well: man, caught in the trap of a joke, suffers a personal catastrophe which, seen from without, is ludicrous. His tragedy lies in the fact that the joke has deprived him of the right to tragedy. He is condemned to triviality. The mourning with which the Helena story ends is of a different weave from the mourning that becomes Electra.

But if a character is condemned to triviality in his private life, can he escape to the stage of history? No. I have always been convinced that the paradoxes of history and private life have the same basic properties: Helena ends up in the hoax of the trap Ludvik has set for her; Ludvik and all the others end up in the trap of the joke history has played on them: lured on by the voice of utopia, they have squeezed their way through the gates of paradise only to find, when the doors slam shut behind them, that they are in hell. Those are the times that give me the feeling history enjoys a good laugh.

If a man loses the paradise of the future, he still has the paradise of the past, paradise lost. From childhood I have been fascinated by the folk tradition called the Ride of the Kings: a singularly beautiful ceremony whose meaning has long been lost and which survives only as a string of obscure gestures. This rite frames the action of the novel; it is a frame of forgetting. Yesterday's action is obscured by today, and the strongest link binding us to a life constantly eaten away by forgetting is nostalgia. Remorseful nostalgia and remorseless skepticism are the two pans of the scales that give the novel its equilibrium.

I presented the manuscript of *The Joke* to the editors of a Prague publishing house in December 1965, and though they promised to do their best to bring it out, they never really believed they would succeed. The spirit of the work was diametrically opposed to the official ideology. Yet *The Joke* did come out two years later—and without a trace of censorship! How was that possible in Communist Czechoslovakia one year before the Prague Spring?

By today that state of affairs has also become obscure, the dissolution of Stalinism in Central Europe difficult to explain. Russian Communism (no other has existed in Czechoslovakia) was so completely foreign to Central European (Polish, Hungarian, Czech) traditions that the large majority of people spontaneously rejected it. Behind the Communist façade a gradual liberalization process took place, a process that saw the creation (in spite of the official ideology, which no one could question but no one took seriously) of many outstanding films, plays, and works of literature.

Three editions of *The Joke* appeared in quick succession and incredibly large printings, and each sold out in a matter of days, as though people realized the moment of freedom would be short. It was. The Russians could not tolerate a free atmosphere in a country that since 1948 they had considered their *gubernia*, and in 1968 they launched a military invasion of Czechoslovakia. Immediately thereafter *The Joke* (together with many other books) was banned, removed from all public libraries, erased from the history of Czech literature; its author was named in official documents as one of the initiators of the "counterrevolution," deprived of the right to work, and finally forced to emigrate.

Two months after Russian troops occupied Czechoslovakia with the kind consent of the entire world (the American government issued a single sharp protest—when Russian soldiers were caught picking pears in the garden of its embassy), *The Joke* was published in Paris with a foreword by Louis Aragon, who called the book "one of the greatest novels of the century." The foreword, which created a worldwide sensation, is another aspect of the paradoxical fate of the book. Aragon is not merely a famous figure in the surrealist movement and a great novelist but also a member of the Central Committee of the French Communist Party, its untouchable demiurge.

I remember meeting him during my stay in Paris in the autumn of 1968. He was entertaining two guests from Moscow, friends of Sakharov's, when I arrived. They were trying to persuade him to maintain his contacts with the Soviet Union. Incensed, irate over the Russian invasion of Czechoslovakia, Aragon told them pointblank that he would never again set foot on Russian soil. "Even if I wanted to, my legs would refuse," he said, pacing the floor like a character from a Corneille tragedy pacing the boards of the Comédie Française. I admired him. Four years later his legs consented to take him to Moscow to receive a decoration from Brezhnev; fourteen years later they took him up to the tribune of the French Communist Party congress that condoned both the atrocities in Afghanistan and the enslavement of Poland. And yet the very same Aragon wrote what is probably the most eloquent and penetrating piece anyone has written on the Russian invasion of Czechoslovakia: his foreword to *The Joke*

"Some day the mythographers who assume the name of historians will write their version of the history of Czechoslovakia . . . and we may be sure that they will write it through the eyes of the victors. . . . People will not find the true explanation of what we have witnessed." And a few pages later: "*O mes amis,* is everything lost?" And farther on: "I refuse to believe that a Biafra of the spirit is in the offing. Yet I see no light at the end of the path of violence."

At first reading I found the pessimism of these words a bit exaggerated. I still maintained the naïve democratic illusion (Americans know it well) that no force can withstand the will of the people. But Aragon knew both Communism and Russia better than I. He knew whereof he spoke. He knew the ways of totalitarian power. He knew the power of its mythographers, their ability to organize forgetting ("people will not find the true explanation of what we have witnessed"). He knew that if culture is massacred in a "Biafra of the spirit" (let me remind those who find the metaphor abstruse that Biafra was then the scene of African tribal genocide), there will be "no light at the end of the path of violence."

What Aragon knew then—and what he no longer wished to know later—was something the rest of the world did not see. De Gaulle's government regarded the attack on Czechoslovakia as nothing more than a localized spat "within the Communist family." As if a "family" were what was at stake! What was actually at stake behind the smokescreen of political terminology (revolution, counterrevolution, socialism, imperialism, and so on, and so forth) was nothing less than a shift in the borders between two civilizations: the Russian imperium had once and for all conquered a piece of the West, a piece of Europe, the better to watch it founder, together with the other countries of Central Europe, in its own civilization. (The fact that the countries in question have belonged to the history of the West for six or seven centuries longer than the United States has been forgotten.) That is what Aragon called the "Biafra of the spirit." Some day Russian mythographers will write about it as a new dawn of history. I see it (rightly or wrongly) as the beginning of Europe's end.

In 1968 and 1969 *The Joke* appeared not only in French, but in all the languages of European countries not occupied by Russia, and Japanese and Hebrew as well. It also appeared in Polish, conditions in Poland being as liberal as in Czechoslovakia before 1968, and the Hungarian translation, though banned as it came off the press in September 1968 and therefore never officially distributed, has circulated clandestinely and is well known in Hungarian intellectual circles.

It also appeared in English. I was appalled by the British edition. The number of chapters was different; the order of chapters was different; a number of passages were omitted. I published a letter of protest in *The Times Literary Supplement* requesting readers not to accept the English version of *The Joke* as my novel; the publisher apologized and authorized a paperback edition which restored the order of the chapters. At about the same time, the British translation was published in New York—but even more simplified, more mutilated! I was powerless. Contact with the outside world was becoming more and more difficult in occupied Prague, and what with house searches and arrests, I had other things to worry about. I had no idea that a young American professor of literature, indignant at the mutilation of *The Joke*, had translated the most important of the omitted passages and published them in an American journal.

When Goethe was working on *Wilhelm Meister*, he allowed his secretary Riemer to read proof for him and strike out a superfluous word or touch up a phrase here or there, though he would never have entrusted his poetry to him. In Goethe's time prose could not make the aesthetic claims of poetry; perhaps not until the work of Flaubert did prose lose the stigma of aesthetic inferiority. Ever since *Madame Bovary*, the art of the novel has been considered equal to the art of poetry, and the novelist (any novelist worthy of the name) endows every word of his prose with the uniqueness of the word in a poem.

Once prose makes such a claim, the translation of a novel becomes a true art. A novelist whose works are banned in his own country is doubly conscious of the difficulties involved. Three years ago, returning to the original French translation of *The Joke*, I discovered that its style did not resemble mine, and I reworked it completely myself, taking advantage of the occasion to introduce some modifications in my original text. *The Joke* is also appearing in new translations in Italy and Spain, and now the same professor of literature who ten years ago published the material omitted from the English edition has done the first valid and authentic version of a book that tells of rape and has itself so often been violated.

Habent sua fata libelli. Books have their fates. The fate of the book called *The Joke* coincided with a time when the combined inanity of ideological dictatorship (in the Communist countries) and journalistic oversimplification (in the West) was able to prevent a work of art from telling its own truth in its own words. The ideologues in Prague took *The Joke* for a pamphlet against socialism and banned it; the foreign publisher took it for a political fantasy that became reality for a few weeks and rewrote it accordingly.

Today, in a world of ever accelerating forgetting, Prague has long since lost its topicality. Surely no one at the American Embassy there has an inkling that Russian soldiers stole pears from the garden fourteen years ago. Yet only thanks to that forgetting (and here we have the final paradox of *The Joke*) can the novel ultimately be what it has always meant to be: *merely* a novel.

June 1982

CONTENTS

THE JOKE

PART ONE

So here I was, home again after all those years. Standing in the main square (which I'd crossed countless times in my childhood, boyhood, and youth), I felt no emotion whatsoever; all I could think was that the flat space, with the spire of its town hall (like a soldier in an ancient helmet) rising above the rooftops, looked like a huge parade ground and that the military past of the Moravian town, once a bastion against Magyar and Turk invaders, had engraved a set of irrevocably hideous features on its face.

For years there had been nothing to attract me; I'd told myself I had no feeling left for the place, which seemed perfectly natural: I'd been away for fifteen years, I had almost no friends or acquaintances left (and wished to avoid the ones I did have), and my mother was buried among strangers in a grave I had never tended. But I'd been deceiving myself: what I'd called indifference was in fact aversion; the motivations for it had escaped me, because here as elsewhere I had had both good and bad experiences, but there it was; and it was this trip that had made me conscious of it: the mission that had brought me here could easily have been accomplished in Prague, and if I suddenly felt irresistibly drawn to the prospect of seeing it through here in my hometown, it was because the whole idea was so cynical and base as to make a mockery of any suspicion that I had come out of any maudlin attachment to things past.

I gave the unsightly square a final sardonic glance and, turning my back on it, set off for the hotel where I had booked a room for the night. The porter handed me a key hanging from a wooden pear and said, "Second floor." The room was not exactly attractive: a bed along one wall, a small table and chair in the middle, an ostentatious mahogany chest of drawers cum mirror next to the bed, and a minuscule cracked washbasin by the door. I put my briefcase down on the table and opened the window: it looked out onto a courtyard and the bare grubby backs of neighboring buildings. I closed the window, drew the curtains, and went over to the washbasin, which had two taps—one blue, the other red; I turned them on; cold water trickled out of both. I looked over at the table, which wasn't all that bad; at least it had room for a bottle and two glasses; the trouble was, only one person could sit at it: there was only one chair. I pushed the table up to the bed and tried sitting at it, but the bed was too low and the table too high; besides, the bed sank so low under my weight that I realized right away it was not only unsatisfactory as a seat, but equally unlikely to perform its function as a bed. I leaned down on it with my fists, then lay down on it, carefully lifting my legs so as not to dirty the blanket. The bed sagged so much I felt I was in a hammock. It was impossible to imagine anyone sharing the bed with me.

I sat down on the chair and, staring up at the transparent curtains, began to turn things over in my mind. Just then the sound of steps and voices penetrated the room from the corridor; two people, a man and a woman, were having a conversation, and I could understand their every word: it was about a boy named Petr who'd run away from home and his Aunt Klara, who was a fool and spoiled the boy. Then a key turned in a lock, a door opened, and the voices went on talking in the next room; I heard the woman sighing (yes, even her sighs were audible!) and the man resolving to give Klara a piece of his mind once and for all.

By the time I stood up, my decision was firm; I washed my hands in the basin, dried them on the towel, and left the hotel, though I had no clear idea of where to go. All I knew was that if I didn't wish to jeopardize the success of my journey (my long, arduous journey), I would have no choice, much as I hated the idea, but to ask a discreet favor of a local acquaintance. I ran through all the old faces from my youth, rejecting each in turn, if only because the confidential nature of the service to be rendered would require me to bridge the gap, account for my long years of absence—something I had no desire to do. But then I remembered someone else, a newcomer, a man whom I'd helped to find a job and who would be only too glad, if I knew him at all, to repay one good turn with another. He was a strange character, both scrupulously moral and oddly unsettled, unstable, whose wife, as far as I could tell, had divorced him years before for living anywhere and everywhere but with her and their son. I was a little nervous: if he had remarried, it would complicate matters considerably; I walked as fast as I could in the direction of the hospital.

The local hospital was a complex of buildings and pavilions scattered over a large landscaped area; I went into the booth at the gate and asked the guard to connect me with Virology; he shoved the telephone over to the edge of his desk and said, "02." I dialed 02, only to learn that Dr. Kostka had just left and was on his way out. I sat down on a bench near the gate so I couldn't miss him, and watched the men wandering here and there in blue-and-white-striped hospital gowns. Then I saw him: he was walking along deep in thought, tall, thin, attractively unattractive; yes, that was Kostka, all right. I stood up and headed straight towards him, as if meaning to bump into him; first he gave me an irritated look, but then he recognized me and opened his arms. I had the feeling he was more pleasantly than unpleasantly surprised, and the spontaneity of his welcome was quite encouraging.

I explained I'd arrived less than an hour before and was here on some unimportant business that would last two or three days; he immediately told me how surprised and gratified he was that my first thought had been to come to see him. Suddenly I felt bad about having an ulterior motive and asking my question (I put it jovially: "Well? Remarried?") out of calculation rather than genuine interest. He told me (to my relief) that he was still on his own. I suggested we had a lot to catch up on. He agreed and regretted that he had only a little over an hour before he was due back at the hospital and in the evening he was leaving town. "You mean you don't live here?" I asked in dismay. He assured me that he did, that he had a bachelor flat in a new complex, but that "it's no good living alone." It turned out that Kostka had a fiancée in another town fifteen miles away, a schoolteacher with a two-room flat of her own. "So you'll be moving in with her eventually?" I asked. He said he was unlikely to find as interesting a job there as the one I had helped him to find and his fiancée would have trouble finding a job here. I began (quite sincerely) to curse the ineptitude of a bureaucracy unable to arrange for a man and woman to live together. "Calm down, Ludvik," he said with gentle indulgence. "It's not so bad as all that. Traveling back and forth does cost time and money, but I keep my privacy intact—and my freedom." "Why is your freedom so important to you?" I asked him. "And why is your freedom so important to *you*?" he countered. "I'm a ladies' man," I replied. "I don't need freedom for women," he said. "I need it for myself. Say, how about coming over to my place until I have to leave?" I couldn't have wished for anything better.

Soon after leaving the hospital grounds, we came to a group of buildings jutting up fitfully one after the next from an unleveled, dust-laden plot of land (without lawns, paths, or roads) and forming a pitiful screen between the town and the flat, open fields in the distance. We went in one of the doors and climbed a narrow staircase (the elevator was out of order) to the third floor, where I saw Kostka's card. As we walked from the entrance hall into the main room, I was pleased to see a wide, comfortable daybed in the corner along with a table, an easy chair, a large collection of books, a record player, and a radio.

I praised the setup and asked about the bathroom. "Nothing luxurious," said Kostka, pleased by my interest. He took me back to the entrance hall and opened a door to a small but pleasant bathroom complete with tub, shower, and washbasin. "Seeing this attractive place of yours has given me an idea," I said. "What are you doing tomorrow afternoon and evening?" "Unfortunately I have to work late tomorrow," he answered apologetically. "I won't be back until seven or so. Are you free in the evening?" "Possibly," I answered, "but do you think you could lend me the place for the afternoon?"

My question surprised him, but immediately (as if worried I might think him unwilling) he replied, "I'd be only too glad to share it with you." Then, deliberately trying to avoid guessing my plans, he added, "And if you need a place to sleep tonight, you're welcome to stay here. I won't be back until morning. No, not even then. I'll be going straight to the hospital." "No, there's no need. I have a room at the hotel. The thing is, the hotel room isn't very pleasant, and tomorrow afternoon I need a pleasant atmosphere. Not just for myself, of course." "Of course," said Kostka, lowering his eyes. "I thought as much." He paused, then added, "I'm glad to be able to do you a favor." And after another pause: "Providing it really is a favor."

Then we sat down at the table (Kostka had made coffee) and had a short chat (I tested the daybed and found to my delight that it was firm and neither sagged nor creaked). Before long Kostka announced it was time for him to be getting back to the hospital and quickly initiated me into the major mysteries of the household: the taps in the bathtub needed extra tightening, contrary to generally accepted procedure hot water was available exclusively from the tap marked C, the socket for the radio was hidden under the daybed, and there was a newly opened bottle of vodka in the cupboard. He gave me two keys on a ring and showed me which one opened the main door of the building and which one opened his flat. During a lifetime of switching beds I'd developed a personal cult of keys, and I slipped Kostka's into my pocket with silent glee.

On our way out Kostka expressed the hope that his flat would be the basis of "something really beautiful." "Yes," I said, "it will help me to do a beautiful demolition job." "So you think destruction can be beautiful," said Kostka, and I smiled inwardly, recognizing in his response (delivered nonchalantly, but conceived as a challenge) the Kostka I had first met more than fifteen years before. Although I liked him, I also found him a bit laughable, and so I replied, "I know you're a quiet workman on God's eternal construction site and don't like hearing about demolition jobs; but what can I do? I'm just not one of God's masons. Now, if God's masons built real walls, I doubt we'd be able to destroy them. But instead of walls all I see is backdrops, sets. And sets are made to be destroyed."

Which brought us back to where (some nine years before) we had parted ways. This time, however, our quarrel had a decidedly abstract cast to it: we were well aware of its concrete foundations and did not feel the need to reiterate them. All we needed was to note how little we'd changed, how similarly unlike each other we'd remained (though I must say, it was our differences that endeared him to me and made me enjoy our arguments; I used them as a touchstone of who *I* was and what *I* thought). But to clarify his position unequivocally, he replied, "That's all well and good, but tell me, how can a skeptic like you be so sure he knows how to tell a set from a wall? Haven't you ever doubted that the illusions you ridicule *are* illusions? What if you're wrong? What if it's genuine values you're so busy destroying?" And then: "A value debased and an illusion unmasked have the same pitiful shell. They are identical. There is nothing easier than to take one for the other."

I walked Kostka back through town to the hospital, playing with the keys in my pocket and thinking how good it felt to be back with an old friend willing to argue me over to his truth anytime, anyplace, even here and now on our way across the bumpy surface of a new housing complex. Since Kostka knew we had all the following evening to look forward to, he allowed himself the luxury of turning from philosophizing to more mundane affairs: he wanted to make sure I would wait for him until he came back at seven the next day (he didn't have another set of keys) and asked me whether there was really nothing else I needed. I put my hand up to my face and said, "Just a trip to the barber's," because it felt disagreeably stubbly. "Leave it to me," said Kostka. "I'll see you get a first-rate shave."

I accepted Kostka's patronage and let him take me to a small barbershop with three large revolving chairs towering before three mirrors. Two of the chairs were occupied by men with heads bent back and faces covered with soap; two women in white smocks were leaning over them. Kostka went up to one of them and whispered something in her ear, and the woman wiped her razor on a cloth, called something to the back of the shop, and out came another girl in white. The new girl took over the abandoned gentleman, while the woman Kostka had talked to nodded to me and motioned me to the remaining chair. Kostka and I shook hands, and as he left, I took my place in the chair, leaning my head back against the headrest. Since many years of experience had taught me not to look at my own face, I avoided the mirror directly opposite me and raised my eyes, letting them wander over the blotchy white ceiling.

I kept my eyes on the ceiling even after I felt the girl's fingers tucking the white sheet into my shirt collar. Then she stepped back, and all I could hear was the sound of the razor sliding up and down the leather strap. I sank into a kind of blissful lethargy. Feeling her wet, slippery fingers smearing soap over my face, I mused at how strange and laughable it was to be caressed so tenderly by an unknown woman who meant nothing to me and to whom I meant nothing. Then (since the mind, even when at rest, never stops playing its tricks) I fantasized I was a defenseless victim entirely at the mercy of the woman with the razor. And because my body had dissolved in space and all I could feel was the touch of her fingers on my face, I fantasized that the gentle hands holding (turning, stroking) my head did so as if it were unattached to my body, as if it existed independently and the sharp razor waiting on the nearby table were there merely to consummate that independence.

Then the caressing stopped, and when I heard the girl step back and actually pick up the razor, I said to myself (since my mind had not stopped playing its tricks) I absolutely had to see what she looked like, this keeper (custodian) of my head, my tender assassin. I looked down from the ceiling into the mirror and felt a chill run up my spine: the game I was playing had suddenly, uncannily taken a turn towards reality; the woman leaning over me in the mirror—I thought I knew her.

She was holding my earlobe with one hand and carefully scraping the soap off my face with the other; as I watched her work, the likeness that had so astonished me a minute before began slowly to dissolve and disappear. She leaned down over the basin, slid two fingers along the razor to remove the foam, straightened up again, and gave the chair a gentle turn; again our eyes met for an instant, and again I thought I knew her. True, the face was somewhat different, an older sister's face: grayed, faded, slightly sunken; but then I hadn't seen her for fifteen years! During that period, time had superimposed a mask on her true face, but fortunately the mask came with two holes that allowed her real eyes, her true eyes, to shine through, and they were just as I had known them.

Then the trail became muddled again: a new customer came in and sat down behind me to wait his turn; he struck up a conversation with my girl, going on about the fine summer we were having and the swimming pool they were building outside of town; when she responded (I paid more attention to her intonation than to her words, which were of no significance), I was certain I didn't recognize the voice; it sounded matter-of-fact, casual, nonchalant, almost coarse; it was the voice of a stranger.

By that time she was washing off my face, pressing it between her palms, and (in spite of the voice) I began to believe once more that I knew her, that after fifteen years here she was, caressing me again, caressing me with long gentle strokes (I had completely forgotten she was washing, not caressing me). Her stranger's voice babbled away to the talkative customer, but I refused to believe it; I wanted to believe her hands, to recognize her by her hands; I wanted the degree of tenderness in her touch to determine whether I knew her, whether she recognized me.

She took a towel and dried my face. The talkative customer was laughing loudly at one of his own jokes, and I noticed that my girl had not joined in. In other words, she probably hadn't heard a word he'd said. That excited me: I took it as proof she'd recognized me and was shaken by it. I decided to say something to her as soon as I got out of the chair. She pulled the cloth from my neck. I stood up. I dug into my breast pocket for a five-crown note. I waited for our eyes to meet so I could call her by her name (the customer was still going on about something), but she kept her head turned away from me and took the money so briskly and impersonally that I suddenly felt like a madman fallen prey to his own hallucinations and could not find the courage to say anything to her.

I left the barbershop feeling oddly frustrated. All I knew was that I knew nothing and that failing to recognize a face once dearly loved was a sign of great *callousness*.

I hurried back to the hotel (on the way I caught a glimpse of an old friend, Jaroslav, first fiddle of our folk ensemble, but avoided his eyes as if fleeing his loud, insistent music) and phoned Kostka. He was still at the hospital.

"That girl you had shave me—could her name be Lucie Sebetka?"

"She goes under a different name now, but that's who she is. Where do you know her from?" asked Kostka.

"Oh, it's been ages," I answered, and not even thinking about dinner, I left the hotel again (it was getting dark) and set off wandering through the town.

PART TWO

═══════

1

Tonight I'm going to bed early, I may not fall asleep, but I'm going to bed early, Pavel left for Bratislava this afternoon, I'll fly to Brno early tomorrow morning and go the rest of the way by bus, little Zdena will have to be on her own for two days, she won't mind, she doesn't care much for our company anyway, at least not mine, she worships Pavel, Pavel is the first man in her life, he knows how to handle her, he knows how to handle all women, knew how to handle me, still does, this week he was his old self again, stroking my face and promising to stop off for me in Moravia on his way back from Bratislava, he said it was time we started talking things over, he must have realized we couldn't go on like this, I hope he wants it to be the way it was before, but why did he have to wait until now, now that I've met Ludvik? Oh, the pain of it all, but no, I mustn't give in to melancholy, *may melancholy never taint my name,* as Fucik said, his words are my motto, even when they tortured him, even in the shadow of the gallows Fucik never lost heart, and what do I care if he's out of fashion nowadays, maybe I'm just an idiot, but they're idiots too with their fashionable skepticism, why shouldn't I trade my idiocy for theirs, I don't want to split my life down the middle, I want it to be one from beginning to end, that's why I'm so wild about

Ludvik, when I'm with him I don't have to alter my ideals and tastes, he's so normal, straightforward, cheerful, definite about everything, that's what I love, that's what I've always loved.

I'm not ashamed of the way I am, I can't be anything but what I've always been, until I was eighteen all I knew of life was the well-ordered flat of a well-ordered bourgeois clan and schoolwork, schoolwork, schoolwork, I was as isolated from the real world as I could be, and when I arrived in Prague in forty-nine it was like a miracle, I was so happy, I'll never forget it, and that's why I can never erase Pavel from my heart, even though I don't love him anymore, even though he's hurt me, no, I can't, Pavel is my youth, Prague, the university, the dormitory, and most of all the Fucik Song and Dance Ensemble, nowadays no one knows what it meant to us, that's where I met Pavel, he sang tenor, I sang alto, we gave hundreds of concerts and demonstrations, we sang Soviet songs and our own socialist-construction songs and of course folk songs, we liked those the best, I fell so in love with Moravian folk songs they became the leitmotiv of my existence.

As for how I fell in love with Pavel, I could never tell anyone today, it was like a fairy tale, the anniversary of the Liberation, a big demonstration in Old Town Square, our ensemble was there too, we went everywhere together, a handful of people among tens of thousands, and up on the rostrum sat all kinds of important statesmen, Czech and foreign, and there were all kinds of speeches and applause, and then Togliatti himself went up to the microphone and said a few words in Italian, and the whole square responded as usual by shouting and clapping and chanting slogans. Pavel happened to be standing next to me in the crush, and I heard him shouting something of his own into the general hubbub, something different, and when I looked over at his lips, I realized he was singing, or rather screaming, a song, he was trying to get us to hear him and join him, he was singing an Italian revolutionary song that was in our repertory and very popular at the time: *Avanti popolo, a la riscossa, bandiera rossa, bandiera rossa . . .*

That was Pavel all over, he was never satisfied with reaching the mind alone, he had to get at the emotions, wasn't it wonderful,

I thought, saluting the leader of the Italian workers' movement in a Prague square with an Italian revolutionary song, I wanted more than anything for Togliatti to be moved the way I was, so I joined in with Pavel as loud as I could, and others joined us and others and others, until finally the whole ensemble was singing, but the shouting was terribly loud and we were no more than a handful, there were fifty of us to at least fifty thousand of them, the odds were overwhelming, but we fought a desperate fight, for the whole first stanza we thought we wouldn't make it and our singing would go unheard, but then a miracle occurred, little by little more voices broke into song, people began to realize what was going on, and the song rose up slowly out of the pandemonium in the square like a butterfly emerging from an enormous rumbling chrysalis. And finally that butterfly, that song, or at least the last few bars, flew up to the rostrum, and we gazed eagerly at the face of the graying Italian, and we were happy when we thought we saw him respond to the song with a wave of the hand, and I was certain, even though I was too far away to tell, I was certain I saw tears in his eyes.

And in the midst of all the enthusiasm and emotion, I don't know how it happened, I suddenly seized Pavel's hand, and he squeezed mine, and when things died down and another speaker stepped up to the microphone, I was afraid he'd let go, but he didn't, we held hands all the way to the end of the demonstration and didn't let go even afterwards, the crowds broke up, and we spent several hours together roaming through Prague in all its spring finery.

Seven years later, when little Zdena was five, I'll never forget it, he told me *we didn't marry for love, we married out of Party discipline,* I know he said it in the heat of an argument, I know it was a lie, Pavel married me for love, he didn't change until later, but still what a terrible thing to say, wasn't he the one who was always telling everybody that love was different nowadays, a support in battle rather than an escape from the world, that was how it was for us anyway, we didn't even take the time out to eat, after two dry rolls at the Youth League office we might not meet again all day, I'd wait up for Pavel until midnight when he came home from those endless, six-hour, eight-hour meetings, in my free time I copied out the talks he gave at all sorts of conferences and political training sessions, he attached a great deal of importance to them, only I know how much the success of his political appearances meant to him, he never tired of repeating that the new man differed from the old insofar as he had abolished the distinction between public and private life, and now, years later, he complains about how back then the Comrades never left his private life alone.

We went together for nearly two years, and I was getting a little impatient, and no wonder, no woman can be content forever with puppy love, Pavel was perfectly content, he enjoyed the convenient lack of commitment, every man has a selfish streak in him, it's up to the woman to stand up for herself and her mission as a woman, unfortunately Pavel was less attuned to the problem than the rest of our ensemble, especially a few of the girls I was close to, and they had a talk with the others, and the upshot of it all was that they called Pavel before the committee, I have no idea what they said to him there, we've never discussed the matter, but they must have been tough on him, morals were pretty strict in those days, people really overdid it, but maybe it's better to overdo morality than immorality the way we do now. Pavel kept out of my way for a long time, I thought I'd ruined everything, I was desperate, I was ready to commit suicide, but then he came back, oh, how my knees trembled, he asked me to forgive him and gave me a locket with a picture of the Kremlin on it, his most treasured possession, I never take it off, it's more than just a reminder of Pavel, much more, and I cried tears of joy, and two weeks later we were married, and the whole ensemble came to the wedding, sang and danced for almost twenty-four hours, and I told Pavel that if we ever betrayed each other it would be tantamount to betraying everyone at the wedding, everyone at the demonstration in Old Town Square, Togliatti included, it makes me laugh when I look back on everything we ultimately *did* betray. . . .

2

Let's see, what shall I wear tomorrow, the pink sweater, the plastic raincoat, they show off my figure best, I'm not as slim as I used to be, but then again I've got something to make up for the wrinkles, something none of the young girls have, the charm of a life lived to the hilt, that's what draws Jindra to me, the poor boy, I can still see the disappointment in his face when I told him I'd be taking the plane and he'd have to go by himself, he's happy for every minute he can spend with me and show off his nineteen-year-old virility, he'd have broken all speed records just to impress me, oh, he's not much to look at, but he's good with the equipment and an excellent driver, people at the station enjoy taking him along for minor jobs, and why not, it's nice to know there's someone around who likes me, I haven't been particularly popular at the station these past few years, people call me a hard-liner, a fanatic, a dogmatist, a Party bloodhound, and I don't know what else, but they'll never make me ashamed of loving the Party and sacrificing all my spare time to it. What else do I have to live for? Pavel has other women, I don't even bother to check on them anymore, little Zdena worships him, for ten years now my work has been absolutely routine, features, interviews, programs about plans fulfilled, model barns and model milkmaids, that and the hopeless situation at home, only the Party has never done me any harm, and I've never harmed the Party, not even in the days when almost everyone was ready to desert it, in fifty-six when there was all that talk about Stalin's crimes, and people went wild and began rejecting everything, saying our papers were a pack of lies, nationalized stores were worthless, culture was in decline, farms should never have been collectivized, the Soviet Union had no freedom, and the worst part of it all was that even Communists went around talking like that, and at their own meetings, Pavel too, and again they all applauded him, Pavel was always being applauded, it began when he was a child, he was an only child, his mother took his picture to bed with her, her prodigy, child prodigy but adult mediocrity, he doesn't smoke, doesn't drink, but he can't live without applause, it's his alcohol and nicotine, how thrilled he was at the new chance to pull at people's heartstrings, he spoke about those awful judicial murders with such emotion that people all but wept, I could tell how much he enjoyed his indignation, and I hated him.

Luckily the Party gave the squawkers a good rap on the knuckles, and when they calmed down Pavel calmed down too, he didn't want to risk his cushy lectureship in Marxism at the university, but something did remain behind, a germ of apathy, mistrust, misgiving, a germ that reproduced in silence, in secret, I didn't know how to counter it, I just clung to the Party more tightly than ever, the Party is almost like a living being, I can tell it all my most intimate thoughts now that I have nothing to say to Pavel, or anyone else for that matter, the others don't like me either, it all came out when we had to take care of that awful business, one of my colleagues at the station, a married man, was having an affair with a girl in the technical department, single, irresponsible, and cynical, and in desperation his wife turned to our Party committee for help, we spent hours going over the case, we interviewed the wife, the girl, various witnesses from work, we tried to get a clear, well-rounded picture of things and be scrupulously fair, the man was given a reprimand by the Party, the girl a warning, and both had to promise the committee to stop seeing each other. Unfortunately, words are not deeds, they agreed to split up only to keep us quiet and in fact went on seeing each other on the sly, but the truth will out, we soon found out about it, and I took a firm stand, I proposed that the man be expelled from the Party for having deliberately deceived and misled it, after all, what kind of Communist could he be if he lied to the Party, I hate lies, but my proposal was defeated, and the man got off with another reprimand, at least the girl had to leave the station.

And did they take it out on me for that, they made me look like a monster, a beast, it was a regular smear campaign, they started poking about in my private life, and that was my Achilles' heel, no woman can live without feelings, she wouldn't be a woman if she did, so why deny it? Since I didn't have love at home, I sought it out elsewhere, not that I found any, but they laid into me at a public meeting, called me a hypocrite, trying to pillory others for breaking up marriages, trying to expel, dismiss, destroy, when I myself was unfaithful to my husband at every opportunity, that was how they put it at the meeting, but behind my back they were even more vicious, they said I was a nun in public and a whore in private, as if they couldn't see that the only reason I was so hard on others was that I knew what an unhappy marriage meant, it wasn't hate that made me do what I did, it was love, love of love, love of their house and home, love of their children, I wanted to help them, I too have a child, a home, and I tremble for them!

Though maybe they're right, maybe I am just a bitter old witch and people should be free to do as they please and no one has the right to go sticking his nose into their private lives, maybe this world we've thought up isn't so wonderful and I really am a dirty commissar and won't mind my own business, but that's the way I do things, all I can do is act on my feelings, it's too late now, I've always believed that man is one and indivisible and that only the petty bourgeois divides him hypocritically into public self and private self, such is my credo, I've always acted on it, and that time was no exception.

As for my being bitter, I am perfectly willing to admit I can't stand those young girls, those little bitches, so sure of themselves and their youth and so lacking in compassion for older women, they'll be thirty one day, and thirty-five, and forty, and don't try to tell me she loved him, what does she know about love, she'll sleep with any man the first night, no inhibitions, no sense of shame, why, I'm mortified when they compare me to girls like her just because I, a married woman, have had a few affairs, the difference is I was always looking for love, and if I made a mistake, if I didn't find it, I'd turn away in horror and look elsewhere, even though it would have been much simpler to forget my girlish dreams of love, forget them and cross the border into the realm of that monstrous freedom where shame, inhibitions, and morals have ceased to exist, that vile, monstrous freedom where everything is permitted, where the single strongest force is the beast of sex pulsating in the heart of man.

And I know that if I crossed that border, I would stop being myself, I'd be somebody else, I don't know who, and I'm terrified of that awful transformation, so I keep looking for love, desperately looking for love, a love I can embrace just as I am, with all my old dreams and ideals, because I don't want my life to split down the middle, I want it to remain whole from beginning to end, which is why you took my breath away that day we met, Ludvik, dear, dear Ludvik....

3

It was really awfully funny the first time I went into his office, he didn't even make much of an impression on me, I got right down to business, explaining what I needed from him for the story and how I pictured the end result, but when he started talking to me I suddenly felt confused, tongue-tied, inarticulate, and when he noticed how uncomfortable I was he immediately switched to more general topics, asked whether I was married, whether I had any children, where I took my vacation, told me how young I looked, how pretty, it was nice of him, he wanted to get me over my stage fright, when I think of all the braggarts I meet, never let you get a word in edgeways and can't hold a candle to Ludvik, Pavel would have talked about himself the whole time, but it was really funny, I spent a full hour with him and didn't know any more about his institute than when I came, back home I quickly put something down on paper, but it just wasn't right, maybe I was glad, it gave me an excuse to phone him and ask if he wouldn't mind reading over what I'd written. We met at a café, my story was a pitiful four pages long, he read it through, gave me a gallant smile, and said it was excellent, he'd made it clear from the start he was interested in me more as a woman than as a reporter, I wasn't sure whether to feel flattered or insulted, but he was so nice to me, and we understood each other, he wasn't one of your egghead types, they really turn my stomach, he had a rich life behind him, he'd even worked in the mines, that's the kind of person I really liked, I told him, but the thing that excited me most was he was from Moravia, he'd even played in a cimbalom orchestra, I couldn't believe my ears, it was like hearing the leitmotiv of my life again, seeing my youth return from the shadows, my heart and soul went out to him.

He asked me what I did all day, and when I told him he said, I can still hear his voice, half joking, half sympathetic, that's no kind of life for someone like you, it's time for a change, he said I should turn over a new leaf, devote more time to the *joys of life*. I told him that was fine with me, joy had always been part of my credo and there was nothing I hated more than today's spleen and ennui, and he said credos don't mean a thing, people who shout joy from the rooftops are often the saddest of all, oh, how true, I felt like shouting, and then he told me point-blank, no beating about the bush with him, that he'd be by to pick me up the next day at four in front of the station, we'd take a drive out into the country. But I'm a married woman, I protested, I can't just run off into the woods with a strange man, and Ludvik responded jokingly that he wasn't a man, he was a scholar, but how sad he looked when he said it, how sad! Seeing him that way made me hot all over, what joy, he wanted me, he wanted me all the more after I reminded him I was married, because it made me more inaccessible, and men desire most what they consider inaccessible, and I drank in all the sadness from his face and realized he was in love with me.

The next day we heard the Vltava murmuring on one side of us, saw the forest rising abruptly on the other, it was all so romantic, I love life to be romantic, I'm sure I behaved like a silly young thing, which may not have been becoming to the mother of a twelve-year-old, but I couldn't help it, I laughed and skipped, pulling him along with me, and when we stopped my heart was pounding, there we stood face to face, and Ludvik bent over slightly and gave me a gentle kiss, I tore myself away from him, but then took him by the hand and started running again, I have a little trouble with my heart now and then, it starts beating wildly after the slightest bit of exertion, all I have to do is run up a flight of stairs, so I slowed down a little and got back my breath, and suddenly I heard myself humming the opening two bars of my favorite song, *Oh, brightly shines the sun on our garden . . .* , and sensing he recognized it, I began to sing it out loud, without shame, and I felt years, cares, sorrows, thousands of gray scales peeling off me, and then we found a little inn and had some bread and sausage, everything was perfectly ordinary and simple, the surly waiter, the stained tablecloth, and yet what a wonderful adventure, I said to Ludvik, did you know I was going to Moravia for three days to do a feature on the Ride of the Kings? He asked me where in Moravia, and when I told him he said that was his hometown, another coincidence, it took my breath away, I'll take some time off and go with you, he said.

I was afraid, I thought of Pavel, of the spark of hope he'd kindled in me, I'm not cynical about my marriage, I'm ready to do anything to save it, if only for little Zdena's sake, no, that's not true, mostly for my own sake, for the sake of the past, in memory of my youth, but I didn't have the strength to say no to Ludvik, I just didn't have the strength, and now the die is cast, Zdena is asleep, I'm frightened, at this very moment Ludvik is in Moravia, and tomorrow he'll be waiting for me when my bus pulls in.

PART THREE

=====

1

Yes, I went wandering. I stopped for a moment on the bridge that spanned the Morava and gazed downstream. What an ugly river (and so brown it looked more like viscous clay than water) and how depressing its embankment: a street of five stolid single-story houses, each standing on its own like a freakish orphan; apparently they were meant to constitute the embryo of a grandiose ensemble, but it never came to anything; two of them were decorated with ceramic angels and small stucco bas-reliefs; needless to say, they were badly chipped and cracked: the angels had lost their wings and the bas-reliefs, worn down in places to bare brick, had lost their meaning. Beyond the orphan houses the street petered out into a row of iron pylons and high-tension wires, then grass with a few straggling geese, and finally fields, horizonless fields, fields stretching out into nowhere, fields camouflaging the Morava's viscous brown clay.

Towns have a propensity to produce mirror images of themselves, and this view (I'd known it from childhood, and it had no significance for me whatsoever) suddenly reminded me of Ostrava, that huge, cheap boardinghouse of a mining town full of deserted houses and dirty streets leading into the void. I felt I'd fallen into a trap, standing up there on the bridge like a target for stray machine-gun fire. I couldn't bear to go on looking at that woebe-gone street of five solitary houses because I couldn't bear to think about Ostrava, and so I turned my back on it and started walking upstream.

I walked along the bank on a narrow path flanked on one side by a thick row of poplars. To the right of the path a mixture of grass and weeds sloped down to the level of the water, and across the river, on the opposite bank, stood the warehouses, workshops, and courtyards of several small factories; to the left of the path beyond the trees there was a sprawling rubbish heap and, farther on, open fields punctuated by more metal pylons and high-tension wires. Making my way along the path, I felt I was crossing a foot-bridge over a broad expanse of water. And if I compare that land-scape to an expanse of water, it is because, first, it gave me the shivers, and second, I was constantly on the verge of crashing down off the path. I was well aware that the nightmarish phantas-magoria of the landscape was merely a metaphor for everything I had tried not to recall after my encounter with Lucie; I seemed to be projecting suppressed memories onto everything I saw around me: the desolation of the fields and courtyards and warehouses, the murk of the river, and the pervasive chill that gave the land-scape its unity. But I understood there was no escaping those memories; they were all around me.

2

The events leading to my first major disaster (and, as a direct result of its uncharitable intervention, to my acquaintance with Lucie) might well be recounted in a detached, even lighthearted tone: it all goes back to my fatal predilection for silly jokes and Marketa's fatal inability to grasp any joke whatsoever. Marketa was the type of woman who takes everything seriously (which made her totally at one with the spirit of the age); her major gift from the fates was an aptitude for credulity. Now, I am not using credulity as a euphemism for stupidity; not in the least: she was moderately bright and in any case young enough (nineteen, a first-year student) so that her trustful naïveté seemed more charm than defect, accompanied as it was by undeniable charms of a physical nature. Everyone at the university liked her, and we all made more or less serious passes at her, which didn't stop us (at least some of us) from poking gentle, perfectly innocent fun at her.

But that kind of fun did not go over very well with Marketa, to say nothing of the spirit of the age. It was the first year after February 1948. A new life had begun, a genuinely new and different life, and its features—they are imprinted upon my memory—were rigid and grave. The odd thing was that the gravity of those features took the form of a smile, not a frown. That's right, those years told the world they were the most radiant of years, and anyone who failed to rejoice was immediately suspected of lamenting the victory of the working class or (what was equally criminal) giving way *individualistically* to inner sorrows.

Not only was I unencumbered with inner sorrows; I was blessed with a considerable sense of fun. And even so I can't say I wore the joyous physiognomy of the times: my sense of fun was too frivolous. No, the joy in vogue was devoid of irony and practical jokes; it was, as I have said, of a highly serious variety, the self-proclaimed *historical optimism of the victorious class,* a solemn and ascetic joy—in short, Joy with a capital J.

I remember how we were all organized into "study groups" that met for frequent criticism and self-criticism sessions culminating in formal evaluations of each member. Like every Communist at the time, I had a number of functions (I held an important post in the League of University Students), and since I was quite a good student as well, I could pretty well count on receiving a positive evaluation. If the public testimonials to my loyalty to the State, my hard work, and my knowledge of Marxism tended to be followed by a phrase along the lines of "harbors traces of individualism," I had no reason to be alarmed: it was customary to include some critical remark in even the most positive evaluations, to censure one person for "lack of interest in revolutionary theory," another for "lack of warmth in personal relations," a third for "lack of caution and vigilance," a fourth for "lack of respect for women." But the moment a remark like that was not the only factor under consideration (when it was joined by another or when we came into conflict with a colleague or under suspicion or attack), those "traces of individualism," that "lack of respect for women," could sow the seeds of our destruction. And every one of us carried the first fatal seed with him in the form of his Party record; yes, *every* one of us.

Sometimes (more in sport than from real concern) I defended myself against the charge of individualism. I demanded that my colleagues prove to me why I was an individualist. For want of concrete evidence they would say, "Because you act like one." "How do I act?" "You have a strange kind of smile." "And if I do? That's how I express my joy." "No, you smile as though you were thinking to yourself."

When the Comrades branded my conduct and my smile as *intellectual* (another notorious pejorative of the times), I actually believed them. I couldn't imagine (I wasn't bold enough to imagine) that everyone else might be wrong, that the Revolution itself, the spirit of the times, might be wrong, and I, an individual, might be right. I began to keep tabs on my smiles, and soon I felt a tiny crack opening up between the person I'd been and the person I should be (according to the spirit of the times) and tried to be.

But which was the real me? Let me be perfectly honest: I was a man of many faces.

And the faces kept multiplying. About a month before summer I began to get close to Marketa (she was finishing her first year, I my second) and like all twenty-year-olds I tried to impress her by donning a mask and pretending to be older (in spirit and experience) than I was: I assumed an air of detachment, of aloofness; I made believe I had an extra layer of skin, invisible and impenetrable. I thought (quite rightly) that by joking I would establish my detachment, and though I'd always been good at it, the line I used on Marketa always seemed forced, artificial, and tedious.

Who was the real me? I can only repeat: I was a man of many faces.

At meetings I was earnest, enthusiastic, and committed; among friends—a provocative busybody; with Marketa—cynical and fitfully witty; and alone (and thinking of Marketa)—unsure of myself and as excited as a schoolboy.

Was that last face the real one?

No. They were all real: I wasn't a hypocrite, with one real face and several false ones. I had several faces because I was young and didn't know who I was or wanted to be. (I was frightened by the differences between one face and the next; none of them seemed to fit me properly, and I groped my way clumsily among them.)

The psychological and physiological mechanisms of love are so complex that at a certain point in life a young man must concentrate all his energy on coming to grips with them and often loses sight of the object of his desires: the woman he loves. (In this he is much like a young violinist who cannot concentrate on the emotional content of a piece until the technique required to play it comes automatically.) Since I've spoken of my schoolboy-like crush on Marketa, I should point out that the excitement I felt stemmed not so much from my being in love as from my awkward lack of self-assurance; it weighed heavily on me and exerted much more of an influence on my thoughts and feelings than Marketa herself.

To ease the burden of my embarrassment, I flaunted my knowledge, disagreeing with her at every opportunity and poking fun at all her opinions. It wasn't hard to do because despite her brains (and beauty, which, like all beauty, had an aura of inaccessibility to it) she was innocent and trusting. She was constitutionally unable to look behind anything; she could only see the thing itself; she had a remarkable mind for botany, but would often fail to understand a joke told by a fellow student; she let herself be carried away by the enthusiasm of the day, but when confronted with a political deed based on the principle that the end justifies the means, she would be as bewildered as when told a joke. That was why the Comrades decided she needed to fortify her zeal with concrete knowledge of the strategy and tactics of the revolutionary movement, and sent her during the summer to a two-week Party training session.

The training session put a definite damper on my plans: those were the two weeks I'd planned to spend alone with Marketa in

Prague with an eye to putting our relationship (which until then had consisted of walks, talks, and a few kisses) on a more concrete footing, and since they were the only weeks I had (I was required to spend the next four on a student agricultural brigade and had promised the last two to my mother in Moravia), I reacted with painful jealousy when Marketa, far from sharing my feeling, failed to show the slightest chagrin and even told me she was looking forward to it.

From the training session (it took place at one of the castles of central Bohemia) she sent me a letter that was one hundred percent Marketa, chock-full of earnest enthusiasm for everything around her. It was all so wonderful: the early-morning calisthenics, the talks, the discussions, even the songs they sang; she praised the "healthy atmosphere" that reigned there and diligently added a few words to the effect that the revolution in the West would not be long in coming.

Actually I quite agreed with what she said; I even believed in the imminence of a revolution in Western Europe; there was only one thing I could not accept: her happy, buoyant mood in the face of my desire. So I bought a postcard and (to hurt, shock, and confuse her) wrote: Optimism is the opium of the people! A healthy atmosphere stinks of stupidity! Long live Trotsky! Ludvik.

3

Marketa responded to my provocative postcard with a brief and banal note and left the rest of the letters I sent her during the summer unanswered. I was up in the mountains pitching hay with my student brigade, and Marketa's silence was very hard on me. I wrote her almost daily letters overflowing with prayerful, mournful infatuation: Couldn't we at least see something of each other the last two weeks of the summer, I begged her; I was willing to give up the trip home, the visit to my poor deserted mother; I was willing to go anywhere just to be with Marketa. And it was not merely because I loved her; more than anything it was because she was the only woman on my horizon and I found the state of boy without girl intolerable. But Marketa didn't answer my letters.

I couldn't understand what had happened. I arrived back in Prague in August and managed to catch her at home. We took our usual walk along the Vltava and over to Imperial Meadow (a melancholy island of poplars and deserted playgrounds), and Marketa not only claimed that nothing had changed between us, but acted accordingly. The trouble was that the rigid, unwavering *sameness* of everything (sameness of kiss, sameness of conversation, sameness of smile) proved more depressing than my worst fears. When I asked if I could see her the next day, she told me to phone and we'd set a time.

I did phone; an unfamiliar woman's voice informed me that Marketa had left Prague.

I was unhappy as only a womanless twenty-year-old can be, a rather shy young man who has known few encounters with physical love, few and fleeting and gauche, and who is constantly preoccupied with it. The days were unbearably long and futile; I couldn't read, I couldn't work, I went to three different films a day, one showing after another, just to kill time, to drown out the screech of the hoot owl issuing from deep inside me. Although thanks to my own laborious attempts Marketa thought of me as a roué quite surfeited with women, I could not get up the courage to talk to girls walking along the street, girls whose beautiful legs made my heart ache.

And so I was very glad when September came at last, bringing classes and (several days before classes began) my work at the League of Students, where I had an office to myself and all kinds of things to keep me busy. The day after I got back, however, I received a phone call summoning me to District Party Headquarters. From that moment I remember everything in perfect detail. It was a sunny day, and as I came out of the League of Students building I felt the grief that had plagued me all summer slowly dissipating. I set off with an agreeable feeling of curiosity. I rang the bell and was let in by the chairman of the Party University Committee, a tall gaunt youth with fair hair and ice-blue eyes. I gave him the standard Party greeting of the time, "Honor to Labor," but instead of responding he said, "Go straight back.

They're waiting for you." In the last room I found three more members of the committee. They told me to sit down.

Their first question was whether I knew Marketa. They asked me whether I had corresponded with her. I said I had. They asked me whether I remembered what I wrote. I said I didn't, but immediately the postcard with the provocative text materialized before my eyes and I began to have an inkling of what was going on. Can't you recall anything? they asked. No, I said. Well, then, what did Marketa write to you? I shrugged my shoulders to give the impression she'd written about intimate matters I couldn't possibly discuss in public. Didn't she write anything about the training session? they asked. Yes, I said. What did she say? That she liked it there, I answered. And? That the talks were good, I answered, and the group spirit. Did she mention that a healthy atmosphere prevailed? Yes, I said, I think she did say something like that. Did she mention she was discovering the power of optimism? Yes, I said. And what do *you* think of optimism? they asked. Optimism? I asked. Why, nothing special. Do you consider yourself an optimist? they went on. I do, I said uneasily. I like a good time, a good laugh, I said, trying to lighten the tone of the interrogation. A nihilist likes a good laugh, said one of them. He laughs at people who suffer. A cynic likes a good laugh, he went on. Do you think socialism can be built without optimism? asked another of them. No, I said. Then you're opposed to our building socialism, said the third. What do you mean? I protested. Because you think optimism is the opium of the people, they said, advancing their attack. The opium of the people? I asked defensively. Don't try to dodge the issue. That's what you wrote. Marx called religion the opium of the people, and you think our optimism is an opiate! That's what you wrote to Marketa. I wonder what our workers, our shock workers, would say if they were to learn that the optimism spurring them on to overfulfill the plan was an opiate. To which another added, for a Trotskyite the optimism that builds socialism can never be more than a opiate. And you are a Trotskyite. For heaven's sake, what ever gave you that idea? I protested. Did you write it or did you not? I may have written something of the kind as a joke, but that was two months ago, I don't remember. We'll be glad to refresh your memory, they said, and read me my postcard aloud: Optimism is the opium of the people! A healthy atmosphere stinks of stupidity! Long live Trotsky! Ludvik. The words sounded so terrifying in the small Party Headquarters office that they frightened me out of my wits. I realized they had a destructive force I was powerless to counter. But, Comrades, it was meant to be funny, I said, knowing they couldn't possibly believe me. Do you feel like laughing? one of the Comrades asked the other two. Both shook their heads. You have to know Marketa, I said. We do, they replied. Then don't you see? Marketa takes everything seriously. We've always poked a little fun at her, tried to shock her. Interesting, replied one of the Comrades. Your other letters give no sign that you fail to take Marketa seriously. You mean you've read all my letters to Marketa? So the reason you make fun of Marketa, said another one, is that she takes everything seriously. Tell us now, what is it she takes seriously? Things like the Party, optimism, discipline, right? Are those the things that make you laugh? Try to understand, Comrades, I said. I don't even remember writing it, I must have dashed it off, it was just a few sentences, a joke, I didn't give it a second thought. If I'd meant anything bad by it, I wouldn't have sent it to a Party training session! How you wrote it is immaterial. Whether you wrote it quickly or slowly, in your lap or at a desk, you could only have written what was inside you. That and nothing else. If you'd thought things through, you might not have written it. As it is, you wrote what you really felt. As it is, we know who you are. We know you have two faces—one for the Party, another for the rest of the world. I felt I had run out of arguments and kept reiterating the old ones: that it was all in fun, that the words were meaningless, that my mood at the time was to blame, and so on. I failed completely. They said I'd written what I had to say on an open postcard, that it was there for everyone to see, that my words had an *objective* significance which could not be explained away by my mood at the time. Then they asked me how much Trotsky I had read. None, I said. They asked me who had lent me the books. No one, I said. They asked me what Trotskyites I had met with. None, I said. They told me they were relieving me of my post in the League of Students, effective immediately, and asked me to give them the keys to my office. I took them out of my pocket and handed them over. Then they said my case would be handled on the Party level by the Party Organization at the Division of Natural Sciences. They stood up and looked past me. I said "Honor to Labor" and left.

Later I remembered I had a lot of things at the League office. My desk drawer had socks in it as well as personal papers, and in my cupboard there was a half-eaten rum cake from my mother's oven alongside the dossiers. Although I had just given up my keys at Party Headquarters, the downstairs porter knew me and gave me the house key, which hung with all the others on a wooden board. I remember everything down to the last detail: the key was attached by strong cord to a small wooden board with the number of my office painted on it in white; I unlocked the door and sat down at my desk; I opened the drawer and took out my things; I was slow and absentminded; in that short period of relative calm I was trying to come to grips with what had happened to me and what I ought to do about it.

It wasn't long before the door opened and in came the three Comrades from Party Headquarters. This time they were far from cold and reserved; this time their voices were loud and agitated, especially the shortest of the three, the official in charge of Party cadres. How did I get there? he snapped at me. What right did I have to be there? Did I want him to have me hauled off by the police? What was I doing rummaging around in the desk? I told him I'd come for the rum cake and the socks. He said I had no right whatsoever to be there even if my socks were all over the place. Then he went up to the desk and looked through the contents paper by paper, notebook by notebook. Since they were in fact my personal belongings, he finally allowed me to put them into a suitcase while he looked on. I stuck them in with my dirty, crumpled socks, and managed to squeeze in the rum cake, by wrapping it in the greasy paper that had caught the crumbs during its stay in the cupboard. He followed my every move, and as I left, his parting words were: Never show your face here again.

No sooner was I released from the spell of the Comrades from the District Headquarters, from the invincible logic of their interrogation, than I felt I was innocent, that there wasn't anything so terrible in what I'd said, and that the best thing to do would be to go and talk to someone well acquainted with Marketa, someone I could confide in, someone who would tell me the whole business was absurd. I looked up a fellow student, a Communist, and when I'd told him the story from beginning to end, he said that District Headquarters had a reputation for being bigoted and humorless and that he, knowing Marketa, had a clear idea of what it was all about. In any case, the man for me to see was Zemanek, who was going to be Party Chairman of Natural Sciences and knew both Marketa and me very well.

<h1 style="text-align:center">4</h1>

I had no idea Zemanek had been chosen Party Chairman, and it seemed a stroke of luck: not only did I in fact know him well, I was confident he'd be sympathetic if for no other reason than my Moravian background. For Zemanek loved singing Moravian folk songs, and at the time it was very fashionable to sing folk songs not like schoolchildren but with a rough voice and an arm thrust upwards, that is, in the guise of a *man of the people,* born under the cimbalom just off the dance floor.

Being the only genuine Moravian in Natural Sciences had won me certain privileges: on every special occasion, at meetings, celebrations, on the First of May, I was always asked to take up my clarinet and join two or three other amateurs from among my fellow students in a makeshift Moravian band. The three of us (clarinet, fiddle, and bass) had marched in the May Day parade for the past two years, and Zemanek, who was good-looking and liked being the center of attention, put on a borrowed folk costume and joined us, dancing, waving his arms in the air, and singing. Though he was born and bred in Prague and had never set foot in Moravia, he enjoyed playing the village swain, and I couldn't help liking him. I was glad that the music of the region where I grew up, from time immemorial a paradise of folk art, was so popular, so admired.

Another advantage was that Zemanek knew Marketa. The three of us often attended the same student functions. On one occasion (there was a large group of us) I made up a story about some dwarf tribes living in the Czech mountains, documenting it with quotes from an alleged scholarly paper devoted to the subject. Marketa was astonished that she'd never heard of them. It wasn't surprising, I said. Bourgeois scholarship had deliberately concealed their existence, because they were bought and sold as slaves by capitalists.

But somebody ought to bring it out into the open! cried Marketa. Why doesn't somebody write about it? It would make a really strong case against capitalism!

Perhaps the reason no one writes about it, I said pensively, is that the whole thing is rather delicate. You see, the dwarfs had an extraordinary capacity for the act of love, which was why they were so much in demand and why our Republic exported them for hard currency, especially to France, where they were hired by aging capitalist ladies as servants, though obviously used for different purposes altogether.

The others stifled their laughter, which resulted not so much from the wittiness of my invention as from Marketa's attentive expression, her passion for supporting (or opposing) the issue at hand; they bit their lips to keep from spoiling Marketa's pleasure at learning something new, and some of them (Zemanek, in particular) joined in and confirmed my account of the dwarfs.

When Marketa asked what they looked like, I remember Zemanek telling her with a straight face that Professor Cechura, whom Marketa and the assembled company had the honor of seeing regularly on the lecture hall podium, was of dwarf descent, possibly on both sides, but most definitely on one. Zemanek claimed to have it from Cechura's assistant, who had once spent a summer in the same hotel as the professor and his wife and could vouch for the fact that between them they were not quite ten feet long. One morning he'd gone into their room not realizing they were still asleep, and he was amazed to find them lying not side by side, but head to foot: Professor Cechura curled up in the lower half of the bed and Mrs. Cechura in the upper.

Yes, I said by way of confirmation, then it is absolutely clear that both Cechura *and* his wife are of dwarf extraction. Sleeping head to foot is an atavistic custom of all dwarfs from that region, and in olden days they built their huts on long, rectangular plots rather than circular or square ones, because not only husband and wife, but entire clans, slept in long chains, one below the other.

Recalling our fabrication, I felt a faint glimmer of hope even on that black day. Zemanek, who would have the main say in my case, knew both Marketa and my sense of humor and would understand that the postcard was nothing but a silly bit of provocation aimed at a girl we all admired and (probably for that very reason) liked to pull down a peg. So at the first opportunity I gave him a full account of my misfortune. He listened attentively, frowning all the while, then said he'd see what he could do.

In the meantime, I lived in a state of suspended animation, attending lectures as before and waiting. I was called before numerous Party commissions, whose job it was to establish whether or not I belonged to a Trotskyite group; I tried to prove I didn't have the faintest idea of what Trotsky stood for; I met the glances of my interrogators head-on; I was looking for trust, and the few times I found it, I would carry that glance with me for a long time, nurture it, try patiently to kindle a spark of hope from it.

Marketa continued to avoid me. I realized it was on account of the postcard, and I was too proud and sensitive to ask her for anything. Then one day she herself stopped me in a corridor at the university and said, "There's something I'd like to talk to you about."

So once again after a few months' break we took one of our walks. It was autumn by then, and we were both wearing long trench coats—yes, very long, down below the knee, as was the style in those days of extreme inelegance. It was drizzling, and the trees on the embankment were leafless and black. Marketa told me how the whole thing had come about. While still at the training session, she had been called in by the Comrades in charge and asked whether she'd been receiving any letters there. She said she had. From whom, they asked. She said her mother had written to her. Anyone else? Oh, a friend now and then, she said. Can you tell us his name? they asked. She gave them my name. And what did Comrade Jahn write about? She shrugged her shoulders, not wanting to quote my card. Did you write back to him? they asked. I did, she said. What did you write? they asked. Oh, nothing much, about the training session, that kind of thing. Are you enjoying the session? they asked her. Oh, yes. I love it, she answered. And did you write that to him? Yes, I did, she answered. And what was his response? they went on. His response? she asked after a pause. Well, he's a little odd, you have to know him. We do know him, they said, and we would like to know what he wrote. Can you show us his card?

"You're not angry with me, are you?" said Marketa. "I had to show it to them."

"You don't have to apologize," I said. "They knew all about it before talking to you. Otherwise they wouldn't have called you in."

"I'm not apologizing," she protested, "and I'm not ashamed of having given them the card. That's not what I meant at all. You're a Party member, and the Party has a right to know exactly who you are and what you think." She'd been shocked by what I'd written, she told me. After all, didn't everybody know that Trotsky was the archenemy of everything we stood for, everything we were fighting for?

What could I say? I asked her to tell me what had happened after that.

After that, they read the card and were horrified. They asked her what she thought of it. She said it was disgraceful. They asked her why she hadn't brought it to them of her own accord. She shrugged her shoulders. They asked her if she knew what it meant to be vigilant, on guard. She hung her head. They asked her if she knew how many enemies the Party had. She said yes, she knew, but she would never have believed that Comrade Jahn . . . They asked her how well she knew me. They asked her what I was like. She said I was a bit odd, I was a staunch Communist all right, but there were times I would come out with things a Communist had no business saying. They asked her to give an example. She said she couldn't remember anything specific, but that nothing was sacred to me. They said that was obvious from my postcard. She told them we often argued about things and that I said one thing at meetings and another when I was with her. At meetings I was all enthusiasm, while with her I made a joke of everything, made everything seem ridiculous. They asked her if she thought a man like that was worthy of his Party membership. She shrugged. They asked her if the Party could encourage the building of socialism when its members went around proclaiming that optimism was the opium of the people. She said no, it would never build socialism that way. They told her she could go, but not to tell me anything about all this: they wanted to see what else I would write. She told them she never wanted to see me again. They replied that would be a mistake on her part, and she should keep writing so they could find out more about me.

"And then you showed them my letters?" I asked Marketa, turning bright red at the thought of my romantic effusions.

"What else could I do?" said Marketa. "But I couldn't go on writing after what had happened. I couldn't write just to trap you. So I sent you one more card and quit. The reason I didn't want to see you is I wasn't supposed to tell you anything, and I was afraid you'd ask me and I'd have to lie to your face. I don't like telling lies."

I asked Marketa what had inspired her to see me today.

She told me it was Comrade Zemanek. He had met her in the corridor of the university and taken her into the cubbyhole of a room where the Party Organization of the Division of Natural Sciences had its office. He told her he'd heard I'd written her a postcard with some anti-Party statements on it. He asked her what they were. She told him. He asked her what she thought of them. She said she condemned them. He told her that was the right thing to do and asked if she was still seeing me. She was embarrassed and tried to evade the question. He told her the Division had received a highly favorable report on her from the training session and that the Party Organization was counting on her. She said she was glad to hear it. He told her he didn't want to interfere in her private affairs, but that as far as he was concerned, a person was judged by the company he kept and I wasn't the most promising company for her.

For weeks thereafter, she told me, his words kept running around in her head. Since we had stopped seeing each other months before, Zemanek's admonition was basically superfluous. Yet it was that very admonition that started her thinking about whether it wasn't cruel and morally inadmissible to encourage a person to break up a friendship merely because the friend had made a mistake, whether it hadn't been unjust on her part to break up with me in the first place. She went to see the Comrade who had run the training session and asked him whether she was still forbidden to talk to me about the postcard incident, and learning that there was no longer reason for secrecy, she had stopped me and asked for a chance to talk.

She then confided to me all the things that had been worrying, torturing her: yes, she'd acted badly in deciding not to see me anymore; no man is completely lost, however great his mistakes. She recalled the Soviet film *Court of Honor* (at that time very popular in Party circles), in which a Soviet medical researcher places his discovery at the disposal of other countries before his own, an act bordering on treason. She had been especially touched by the film's conclusion: though the scientist is in the end condemned by a court of honor of his colleagues, his wife does not desert him; she does her best to infuse in him the strength to atone for his egregious error.

"So you've decided not to leave me," I said.

"Yes," said Marketa, taking my hand.

"But tell me, Marketa, do you really think I've committed a great crime?"

"Yes, I do," said Marketa.

"And do you think I have the right to remain in the Party? Yes or no?"

"No, Ludvik, I don't."

I saw that if I entered into the game that Marketa took for reality (and that she was living for all she was worth), I would gain everything that for months I had sought in vain: powered by a passion for salvation as a steamboat is powered by steam, she was all ready to give herself to me, body and soul. The only condition was that her evangelical spirit be satisfied. For that, the object of her salvation (I myself, alas) would have to concede his profound, his innermost guilt. And that I was unwilling to do. I was minutes away from the long-desired goal of her body, but I could not accept it at that price; I could not admit to a guilt I did not feel; I could not vindicate an intolerable verdict; I could not stand to hear a person supposedly close to me acknowledge that guilt, that verdict.

I didn't give in to Marketa, and I lost her. But is it true I felt completely innocent? I kept assuring myself of the absurdity of the whole affair, of course, but even as I did so (and here we come to what now, with hindsight, I find most upsetting and most revealing) I began to see the three sentences on the postcard through the eyes of my interrogators; I began to feel their horror and fear that something serious did in fact lurk behind the façade of my humor, that I never really had been one with the body of the Party, that I'd never been a true proletarian revolutionary, that I'd "gone over to the revolutionaries" on the basis of a *simple* (!) decision (we felt participation in the proletarian revolutionary movement to be a matter of, how shall I put it, *essence,* not a matter of *choice;* a man either was a revolutionary, in which case he completely merged with the movement into one collective entity, or he wasn't, and could only *hope* to be one, and therefore suffered constant guilt over not being one).

Looking back on my state of mind at the time, I am reminded by analogy of the enormous power of Christianity to convince the believer of his fundamental and never-ending guilt. Because I (like the rest of us) stood before the Revolution and its Party with permanently bowed head, I gradually became reconciled to the idea that my words, though genuinely intended as a joke, were still a transgression of sorts, and torrents of tortured self-criticism started whirling through my head. I told myself that it was no accident those thoughts had occurred to me, that the Comrades had long since reproached me for "traces of individualism" and "intellectual tendencies" (how right they were); I told myself that I'd taken to preening myself on my education, my university status, and my future as a member of the intelligentsia, that my father, a worker who died during the war in a concentration camp, would never have understood my cynicism; I reproached myself for letting his workingman's mentality die in me; I reproached myself on every possible score and in the end came to accept the necessity for some kind of punishment; I resisted one thing and one thing only: expulsion from the Party and the concomitant designation of *enemy*. To live as the branded enemy of everything I'd stood for since early childhood and still clung to seemed unbearably bleak.

Such was the self-criticism (and plea for mercy) I recited a hundred times to myself and at least ten times to various committees and commissions and finally to the plenary session of the Division of Natural Sciences, at which Zemanek delivered the opening address (highly effective, brilliant, unforgettable), recommending in the name of his commission that I be expelled from the Party. The discussion following my public self-denunciation went solidly against me: no one spoke on my behalf, and everyone present (and there were about a hundred of them, including my teachers and my closest friends), yes, every last one of them raised his hand to approve my expulsion not only from the Party but (and this came as a complete surprise to me) from the university as well.

That night, I took the train home to Moravia. I found no comfort there: for days I was unable to work up the courage to break the news to my mother, who took great pride in my studies. But the day after I arrived, Jaroslav, a school friend who'd played in the cimbalom ensemble with me, dropped by and was delighted to find me in town: it turned out he was getting married in two days and immediately asked me to be his best man. Since I couldn't refuse an old friend, I found myself celebrating my downfall with a wedding ceremony.

On top of it all, Jaroslav was a dyed-in-the-wool Moravian patriot and an expert on local traditions, and in his passion for folklore he was turning the wedding into a showcase of traditional rituals and customs: the cimbalom ensemble, the "patriarch" and his flowery speeches, the rite of carrying the bride over the threshold, the songs, the costumes, and any number of details to fill up the day, all reconstructed more from textbooks of ethnography than from living memory. I was struck by one thing: friend Jaroslav, the new head of a flourishing song and dance ensemble, clung to all the old customs, but (presumably mindful of his career and submissive to the atheistic slogans of the day) gave the church a wide berth, even though a traditional wedding was unthinkable without a priest and God's blessing; he had the patriarch give all the ritual speeches, but purged them of all Biblical motifs, even though it was Biblical imagery that held them together. The sorrow that kept me from joining the drunken wedding party had sensitized me to the chloroform seeping into the clear waters of these folk rituals, and when Jaroslav asked me (as a sentimental reminder of the days when I'd played in the ensemble with him) to grab a clarinet and sit in with the other players, I refused. I suddenly saw myself playing in the last two May Day parades with Prague-born Moravian-clad Zemanek singing and dancing and waving his arms alongside me, and I was unable to pick up the instrument. Suddenly all the folksy squealing made me sick, nauseous. . . .

5

Having lost the right to continue my studies, I lost the right to defer military service, and I was certain to receive notification that autumn. To fill in the time, I signed up for two long work brigades: one, repairing roads near Gottwaldov; the other, towards the end of summer, helping with seasonal labor at a fruit-processing plant; but autumn finally came, and one morning (exhausted after a sleepless night on the train) I reported to camp in an ugly, unfamiliar outlying district of Ostrava.

I stood in a courtyard with the other young recruits of my unit, strangers all; in the gloom of initial anonymity, what comes to the fore is coarseness, otherness; that is how it was for us; the only human bond we had was our uncertain future, and conjectures were rampant—some claiming we were to be given black insignia, others denying it, still others not understanding what it meant. I understood all too well and was horrified at the prospect.

Then a sergeant came and took us to one of the barracks. We poured into a corridor and along the corridor into a large room hung all around with enormous posters, photographs, and primitive drawings. A WE ARE BUILDING SOCIALISM sign made of large red construction-paper letters and covering most of the wall facing us dwarfed a wizened little old man standing beneath it next to a chair. The sergeant pointed to one of us and told him to go and sit in the chair. The old man tied a white sheet around the boy's neck, dug into the briefcase that was leaning up against a chair leg, pulled out an electric haircutter, and plunged it into the boy's hair.

The barber's chair inaugurated a production line designed to turn us into soldiers: after being deprived of our hair, we were hustled into the next room, where we were made to strip to the skin, wrap our clothes in a paper bag, tie them up with string, and pass them in at a window; then, naked and shorn, we proceeded across the hall to another room, where we were issued nightshirts; in our nightshirts we went on to the next door, where we received our army boots; in boots and nightshirts we marched across the courtyard to another hut, where we got shirts, underpants, foot wrappings, one belt, and one uniform (with the black insignia of the penal battalion); and finally we came to the last hut, where a noncommissioned officer read out our names, divided us into squads, and assigned us rooms and bunks.

That day we formed ranks again, went to supper, then to bed; in the morning we were wakened, taken out to the mines, and, at the pit head, divided by squads into work gangs and presented with tools (drill, shovel, and safety lamp) which almost none of us knew how to use; then the cage took us below ground. When we surfaced again with aching bodies, the waiting NCOs assembled us and marched us to the barracks; after our midday meal we went out to drill, and after drill we had political instruction, compulsory singing, and kit cleaning. Our only privacy was a room with twenty bunks. And so it went, day after day.

During those first days the penumbra of depersonalization seemed absolutely opaque to me; the impersonal orders we carried out took the place of all human expression; of course, the opacity was merely relative; it stemmed not only from the situation itself, but also from the difficulty we had in adjusting our sight (it was like entering a dark room from broad daylight); with time our sight improved, and we began to see the human in human beings even through the penumbra. I must confess, however, that I was one of the last to make the necessary adjustments.

The reason was that my entire being refused to accept its lot. The soldiers with black insignia, the soldiers whose lot I shared, went through only the most perfunctory drills and were given no weapons; their main job was to work in the mines. They were paid for their work (in which respect they were better off than other soldiers), but I found that a poor consolation; after all, they consisted entirely of elements that the young socialist republic was unwilling to entrust with arms and regarded as its enemies, which meant they received rougher treatment and had to live with the threat that their period of service would be extended beyond the compulsory two years. But what horrified me more than anything was being branded for life, being condemned (once and for all, definitively and by my own Comrades) to the company of men I considered my mortal enemies. I spent those early days among the black insignia as a hardheaded recluse, refusing to make friends with my enemies, refusing to accommodate myself to them. Passes were hard to come by at the time (no soldier had a right to a pass; he received a pass only as a privilege, which to all intents and purposes meant he was allowed out once every two weeks—on Saturday), but even when the soldiers surged out in gangs to ransack the bars for girls, I preferred my solitude; I would lie on my bunk and try to read or even study, drawing nourishment from my nonconformity; it was my firm belief I had only one thing to accomplish: fight the fight for my right "not to be an enemy," for my right to get away.

I paid several visits to the company's political commissar in an attempt to convince him that my presence there was a mistake, that I had been expelled from the Party for intellectualism and cynicism, not as an enemy of socialism. Once again (for the ump-teenth time) I recounted the ridiculous story of the postcard, but unfortunately it no longer seemed laughable; in fact, given my black insignia, it sounded more and more suspicious, like a cover-up for something even worse. In all fairness I must point out that the commissar heard me out patiently and showed a somewhat unexpected understanding of my desire for justice; he actually did make inquiries about my case somewhere higher up (O inscrutable topography!), but when he finally called me, it was to say, with unconcealed resentment, "Why did you try to fool me? They told me all about you. A known Trotskyite!"

Slowly I came to realize that there was no power capable of changing the image of my person lodged in the supreme court of human destinies, that the image in question (even though it bore no resemblance to me) was much more real than my actual self; that I was its shadow and not the other way round; that I had no right to accuse it of bearing no resemblance to me, because I bore the guilt for the lack of resemblance; that the lack of resemblance was my cross, to bear on my own.

And yet I refused to give in. I really wanted to *bear* my lack of resemblance, to be the person they had decided I was not.

It took me about two weeks to become more or less accustomed to hard labor in the mines, to the pneumatic drill, whose vibra-tions I felt pulsating through my body even as I slept. But I worked hard, with a frenzy. I wanted to break all records, and before long I was on my way.

The trouble was that no one took it as an expression of my political convictions. Since we were all paid piece rates (true, they deducted room and board, but there was still quite a bit left over), many others, no matter what their politics, worked with consider-able energy to wrest at least something worthwhile from all those wasted years.

Even though everyone looked on us as sworn enemies of the regime, we were required to maintain all the formalities of public life characteristic of socialist collectives: we, the enemy, the foe, took part in discussions of current events (under the watchful eye of the political commissar) we went to daily political pep talks, we covered the bulletin boards with pictures of socialist statesmen and slogans about the radiant future. At first I made a point of volunteering, but nobody took that as a sign of my political maturity either: the others volunteered too when they needed to attract the company commander's attention for an evening's leave. None of them thought of this political activity as political; it was an empty gesture required of them by the powers that be.

It didn't take me long to realize that resistance would get me nowhere, that I was the only one who had noticed my "lack of resemblance," that it was invisible to others.

Among the NCOs who had us at their mercy was a short, dark corporal, a Slovak, whose mild manners and utter lack of sadism set him off from the others. He was generally well liked, though there were those who claimed maliciously that his kind heart was more dim wits than anything else. Unlike us, of course, the noncoms carried arms, and from time to time they would go off for target practice. Once the dark corporal came back from practice basking in the glory of a first in marksmanship. A number of us were particularly boisterous in our congratulations (half sympathetic, half mocking), but the corporal merely blushed.

Later that day I happened to be alone with him and, just to keep the conversation going, asked how he'd come to be such a good shot. Looking up at me with a quizzical glance, he said, "It's this trick I've worked out for myself. I pretend the bull's-eye is an imperialist, and I get so mad I never miss." And before I could ask him what his imperialist looked like, he added in a serious, pensive voice, "I don't know what you're all congratulating me for. If there was a war on, you're the ones I'd be shooting at."

Hearing those words from the mouth of that nice little man so incapable of shouting at us that he was later transferred, I realized that the bonds tying me to the Party and the Comrades had been irrevocably broken. I had left the road that was to have been my life.

6

Yes. All ties were cut.

Everything was broken off: studies, work for the movement, friendships, love, and the quest for love—the whole meaningful course of life, broken off. All I had left was time. And I became intimate with time in a way I'd never been before. It was different from the time I'd known before: a time transmogrified into work, love, and exertion, a time I had accepted unthinkingly because it so discreetly hid behind my actions. It was time laid bare, time in and of itself, time at its most basic and primal, and it forced me to call it by its true name (for now I was living pure time—pure, vacant time) so as not to forget it for a moment, keep it constantly before me, and feel its weight.

When music plays, we hear a melody and forget it is only one of the faces of time; when the orchestra falls silent during a rest in the score, we hear time, pure time. Well, I was living a rest, but not the kind whose length is determined by a conventional sign; I was living a rest without end. We could not follow the example of the other battalions and snip off lines on a tape measure to show the two-year stint shrinking day by day: men with black insignia could be kept on indefinitely. Forty-year-old Ambroz from the second company was in for his fourth year.

Doing military service at that time and having a wife or fiancée at home was a bitter fate indeed: it meant keeping constant long-distance guard over her unguardable existence; it meant living in constant fear that the commanding officer would cancel the leave he had promised for one of her rare visits and that she would wait at the camp gates in vain. With a humor as black as their insignia, the men would tell stories of officers lying in ambush for those frustrated women and reaping the benefits that rightly belonged to privates confined to the barracks.

And yet. And yet the men with a woman at home had a thread stretching across that rest in the score. No matter how thin, how agonizingly thin and fragile it might have been, it was still a thread. I had no such thread; I'd broken off all relations with

Marketa, and the only letters I received were from my mother. . . .
Well, wasn't that a thread?

No, it was not. If home is only the parental home, it is no
thread; it is only the past. Letters written by parents are messages
from a shore we are forsaking; all they can do is make us aware of
how far we have strayed from the port we left, enveloped in the
selfless devotion of our loved ones. Yes, their letters say, the port
still exists, it's still there in all its comforting, pristine beauty; but
the *road back,* the *way back* is lost.

Little by little I grew used to the idea that my life had lost its
continuity, that it had been taken out of my hands, and that I had
no choice but to live the internal reality of the external reality I
had actually, inescapably been living all along. And so my eyes
gradually adjusted to the penumbra of depersonalization, and I
began to notice the people around me—later than they noticed
one another, but fortunately not so late as to alienate myself from
them altogether.

The first to emerge from the penumbra was Honza, who spoke
the all but incomprehensible slang of the streets of Brno and had
been issued his black insignia for assaulting a policeman. According to his story he was an old schoolmate of the policeman's and
had beat him up as the result of a personal quarrel, but the court
didn't see it his way, and he had come to us straight from six
months in jail. He was a first-rate mechanic, but seemed completely indifferent about working again as a mechanic or as anything else for that matter; he had no attachments, no concern for
the future, which gave him a carefree, insolent feeling of freedom.

The only other one of us with a feeling of inner freedom was
Bedrich, the most eccentric member of our twenty-bunk quarters.
Bedrich came to us two months after the usual September influx,
having originally been assigned to an infantry battalion; but first
he'd stubbornly refused to bear arms on strict religious grounds,
then the authorities intercepted letters he'd addressed to Truman
and Stalin, passionately appealing for the disbanding of all armies
in the name of socialist brotherhood. In their confusion they even
let him take part in drill, where, though the only man without a

weapon, he went through the motions of sloping and ordering arms with great precision; he also took part in political sessions, inveighing enthusiastically against imperialist warmongers. But when on his own initiative he made a poster calling for total disarmament and hung it in the barracks, he was court-martialed for mutiny. The judges, disconcerted by his pacifist harangues, had ordered him examined by a team of psychiatrists, and after a good deal of temporizing, had withdrawn their charges and transferred him to us. Bedrich was delighted: he was the only one who'd deliberately earned his black insignia and took pleasure in wearing them. That was why he felt free—though unlike Honza and his cheek, he expressed his independence by means of quiet discipline and industry.

All the others were plagued by fear and despair: Varga, a thirty-year-old Hungarian from southern Slovakia, who, oblivious of national prejudices, had fought the war in several armies and been in and out of prisoners' camps on both sides of the front; Petran the carrot top, whose brother had escaped across the border, shooting a soldier guard as he went; Stana, a twenty-year-old dandy from the Prague working-class district of Zizkov, whose pranks—not only did he march in the May Day parade while inebriated, he *deliberately* urinated on a curb in full sight of the cheering citizens—had earned him the local council's wrath; Pavel Pekny, a law student, who at the time of the February Communist coup had demonstrated against the Communists with a handful of his fellow students (he soon discovered I belonged to the same camp as those who had kicked him out of the university after the coup, and he alone showed a malicious satisfaction at the thought that we had both ended up in the same boat).

I could tell about numerous other soldiers who shared my fate, but I will concentrate instead on the one I liked best: Honza. I remember one of the first conversations we had together: it took place during a break in a pit gallery where we happened to be sitting (chewing on some bread rations) side by side. Suddenly Honza gave me a slap on the knee and said, "Hey, you there! You deaf and dumb or something? What makes you tick anyway?" Since I really was deaf and dumb at the time (entirely absorbed by my endless attempts at self-justification), I was hard put to explain (all at once I felt how forced and affected my choice of words must have sounded to him) how I'd ended up in the mines and why I actually didn't belong there. "Why, you fucking bastard! You mean *we* belong here?" I tried to make my position more clear (and choose more natural-sounding words), but Honza, swallowing his last mouthful, interrupted. "You know, if you were as tall as you are stupid, the sun'd burn a hole through your head." That little bit of good-natured plebeian mockery made me ashamed of worrying my self-indulgent head off over the privileges I had lost—I who had always taken such a firm stand against privilege and self-indulgence.

As time went on, Honza and I became fast friends (Honza respected me for my skill at mental arithmetic; more than once a fast calculation on my part had saved us from being shortchanged on payday). One night he called me an idiot for spending my leaves in camp and dragged me along with the rest of the gang. I'll never forget it. We were a pretty big group, about eight in all, including Stana, Varga, and a former student of applied art by the name of Cenek (Cenek was put in with us because he'd insisted on doing cubist paintings at school; now, for an occasional favor, he covered the barracks walls with oversized charcoal drawings of medieval warriors, Hussites, complete with flails and spiked clubs). We didn't have much choice where to go: the center of town was off limits, and even in the districts open to us we were limited to certain places. But that night we were in luck: there was a dance going on at a nearby hall where none of our restrictions applied. We paid the nominal entrance fee and surged in. The hall had lots of tables, lots of chairs, but not that many people: ten girls, no more, and about thirty men, half of them soldiers from the local artillery barracks; the minute they saw us, they were on their guard; we could feel their eyes on us, counting heads. We sat down at a long empty table and ordered a bottle of vodka, but the ugly waitress announced in no uncertain terms that no alcohol was to be served, so Honza ordered soft drinks all around; then he collected money from each of us and returned a short while later with three bottles of rum, which we immediately added to our soft drinks underneath the table. We had to act with the utmost circumspection because we knew the artillerymen were watching us and wouldn't hesitate to report us for illegal consumption of alcoholic beverages. The armed forces, it must be said, were extremely hostile to us: on the one hand, they looked upon us as suspicious elements (criminals, murderers, and monsters, as the propaganda spy novels put it) ready to cut the throats of their poor innocent families; on the other hand (and probably more important), they envied us for earning five times what they did.

That was what made our position so unusual: all we knew was drudgery and fatigue; we had our heads shaved clean every two weeks to rid them of all thoughts of self-esteem; we were the disinherited of the earth with nothing more to look forward to in life; but we had money. Oh, not much; but for a soldier with only two nights free a month it was a fortune: in those few hours (and in those few places not off limits) he could act like a millionaire and make up for the chronic frustration of all the other endless days.

Up on the platform a miserable band oompahpahed its way between polka and waltz for the few couples on the floor, while we coolly eyed the girls and sipped our drinks, whose alcoholic content soon lifted us far above anyone else in the hall. We were in a fine mood. I could feel a heady conviviality taking hold of me, a sense of companionship I hadn't experienced since the last time I played with Jaroslav and the boys in the cimbalom ensemble. In the meantime, Honza had come up with a plan to whisk as many girls as possible from the gunners. The plan was admirable in its simplicity, and we lost no time putting it into action. Cenek, extroverted clown that he was, had the most energy, and to our great delight he played his role to the hilt: after dancing with a dark-haired, heavily made-up girl, he brought her over to our table, poured out two of our concoctions, and said, "Fine, let's drink on it." The girl nodded, and they clinked glasses. At that moment a runt in an artillery uniform decorated with two stripes walked up to the girl and said to Cenek in the rudest tone he could muster, "She free?" "Why, of course, dear boy," said Cenek. "She's all yours." And while the girl hopped and skipped to the inane rhythm of the polka with her lovesick corporal, Honza was off phoning for a taxi. As soon as it arrived, Cenek went over and stood by the exit; when the girl finished the dance, she told the corporal she had to go to the ladies' room, and a few seconds later we heard the taxi pull away.

The next to score was old Ambroz from B Company. (The fact that his girl had definitely seen better years and always been less than attractive had not stopped four artillerymen from besieging her all evening.) Ten minutes later, Ambroz, the girl, and Varga (who was sure no girl would dream of going with him) climbed into a cab and sped off to meet Cenek in a bar at the other end of town. Before long two more of our group had persuaded another girl to go with them, and that left only Stana, Honza, and me. By now the gunners were eyeing us more and more ominously: the connection between our diminishing numbers and the disappearance of the three women from their lair had finally begun to dawn on them. We tried to look innocent, but it was clear a fight was brewing. "How about one more taxi and an honorable retreat," I said, looking wistfully at a blonde I'd managed to dance with once early in the evening without plucking up the courage to suggest we leave together; I'd hoped to have another chance later on, but the gunners had guarded her so zealously that I never got near her again. "Nothing else we *can* do," said Honza, starting off to the phone. But as he walked across the floor, the gunners all stood up from their tables and moved quickly to surround him. The fight now seemed imminent, and Stana and I had no choice but to get up from our table and make our way over to our threatened companion. For a while the crowd of gunners simply stood there in ominous silence, but suddenly one of them who was less than sober (he'd probably had his own bottle under the table) launched into a long tirade about how his father had been unemployed under capitalism and it made him sick to stand by and watch these bourgeois brats with their black insignia lord it over them, it made him sick, so if his comrades didn't hold him back, he might just give that bastard (meaning Honza) a good sock in the jaw. At the first pause in the trooper's tirade Honza inquired civilly what the Comrades from the artillery wanted of him. We want you out of here, and on the double, they said. To which Honza replied that

49

was exactly what we wanted and would they please let him call a taxi. By this point the trooper looked ready to have a fit. The bastards, he screamed in a high-pitched voice, the fucking bastards! Here we work our guts out, day and night, with nothing to show for it, and these capitalists, these foreign agents, these dirty bastards ride around in taxis! Well, not this time, let me tell you; not if I have to strangle them with my bare hands!

Soon everyone had joined in, civilians and soldiers alike, and the staff of the hall was trying hard to avoid an incident. Suddenly I caught sight of my blonde. She had been left alone at her table and (keeping aloof from the mêlée) was making her way to the ladies' room. I detached myself from the crowd as inconspicuously as I could and followed her into the vestibule, where the cloakroom and toilets were. I felt like a beginning swimmer who'd been thrown in the deep end; shy or not, I had to act; I rummaged around in my pocket, pulled out several crumpled hundred-crown notes, and said to her, "How about coming with us? You'll have a better time." She looked down at the money and shrugged her shoulders. I told her I'd wait outside; she nodded, disappeared into the ladies' room, and soon came outside with her coat on; she smiled at me and said she could tell right off I wasn't like the rest of them; it made me feel good, and I took her arm; we walked across the street and around the corner and waited for Honza and Stana to make their appearance at the entrance to the hall (it was lit by a streetlamp). The blonde asked me if I was a student, and when I said I was, she told me she'd had some money stolen from her the day before in the factory cloakroom, and since it belonged to the factory, she was terribly afraid they'd take her to court: Could I lend her a hundred crowns? I reached into my pocket and gave her two crumpled slips of paper.

Before long out came Honza and Stana with their caps and coats on. But the moment I whistled to them, three other soldiers (capless and coatless) rushed out of the hall on their heels. All I could hear was the intonation of their questions, but I didn't need words to guess their meaning: it was my blonde they were after. Then one of them lunged at Honza, and the fight was on. Stana had only one to deal with, Honza two. They were just about to pin him to the ground when I ran up and laid into one of them. The gunners had assumed they'd be numerically superior, and as soon as the sides were equal, they lost their momentum; when one of them folded under Stana's fist, we took advantage of their confusion and beat a hasty retreat.

The blonde was waiting obediently for us around the corner. When Honza and Stana saw her, they went wild with joy. They told me I was the greatest and tried to hug me, and for the first time in as long as I could remember I felt truly happy. Honza pulled a full bottle of rum from under his coat (how he'd managed to keep it intact through the fight was beyond me) and swung it above his head. Everything was perfect except we had nowhere to go: we'd been thrown out of one place, and the rest were off limits; our ranting rivals had cut off our taxi supply and might at any moment threaten our very existence with a newly mounted campaign. We set off quickly down a narrow alley between some houses; after a short distance the houses gave way to a wall on one side, a fence on the other; up against the fence stood a hay wagon and a tractor-like contraption with a tin seat. "Your throne," I said, and Honza sat the blonde on the seat, which was a few feet off the ground. The bottle passed from hand to hand; all four of us drank from it; the blonde soon became voluble and said to Honza, "Hey, I bet you wouldn't lend me a hundred crowns," whereupon Honza slipped her a hundred-crown note and she opened her coat, hitched up her skirt, and pulled down her panties. She took my hand and pulled me towards her, but I was scared and broke away from her, pushing Stana into the breach; Stana showed no qualms whatsoever and moved right up between her legs. They lasted less than twenty seconds together. I planned to let Honza have his turn next (partly because I was trying to play the host, partly because I was still scared), but this time the girl was more determined and pulled me against her hard, and when, aroused by her caresses, I was finally ready to oblige her, she whispered tenderly in my ear, "I only came along because of you, silly," and began to sigh, and all at once I genuinely felt she was a nice girl in love with me and worthy of my love, and she went on sighing, and I went at it with abandon, but suddenly

Honza came out with some obscenity, and again I realized I wasn't in love with her in the least, so I pulled away from her without climaxing, and she looked up at me almost frightened and said, "Hey, what's going on?" but by then Honza had taken my place, and the sighs started up again.

We didn't get back to camp that night until nearly two in the morning, and at half past four we were up for that voluntary Sunday shift that earned the commanding officer a bonus and us our biweekly Saturday passes. Groggy and still under the influence of the rum, we moved like zombies through the gloom of the gallery, but I reveled in the memories of an evening pleasurably spent.

Our next leave two weeks later didn't measure up at all. Honza had his pass revoked for some incident or other, and I was stuck with two more or less unknown quantities from another platoon. We immediately set our sights on a sure thing—a woman whose monstrous height had earned her the nickname Candlestick. She was ugly, but what could we do? The circle of women at our disposal was severely limited, not the least by constraints of time. The necessity of taking full advantage of every leave (they were so short and so hard to come by) meant that the men invariably preferred the accessible to the attractive. By comparing notes, they gradually put together a rather pitiful pool of more or less accessible (read: unattractive) women and made it available for general use.

That Candlestick was part of the pool made no difference to me; the other two joked on and on about how unbelievably tall she was, about how we'd have to find a brick to stand on when the time came, and I actually enjoyed it: it intensified my own raging lust for a woman; any woman; the less individualized, the less personalized, the better; any woman *whatsoever*.

But even though I'd had quite a bit to drink, my burning desire suddenly subsided the moment I laid eyes on her. It all seemed revolting and pointless, and because neither Honza nor Stana nor anyone I liked had been there, I woke up the next morning with a hangover so fierce that the doubts it spawned included retroactively the events of the previous leave.

Had I perhaps felt the stirrings of some moral principle? Nonsense: it was revulsion, pure and simple. But where had it come from, when a few short hours before I had been consumed by burning desire for a woman and the fury of that desire was intimately bound up with my not knowing who the woman would be? Was I perhaps more delicate than the others? Did I have an aversion to prostitutes? Nonsense: I was simply overcome by depression.

Depression over the sudden realization that there was nothing exceptional about what I'd been through, that I hadn't chosen it out of excess or caprice or an obsessive desire to know and experience everything (the sublime and the despicable), that it had simply become the *norm* of my existence. That it precisely defined the range of my opportunities, that it accurately depicted the horizon of my love life from then on. That it was an expression not of my freedom (as I might have seen it, say, a year earlier), but of my submission, my limitation, my *sentence*. And I felt fear. Fear of that bleak horizon, of that destiny. I felt my soul contracting, retreating, then cringing at the realization that it was completely encircled and could not escape.

7

Depression over the bleakness of our erotic horizons was something nearly all of us went through. Bedrich (the author of the peace manifestos) resisted it by withdrawing into the depths of his being to commune with his mystic God, the erotic complement to this religious turn inward being a ritualistic regime of self-stimulation. Others exhibited a much greater degree of self-deception, supplementing their cynical whoring expeditions with the most maudlin romanticism: many had their own loves at home and burnished their memory to a brilliant sheen; many put their faith in never-ending faithfulness and faithful expectation; many tried to convince themselves in secret that the girls they'd picked up drunk in a bar burned for them with a holy fire. Stana had two visits from a girl in Prague he'd gone with before being drafted (but had never taken seriously), and suddenly he was head over heels in love and (true to his impetuous nature) couldn't wait to marry her. He claimed to have thought it all up for the two days' marriage leave, but I could see through his cynical façade. It was early March when the commanding officer gave him his pass and Stana went off to Prague with exactly one weekend to get married. I remember it all so well because the day of Stana's wedding turned out to be a very important day for me as well.

I too had been granted a pass, and still upset over the last one, squandered on Candlestick, I steered clear of my fellow soldiers and went off on my own. I climbed aboard an ancient narrow-gauge tram, a local linking the outer suburbs of Ostrava, and let it carry me away. I got off at a random stop and changed to a random tram belonging to a different line; the endless outskirts with their curious mixture of factories and fields, natural beauties and rubbish heaps, woods and slag heaps, tenements and farmhouses, both attracted and disturbed me; again I got off the tram, but this time I took a long walk, drinking in the peculiar landscape with something akin to passion and trying to grasp what made it what it was, trying to put into words what gave its multiplicity of elements their unity and order. As I walked past an idyllic little house covered with ivy, it occurred to me that the reason it belonged there was that it differed so from the shabby buildings all around it, from the silhouettes of bulky headframes and chimneys and furnaces that served as its backdrop; and as I walked past the squat temporary huts and saw a house not too far off, a dirty, gray old house, but with its own garden and iron fence and large weeping willow, a real freak in such surroundings, I said to myself that that must have been the reason *it* belonged there. I was disturbed by all these minor *incompatibilities* not only because they struck me as the common denominator of the surrounding area, but because they provided me with an image of my own exile there; and also, of course, projecting my personal history onto the objective backdrop of an entire city offered me a certain relief: I understood that I no more belonged there than did the weeping willow and the little ivy-covered house, than did the short streets leading nowhere, into the void, streets lined with houses, each of which seemed to come from a different place; I no more belonged in that region once pleasantly rustic than did the hideous districts of temporary housing, and I realized that the real reason I had to be there in that disconcerting city of incompatibility, of indiscriminate embrace, was that I didn't belong.

I ended up walking down a long street—once a village in and of itself, now a suburb close to town—and stopping in front of a large one-story building with a vertical CINEMA sign attached to one corner. I speculated idly, as chance passersby are wont to do, on why the sign said only CINEMA with no name. I searched all over the outside of the building (which looked singularly unlike what it purported to be), but found no other sign. What I did find was an alley about five feet wide, separating it from the building next door, and after following it into a courtyard, I saw that the cinema had a one-story wing tacked on in the back with glass cases along the walls for film advertisements. I went up to them, but still found no indication of a name. I looked around, saw a little girl behind a wire fence in a neighboring backyard, and asked her what its name was, but she gave me a surprised look and said she didn't know, and finally I resigned myself to its anonymity: in this Ostrava exile even cinemas had no names.

I drifted back (for no particular reason) to the glass cases and noticed for the first time that the show of the day, as announced by a poster and two stills, was none other than the Soviet film *Court of Honor,* whose heroine Marketa had alluded to when she took it upon herself to play the angel of mercy in my life, the film whose harsher aspects the Comrades had alluded to when instituting Party proceedings against me. It had caused me enough grief, and I had hoped never to hear of it again, but no, not even here in Ostrava could I escape its pointing finger. . . . At least this time I could turn my back on it. And I did, heading for the alleyway back to the street.

It was then I first set eyes on Lucie.

She was coming in my direction, in the direction of the courtyard. Why didn't I simply walk past her? Was it because I was merely drifting aimlessly or because the unusual late-afternoon lighting in the courtyard held me back? Or was it something in the way she looked? But her appearance was utterly ordinary.

55

True, later that *ordinary* quality about her was what touched and attracted me, but how was it she caught my eye and stopped me in my tracks the first time I saw her? Hadn't I seen enough ordinary girls in the streets of Ostrava? What was so extraordinary about her ordinariness? I don't know. I only know I stood and watched, watched her walk slowly and deliberately up to the glass case, stop in front of the *Court of Honor* stills, then turn towards the entrance and walk through the open doors into the lobby. Yes, it must have been the slow pace that fascinated me; she had a slowness about her that radiated resignation: there was nowhere worth hurrying to, nothing worth fretting over. Yes, maybe it really was that melancholy slowness that made me follow her as she went up to the box office, took out some change, bought a ticket, glanced into the auditorium, then turned around and came back out into the courtyard.

I couldn't take my eyes off her. She stood with her back to me, looking out past the courtyard to where a group of cottages and gardens, each enclosed by its own picket fence, crept up a hill until the outline of a quarry cut them off. (I'll never forget that courtyard; I remember its every detail, I remember the wire fence separating it from the backyard where the little girl sat staring out into space, I remember the steps where she sat being flanked by a low wall with two empty flowerpots and a gray washtub on it, I remember the smoky sun edging its way down over the quarry.)

It was ten to six, which meant the showing wouldn't begin for ten minutes. Lucie turned and walked slowly across the courtyard and out into the street. I followed, exchanging the picture of ravaged rural Ostrava behind me for a more urban landscape. Fifty steps away was a pleasant little square, neatly kept up, with a tiny park and benches in front of a redbrick building with a pseudo-Gothic clock tower. I followed her: she sat down on a bench; her slowness never left her for an instant; she seemed almost to be *sitting slowly;* she didn't look around, didn't let her eyes wander; she sat the way we sit when waiting to go in for an operation, waiting for something that so engages us it drives us inwards, away from our surroundings. It must have been that inward concentration that allowed me to hover over her, look her up and down, without her noticing me.

A great deal has been said about love at first sight, and since I am perfectly aware of love's retrospective tendency to make a legend of itself, turn its beginnings into myth, I will even refrain from claiming it was *love;* but I have no doubt there was a kind of clairvoyance at work: I immediately felt, sensed, grasped the essence of Lucie's being or, to be more precise, the essence of what she was later to become for me; Lucie had revealed herself to me the way *religious truth* reveals itself to others.

I saw a slipshod permanent crumpling her hair into a shapeless mass of curls; I saw a brown overcoat, pitifully threadbare and none too long either; I saw a face both unobtrusively attractive and attractively unobtrusive; I saw an inborn tranquillity, simplicity, modesty; and I felt how much I needed them; I saw how similar we were: all I had to do was to go up and start talking to her and she would smile as if a long-lost brother had suddenly appeared before her.

She raised her head to look at the clock tower. (Even this slight movement is fixed in my memory, the movement of a girl who has no watch and instinctively sits facing a clock.) She stood up and started back to the cinema. I wanted to go up to her, but lacked not so much the courage as the words; my heart was full, but my mind was a blank; so I merely followed her into the small lobby. All at once a handful of people rushed in and made a beeline for the box office. I stepped ahead of them and bought a ticket for the film I so detested.

Meanwhile she had gone in; in the nearly empty auditorium numbered tickets lost all significance, and we sat where we pleased; I turned into Lucie's row and took the seat next to her. At that moment a scratchy fanfare blared out into the hall, the lights dimmed, and the advertisements started appearing on the screen.

Lucie must have realized that the soldier with black insignia had not sat next to her by chance; she must have been aware of me the whole time, must have felt my presence, if only because I concentrated entirely on her and paid no attention whatsoever to what was happening on the screen (enjoying an admittedly laughable revenge as the film so often quoted at me by my moral guardians flashed before me unheeded).

Finally the film was over, the lights came on, and the tiny audience stood up and stretched. Lucie stood up too; she took the folded brown overcoat from her lap and placed one arm in the sleeve. I quickly put on my cap to hide my clean-shaven skull, and without a word helped her into the other sleeve. She looked up at me briefly, mutely, and gave me a slight nod, but I couldn't tell whether to interpret it as a sign of thanks or as a purely instinctive gesture. Then she inched her way out of the row. I immediately threw on my green coat (it was too long on me and probably not very becoming) and went after her. We were still inside the auditorium when I first spoke to her.

Those two hours of sitting next to her, thinking of her, must have put me on her wavelength: from the very start I was able to talk to her as if I knew her well; for once I started a conversation naturally, without a joke or an ironic remark, and I was surprised at how easy it was after all the masks I'd hidden behind.

I asked her where she lived, what she did, whether she went to the pictures a lot. I told her that I worked in the mines, that it was hard work, that I didn't have much time off. She said that she worked in a factory and lived in a dormitory, that she had to be in by eleven, that she went to the pictures a lot because she didn't like going to dances. I told her I'd be glad to go to the pictures with her anytime she was free. She said she'd rather go alone. I asked her if it was because life was so depressing. She said it was. I told her I wasn't particularly enjoying it either.

Nothing brings people together more quickly and easily (though often spuriously and deceitfully) than shared melancholy; an atmosphere of undemanding sympathy puts to rest all manner of fears and defenses and is easily comprehended by the refined and vulgar, the erudite and unlettered, and while it is the most simple means of bringing people together, it is extremely rare. It requires the individual to lay aside his culture-induced "psychological restraints," culture-induced gestures and facial expressions, and be himself. How I managed to accomplish this feat (out of the blue, with no preparation), I who'd always felt my way cautiously behind one false front or other, I do not know; I do not know, but it was like an unexpected gift, a miraculous release.

We told each other the most ordinary things about ourselves; our confessions were short and to the point. When we reached the dormitory, we stood outside for a while under a streetlamp that bathed Lucie in light, and I found myself stroking not her cheeks or her hair, but the shabby material of her touching brown coat.

I still remember the streetlamp swaying and the girls laughing raucously as they passed us on their way into the dormitory; I remember looking up at Lucie's building, at the bare gray wall and unrecessed windows; and I remember watching Lucie's face, which (unlike the faces of other girls I'd known in similar situations) was calm, almost blank, rather like the face of a schoolgirl standing at the blackboard (without artifice or guile), humbly reciting what she knows, seeking neither high marks nor high praise.

We agreed I'd send a postcard to let her know when I had my next leave and could see her. We said good night (without kissing or touching), and I walked away. After a few steps I turned and saw her standing in the doorway, not unlocking the door, just standing there, watching me. Now that I had moved away a bit, she could drop her reserve and allow her eyes (so timid before) a long stare. Then she lifted her arm—like someone who has never waved, who doesn't know how to wave, who only knows that when one person leaves, the other person waves—and did her awkward best to make the gesture. I stopped and waved back, and we stood there looking at each other. Then I started off again, stopped once more (Lucie's hand was still going), and went on, starting and stopping, until finally I turned the corner and we vanished from each other's sight.

8

From that evening I was different inside; I was inhabited again; my inner space was clean and tidy; there was someone living there. The clock that for months had hung silent on the wall had suddenly begun to tick. It was an event of major significance: time, which until then had flowed like a lazy stream from nowhere to nowhere devoid of signposts, devoid of time signatures (I had been living an indefinite rest), had begun to wear its human face again, to mark itself off, measure itself out. I came to live for my passes, and each day was a rung on the ladder to Lucie.

Never in my life have I devoted such thought, such concentration, to a woman (though, of course, I've never had so much time for it either). To no other woman have I felt such gratitude.

Gratitude? For what? First and foremost for releasing me from the pathetically limited erotic horizon we were all faced with. True, Stana the newlywed had found a way out: he had a beloved wife at home in Prague. But Stana was not to be envied. By marrying, he had set his destiny in motion, and the minute he boarded the train back to Ostrava, he lost all control over it.

By establishing an acquaintance with Lucie, I too had set my destiny in motion, but I never let myself lose sight of it. Though we didn't meet very often, at least our meetings were more or less regular, and I knew she was capable of waiting several weeks and then greeting me as if we'd seen each other the day before.

But Lucie did more than free me from the depression I felt after our bleak erotic adventures. Even if by that time I knew I'd lost my fight and would never be able to do anything about my black insignia, even if I knew it was senseless to alienate myself from people I'd be living with for another two years or more, senseless to trumpet my right to the career I'd chosen for myself (it took me a while to realize how privileged a career it was), still I'd accepted the change on an intellectual level only and was therefore unable to root out the deep pain I felt for my "lost destiny." Lucie had a miraculous healing effect on that deep pain. All I needed was to feel her close to me, feel the warmth of her way of life, a life outside the issues of cosmopolitanism and internationalism, vigilance and the class struggle, and what constitutes the dictatorship of the proletariat—a life outside the whole gamut of politics, its strategy and tactics.

These were the concerns (so much a part of the times that they will soon be nothing but incomprehensible jargon) which had led to my downfall, and yet I could not let go of them. I had all kinds of answers ready for the commissions that called me in and asked me what had made me become a Communist, but what had attracted me to the movement more than anything, dazzled me, you might say, was the feeling (real or apparent) of standing near the *wheel of history*. We really did decide the fate of men and events, especially at the universities. In those early years there were very few Communists on the faculty, and the Communists in the student body ran the universities almost single-handedly, making decisions on academic staffing, teaching reform, and the curriculum. The elation we experienced is commonly known as the intoxication of power, but (taking a more benevolent stance) I would suggest something milder: we let history bewitch us; we were drunk with the thought of jumping on its back and feeling it beneath us, and if, more often than not, the result was an ugly lust for power, still (given that all human affairs are ambiguous) an idealistic illusion remained (especially, perhaps, in us, the young), the illusion that we were the ones to inaugurate the era in which man (all men) would no longer stand *outside* history, no longer cringe *under its heel*, but direct and create it.

I was convinced that far from the wheel of history there was no life, only vegetation, boredom, exile, Siberia. And suddenly (after six months of Siberia) I'd found a completely new and unexpected opportunity for life: I saw spread before me a long-lost meadow (lost beneath history's soaring wings), the meadow of day-to-day existence, and in that meadow I saw a poor, a pitiful girl, but a girl eminently worthy of love—Lucie.

What did Lucie know of the great wings of history? When could she have heard their sound? She knew nothing of history, she lived *beneath* it; history held no attraction for her, it was alien to her; she knew nothing of the *major problems of our times,* the problems she lived with were *trivial and eternal*. And suddenly I'd been released; Lucie had come to take me off to her *gray paradise,* and the step that until such a short time before had seemed unthinkable, the step enabling me to "make my exit from history," was suddenly a cause for relief and rejoicing. Lucie held me shyly by the arm, and I let myself be led. . . .

Lucie was my gray guide. And in more concrete terms?

She was nineteen, though in fact much older, as women tend to be when they've led a hard life and been catapulted from childhood to adulthood. She said she was from western Bohemia and had finished school before becoming an apprentice. She didn't enjoy talking about home and wouldn't have said anything if I hadn't pressed her. She had been unhappy there. "My parents never liked me," she said, and as proof she told me about how her mother had remarried and her stepfather drank and was cruel to her and how once they'd accused her of hiding some money from them and how they always beat her. When their disagreements finally became unbearable, she had picked up and left. She'd been living in Ostrava for a whole year. Oh, she had friends, but she preferred keeping to herself; her friends went out dancing and brought boys back to the dormitory, and Lucie was against that; she was serious, she preferred going to the pictures.

Yes, she thought of herself as "serious" and identified being serious with going to the pictures. Her favorites were the war pictures so prevalent at the time, perhaps because they were exciting, but more likely because the unmitigated suffering in them filled her with the feelings of pity and compassion she found uplifting and indicative of the "serious" part of herself she prized so highly.

But it would not be accurate to say I was attracted to Lucie only by her exotic simplicity. Her simplicity, the gaps in her education, did not prevent her from understanding me, but her understanding had nothing to do with experience or knowledge or the ability to argue and advise; it was more a matter of the receptive way she listened to me.

I remember one summer day when my leave happened to begin before Lucie's shift was over. I had taken a book along and sat down on a garden wall to read; I'd been having a hard time keeping up with my reading; there was so little time, and communications with my Prague friends were poor; but I'd packed three small books of poetry into my bag and read them over and over for the comfort they gave me. They were poems by Frantisek Halas.

Those three books played a strange role in my life, strange if only because I am not a great poetry-lover and they were the only books of poetry I ever really cared for. I discovered them just after I'd been expelled from the Party, during the period when the name of Halas was coming back into the public eye: the leading ideologue of the time had seen fit to accuse the recently deceased poet of morbidity, depression, bad faith, existentialism—in other words, everything that smacked of political anathema in those days. (The book in which he set forth his views on Czech poetry in general and Halas in particular came out in an enormous printing and was required reading in all Czech schools.)

In times of distress we seek comfort by linking our own grief with the grief of others, and laughable as it may sound, I confess that the reason I'd sought out Halas's verse was that I wanted to commune with someone else who had been *excommunicated;* I wanted to find out whether my own mentality had any similarity to the mentality of a recognized apostate; and I wanted to test whether the grief which the powerful ideologue had proclaimed pernicious and cankered might not hold some joy for me given my own affinitive condition (under the circumstances, I could scarcely have been expected to find joy in joy). Before leaving for Ostrava, I borrowed the three books from a former fellow student, a lover of literature, and then begged and begged until he agreed not to ask for them back. And so they had accompanied me into exile.

When Lucie found me at the appointed place with a book in my hand, she asked me what I was reading. I showed her the pages it was open to. "Poetry!" she said in amazement. "Do you find it strange for me to be reading poetry?" She shrugged her shoulders and said, "No, why should it be?" But I think she did, because in all probability she identified poetry with children's books. We wandered through Ostrava's odd sooty summer, a black summer of coal cars rumbling along overhead cables rather than fleecy clouds scudding across the sky. I noticed that Lucie was still somehow drawn to the book, and so when we found a small grove and sat down, I opened it and asked, "Are you interested?" She nodded.

I'd never recited poetry to anyone before; I've never done it since. I have a highly sensitive, built-in fuse mechanism that keeps me from opening up too far, from revealing my feelings, and reciting poetry makes me feel as though I'm talking about my feelings and standing on one leg at the same time; there is something in the very principle of rhythm and rhyme that embarrasses me when I think of indulging in it in all but the strictest solitude.

But Lucie had the miraculous power (that no one after her has ever had) to bypass the fuse and rid me of the burden of my diffidence. In her presence I could dare to show everything: sincerity, emotion, pathos. And so I recited:

Your body is a slender ear of corn
From which the grain has dropped and won't take root
Your body's like a slender ear of corn

Your body is a skein of silk
With longing written into every fold
Your body's like a skein of silk

Your body is a burnt-out sky
And death dreams under cover in its weave
Your body's like a burnt-out sky

Your body is so silent
Its tears quiver beneath my lids
Your body is so silent

I had my arm around Lucie's shoulders (which were covered only by the thin material of her flowered dress), I could feel them in my fingers, and I so wanted to believe that the poem I was reading (a slow-moving litany) referred to the anguish of that body: mute, resigned, condemned to death. I read her some more poems, including the one that to this day calls forth her image to me and ends with the lines:

Fatuous words I don't trust you I trust silence
More than beauty more than anything
A festival of understanding

Suddenly I felt Lucie's shoulders shaking in my fingers; she was crying.

What had made her cry? The meaning of the words? The ineffable sadness flowing from the melody of the verse and timbre of my voice? Had she perhaps been elated by the hermetic solemnity

of the poems and moved to tears by that *elation?* Or had the lines
simply broken through a secret barrier within her and lifted a
weight long accumulating there?

I do not know. Lucie clung to my neck like a child; her head
pressed up against the cloth of the green uniform stretched across
my chest, and she cried and cried and cried.

9

How many times in recent years have women of all kinds reproached me (because I was unable to reciprocate their feelings)
with being conceited. Nonsense, I'm not in the least conceited; but
to be frank, it does pain me to think that not since reaching maturity have I been able to establish a true relationship with a woman, that I have never, as they say, been in love with a woman. I'm
not sure I know the reasons for my failure, whether they lie in
some innate emotional deficiency or in my life history; I don't
mean to sound pompous, but the truth remains: the image of that
lecture hall with a hundred people raising their hands, giving the
order to destroy my life, comes back to me again and again. Those
hundred people had no idea that things would one day begin to
change; they counted on my being an outcast for life. More out of
malicious obstinacy (the proper domain of meditation) than a desire for martyrdom, I've made up numerous variations on the situation: what it would have been like, for example, if instead of expulsion from the Party the verdict had been hanging by the neck.
No matter how I construe it, I can't see them doing anything but
raising their hands again, especially if the utility of my hanging
had been movingly argued in the opening address. Since then,
whenever I make new acquaintances, men or women with the potential of becoming friends or lovers, I project them back into that
time, that place, and ask myself whether they would have raised
their hands; no one has ever passed the test: every one of them
has raised his hand in the same way my friends and colleagues
(willingly or not, out of conviction or fear) raised theirs. You must
admit: it's not easy to live with people willing to send you to exile

or death, it's not easy to become intimate with them, it's not easy to love them.

Perhaps it was cruel of me to submit the people I met to such merciless scrutiny when it was highly likely they would have led a more or less peaceful existence in my company and never set foot in that hall where hands are raised. There are those perhaps who will say I did it for one reason only: to look down on others from the heights of my moral superiority. But to accuse me of pride would be quite unjust; if I have never voted for anyone's downfall, I am perfectly aware that my merit in the matter is hypothetical: I was deprived of the right to raise my hand quite early in the game. I've long tried to convince myself that if I *had* been in their position I wouldn't have acted as they did, but I'm honest enough to laugh at myself. Why should I have been the only one not to raise his hand, the one just man? No, there is no guarantee I would have acted any better. And how has that affected my relationship with the rest of the world? The consciousness of my own baseness has done nothing to reconcile me to the baseness of others. Nothing is more repugnant to me than brotherly feelings grounded in the common baseness people see in one another. I have no desire for that rank brand of brotherhood.

Then how is it I was able to love Lucie? Fortunately, the observations I have just made date from a later period, and so (a mere adolescent and more prone to sorrow than reflection) I was still able to accept Lucie with open arms and a trusting heart, accept her as a gift, a gift from heaven (a heaven of benevolent, gray skies). That was a happy time for me, the happiest in my life, perhaps. I was run down, worn out, harassed half to death, but day by day I felt a growing sense of inner peace. It's funny: if the women who now hold my arrogance against me and suspect me of considering everybody a fool—if those women knew about Lucie, they'd call *her* a fool and completely fail to understand how I loved her. And I loved her so much I couldn't conceive of ever parting from her; true, we never talked about marriage, but I at least was absolutely serious about marrying her one day. And if it did enter my mind that the match was an unequal one, the inequality of it attracted more than repelled me.

For those few happy months I can be grateful to my commanding officer as well; the noncoms pushed us around as much as they could, searching for specks of dirt in the folds of our uniforms, tearing apart our beds if they found the slightest crease in them; but the commanding officer was a good man. He was beginning to show his age and had been transferred to us from an infantry regiment—a step down, it was rumored. In other words, the fact that he too had been through the mill may have disposed him in our favor. Not that he didn't require order, discipline, and an occasional voluntary Sunday shift (to give his superiors evidence of his political activism), but he never assigned us backbreaking busy work, and he issued our biweekly Saturday passes with a minimum of fuss and bother; if I remember correctly, I managed to see Lucie as often as three times a month that summer.

And when I wasn't with her, I wrote to her, wrote innumerable letters and cards. Looking back, I can't quite picture what I put in them. But that's not the point; the point is that I wrote Lucie any number of letters and Lucie never wrote me one.

I simply could not get her to write to me. Perhaps I intimidated her with my own letters; perhaps she felt she had nothing to write about or would make spelling mistakes; perhaps she was ashamed of the awkward penmanship I knew only from the signature on her identity card. It was not within my power to make her see that I actually admired her awkwardness, her ignorance. I did not value her simplicity in an abstract way; I saw it as a sign of her purity, of a tabula rasa enabling me to make my imprint on her all the more profound and indelible.

At first, Lucie merely thanked me shyly for my letters, but soon she found a way to repay me: instead of writing, she gave me flowers. It all began like this: We were strolling through a wooded area when Lucie suddenly bent down, picked a flower, and handed it to me. I was touched; it didn't embarrass me in the least. But when the next time we met she stood waiting with a whole bunch of them, I began to feel a little uncomfortable.

I was twenty-two and painstakingly careful to avoid everything liable to cast doubts on my virility or maturity. I felt uncomfortable having to walk along the street carrying flowers; I cringed at the thought of buying them, let alone receiving them. In my embarrassment I pointed out to Lucie that it was men who gave flowers to women, not vice versa, but when I saw the tears well up in her eyes, I hastened to add how beautiful they were, and accepted them.

From then on there was no stopping her. There were flowers waiting for me every time we met, and in the end I gave in, disarmed by the spontaneity of the giving and its meaning for the giver. Perhaps her tongue-tied state, her lack of verbal eloquence, made her think of flowers as a form of speech—not the heavy-handed imagery of conventional flower symbolism, but an older, vaguer, more instinctive *precursor of language;* perhaps, having always been sparing of words, she instinctively longed for a mute, preverbal stage of evolution when people communicated with a minimum of gestures, pointing at trees, laughing, touching one another. . . .

Whether or not I grasped the essence of Lucie's flower-giving, I was moved enough by it to feel the desire to reciprocate. Lucie's entire wardrobe amounted to three dresses, and since she always wore them in the same order, our rendezvous followed one another in strict three-four time. I liked them all for being frayed, threadbare, and not very tasteful; I liked her brown overcoat too (short and worn at the cuffs), which, after all, I'd stroked before stroking her face. Yet I took it into my head to buy Lucie a dress, a beautiful dress, many dresses. And one day I suggested we go to a department store.

At first, she thought it was just for fun, to watch the people streaming up and down the stairs. But on the second floor I stopped at a long rack of tightly packed dresses, and Lucie, seeing me eye them with interest, went up closer and began to comment on some of them. "That's a nice one," she said, pointing at a dress with a busy red floral pattern. There were very few good-looking dresses, but some were a bit more presentable than others; I pulled one out and called over to the salesman, "Could the young lady try this one on?" If not for the salesman, Lucie might have put up some resistance, but in front of a stranger she didn't dare, and before she knew what had happened, she found herself in the dressing room.

I gave her some time, then pulled open the curtain slightly to see how she looked; although the dress she was trying on was not particularly attractive, I was flabbergasted: its more or less modern cut had completely transformed her. "May I have a look?" I heard the salesman asking behind me, whereupon he went into an extended paean to Lucie and the dress. Then he turned, looked straight at my insignia, and (knowing full well the answer in advance) asked if I was a political. I nodded. He gave me a wink and said with a smile, "I may have a few things in a better line to show you. Would you care to see them?" And he immediately produced an assortment of stylish summer dresses and a dazzling evening gown. Lucie tried on one after the other; they all looked good on her, and she looked different in each; in the evening gown I didn't recognize her at all.

Turning points in the evolution of a relationship are not always the result of dramatic events; they often stem from something that at first seems completely inconsequential. In the evolution of my love for Lucie the dresses were just such a thing. Until that day at the dress department Lucie had been many things to me: a child, a source of comfort and affection, a balm, an escape from myself—everything, in fact, but a woman. Our love in the physical sense of the word had proceeded no farther than the kissing stage, and the way she kissed was as childish as everything else about her (I'd fallen in love with those kisses—long, but chaste, with dry closed lips counting each other's fine striations as they touched in tender emotion).

In short, until then I had felt affection for Lucie, but no physical desire; I'd grown so accustomed to the absence of desire that I wasn't even conscious of it, and my relationship with Lucie seemed so ideal that I could never have dreamed anything was missing. Everything fit so harmoniously together. Lucie with her cloister-gray outfits and I with my cloister-innocent outlook. But the moment she put on another dress, the equation failed to balance. Suddenly the Lucie I saw lost all connection with the Lucie I'd imagined, and I realized she had potential far beyond that of the touching provincial I'd taken her for. I suddenly saw an attractive woman with a graceful, well-proportioned figure and shapely legs set off alluringly by the elegant cut of the skirt. Her drab protective covering had dissolved instantly in the bright, tasteful, well-made clothes. I was bowled over by the *revelation of her body*.

Lucie shared her room at the dormitory with three other girls. Visitors were permitted two days a week and three hours only, from five to eight; they were required to sign in when they arrived, hand over their identity cards, and sign out when they left. To make matters worse, each of Lucie's roommates had her own boyfriend (or boyfriends), and each of them needed the intimacy of the room for trysts, which meant they were involved in constant bickering and backbiting and kept careful record of every minute one stole from the others. It was all so unpleasant that I'd never once tried to visit Lucie there. But I happened to know that in about a month's time all three were going off on an obligatory agricultural brigade. I told Lucie I wanted to take advantage of the situation and see her in her room. She was far from overjoyed; she told me sadly that she preferred meeting me out of doors. I told her I was longing to spend some time with her in a place where no one would intrude and we could concentrate entirely on each other; I told her I wanted to see how she lived. She was powerless to refuse, and I remember to this day how excited I was when she finally agreed.

10

By that time I had been in Ostrava nearly a year, and military service, so unbearable at first, had become habitual, routine; it was still unpleasant and exhausting, of course, but I had found a way to live with it, make a few friends, and even be happy; for me the summer was radiant (the trees were coated with soot, but they seemed a rich, deep green when I gazed on them with my coalmine eyes); yet as is so often the case, joy concealed the germ of sadness: the sad events of autumn were conceived in green-black summer.

It all began with Stana. Within several months of his March marriage he'd begun to hear rumors that his wife was hanging around the bars; he was terribly upset and wrote her letter after letter; her replies calmed him down for a while, but then (about the time it started getting warm) he had a visit from his mother; he spent an entire Saturday with her and came back to the barracks pale and tight-lipped; at first he was too ashamed to tell anyone anything, but the next day he opened up to Honza, then to others, and soon we all knew; and when Stana saw that we all knew, he talked about it even more, all the time; it became an obsession: his wife had been sleeping around, and he was going to go and wring her neck for her. He tried to get a two-day pass from the commanding officer, but found him none too willing: he had been getting nothing but complaints about Stana from both the mines and the barracks, complaints about his absentmindedness and irritability. So Stana asked for a twenty-four-hour pass. The CO took pity on him and granted it. We never saw him again. All I know about what happened I know from hearsay:

As soon as he got to Prague, he pounced on his wife (I call her his wife, but she was actually just another nineteen-year-old girl), and she admitted everything brazenly (perhaps even eagerly); he started beating her; she fought back; he started choking her and smashed a bottle over her head; she fell to the floor and lay there motionless. He immediately realized what he had done, panicked, and fled; somehow or other he found an empty summer cottage in the mountains and holed up there in terrified anticipation of being caught and hanged for murder. When they found him two months later, they put him on trial for desertion rather than murder. His wife, it turns out, had regained consciousness shortly after he ran out and had nothing to show for the adventure but a bump on the head. While he was serving his time, she divorced him, and today she is the wife of a famous Prague actor. I go to his plays from time to time just to remind myself of Stana and his unhappy end: after his term of service was up, he stayed on in the mines; an accident cost him a leg, the amputation took his life.

That woman, a mainstay, I am told, of various bohemian circles, was the downfall of more than Stana; she was the downfall of us all. At least that's the way it seemed to us. Of course, we can never be absolutely certain whether (as everyone assumed) there was a causal connection between the scandal surrounding Stana's disappearance and the ministerial commission visiting our barracks shortly thereafter; nonetheless, our commanding officer was given his walking papers and replaced by a young officer (he couldn't have been older than twenty-five). And from the day he arrived, everything was different.

He was, as I say, about twenty-five. Unfortunately, he looked a good deal younger, like a little boy in fact, which made it all the more important to him to command our respect. We used to say among ourselves that he rehearsed his speeches in front of the mirror, that he learned them by heart. He was dry and didn't like to shout; with the utmost composure he would make it perfectly clear he regarded us all as criminals. "I know you'd all be happy to see me strung up," the boy commander told us the first time he had us all together, "but if anybody does get hanged around here, it's going to be you, not me."

The first clashes were not long in coming. The incident that sticks most in my mind, perhaps because we found it so hilarious, involved the artist Cenek. During his first year of military service Cenek had done a large number of murals, which under the previous commanding officer had always received their due. As I've said before, Cenek was partial to the Hussite warriors and their leader Jan Zizka, but he always threw in a naked female figure for the pleasure of his friends, justifying her to the CO as a symbol of Liberty or the Motherland. The new CO, every bit as eager to make use of Cenek's services, called him in and asked him to do something for the room where political instruction classes were given. He took the opportunity to tell him to forget about all those Zizkas and "pay more attention to the present," to show the Red Army and its alliance with our working class, its role in the victory of socialism in February 1948. "Yes, sir!" said Cenek, and set to work. After several afternoons spent on the floor painting, he tacked up a series of large sheets of paper along the far wall of the room. When we first saw the finished product (it was a good five feet high and twenty-five feet long), we stood there with our mouths hanging open. In the center stood a heroically posed, warmly clad Soviet soldier with a submachine gun slung over his shoulder, a shaggy fur cap pulled down over his ears, and eight or nine naked women crowding round him. The two standing on either side were gazing up at him coquettishly; he had an arm around the shoulders of each and was laughing a jubilant laugh. The others had draped themselves in such a way as to be looking up at him, holding out their arms towards him, or simply standing there (though one was lying there), showing off their stunning figures.

Cenek took up a position in front of the picture (we were waiting for the political officer to arrive and had the room to ourselves) and gave us a talk that went something like this: Now, here to the right of our sergeant, that's Alena, the first woman I ever had. I was sixteen at the time, and she was the wife of an officer, so she should feel right at home here. I've painted her the way she looked at the time; you can be sure she's gone downhill since. Even then she was on the plump side, right here (he used his finger as a pointer) around the thighs. And because she was much more attractive from the rear, I've done another one of her here (he walked over to one edge of the picture and pointed to a woman whose bare behind seemed on the verge of backing into the room). I may have made her regal posterior a bit larger than life, but that's the way we like them, isn't it? Anyway, I was young and foolish then and had no idea why she kept asking me to give her "love taps" back there. One day, she got fed up and said, That's not what I mean. Here, pull the little lady's skirt up, and I had to pull her skirt up and her panties down, and still all I did was to pat her like before, and she got really annoyed and started yelling, Beat me, you little snot-nose, you! Beat me hard! What an idiot I was. Anyway, this one (he pointed to the girl on the sergeant's left), this one is Lojzka, I was much more experienced by the time I got to her, she had small breasts (he pointed to them), long legs (he pointed to them), and very pretty features (he pointed to them too), and she was in my year at school. And this is our model from live drawing class, I knew her inside out; we all did, all twenty of us; she would stand in the middle of the classroom while we used her body to study the human form, but none of us ever laid a finger on her: her mother was always there waiting at the end of the class to whisk her off, so she could show herself off without taking the consequences. Now this one (he pointed to a woman lolling on a stylized divan), this one was a whore from the word go, come up a little closer (we did) and have a look at that little mark on her stomach, it's a cigarette burn they say she got from a jealous woman she was having an affair with because, yes, gentlemen, she liked it both ways, and by the way, she had a box that would accommodate anything you cared to stick up it, a real accordion it was, why, she had room for the whole lot of us, to say nothing of our wives and girls and kids and all the folks back home. . . .

Cenek was obviously hitting his stride, but he was interrupted by the political commissar, and we had to go back to our seats. The commissar, who was used to Cenek's murals from the days of the old CO, launched into a stentorian reading of a pamphlet elucidating the differences between socialist and capitalist armies without even glancing up at Cenek's latest creation. Just as Cenek's commentary was fading away in our minds and we were settling down to our own quiet reveries, in walked the boy commander and up we jumped. He had come to check up on the commissar's talk, but before he could motion us to our seats, he was transfixed by what he saw on the far wall. Instead of letting the commissar go on with his talk, he barked out at Cenek, What is the meaning of this? Cenek broke ranks and planted himself in front of the picture: Here we have an allegorical representation of the significance of the Red Army for the struggle currently engaged in by our nation, he declaimed. Here (he pointed to the sergeant) we see the Red Army, and flanking the Red Army (he pointed to the officer's wife) the working class and (he pointed to his schoolmate) the revolutionary month of February. Now, these (he pointed to the other ladies in turn) are symbolic of liberty, victory, and equality, and here (he pointed to the officer's wife displaying her hindquarters) we find the bourgeoisie making its exit from the stage of history.

When Cenek had finished, the CO declared the mural an insult to the Red Army and ordered it removed at once. He told Cenek he would have to take the consequences. What for? I asked (under my breath). The CO heard me and asked if I had any objections. I said I liked the mural. The CO said he wasn't surprised; it was perfect for masturbators. I reminded him that none other than Myslbek had sculpted Liberty as a nude, that Ales had a famous painting of the River Jizera as *three* nudes, that painters had used nudes allegorically throughout history.

The boy commander gave me a dubious look and repeated that the mural was to be taken down. Perhaps we had managed to throw him off guard, though, because Cenek was not punished, not this time, at least. But the CO had taken a real dislike to him and to me as well, and it wasn't long before he had first Cenek, then me, up on disciplinary charges.

This is how it happened: One day our company was working with picks and shovels in an out-of-the-way section of camp. Since we were under the none too watchful eye of a lethargic corporal, we spent most of the time leaning on our shovels discussing this and that, and failed to notice the boy commander observing us from a distance. The first hint we had of his presence was his peremptory "Private Jahn, come here immediately!" I grabbed my shovel with a great show of energy and went and stood at attention before him. "Is that your idea of work?" he asked. I can't quite remember how I responded, but I know I wasn't insolent: I had no intention of making life in the barracks any harder for myself or needlessly antagonizing a man who had complete power over me. But after my innocent, even embarrassed reply, his eyes hardened. He stepped up close to me, grabbed hold of my arm, and flipped me over his shoulder in a perfectly executed feat of jujitsu. Then he squatted down beside me and pinned me to the ground (I made no attempt to defend myself, I was so surprised). "Had enough?" he asked in a loud voice (so everyone could hear). I told him I had. He ordered me back to attention and announced to the assembled company, "I am giving Private Jahn two days' detention. Not for insubordination. That, as you all saw, I took care of with my own hands. No, I am giving him two days for lying down on the job. And next time the rest of you can expect the same." Then turning on his heel, he strode off with style.

At the time my feeling for the man was one of unqualified hatred. But hatred shines too bright a light on things, deprives them of their relief. At the time all I could see in him was a vindictive, wily bastard; now I see him as a young man playing a part. The young can't help acting: they're thrust immature into a mature world and must *act* mature. They therefore adopt the forms, patterns, and models of anyone who appeals to them, seems fashionable enough, and suits their purposes—and try to act like him.

Take the boy commander. Immature and inexperienced, he suddenly found himself at the head of a group of soldiers he couldn't possibly understand. If he was able to come to grips with the situation, it was only because so much of what he had read and heard offered him a ready-made mask: the cold-blooded hero of the cheap thriller, the tough guy with nerves of steel, the man who can lay low any gang, who lives by his wits not his words, whose faith in his fists gives him faith in himself as a whole. The more self-conscious he was about his boyish appearance, the more fanatical his devotion to the iron man persona, the more forced his performance.

Of course, this wasn't the first time I'd come up against adolescent role playing. At the time of the postcard interrogation I had just turned twenty and my interrogators couldn't have been more than a year or two older. They too were basically *boys* covering their nakedness with the mask they found most suitable, the mask of the hard, ascetic revolutionary. What about Marketa? Hadn't she modeled herself after the female savior in some grade B film? And Zemanek, suddenly seized by a sentimental morality? Wasn't that a mask as well? And myself? Didn't I run back and forth among several masks until I was tripped up and lost my balance?

Youth is a terrible thing: it is a stage trod by children in buskins and fancy costumes mouthing speeches they've memorized and fanatically believe but only half understand. History too is a terrible thing: it so often ends up a playground for youth—the young Nero, the young Napoleon, fanaticized mobs of children whose simulated passions and primitive poses suddenly metamorphose into a catastrophically real reality.

When I think of all this, my whole set of values goes awry and I feel a deep hatred towards youth, coupled with a certain paradoxical indulgence towards the criminals of history, whose crimes I suddenly see as no more than the terrible restlessness of waiting to grow up.

And when I think back on all the children waiting to grow up, I can't help recalling Alexej. He too had a large part to play, one that went beyond both his reason and his experience. Like the commanding officer, he looked young for his age, though he lacked the CO's charm: he had a puny build, shortsighted eyes peering out from behind thick glasses, and a complexion studded with blackheads (the gift of a potentially eternal puberty). He'd begun his service at an infantry officers candidate school, but was suddenly transferred to us. As it turns out, the notorious show trials were about to begin, and every day, in Party headquarters, courtrooms, and police stations all over the country, hands were being raised to strip the accused of all confidence, honor, and freedom. Alexej was the son of a highly placed Communist official who had been recently arrested.

He appeared out of nowhere one day and was given Stana's empty bunk. He showed us the same reserve I had shown my new companions at first, and when it became known he was a member of the Party (he hadn't yet been expelled), the others began watching what they said in his presence.

As soon as he found out I had been a Party member myself, he opened up a bit; he told me that come what might, he was determined to pass the supreme test life had placed before him and never betray the Party. Then he read me a poem he had written (the first he had ever written) when he heard he was to be transferred to our regiment. One of the verses went like this:

> *Do as you please, Comrades,*
> *Drag me through the mud and spit on me too.*
> *But caked in mud and spittle, Comrades,*
> *I shall remain steadfast in the ranks with you.*

I understood what he meant, because I'd felt just the same a year before. But with time it bothered me a good deal less: Lucie, my guide back into the everyday world, had removed me from the regions where Alexej and his kind live in desperate torment.

While the boy commander was busy setting up his new regime, I was concerned mainly with getting myself a pass; Lucie's roommates had gone off to work in the fields, and I hadn't been let out of camp for a month; the CO had taken careful note of my face and name, and in the army that's the worst thing that can happen to you. He lost no opportunity to make it clear that every hour of my life was dependent on his fancy. As for my pass, the outlook was grim; at the very beginning he'd announced that leave would be granted only to men taking voluntary Sunday shifts on a regular basis, so we all did; but it was a miserable existence, working all month without any time away from the mines, and when one or another of us actually did get a Saturday off and staggered back at two in the morning, he went to work the next day dead tired and looked like a sleepwalker a long time thereafter.

I started working Sunday shifts with the rest of them, although that in itself was no guarantee of a pass: the merits earned by a Sunday shift could easily be offset by a poorly made bed or some other such infraction of the rules. But (occasionally, at least) power manifests its arbitrary will in the form of mercy as well as malice. The boy commander's ego must have been gratified when after several weeks of the latter he could show me the former, and at the last moment, two days before Lucie's roommates were due back, I got my pass.

I was trembling with excitement when the old woman at the desk signed me in and told me to go up to the fourth floor, where I knocked on a door at the far end of a long hallway. The door opened, but Lucie stood hidden behind it, and all I could see was the room itself; at first glance, it bore no resemblance to a dormitory room; I seemed to have entered a sanctuary of some kind: the desk was decorated with a bunch of sparkling gold dahlias, the window flanked by two enormous rubber plants, and everything (the vase, the bed, the floor, even the pictures) was festooned with green sprays (asparagus fern, I recognized them immediately), as if Jesus Christ were expected to ride in on a donkey.

I took Lucie in my arms (she was still hiding behind the door) and kissed her. She was wearing the black evening gown and high heels I had bought for her the day we went shopping for clothes. Standing there in black amidst all the festive greenery, she looked like a priestess.

We closed the door behind us, and it was only then I recognized the room for what it was, saw the four iron beds, four chipped night tables, desk, and three chairs under the greenery. But nothing could dampen the delight that had overcome me the minute Lucie opened the door: not only did I have a few hours to myself for the first time in a month; for the first time in a year I was in a *small room;* the intoxicating intimacy of it was overpowering.

Whenever I went walking with Lucie, the open spaces kept me tied to the barracks and my lot there; the ever-present air currents were like an invisible chain binding me to the camp gate and its inscription: WE SERVE THE PEOPLE; I felt there was nowhere I could ever stop "serving the people"; I hadn't been inside a small private room for an entire year.

And here I was all at once in a totally new situation: I had three hours of absolute freedom ahead of me; I could fearlessly (and against all military regulations) throw off my cap and belt, I could throw off my shirt, trousers, boots, everything, I could even jump up and down on them if I so desired; I could do whatever I pleased and never worry about being observed; besides, the room was so nice and warm, and the warmth and freedom went to my head like piping hot wine; I put my arms around Lucie, kissed her, and took her over to the bed. The sprays on the bed (which was otherwise covered by a cheap gray blanket) moved me deeply; the only way I could interpret them was as symbols of wedlock, and I was struck (and touched) by the idea that Lucie in her innocence had resurrected a time-honored popular custom, that she wished to bid her virginity farewell with all due ceremony.

It was some time before I realized that although Lucie was responding to my kisses and embraces, she was also holding back. Her lips kissed me hungrily, but remained closed; she pressed her whole body up against mine, but when I slipped my hand under her skirt to feel the warmth of her thighs, she pulled away. I was beginning to see that my desire to let myself go and be carried away blindly was not being reciprocated, and I remember at that point (no more than five minutes after I'd entered the room) feeling my eyes well up with tears of disappointment.

We sat down side by side (crushing the unfortunate sprays beneath us) and began to make conversation. After a few minutes (the conversation never got off the ground) I tried putting my arms around her again, but she resisted; I began struggling with her, but soon realized that ours was anything but an amorous tussle, that it was threatening to turn our loving relationship into something ugly, that Lucie was putting up a real fight, a furious, almost desperate fight. My only choice was retreat.

I tried to bring her round with words; I talked and talked; I suppose I told her that I loved her and that loving meant giving yourselves to each other, fully; I didn't say anything original, of course (my goal wasn't particularly original either); but even if my argumentation was less than brilliant, it was irrefutable; nor did Lucie try to refute it. Instead, she remained silent or said, "Don't, please, no," or "Not now, not today . . ." and tried (with rather touching ineptitude) to change the subject.

I tried another line: You don't mean to tell me you're the type who leads a man on just to have a laugh at his expense; you don't have it in you to be so heartless and cruel. . . . Again I put my arms around her, again we had a brief, depressing struggle, and (again) I felt the ugliness of it all.

Suddenly it came to me, the reason why she was putting up such resistance; God, why hadn't I thought of it before? She was just a child, afraid of love, a virgin, frightened, frightened of the unknown. I determined to camouflage my urgency—how it must have terrified her—to be tender, loving, and make the act of love no more than an extension of the tender, loving caresses we had known together. I stopped insisting and began fondling. I kissed her (for what seemed like an age), pressed her to me (deceitfully, guilefully), and tried as surreptitiously as possible to work her into a reclining position. I finally succeeded. I stroked her breasts (something she'd never resisted); I told her I wanted to be gentle to her whole body, because she *was* her body, and I wanted to be gentle to all of her; I even managed to raise her skirt a little and kiss her five, then eight or nine inches above the knee; I didn't get any farther; when I tried to move my head as far as her lap, she jerked away from me in terror and jumped off the bed. Her face had a convulsive look about it I'd never seen before.

Lucie, Lucie, is it the light that makes you so ashamed? Would you rather it were dark? She clutched at my question as if it were a life preserver. Yes, she was ashamed of the light. I went over to the window to pull the blinds, but Lucie shouted out, "No, don't do it! Don't draw the blinds!" "Why not?" I asked. "Because I'm afraid," she said. "What are you afraid of, the light or the dark?" Instead of answering, she burst into tears.

Her resistance aroused no pity in me whatsoever; it seemed senseless to me, unmerited, unjust; it tortured me, I couldn't comprehend it. I asked her whether she was putting up such a fight because she was a virgin, whether she was afraid of the pain. Each of my questions she answered with an obedient nod of the head, hoping one or another would give her a way out. I told her how wonderful it was that she was a virgin and would learn all about love from someone who loved her. "Aren't you looking forward to being mine and all that goes with it?" Yes, she was, she said. I put my arms around her again, and again she resisted. It was all I could do to keep from losing my temper once and for all. "Why do you keep fighting me?" "Next time," she said. "I will, I want to, but next time, please, some other time, not today." "Why not today?" "Not today," she answered. "But why?" "Please not today," she answered. "But when? You know very well this is our last chance to be alone together. Tomorrow your roommates are coming back. Where else can we be alone?" "You'll find a place," she said. "All right," I said, "I'll find a place. But promise you'll come with me. It's not likely to be as nice a room as this one." "That doesn't matter," she said. "That doesn't matter. It can be wherever you like." "All right then, but promise you'll be my wife there, promise you won't put up a fight." "All right," she said. "Promise?" "Yes."

That promise, I realized, was the most I'd get out of Lucie for the time being. It wasn't much, but it was more than nothing. I swallowed my indignation, and we spent the rest of the time talking. When it was time to go, I shook my uniform free of asparagus fern, patted Lucie on the cheek, and told her I'd be thinking of nothing but our next time together (and I wasn't lying).

12

Not long after (it was a rainy autumn day), we trudged our way from the mine to the barracks on a road full of pothole puddles. We were muddy, drenched, and yearning for a little rest: most of us hadn't had a single Sunday off all month. But as soon as dinner was over we were called out by the boy commander and informed that during the afternoon inspection of our quarters he had uncovered certain irregularities. He then handed us over to the noncoms and ordered them to drill us for an extra two hours as punishment.

Since we had no weapons, the drills and combat exercises were particularly nonsensical; their only purpose was to devalue our time in as debasing a manner as possible. At one point during the boy commander's reign I remember our spending a whole afternoon hauling heavy boards from one end of the camp to the other; the next afternoon we hauled them back; and we went on alternating for ten more days. But everything we did in camp after a day in the mines was on the board-hauling level. The only difference this time was that instead of boards it was our bodies we were hauling back and forth; we turned them about face and right face, we flung them to the ground and picked them up again, we ran here and there with them and dragged them through the mud. Three hours later the boy commander showed up and motioned to the noncoms to take us off for physical training.

Tucked away behind the barracks was a small field that could be used for soccer or battle exercises or races. The noncoms decided to stage a relay race. Our company was made up of nine squads of ten men each, so we formed nine ten-man teams. The noncoms needed no excuse to run us into the ground, but because they were for the most part between eighteen and twenty and consequently

couldn't resist a chance to show off, they decided to pit themselves against us and put together their own team.

It took a long time for them to explain what they had in mind
and for us to understand it, namely, that the first ten men would
sprint from one end of the field to the other, where each would
find a man waiting for him, and those men would sprint back to
where the first men had started off from, by which time another
ten men would be waiting for them, and so on. Then they counted
us off laboriously and dispatched us to opposite ends of the field.

We were dead tired after the mines and the drills, and furious
at the thought of having to run a race besides. And then I had a
primitive idea: why not stage a showdown? I tried it out on a
friend or two, and it caught on right away. A wave of muffled
laughter ran through the mass of weary soldiers as the plan passed
from mouth to mouth.

At last we were in place and ready to go, ready to run a race
whose entire concept was absurd from start to finish: although we
would be racing in uniform and heavy boots, we had to kneel
down at the starting line; although we would be passing on the
baton in a most unorthodox manner (the runner we handed it to
would be facing us), we had genuine batons to do it with and a
genuine pistol shot to start us off. The corporal in the tenth line
(the first runner for the noncoms) shot out at breakneck speed,
while we (I was in the first heat) straightened up slowly and started off in a slow jog; after twenty yards it was all we could do to
keep from guffawing: the corporal had nearly reached the other
end of the field while we straggled along together, huffing and
puffing in an excess of effort. Soon the soldiers on both sides of
the field were shouting us on: "Go! Go! Go!..." Halfway down the
field we passed the second runner for the noncom team tearing
towards the starting line. By the time we'd made it to the other
end of the field and handed over our batons, the third noncom
had darted out with his baton and was preparing to lap us.

Today I look back on that race as the last stand of the black
insignia. The men's ingenuity knew no bounds: Honza limped terribly, but we cheered him on with all our might, and he scored a
hero's victory (to great applause) by coming in two steps before

the others; Matlos the Gypsy fell to the ground eight or nine times; Cenek lifted his knees to his chin with each step (which must have been much more tiring than running normally at top speed). No one let us down: not Bedrich, the disciplined (and resigned) drafter of peace manifestos, who trotted along at the same speed as the others but with great dignity; nor Pavel Pekny, who disliked me; nor old man Ambroz, who ran bolt upright, his hands clasped behind his back; nor redheaded Petran, who gave out a high-pitched screech as he ran; nor Varga the Hungarian, who shouted "Hurrah!" all the way—not one of them spoiled this wonderful little game that had us all holding our sides.

Then we saw the boy commander walking towards the field from the barracks. One of the corporals saw him too and went over to report. The captain heard him out, then went up to the edge of the field to watch the race for himself. The NCOs (whose anchorman had long since crossed the finish line) started getting nervous and shouting, "Get a move on there! Faster! Hurry it up!" but our cheers completely drowned them out. The NCOs didn't know whether to stop the race or not; they ran back and forth to confer, keeping an eye on the CO, but the CO never even glanced in their direction; he was watching the race, watching it with an icy stare.

The time had finally come for our last group of runners. It happened to include Alexej, and I was very curious to see how he would react. Sure enough, he wanted to spoil the fun. Running ahead full force, he gained five meters in the first twenty. But then something peculiar happened: his pace slowed down, he stopped gaining. I realized in a flash that as much as Alexej wished to spoil the fun, he was incapable of it; he was so sickly, he had so little strength and stamina, that they'd had to take him off heavy work in the mines after two days. That realization made his run the highlight of the entire farce for me. There he was, driving himself as hard as he could, yet he was indistinguishable from the boys idling along five paces behind him at the same speed. The noncoms and the commanding officer must have been convinced that Alexej's brisk start was as much a part of the comedy as Honza's feigned limp, Matlos's tumbles, and our cheering. Alexej's fists were every bit as clenched as those of the runners behind him; they strained and wheezed every bit as much as Alexej. The difference was that Alexej felt *real* pain and his efforts to overcome it sent *real* sweat pouring down his face. Halfway across the field Alexej slowed down even more, and a few of the clowning runners gradually caught up with him; thirty meters from the finish line he stopped running altogether and hobbled his way to the finish line, one hand clamped to the left side of his groin.

The CO ordered us to fall in. He asked why we'd run so slowly. "We were tired, Comrade Captain." He told everyone who was tired to raise his hand. We raised our hands. I looked over at Alexej (who was standing in the row in front of me); he was the only one whose hand had not gone up. The CO hadn't noticed, and said, "I see, all of you." "No, Comrade Captain." "Who wasn't tired?" "I wasn't," said Alexej. "You weren't?" asked the CO, staring at him. "And why is that, if I may ask?" "Because I'm a Communist," answered Alexej. The company half grumbled, half laughed. "Are you the one who finished last?" asked the CO. "I am," said Alexej. "And you weren't tired," said the CO. "No," answered Alexej. "If you weren't tired, then you sabotaged the race on purpose. That's two weeks for attempted mutiny. The rest of you were tired, you have an excuse. But since your output in the mines is so low, you must be using up all your energy on your days off. Out of concern for your health I am canceling all leaves for the next two months."

Before leaving for the guardhouse, Alexej had a talk with me. He reproached me for not behaving like a Communist and asked me with a stern look whether I was for or against socialism. I replied that I was for socialism, but that here in camp it made no difference whatsoever, because the lines were drawn differently, the only valid line being the one between those who had lost control over their own destinies and those who had taken it away from them and could do with it as they pleased. But Alexej did not agree; he insisted that the line between socialism and reaction held everywhere and that the whole purpose of our camp was to defend good Communists against the enemies of socialism. I asked him how the boy commander was defending socialism against its enemies by sending him, Alexej, to the guardhouse for two weeks and by treating all the men in a way calculated to make them confirmed enemies of socialism, and Alexej admitted disliking him. But when I said that if here in camp there was a dividing line between socialism and reaction, then he ought to be on the other side, he replied brusquely that this was where he belonged. "My father was arrested for espionage. Do you understand what that means? How can the Party trust me? It is the Party's *duty* not to trust me."

A few days later I had a talk with Honza. The topic was quite different: I was bemoaning (with Lucie in mind) our two months without leave. "Don't you worry, Ludvik old boy," he said. "We'll be out more than ever."

The good-natured sabotage of the relay race strengthened our sense of solidarity and led to a flurry of activity. Honza put together a small committee to research various AWOL possibilities. Within forty-eight hours everything was ready: a bribery fund had been set up; the two noncoms in our hut had been bought off; and several strands of wire had been unobtrusively cut at the most strategic spot in the fence, near the infirmary, only fifteen feet from the first few cottages in the village. The closest cottage belonged to a miner we knew from the mines; it didn't take long for the boys to get him to leave his gate unlocked; all the soldier had to do was to make his way unnoticed to the camp fence, crawl under, and sprint the fifteen feet to the cottage gate; once inside, he was in complete safety: he simply walked through the house and out onto the street.

Although the route was relatively sure, we had to be careful not to abuse it. If too many men sneaked out of camp at once, their absence would be noticed immediately. As a result, Honza's ad hoc committee had to regulate the number of AWOLs per day and establish a long-term schedule.

But before I ever had my turn, the whole operation came to grief. One night the commanding officer made a personal inspection of our quarters and discovered three men missing. He cornered the noncom in charge (who hadn't reported the men's absence) and asked him with complete self-assurance how much we'd shelled out to him. The corporal, assuming the commanding officer knew the whole story, made no attempt to hide it. When the CO confronted him with Honza, he confirmed that Honza was the one who had given him the money.

The boy commander had us where he wanted us. First, he arranged for the NCO, Honza, and the three soldiers on AWOL to be court-martialed. (I didn't even have time to say good-bye to my best friend; it all took place the next morning while we were in the mines; not until years later did I learn they'd all been convicted and Honza got a year in prison.) Then, at the next assembly, he announced he was extending the ban on leaves for an additional two months and putting us all under a special disciplinary regime. He had also requested the construction of two watchtowers—one for each end of the camp—a system of searchlights, and two patrols of German shepherds specially trained for guarding camps.

The commander's attack was so sudden and effective that we were all positive someone had squealed on Honza and his operation. Not that our battalion was a hotbed of informers (we were unanimous in our scorn for the practice), but we knew the possibility was always there: it was the most effective means at our disposal for bettering our lot, getting released on time, receiving good character references, and laying the foundation for some sort of future. Though we ourselves (the great majority of us) resisted this most abominable of abominations, we couldn't quite resist suspecting others of it.

On this occasion suspicion spread like wildfire, quickly turned into collective conviction (though other explanations of the commander's attack were perfectly reasonable), and settled unconditionally on Alexej. He was in the guardhouse serving out his sentence when it happened, but he still had to put in his time down in the mines and spent a good part of the day with us, so everyone was certain he'd had ample opportunity ("with those well-trained ears of his") to pick up something of Honza's scheme.

Poor puny Alexej really went through the mill: the foreman (one of us) started giving him the toughest jobs again; his tools suddenly began vanishing, and he had to pay for replacements out of his wages; he was the constant butt of insults and insinuations, had to put up with an infinite variety of pranks; and the day he returned to the barracks someone decorated the wooden wall above his bunk with a sign in big, black, motor-oil letters saying BEWARE OF THE RAT.

Several days after Honza and the other four delinquents were led off under escort, I happened to go into the barracks late in the afternoon. There was no one there but Alexej, who was remaking his bunk. I asked him what had happened. He told me the boys messed up his bed several times a day. I told him they were all convinced he'd informed on Honza. He protested, on the verge of tears, that he knew nothing about it and would never inform on anybody. "How can you say you'd never inform on anybody?" I said. "You think of yourself as the CO's ally. It's only logical you'd pass on information to him." "I'm not the CO's ally!" he said, his voice breaking. "The CO is a saboteur!" Then he poured out the conclusions he'd come to while sitting and thinking things through in the guardhouse: Black insignia were created by the Party for men it could not trust with arms, but deemed capable of reeducation; but the class enemy never sleeps; it does everything in its power to prevent the reeducation process from taking place; and since it looks on the men in penal battalions as reserves for the counterrevolution, it has a real stake in maintaining their virulent hatred for Communism. The way the boy commander treated the men, the way he kept provoking them—it was all clearly part of the enemy's plan. You never know where the enemy might be lurking. The CO was definitely an enemy agent. But Alexej knew his duty and had drafted a detailed account of the CO's activities. I was stunned. "What's that? You've done what? Have you sent it anywhere?" He told me he'd sent his accusations straight to the Party.

We went outside. He asked me if I wasn't afraid of being seen with him. I told him he was a fool for asking and a bigger fool if he thought his letter was going to reach its destination. He replied that he was a Communist and required to act at all times in a manner befitting a Communist. And again he reminded me that *I* was a Communist (even though I'd been expelled from the Party) and should behave accordingly. "As Communists we are responsible for everything that is going on here." I nearly laughed in his face. Responsibility was unthinkable without freedom, I told him. He said he felt free enough to act like a Communist and that he *had* to prove, *would* prove himself a Communist. His jaw trembled as he spoke. Today, years later, I can still remember it clearly, but now I realize that Alexej was not much more than twenty at the time, a child, an adolescent, and his destiny hung on him like the clothes of a giant on a little boy.

Not long after my talk with Alexej, Cenek asked me (just as Alexej had feared) what I was doing talking to that rat. I told him Alexej might be a fool but he was no rat, and I told him about Alexej's complaint about the CO. Cenek was unimpressed. "I don't know if he's a fool or not," he said, "but I'm absolutely positive he's a rat. Anyone who can publicly renounce his father is a rat in my book." I didn't understand at first; he was surprised I hadn't heard; after all, the political commissar himself had shown them the newspaper—a few months old by then—that carried Alexej's statement: he had renounced his father for betraying and defiling the most sacred thing in his life.

That evening the searchlights on the newly constructed watchtowers lit up the camp for the first time, and a guard accompanied by a German shepherd patrolled the barbed wire. Suddenly I felt terribly alone: I yearned to see Lucie and knew I would have to wait two whole months. I sat down and wrote her a long letter; I wrote that I wouldn't be seeing her for some time; we weren't allowed out of camp, and I was sorry she'd denied me what I so desired, the memory of it would have sustained me through these hard weeks.

The day after I sent the letter off was like every other: after the mines we did our compulsory about faces, forward marches, and hit the dirts, and as usual I went through the motions, scarcely noticing the corporal in charge or my friends marching and hitting the dirt around me or the barracks on three sides of us or even the road running along the barbed-wire fence on the fourth side. Now and then someone would walk past the fence; now and then someone would stop (mainly children, alone or with their parents, who would explain that we were soldiers drilling). It was all a lifeless backdrop to me, a painted scrim (everything on the other side of the barbed wire was a painted scrim), so I never would even have looked up if someone hadn't called softly in that direction, "Hey there, girl, what're you staring at?"

Then I saw her. It was Lucie. She was standing by the fence in her old brown overcoat (it never occurred to us as we made our summer purchases that winter was not far behind) and the fashionable black high-heeled shoes I had given her (they clashed ludicrously), standing motionless by the fence and looking in our direction. The men started by commenting on the unusual resigned air she had about her, but gradually their remarks betrayed the desperation of men kept in forced celibacy. The corporal noticed that the men's attention was wandering, and soon realized the cause, but he was powerless to order the girl away from the fence: the realm outside the fence was a realm of relative freedom to which his jurisdiction did not extend. His impotence infuriated him. He ordered the men to keep their comments to themselves, then stepped up the volume of his voice and the pace of the drill.

She began walking back and forth, and for a while I would lose sight of her; but she always returned to the spot where she had stood before. Even when the drill was over, I couldn't go up to her; we still had political instruction; and it wasn't until we'd sat through an hour of stock phrases about the camp of peace and imperialist warmongers that I was able to slip out (it was almost dark by then) and see whether Lucie was still by the fence; she was, and I ran over to her.

She told me not to be angry with her, she loved me, and she was sorry if she'd made me unhappy. I told her I didn't know when I could see her again. She said it didn't matter, she'd come and see me here. (At this point a few of the men walked past and called out something obscene at us.) I asked her whether she would mind having soldiers shout at her like that. She said no, she wouldn't, because she loved me. She slipped me a rose through the fence (the bugle sounded assembly), and we kissed through a gap in the barbed wire.

13

Lucie came to the fence almost every day; I was on the morning shift in the mines, so I spent afternoons in camp. Every day I received a small bunch of flowers (once during kit inspection the sergeant threw them on the floor) and exchanged a few words with her (the same words each time, because we actually had nothing to say to each other; we didn't go into news or ideas; we simply wished to reassure each other of a single constantly reiterated truth), and nearly every day I wrote her letters; it was the most intensive period of our love. The searchlights burning on the watchtowers, the dogs barking at the approach of evening, the cocky little boy reigning over us all—they took up very little of my thoughts; I concentrated entirely on Lucie's visits.

I was actually quite happy in camp, surrounded by killer dogs, and in the mines, vibrating with my pneumatic drill; happy and proud, for in Lucie I possessed a prize vouchsafed neither to my fellow soldiers nor to our officers: I was loved, I was loved publicly and demonstratively. And even if Lucie wasn't their idea of the perfect woman, even if the way she showed her love was—from their point of view—rather odd, it was still the love of a woman and it aroused feelings of wonder, nostalgia, and envy.

The longer we were cut off from the world and women, the more women dominated our talk. Every particular, every detail, was significant: we recalled birthmarks, outlined (pencil on paper, pick in clay, finger in sand) breasts and backsides; we argued over which absent bodies had the most perfect curves; we gave exact renditions of words and sighs uttered during intercourse; and then we started all over again, embroidering more each time. It was only natural for them to be even more curious than normal when my turn came, because they saw my girl daily and were able to picture her and make the connection between her actual appearance and my descriptions. I couldn't disappoint my friends; I had to tell them; I had to expatiate on Lucie's nakedness, which I'd never seen, and our nights of love, which I'd never known. And as I spoke, a precise, minutely detailed picture of her quiet passion rose before my eyes.

What was it like, the first time I made love to her?

It was in her room at the dormitory. She undressed in front of me, docile, devoted, but obviously shy: she was a country girl, and I was the first man to see her naked. It drove me wild—that combination of devotion and shyness. When I went up to her, she shrank back and covered her lap with her hands. . . .

Why does she always wear those black high heels?

I told them I'd bought them for her to wear when she was naked; she was shy about it, but did everything I asked of her; I kept my clothes on till the last possible moment, and she would walk up and down in front of me in those heels (how I loved seeing her naked when I was dressed!) and then go over to the cupboard, where she kept the wine, and, still naked, fill my glass. . . .

So when Lucie came up to the fence, I wasn't the only one looking at her; I was joined by ten or so of my fellow soldiers, who knew precisely what she was like when she made love (what she said, how she moaned) and who would make all kinds of innuendos about the black heels she had on again, and picture her parading naked in them around her tiny room.

Each of my friends could conjure up one or another woman and share her with the rest of us, but I was the only one who could offer a *picture* to go with the words; mine was the only one who was real, alive, there. The feeling of friendly solidarity that had led me to paint so detailed a picture of Lucie's nakedness and erotic behavior had the effect of painfully intensifying my desire for her. I was not the least bit upset by the obscenities they used each time she appeared at the gate; they could never act them out (the barbed wire and dogs protected her from all of us, myself included); besides, they were the ones who actually gave her to me: they brought my fantasy of her into focus and helped me to paint its picture, adding all kinds of ravishingly seductive traits; we all desired her passionately. Whenever I went up to her at the fence, I could feel myself tremble; I was tongue-tied with desire; I couldn't understand how I had taken six months to see the woman in her; I was willing to give anything for a single night alone with her.

Not that my attitude towards her had become violent or coarse or any less affectionate. I'd even go so far as to say that it was the only time in my life I experienced *total desire for a woman;* it encompassed my entire being: body and soul, lust and sensitivity, grief and wanton vitality, the longing for vulgarity as well as consolation, for the moment of ecstasy as well as eternal possession. I was completely involved, focused, centered, and I now think of those days as a paradise lost (an odd paradise—guarded by a pack of dogs and echoing a corporal's commands).

I resolved to arrange a meeting with Lucie at all costs; I had her word that she "wouldn't put up a fight" and would meet me anywhere I chose, and she'd confirmed it many times during our brief talks through the fence. All I had to do was to take the plunge.

It wasn't long before I came up with a plan. Honza's escape route had never been discovered by the CO. The fence still had an imperceptible gap in it, and the arrangement with the miner who lived opposite the barracks merely needed renewing. Of course, the camp was heavily guarded, and escape by day was out of the question. And while at night there were the searchlights and dog patrol to contend with, it was all more for effect and the CO's gratification than from suspicion of a break on our part: attempted escape meant the possibility of court-martial; it was much too risky. That was why I thought I had a chance.

All I had to do was to find a suitable hideaway for Lucie and myself, some place not too far from camp. Most of the men living in the area worked in the same mine as we did, and it wasn't long before I found someone (a fifty-year-old widower) who was willing to lend me his place on my terms (a mere three hundred crowns). The house where he lived was visible from camp; I pointed it out to Lucie through the fence and told her my plan; she was less than thrilled; she begged me not to take any chances for her sake; if she agreed to go through with it in the end, it was only because she didn't know how to say no.

Finally the appointed day arrived. It began rather oddly. Right after we got back from our shift, the boy commander had us fall in for one of his frequent talks. Usually he tried to scare us with the war about to break out and the hard days ahead for all reactionaries (by which he mainly meant us). This time, however, he threw in some new ideas: The class enemy had wormed its way into the heart of the Communist Party, but all spies and traitors were hereby advised that enemies who hid behind masks would be dealt with a hundred times more severely than those who came out and said what they thought, because an enemy who hid behind a mask was no better than a mangy cur. "And we have one such mangy cur here in our midst." He ordered Alexej to step forward, and pulling a piece of paper out of his pocket, thrust it in his face. "Have you seen this letter before?" "I have," said Alexej. "You're a mangy cur, an informer, and a spy. But when a dog squeals, the sound doesn't travel." And he tore the letter to shreds.

"I have another letter for you," he added, handing Alexej an unsealed envelope. "Read it out loud." Alexej took a sheet of paper out of the envelope and skimmed it, but didn't say a word. "Read it out loud!" repeated the CO. Again Alexej said nothing. "Are you going to read it or aren't you?" asked the CO, and when Alexej still said nothing, he barked out, "Hit the dirt!" and Alexej flung himself into the mud. The boy commander stood over him for a moment, and we were all positive he was going to burst into a volley of "Up! Down! Up! Down!" and Alexej would have to pick himself up, fling himself down, pick himself up, fling himself down. But no, the commander left him there, turned away, and started walking slowly along the front rank, carefully inspecting the men's equipment as he went. When he reached the end of the rank (it took him several minutes), he turned around and walked slowly back to where Alexej still lay. "Now read it," he said, and yes, Alexej lifted his muddy chin off the ground, stretched out his right hand (it was still clutching the letter), and, lying there on his stomach, read out loud, "This is to inform you that on September 15, 1951, you were expelled from the Communist Party of Czechoslovakia. Signed on behalf of the Regional Committee by . . ." Then the commanding officer ordered Alexej to fall in again, and handed us over to a corporal for drill.

After drill and political instruction, at about six-thirty (it was dark by then), Lucie was standing by the fence. When I went up to her, she indicated with a simple nod that everything was fine.

and left. Then came mess, singing, cleanup, and finally lights out; I waited in bed until the corporal was asleep, then pulled on my boots and slipped out just as I was, in white longjohns and nightshirt; I walked down the hall and into the yard, feeling quite chilly in my nocturnal attire. The opening in the fence was just behind the infirmary. It couldn't have been better placed: if anyone stopped me, I could say I was feeling sick and on my way to wake the medical officer. But no one stopped me; I skirted the infirmary and crouched down in its shadow; the searchlight idled on one spot (clearly the sentry in the tower no longer took his job very seriously), and the space I had yet to cross lay in darkness; my only problem now was keeping clear of the all-night dog patrol; it was quiet (dangerously quiet: I lost all sense of direction); I had been standing there for about ten minutes when finally I heard a dog's bark; it came from behind, from the other side of camp; I jumped up and dashed across to the fence (a distance of no more than five yards), to where, thanks to Honza's handiwork, the wire didn't quite touch the ground; I dropped on my stomach, crawled under, and ran the last five steps to the wooden fence of the miner's house. Everything was just as we'd planned it: the gate was open, and across the tiny courtyard a light was burning in a window behind a curtain. I tapped at the window, and a few seconds later a giant of a man opened the door and invited me in with a booming voice. (I was terrified at the volume of the voice; I couldn't forget I was a mere five yards away from camp.)

The door led straight into the room. I hesitated for a moment in the doorway, disoriented by what I found: sitting around a table (with an open bottle on it) were five other men; when they saw me, they burst out laughing at my outfit; they said they bet I was cold in that nightshirt and poured me a glass; I took a taste: it was ethyl alcohol, scarcely diluted; they told me to toss it right down; I did, and had a coughing fit; they all laughed again and pulled up a chair for me. They asked how I'd managed to "cross the border," made more fun of my ridiculous getup, and called me "galloping longjohns." They were all miners in their thirties and probably got together there regularly; they'd been drinking, but they weren't drunk, and after my initial surprise (no, shock is more like it) I was considerably calmed by their boisterous presence. I let them pour me another glass of their unusually strong and pungent drink. Meanwhile the man who owned the house had ducked into the room next door and come back carrying a dark suit. "You think it'll fit?" he asked. He was nearly a head taller than I was and quite a bit broader in the beam, but I said, "It'll *have* to." I pulled the trousers on over my longjohns, but the only way I could keep them up was to hold them at the waist. "Anybody got a belt?" asked my benefactor. No one had. "How about a piece of string?" I said. That they did come up with, and it more or less did the job. When I put the jacket on, the men decided (I'm not quite sure why) that all I needed was a bowler hat and walking stick and I'd look just like Charlie Chaplin. To make them laugh, I put my heels together and pointed out my toes. The trouser legs rippled down over the insteps of my boots; the men loved it and told me not to worry: my wish would be any woman's command. Then they poured me a third glass for the road, and the owner assured me I could knock on the window at any hour of the night to change clothes again.

I stepped into the dimly lit street. It took me more than ten minutes to get to the house where Lucie was waiting. I had to circle the entire camp and pass directly in front of the brightly illuminated gates; my fears turned out to be completely ungrounded: the civilian disguise worked perfectly, the guard looked right through me, and I reached my destination safe and sound. I opened the outside door (it was lit by a solitary streetlamp) and made my way by memory (the miner who lived there had given me directions): staircase to the left, up one flight, door straight ahead. I knocked. A key turned in the lock and Lucie opened the door.

I took her in my arms (she'd been in the room since the miner had left for the night shift); she asked if I'd been drinking; I said I had, and told her the story of how I'd sneaked through. She said she'd been trembling, she was so afraid something would happen to me. (It was only then I noticed she actually was shivering.) I told her how much I'd looked forward to seeing her, but I could feel her shaking more and more violently. "What's the matter?" I asked her. "Nothing," she answered. "What are you shaking for, then?" "I was so afraid," she said, freeing herself gently from my embrace.

I looked around. The room was small and furnished austerely: a table, a chair, a bed (with slightly soiled sheets); there was a religious picture above the bed and, against the opposite wall, a cupboard with some jars of fruit preserves along the top (the sole more or less personal touch about the place). A naked bulb hung down from the ceiling, glaring disagreeably into my eyes and throwing my sad, ludicrous figure into sharp relief; it made me painfully aware of my enormous jacket and baggy trousers, my black army boots peeking out down below, and—to crown it all—my clean-shaven skull shining like a pale moon in the bulb's incandescence.

"Forgive me for looking like this, Lucie," I said. "Please!" And again I explained the necessity for my disguise. She assured me it didn't matter; I (carried away by an alcohol-induced impetuosity) declared that no, I couldn't possibly stand there in front of her like that, and threw off the jacket and trousers; but underneath I was wearing a nightshirt and those awful army-issue longjohns, a much more ridiculous outfit than the one I'd just shed. I went over and switched off the light, but no darkness came to my rescue: the streetlamp shone right into the room. And since I was more ashamed of being ridiculous than I was of being naked, I tore off the rest of my clothes. I put my arms around her (once more I felt her shivering) and begged her to undress, to remove all obstacles between us. I ran my hands all over her, repeating my plea again and again, but Lucie asked me to wait a little, she couldn't, not right away, not so soon.

I took her hand and we sat down on the bed. I laid my head in her lap and didn't move for some time; the incongruity of my nakedness (faintly luminous in the dirty yellow of the streetlamp) was suddenly brought home to me when I realized that everything had turned out the opposite of what I'd dreamed: instead of a naked girl serving wine to a fully dressed man, a naked man was lying in the lap of a fully dressed woman. I saw myself as the naked Christ taken down from the cross and placed in the arms of a grieving Mary, and I was horrified, because I hadn't come to Lucie for compassion and consolation, I'd come for something entirely different, and again I forced myself on her, kissing her (her face and dress) and surreptitiously unfastening what I could.

I didn't get very far; Lucie broke loose again; I lost my impetus, my impatient confidence, and ran out of both words and caresses. I simply lay there stretched out on the bed, naked and motionless, while Lucie sat over me stroking my face with her rough fingers. Little by little I was overcome by bitterness and anger: I reminded Lucie, mentally, of all the risks I'd taken to meet with her; I reminded her (mentally) of all the punishment I might yet have to face. But that wasn't what really bothered me (which was why I could tell her about it—even if only mentally); the true source of my wrath lay much deeper (and I would have been ashamed to tell her): in my own misery, the pitiful misery of a failed youth, the misery of endless weeks of frustration, the humiliating eternity of unfulfilled desire. I thought of my vain courtship of Marketa, my repulsive encounter with the blonde on the tractor, my vain courtship of Lucie, and I felt like crying out: Why must I always be an adult—sentenced as an adult, expelled, branded a Trotskyite, sent to the mines as an adult—and only in love be forced to eat the humble pie of my immaturity? I hated Lucie, hated her all the more knowing she loved me, because that made her resistance all the more absurd, incomprehensible, infuriating. And so after half an hour of sullen silence I launched a fresh attack.

I rolled over onto her, using all the strength I could muster, managed to pull up her skirt, tear off her bra, and grab hold of her breasts, but Lucie put up a furious fight and (possessed by the same blind force as I was) finally struggled loose, jumped off the bed, and backed up against the cupboard.

"Why are you fighting me?" I shouted at her. She mumbled something about my not losing my temper and trying to forgive her, but could offer nothing by way of explanation, nothing logical. "Why are you fighting me? Don't you know I love you? You must be crazy!" "Then throw me out," she said, still pressing up against the cupboard. "That's what I'll do, that's just what I'll do! You've been making a fool of me!" I was giving her an ultimatum,

I shouted. Either she gave herself to me, or I never wanted to see her again.

Once more I went up to her and put my arms around her. This time she didn't try to stop me, but she was limp, as if all the life had gone out of her. "What's so special about your virginity? Who are you saving it for?" No answer. "Say something!" "You don't love me," she said. "*I* don't love *you?*" "No, you don't. I thought you did, but you don't. . . ." And she burst into tears.

I got down on my knees, I kissed her feet, I begged her. But she went on crying and saying I didn't love her.

Suddenly I was seized with an insane rage. I felt there was a supernatural force standing in my way, constantly tearing out of my hands everything I wanted to live for, everything I longed for, everything that by rights was mine; I felt it was the same force that had robbed me of my Party, my Comrades, my university degree—of everything, and always senselessly and for no reason. I realized that the same supernatural force was now opposing me in the person of Lucie, and I hated her for becoming its instrument. I gave her a slap across the face, because it wasn't Lucie I was slapping, it was the evil force. I shouted that I hated her, never wanted to see her again, never, as long as I lived.

I threw her brown coat at her (it had been lying on the chair) and yelled at her to get out.

She put on her coat and left.

And I lay down on the bed with a void in my heart. I wanted to call her back, because I missed her even as I threw her out; because I knew that it was a thousand times better to be with a fully dressed, recalcitrant Lucie than to be without any Lucie at all; because to be without Lucie meant living in absolute desolation.

And though I knew it all, I did not call her back.

I lay there naked on that borrowed bed for quite some time: I couldn't face going back to the house the way I felt, joking with the miners, answering their affably lewd questions.

Finally (very late) I picked myself up, dressed, and left. The streetlamp was still shining. Again I circled the entire camp, tapped on the window (now dark) of the house, waited about three minutes, undressed in the presence of the yawning miner, muttered something noncommittal when he asked me how I'd fared, and (once more in nightshirt and longjohns) made for camp. I was in a state of total despair and total indifference. I didn't pay a bit of attention to where the dog patrol or the beam of the spotlight might be. I crawled under the wire and started off unthinkingly in the direction of our barracks. Just as I reached the wall of the infirmary, I heard a sharp "Halt!" I stopped. A flashlight shone in my eyes. A dog began to snarl.

"What are you doing there?"

"Puking, Comrade Sergeant," I replied, leaning against the wall with one hand.

"Well, get on with it, man, and get it over with," said the sergeant, and went back to his rounds with the dog.

14

I got to bed without any further complications, but I couldn't get to *sleep,* and I was glad when the NCO's grating "Everybody up!" put an end to that awful night. I slipped into my boots and ran out to splash some cold, refreshing water over myself. When I got back, I found a group of half-dressed men clustered around Alexej's bed trying hard to muffle their laughter. I immediately guessed what was going on: Alexej (lying on his stomach under the blanket) was still sound asleep. It reminded me of Franta Petrasek, who, to get even with his CO, had simulated a sleep so sound that three consecutive superiors had failed to shake him awake; it wasn't until they'd carried him out into the yard in his bunk and turned the fire hose on him that he started lazily rubbing his eyes. But with Alexej insubordination was out of the question; the only possible explanation was his frailty. While I was thinking, a corporal (our corporal) came in from the hall with a gigantic pail of water in his arms; he was surrounded by another group, which had obviously been egging him on: it was a stupid prank, typical of the NCO mentality and characteristic of all eras and regimes.

I was irritated by this pathetic reconciliation between the men and their NCO (usually a figure of great loathing), irritated that a common hatred for Alexej had suddenly erased all old scores between them. They had obviously interpreted the CO's speech about Alexej in such a way as to confirm their own suspicions and felt a sudden surge of solidarity with the CO's brutal tactics. I was overcome with rage, a blinding rage aimed at the entire lot of them, at their readiness to believe every accusation, at their eagerness to use violence as a salve for battered self-esteem, and I pushed my way in front of the corporal and his band to the head of Alexej's bunk, saying in a loud voice, "Get up, Alexej! Get up, you idiot!"

But someone grabbed my arm and gave it such a twist that I fell to my knees. I looked around and saw Pavel Pekny. "Who asked you to butt in, you Commie bastard!" he hissed at me. I wrenched my arm away from him and gave him a punch in the face. There would have been a fight then and there if the others hadn't quieted us down: they were afraid we'd wake up Alexej before the corporal with the pail could get to him. The corporal then stepped up, roared out "Rise and shine!" and poured the entire contents of the pail (a good two or three gallons) all over him.

Oddly enough, Alexej still didn't move. For a moment the corporal was at a loss. Then he bawled out, "On your feet, soldier! Attention!" But the soldier didn't stir. The corporal bent over and shook him (the blanket was soaking wet, the whole bed was soaked through, and pools of water were forming on the floor). With great difficulty he turned him onto his back. Alexej's face was sunken, pale, and immobile.

"Quick, the MO!" shouted the corporal. But no one moved: we were all staring at Alexej in his sodden nightshirt. "The MO!" the corporal shouted again, pointing at a soldier. The soldier ran out.

(Alexej lay there motionless, smaller and frailer than before, and much younger. He was like a child, though his lips were locked together, the way a child's never are. The drops kept dripping from him. "It's raining," someone said.)

When the medical officer arrived, he took Alexej's wrist and said, "I see." Then he peeled the blanket off him, revealing a pair of wet feet sticking out of a pair of equally wet longjohns. Alexej lay before us at full (puny) length. The doctor looked around and picked up two plastic tubes from the table next to his bunk; he peered into them (they were empty) and said, "Enough for two." Then he pulled a sheet off the nearest bed and used it to cover Alexej.

All this had put us behind schedule, but we ate breakfast on the double, and three-quarters of an hour later we were on our way underground. After our day in the mines came the normal round of drill, political instruction, mess, singing, cleanup, and bed, and all the time I thought of how Stana had gone, my best friend Honza had gone (I never saw him again, but I did hear that he'd crossed the border into Austria after finally completing military service), and now Alexej was gone. He'd played out his madman role brave-ly and blindly, and it wasn't his fault that he was suddenly unable to go on with it, that he lacked the strength to remain *steadfast* and *in the ranks* while they *dragged him through the mud and spit on him too.* He had never been a friend of mine—the virulence of his faith was alien to me—but his fate made me feel closer to him than to any of the others. I felt that his death concealed a reproach: he was trying to tell me that the moment the Party ban-ishes a man from its ranks, that man has no reason to live. I sud-denly felt guilty for not having liked him, because now he was dead, irrevocably dead, and I'd never done anything for him, I, the only one here who could have done something for him.

But I had lost more than Alexej and the irrevocable opportunity to save a fellow man. Looking back on it today, from a distance, I see it was then I lost the warm sense of solidarity and companion-ship I'd had with my fellow politicals, and with that I lost any chance of resurrecting my trust in people. I began to have doubts about the value of a solidarity based solely on the force of circum-stance and the urge for self-preservation. And I began to realize that the collective of the black insignia was as capable of bullying a man (making him an outcast, hounding him to death) as the collective in that lecture hall, as any collective.

I felt I'd been overrun by a desert, I felt like a desert within a desert, and I wanted to call out to Lucie. Suddenly I could not understand why I'd desired her body so compulsively; she *had no body;* she was a transparent pillar of warmth in a land of never-ending frost, a pillar of warmth, and I had let her get away, pushed her away.

The next day during drill I kept my eyes glued to the fence, waiting for her to come; the only person who stopped was an old woman, who pointed us out to her snot-nosed little grandchild. That evening I wrote a long, sorrowful letter begging Lucie to come back. I said I had to see her, I didn't want anything from her, I just wanted her to be there for me to see and know that she was with me, that she was there at all....

As if to mock me, the weather suddenly turned warm, the sky blue, and we had a glorious October. The leaves were a blaze of color; nature (that pitiful Ostrava nature) was feting autumn's departure with an ecstatic celebration. I felt mocked because my letters went unanswered and the people who stopped at the fence (in the arrogant sun) were all utter strangers. After about two weeks one of my letters came back. Someone had crossed out the address with an indelible pencil and written in: Moved. Forwarding address unknown.

I was terror-stricken. A thousand times since my last meeting with Lucie I had turned over in my mind everything I'd said to her, everything she'd said to me; a hundred times I had cursed myself, a hundred times justified myself; a hundred times I had convinced myself I'd driven her away for good, a hundred times reassured myself she'd understand and forgive me. But the note on the envelope had the ring of a verdict.

The anxiety was more than I could bear, and the very next day I embarked on another of my harebrained schemes. And although I say "harebrained," it was no more dangerous than my previous escape. The epithet "harebrained" is more of an afterthought reflecting the fact that the scheme failed. I knew that Honza had carried it off several times during the summer when he was having a fling with a Bulgarian woman whose husband was away at work in the morning, and I based my scheme on his. I arrived at the pithead with everyone else, picked up my number and safety lamp, smudged my face with coal dust, and made a quiet getaway. I ran straight to Lucie's dormitory and questioned the woman at the desk. All I learned was that Lucie had left about two weeks before with a suitcase containing all her worldly possessions; no one knew where she'd gone, she didn't tell anybody. I was beside myself: had anything happened to her? The woman looked at me and said rather airily, "What can you expect? They don't have real jobs. They come and they go. They keep everything to themselves." I went to the place where she'd worked, and asked the personnel department about her, but I didn't find out a thing. I wandered through Ostrava until the shift was almost over and got back in time to mingle with the men as they surfaced. But I must have missed something essential in Honza' technique: the whole thing backfired. In two weeks' time I was hauled before a court-martial and given ten months for desertion.

Yes, the moment I lost Lucie marked the beginning of a long period of hopelessness and emptiness brought back to me now by the muddy outskirts of my hometown on this short visit. Yes, that was when it all began. My mother died while I was in jail; and I couldn't even go to her funeral. After serving out the ten months, I went back to the black insignia in Ostrava for my final year of military service. Then I signed up for another three years in the mines, because rumor had it that anyone who didn't would have to stay on a year with the battalion. And so I spent the next three years mining coal as a civilian.

I take no pleasure in thinking back on all this or talking about it; in fact, I find it offensive to hear men cast out like myself from a movement they had created and trusted boast of their destinies. True, there was a time when I too glorified my destiny as an outcast, but it was false pride. I've had to keep reminding myself that I wasn't assigned to the black insignia for valor in the field or sending my idea out to do battle with the ideas of others. No, my fall did not result from any real drama; I was more the object than the subject of my story, and (unless there is a point in seeing misery, pain, and futility as virtues) I have nothing whatsoever to boast of.

Lucie? Oh, yes: for fifteen years I hadn't set eyes on her, and it was a long time before I even had news of her. After my discharge I heard she was somewhere in western Bohemia. I didn't go looking for her.

PART FOUR

1

I see a road winding through the fields. I see the dirt in that road rutted by the narrow wheels of peasant carts. And I see verges flanking the road, grassy verges so green I cannot help stroking their smooth slopes.

I am completely surrounded by small fields; there is not a collective farm in sight. How can that be? Do these lands I cross belong to another age? What lands are they?

I walk on. A wild rose bush appears before me on the verge. It is covered with tiny roses. I stop, enraptured. I sit awhile in the grass beneath the bush and then lie down. I can sense my back touching the grassy earth. I feel it with my back. I support it on my back and beg it not to be afraid of being heavy and resting its full weight on me.

Then I hear a clattering of hoofs. A small cloud of dust appears in the distance. As it approaches, it thins into transparency, revealing a group of horsemen, young men in white uniforms. But the closer they gallop, the clearer the disarray of those uniforms. If some jackets are fastened with gleaming buttons, others hang open, and there are men in shirtsleeves as well. Some wear caps, others are bareheaded. No, this is no army. They are deserters, these men—turncoats, outlaws! *Our* cavalry! I stand and watch their approach. The first horseman unsheathes his saber and thrusts it in the air. The cavalry comes to a halt.

The man with the drawn saber has leaned down over his horse's neck and is staring at me.

"Yes, it is I," I say.

"The king!" says the man in wonderment. "Now I recognize you."

I bow my head, pleased at being recognized. They have ridden thus for centuries, and still they know me.

"How do you fare, my king?" asks the man.

"I am fearful, my friends."

"Are they after you?"

"Much worse. Something villainous is afoot. I do not know the men who surround me. I enter my house and find a different chamber, different wife—everything is different. I think I am mistaken and rush out, but no, it is indeed my house! Mine without, a stranger's within. I see signs of it wherever I turn. Something villainous is afoot, my friends, and I am sore afraid."

"You have not forgotten how to ride, I trust," says the man. Only now do I note the saddled but riderless mount standing next to his steed. The man points to it. I put my foot in the stirrup and hoist myself up. The horse rears up, but I am firmly in the saddle, my knees gripping its sides with delight. The man pulls a red veil from his pocket and hands it to me, saying, "Veil your face, and they will not know you!" I wind it round my face and am suddenly as blind. "Your horse will lead you," I hear the man's voice say.

The entire formation sets off at a trot. I can feel the riders jogging along on either side of me, feel our calves touching, hear the snorting of their horses. We continue thus for an hour's time. Then we halt. The same voice addresses me. "We have arrived, my king!"

"Arrived?" I ask. "Arrived where?"

"Do you not hear the murmur of a mighty river? We have come to the banks of the Danube. Here you are safe, my king."

"Yes, I feel that I am safe, and I should like to cast off my veil."

"But you may not, my king. Not yet. You do not need your eyes. For they would but deceive you."

"And yet I wish to see the Danube. It is my river, and I wish to see it!"

"You do not need your eyes, my king. For I shall tell you all. It is better thus. We are surrounded by plains, as far as the eye can see. Pasturelands. A clump of bushes here and there, a wooden stake, the crossbar of a well. But we stand hard by the water, where the grass goes into sand. For the river here has a sandy bed. But now pray dismount, my king."

We dismount and sit upon the ground.

"The men are making a fire," I hear the man's voice say, "for the sun will soon merge with the distant horizon and a chill will come over the land."

"I should like to see Vlasta," I say suddenly.

"And see her you shall."

"Where is she?"

"Not far from here. Your horse will take you to her."

I jump up and ask leave to go to her at once. But the man's hand seizes me by the shoulder and forces me to the ground. "Sit here, my king. First you must rest and eat your fill. And for the nonce I shall speak to you of her."

"Where is she, pray tell."

"An hour's ride from here is a wooden cottage with wooden shingles. It is surrounded by a wooden fence."

"Yes, yes." I nod, and my heart feels heavy with joy. "All of wood. That is as it should be. There must not be a single nail."

"Yes," the voice goes on. "The fence is fashioned of wooden pickets roughly hewn. One still discerns the branches in them."

"All things of wood are like cats or dogs," I say. "They are more beings than things. I love the world of wood. It is my only home."

"Beyond the fence grow sunflowers, marigolds, dahlias. An old apple tree grows there too. At this very moment Vlasta stands upon the threshold."

"How is she arrayed?"

"In a skirt of linen, slightly stained, for she is on her way back from the cowshed. In her hand she holds a wooden bucket. She is barefoot. But she is beautiful, for she is young."

"She is poor," I say, "a poor man's daughter."

"But nonetheless a queen. And since a queen, she must be hidden. Even you may not go to her, lest she be revealed. Only in your veil may you go to her. Your horse will lead the way."

So fine was the man's speech that it engulfed me in a sweet languor. I lay upon the grass listening to his voice and when it fell silent, the murmur of the water and crackle of the fire. So beautiful was it that I dared not open my eyes. But I had no choice. I knew the time had come and my eyes must open.

2

Three mattresses separated me from the lacquered wood. I don't like lacquered wood—or the curved metal legs the sofa stands on, for that matter. A pink glass globe with three white bands around it hung from the ceiling above me. I don't like the globe either. Or the buffet facing me, its glass displaying other useless glass. The only wooden object in the room is the black harmonium in the corner. It's the only thing I like in the whole room. It used to be Father's. Father died a year ago.

I stood up from the sofa. I didn't feel rested. It was Friday afternoon, two days before Sunday's Ride of the Kings. Everything was up to me. Everything in our district connected with folklore is my doing. For two weeks now I haven't had a decent night's sleep what with all the errands, the chores, the petty arguments.

Then Vlasta came in. I keep telling myself she ought to put on weight. Fat women are supposed to be good-natured. Vlasta is thin, her face already crisscrossed by fine wrinkles. She asked me whether I'd remembered to stop at the laundry on my way home from school. I'd forgotten. "I might have known," she said, and asked if I planned to stay at home for once. I had to tell her no: I had a meeting in town, a district meeting. "You promised to help Vladimir with his homework." I shrugged. "Who's going to be at the meeting?" I started running down the names, but Vlasta interrupted. "Mrs. Hanzlik?" I nodded. Vlasta looked upset. I knew I was in for it. Mrs. Hanzlik had a bad reputation. It was common knowledge that she slept around. Vlasta didn't suspect me of being involved with her, but she bristled whenever her name came up. She looked down her nose at any meeting Mrs. Hanzlik attended. It was impossible to talk to her about it. I preferred to slip out right away.

The meeting was devoted to last-minute preparations for the Ride of the Kings. The whole thing was a mess. The District Council was starting to cut back on our budget. Only a few years ago the Council had provided lavish subsidies for folk events. Now we had to support the Council. If the Youth League had no way of attracting members anymore, why not let it take over the Ride of the Kings? That would boost its prestige. Gone were the days when profits from the Ride would go to subsidize other, less popular, folk activities. This time the Youth League could have them and do whatever it pleased with them. We asked the police to close off the road for the duration of the Ride. We'd just received their refusal: it was impossible to disrupt traffic just for the sake of the Ride. But what kind of a Ride would it be with cars spooking horses right and left? What a headache!

I couldn't get away from the meeting before eight. And then who did I see in the square but Ludvik! He was walking in the opposite direction. I almost stopped dead in my tracks. What was he doing here? I caught his eye. He looked at me for a second, then turned away, pretending he hadn't seen me. Two old friends. Eight years on the same school bench! And he pretends he doesn't see me!

Ludvik was the first crack to appear in my life. By now I'm used to it. My life is like a none too sturdy house. When I was in Prague not long ago, I went to one of those little theaters, the kind that started springing up in the early sixties and quickly became the rage with their bright new talent fresh from the university. They did a play with very little plot to it, but the songs were clever and the jazz quite good. All of a sudden the musicians donned feathered hats like the ones we wear with our folk costumes, and did a takeoff on a cimbalom ensemble. They screeched and wailed, mimicking our dance steps and the way we throw our arms up in the air. . . . It went on for no more than a few minutes, but it had the audience rolling in the aisles. I couldn't believe my eyes.

Five years ago no one would have dared make clowns of us like that. And no one would have cracked a smile. Now we're a laughingstock. How is it we're suddenly a laughingstock?

Then there's Vladimir. I've been having trouble with him these past few weeks. The District Council proposed him to the Youth League as this year's king. Having a son chosen king has always been a great honor for the father, and this year they were going to honor me, reward me in the person of my son for everything I'd done for folk culture. But Vladimir kept trying to get out of it. He had all kinds of excuses. First he said he wanted to go to Brno on Sunday for the motorcycle races. Then he claimed he was afraid of horses. Finally he came out and admitted he didn't want to be king if the whole thing was fixed. He didn't want to pull strings.

The grief it's caused me. He seems to want to block out everything in his life that might remind him of mine. He always balked at taking part in the children's song and dance group I initiated in conjunction with our ensemble. He was quick with the excuses even then. He had no gift for music, he claimed. Yet he did quite well on the guitar and enjoyed getting together with friends to sing the latest American hits.

Of course, he's only fifteen. And he loves me. He's a sensitive boy. We had a heart-to-heart talk a few days ago. Maybe he understood.

3

I remember it well. I was sitting in the swivel chair, Vladimir across from me on the sofa. My elbow rested on the closed lid of the harmonium, my favorite instrument. I'd heard it ever since I was a child. Father played it every day. Folk songs, mainly, with simple harmonies. It was like the bubbling of a far-off spring. If only Vladimir would think of it like that. If only he'd try to understand.

During the seventeenth and eighteenth centuries the Czech nation almost ceased to exist. In the nineteenth century it was virtually reborn. A child among the old European nations. True, it had its own great past, but it was cut off from that past by a gulf of two centuries, when the Czech language retreated to the countryside, the exclusive property of the illiterate. But even in their midst it continued to create its own culture. A modest culture, completely hidden from the eyes of Europe. A culture of songs, fairy tales, ancient rites and customs, proverbs and sayings. A narrow footbridge spanning the two-hundred-year gulf.

The only bridge, the only link. The only fragile stem of an unbroken tradition. That is why the men who at the turn of the nineteenth century undertook to revive Czech literature and music used it as their point of departure. That is why the first Czech poets and musicians spent so much time collecting tales and songs. And that is why their early attempts were often little more than paraphrases of folk poetry and folk melodies.

If only you'd try to understand, Vladimir. It's not just an addiction, your father's love for folklore. Maybe there is a bit of addiction involved, but it goes deeper than that. What he hears in folk art is the sap that kept Czech culture from drying up.

My love for it dates back to the war, when they tried to make us believe we had no right to exist, we were nothing but Czech-speaking Germans. We needed to prove to ourselves we'd existed before and still did exist. We made a pilgrimage to our sources.

I was playing bass at the time in an amateur jazz band, and one day, out of the blue, we had a visit from some members of the Moravian Association. They said it was our patriotic duty to support their newly resurrected cimbalom ensemble.

Who could have refused under those circumstances? I went and played the violin with them.

We roused old songs from their deathlike slumber. Those nineteenth-century patriots had put folk songs into songbooks in the nick of time. Civilization quickly pushed folklore into the background. By the turn of the century we needed folklore associations to bring them out of the songbooks back to life. First in the towns. Then in the countryside as well. And most of all in our region. They worked to revitalize folk rituals like the Ride of the Kings, gave support to folk ensembles. For a while they seemed to be fighting a losing battle. Folklorists couldn't revive traditions as rapidly as civilization could bury them.

The war gave us new impetus. During the last year of the occupation we organized a Ride of the Kings. There was an army camp in our town, and Wehrmacht officers jostled the local population in the streets. The Ride turned into a demonstration. A host of young men on horseback, wearing colorful costumes and waving sabers. An invincible Czech horde. Shades of Czech history. That's how all the Czechs saw it, and their eyes lit up. I was fifteen at the time, and they chose me king. I rode between two pages with my face veiled. Was I proud! Was my father proud! He knew they had chosen me king in his honor. He was a village schoolmaster, a patriot. Everyone admired him.

I believe things have a meaning, Vladimir. I believe the fates of men are interconnected, cemented together by the mortar of wisdom. I take your being chosen king as a sign. I'm as proud as I was twenty years ago. Prouder. Because in you they wish to honor me. And why deny it? I set great store by the honor. I want to hand my kingdom over to you. And I want you to accept it from me.

Perhaps he did understand me. He promised to accept the offer to be king.

4

If only he would try to understand how interesting it all is. I can't imagine anything more interesting. Or exciting.

Take this, for example. Prague musicologists have long claimed that the European folk song originated in the Baroque, when village musicians playing and singing in the orchestras of the nobility introduced their musical culture into the life of the people. From this they conclude that the folk song is not an artistic form *sui generis*. It is merely a derivative of art music.

Now, that may have been the case in Bohemia, but the songs we sing in southern Moravia can't be explained away by art music. Look at their tonality, for instance. Baroque music was written in major and minor keys. Our songs are sung in modes that castle orchestras never dreamed of!

Here's an example of the Lydian, the scale with the raised

fourth. It never fails to evoke in me the pastoral idylls of antiquity. It makes me think of Pan and hear his pipes.

Baroque and Classical music paid fanatical homage to the power of the major seventh to establish order. Its only path to the tonic was the disciplined, *sensitive* seven. It was frightened of the minor seventh that crept up on the tonic from a major second below. And that minor seventh—be it of the Aeolian, Dorian, or Mixolydian mode—is what I most enjoy in our folk songs. For its melancholy and pensiveness. And for the way it refuses to push on frivolously to the tonic, which puts an end to everything, song and life:

But there are also songs in modes so curious they can't be pinned down by the standard ecclesiastical nomenclature. In these I simply revel:

Moravian songs exhibit an unbelievably wide range of tonality. The rationale behind them is sometimes puzzling. They'll begin in a minor key, end in the major, and modulate several times in the interim. Often I have a terrible time coming to grips with what's going on when I have to harmonize them.

And they're just as ambiguous rhythmically as tonally. Especially when they're meant for rubato-type singing, not dance accompaniment. Bela Bartok called them parlando songs. Their rhythm cannot begin to be recorded by our notation system. Or let me put it differently. From the vantage point of our notation all folk singers sing their songs poorly and unrhythmically.

How can that be explained? Leos Janacek maintained that the complexity which makes it impossible for us to do justice to all the nuances of the rhythm is due to various fleeting moods on the part of the singer. He said that the time, place, and atmosphere of the singing event needed to be taken into account and that during his performance the folk singer reacted to the color of random flowers, to the weather, to the surroundings in general.

But isn't that just a bit too poetic an explanation? During my first year at the university an instructor told us of an experiment he had conducted. He'd asked several folk artists to interpret the same rhythmically indefinable song independently of one another. Measuring the results on highly accurate electronic equipment, he discovered that their interpretations tallied one hundred percent.

The rhythmical complexity of the songs is therefore not a factor of the singer's carelessness, inferiority, or disposition. It follows its own mysterious laws. In one kind of Moravian dance song, for example, the second half of the measure always lasts a fraction of a second longer than the first half. Now, how can that be notated? The metrical system used by art music is based on symmetry. A whole note divides into two halves, a half into two quarters. A bar breaks down into two, three, or four identical beats. But what can be done with a measure that has two beats of unequal length? Our biggest problem today is setting the real rhythm of a Moravian song down on paper.

One thing at least is clear. Our songs do not derive from Baroque music. Bohemian songs, maybe. Perhaps. Bohemia always enjoyed a higher level of civilization, and there was greater contact between city and country, castle and the land. Moravia had its castles too, but the primitiveness of the villages kept them isolated to a much greater extent. There was certainly no question of Moravian country musicians playing in castle orchestras. These conditions enabled us to preserve folk songs from the oldest of times. They derive from various phases of a long, leisurely history.

So when you come face to face with the whole of our folk music culture, it's as if the dancer from *The Thousand and One Nights* were shedding veil after veil for you.

Look. Off comes the first veil. Its cloth is rough and patterned with trivialities. These are the songs of the past fifty, sixty, seventy years. They came to us from the west, from Bohemia's brass bands. Our children were taught to sing them by their teachers. Though slightly adapted to our rhythmic patterns, they are basically run-of-the-mill, major-key, West European folk music.

Here comes the second veil. It is much more colorful. These are songs of Hungarian origin. They came with the encroachment of the Magyar language. Gypsy groups spread them far and wide throughout the nineteenth century. Everyone knew them. Czardases and recruiting songs with that special syncopated rhythm.

Under this veil there is yet another. Look. The songs of the native Slav population during the seventeenth and eighteenth centuries.

But the fourth veil is even more beautiful. Its songs are even older. It goes back as far as the fourteenth century, when the Wallachians made their way across the Carpathians from the east and southeast to the pasturelands of Slovakia. Their songs of shepherds and highwaymen are completely innocent of chords and harmony. They are purely melodic in conception, and the melodies, enhanced by the pipes and fifes that produce them, make full use of the ancient modal scales.

Once this veil has fallen away, there is none left to take its place. Yet utterly naked, the dancer continues. These are the oldest songs of all. They date from ancient pagan times. They are based on the oldest known musical system, the four-tone, tetra-chordal system. Mowing songs, harvest songs. Songs tightly bound up with the rites of the patriarchal village.

Bartok has shown that on this oldest of levels the songs of Slovakia, southern Moravia, Hungary, and Croatia resemble each other to such a degree that is is nearly impossible to tell them apart. Picture the geographical area. What do you see? The first great ninth-century Slav dominion, the Great Moravian Empire. Its borders were swept away a thousand years ago, yet they remain untouched on the oldest level of folk music.

The folk song or rite is a tunnel beneath history, a tunnel that keeps alive much of what wars, revolutions, and brutal civilization have long since destroyed aboveground, and allows us to look far into our past. I see Rostislav and Svatopulk, the first Moravian princes. I see the ancient Slav world.

But why limit ourselves to the Slav world? I remember how we once racked our brains to make sense of an enigmatic folk song text combining hops in some unclear way with a cart and goat. Someone is riding on a goat, someone else in a cart. Then hops are praised for their power of turning maidens into brides. The people who first sang it for us had no idea what it meant either. The tenacity of age-old tradition had preserved a combination of words now lacking all trace of intelligibility. In the end there turned out to be only one possible explanation: the ancient Greek Dionysian festival. A satyr on a billy goat and a god grasping his thyrsus wound round with hops.

Classical antiquity! I couldn't believe it. But then I took a course in the history of musical thought. The structure of our oldest folk songs is in fact analogous to that of ancient Greek music. The same Lydian, Phrygian, and Dorian tetrachords. The same tendency to reckon the scale from the upper, not the lower, note (the lower note did not take precedence until music began to think harmonically). So our oldest songs belong to the same era of musical thought as the songs sung in ancient Greece. They preserve antiquity for us.

5

At supper tonight I kept seeing Ludvik's eyes turn away from me, and I felt more than ever how important Vladimir was to me. Suddenly I felt afraid I'd been neglecting him. That I'd never really succeeded in drawing him into my world. After supper Vlasta stayed in the kitchen, and I went into the living room with Vladimir. I tried to tell him about folk songs. It didn't work. I felt like a schoolmaster. I wondered whether I was boring him. He sat there looking as though he were listening, of course. He's always been a good boy. But how can I tell what's actually going on in that head of his?

I'd been torturing him quite some time with my lecture when Vlasta stuck her head into the room and said it was time for bed. What could I do? She was the heart and soul of the house, its calendar and clock.

We won't argue. Off to bed, my boy. Good night.

I left Vladimir in the room with the harmonium. He sleeps there on the sofa with the metal legs. I sleep next door in the bedroom beside Vlasta in our marriage bed, but I'm not going to bed yet. I'd twist and turn and worry whether I was waking up Vlasta. No, I think I'll take a breath of fresh air. It's a warm night. The garden of the old one-story dwelling where we live is full of old-fashioned rural smells. There's a wooden bench under the pear tree.

Damn that Ludvik. Why did he have to turn up today? I'm afraid it's a bad omen. My oldest friend! This was where we used to sit as boys, under this very tree. I liked him from the start. When we first went to the same school. He had more brains in his little finger than the rest of us put together, but he never showed off. He couldn't have cared less about either school or teachers, and he enjoyed doing anything that was against the regulations.

Why did the two of us become such close friends? Kismet, most likely. We were both half orphans. My mother died in childbirth, and Ludvik's father, who was a bricklayer, was hauled off to a concentration camp. Ludvik was thirteen at the time. He never saw him again.

Ludvik was the elder of two sons, but his brother died, and he and his mother were left alone. They barely managed to make ends meet. School fees were high. For a while it seemed he would have to quit.

But at the eleventh hour he was saved.

Ludvik's father had a sister who, some time before the war, had married a rich local builder. After that she all but broke off relations with her bricklayer brother. But when they took him away, her patriotic feelings took the upper hand. She offered to support Ludvik. Her own daughter wasn't very bright, and Ludvik with all his talents made her jealous. Not only did she and her husband assist him materially; they invited him to their house daily. They introduced him to the cream of local society. Ludvik had to appear grateful to them, because his studies depended on their support. He couldn't bear them. Their name was Koutecky, and from that time on we used it to refer to anyone pompous and pretentious.

Madame Koutecky looked down her nose at Ludvik's mother. She'd always felt her brother had married beneath him. Her brother's arrest did nothing to change her mind. The heavy artillery of her charity was aimed at Ludvik and Ludvik alone. She saw in him her own flesh and blood and longed to make him over into her son. The existence of her sister-in-law she regarded as an unfortunate error. She never invited her to her house. Meanwhile Ludvik looked on, gritting his teeth. He was ripe for rebellion. But his mother would beg him tearfully to be sensible.

That was one reason why he so liked coming to our place. The two of us were like twins. Father loved him almost more than he loved me. It made him happy to see Ludvik devouring the books in his library one by one. When I started playing in the jazz band, Ludvik wanted to play too. He bought a cheap clarinet at the open market and could hold his own on it in no time. We played jazz together and joined the cimbalom ensemble together.

Towards the end of the war the Kouteckys' daughter got married. Ludvik's aunt decided to make it a big affair. She decided to have five pairs of bridesmaids and pages behind the bride and groom. Not only did she include Ludvik; she gave him the eleven-year-old daughter of the local pharmacist for a partner. He was shattered. The shame of playing the fool at that philistine masquerade of a wedding! He wanted to be considered an adult and was mortified by the idea of offering his arm to a mere child. He was furious at being displayed as the Kouteckys' charity case. Furious at being forced to kiss the cross during the ceremony after everyone had slobbered over it. That evening he deserted the festivities for our back room at the local inn. We'd been playing and drinking, and started teasing him. He lost his temper and proclaimed his hatred for the bourgeoisie. Then he cursed Church ritual and said he spat on the Church and was going to leave it.

We didn't take him too seriously, but a few days after the war ended he carried out his threat. By so doing, of course, he mortally offended the Kouteckys. He didn't care. He was only too happy to break all ties with them. He became an avid Communist sympathizer. He went to lectures the Communists sponsored. He bought books they published. Our region was solidly Catholic, our school particularly so. Yet we were willing to forgive Ludvik his Communist eccentricities. We accorded him special privileges.

In 1947 we finished school. That autumn we enrolled at the university—Ludvik in Prague, I in Brno. I didn't see him again until a year later.

6

The year was 1948. Everything was topsy-turvy. When Ludvik came home for the summer, we didn't quite know how to greet him. For us the February Communist coup meant a reign of terror. Ludvik brought his clarinet, but never touched it. We spent the whole night in debate.

Was that when the friction between us began? I don't think so. In fact, he nearly won me over that night. He steered clear of political arguments and stuck to our group. He said we had to look at our work in a broader context. What was the point of merely reviving a lost past? If we looked back, we'd end up like Lot's wife.

Well, what do you propose we do? we cried.

Safeguard the heritage of folk art, he responded, by all means. But that wasn't enough. Times had changed. New horizons were opening. We needed to purge our musical culture of the lifeless hit-tune clichés that the bourgeoisie had used to force-feed the people. We needed to replace them with an original and genuine art of the people.

Strange. What Ludvik was calling for was nothing but the old utopia of the most conservative Moravian patriots. They too went on eternally about the godless depravity of urban culture. They too heard the pipes of Satan in the strains of the Charleston. But what of it? It only made his words seem comprehensible to us.

At any rate, his next point sounded more original. It had to do with jazz. Jazz had grown out of Negro folk music and conquered the whole Western world. Forget the fact that it had gradually become a commercial commodity. We could use it as proof positive that folk music had miraculous powers. That it could engender the musical style of an entire period.

We listened to Ludvik with a mixture of admiration and revulsion. His confidence irritated us. He had the look all Communists had at the time. He looked as if he'd made a secret pact with the future and thereby acquired the right to act in its name. Another reason why we found him so offensive was that all of a sudden he was completely different from the Ludvik we had known. With us he'd always been one of the boys, a real clown. And there he was, shamelessly indulging in inflated rhetoric and high-flown vocabulary. Of course, we were also annoyed at the free and easy way he associated the fate of our ensemble and the fate of the Communist Party. Not one of us was a Communist. And yet there was something attractive in his words. His way of thinking corresponded to our innermost dreams. It elevated us in a flash to the realm of historic grandeur.

I have a private nickname for him: the Pied Piper. All he had to do was blow on his flute and we all flocked after him. Where his arguments were a bit sketchy, we rushed to his aid. I remember my own contributions. I was reviewing the evolution of European music from the Baroque on. After impressionism music had grown weary of itself. It had lost most of its sap in terms of sonatas and symphonies on the one hand and catchy tunes on the other. That was why jazz had had such a miraculous effect on it. It eagerly extracted the fresh sap from the centuried roots of jazz. Jazz captured more than European nightlife; it captured Stravinsky, Honegger, Milhaud, all of whom opened their compositions to its rhythms. But at the same time, or rather a decade or so earlier, the folk music of our own continent injected a supply of fresh, vigorous blood into the veins of European classical music. And nowhere had it remained so alive as here in Central Europe. Think of Janacek and Bartok! So the parallel between folk music and jazz derived directly from the evolution of music in Europe. They had each made an equal contribution to the formation of serious music in the twentieth century. When it came to music for the masses, things were different. Traditional European folk music had left almost no imprint. Jazz had taken over completely. That was where we came in.

Yes, right, we said. The same strength lay in the roots of our folk music as lay in the roots of jazz. Jazz had its own melodic specificity, which still bore traces of the basic six-tone scale of early Negro songs. But our folk songs also had their own specificity, and their melodies were, tonally speaking, much more varied. Jazz had a rhythm of its own, which owed its prodigious intricacies to an African drum culture dating back tens of centuries. But our music was rhythmically original too. Finally, jazz was based on improvisation. But the remarkable ensemble work of our village fiddlers, who can't read a note, also depends on improvisation.

There was only one thing that differentiated us from jazz. Jazz was quick to develop and change. Its style was in constant motion. It had traveled a precipitous road from early New Orleans counterpoint to swing, bop, and beyond. The New Orleans variety had never dreamed of the harmonies used in today's jazz. Our folk music, in contrast, was a languorous Sleeping Beauty of the past. We had to awaken her. She had to merge with the life of today and develop along with it. Without ceasing to be itself, without losing its melodic and rhythmic specificity, folk music had to create its own organically evolving phases of style. It wasn't easy. It was an enormous task. A task that could be carried out only under socialism.

What did it have to do with socialism? we protested.

He explained it to us. The traditional village had lived a collective life. Communal rites marked off the village year. Folk art knew no vitality outside those rites. The romantics imagined that a girl cutting grass was suddenly inspired to pour forth song like a stream from a rock. But folk songs differed in their origins from erudite poetry. Poets wrote verse to express themselves and what made them unique, different. Folk songs brought people together. They came about much like stalactites, developing new motifs and new variations drop by drop. They were passed down from generation to generation, and each singer added something new to them. Every song had many creators, and all of them modestly disappeared behind their creation. No folk song existed purely for its own sake. It had a function. There were songs sung at weddings, songs sung at harvesting, songs sung at Shrovetide, songs for Christmas, for haymaking, for dancing, for funerals. Even love songs existed within the framework of certain recurrent festivities. Evening walks, serenades under maidens' windows, marriage proposals—they all were part of a collective ritual in which song had its established place.

Capitalism had destroyed the collective way of life. Folk art had lost its footing, its sense of itself, its function. There would have been no point in trying to resurrect it while social conditions were such that man lived cut off from man, everyone for himself. But socialism had liberated men from the yoke of their isolation. Their private and public lives would merge. Once more they would be united by dozens of communal rites. They would create their own collective customs. The former would come from the past. Harvests, carnivals, dances, work. The latter would come from the present. May Day, rallies, Liberation celebrations, meetings. Folk art would be welcome everywhere. It would develop, change, renew itself. Did we finally understand?

And before long the unbelievable began to come true. No one had ever done so much for our folk art as the Communist government. It earmarked enormous amounts for the creation of new ensembles. Fiddles and cimbaloms sang forth daily from radio speakers. Moravian and Slovak folk songs inundated the universities, May Day celebrations, youth festivities, and variety theaters. Jazz disappeared from the face of our country. Not only that. It became a symbol of Western capitalism and its decadence. Young people stopped dancing the jitterbug. They grabbed hold of one another's shoulders and danced circle dances. The Communist Party went all out to create a new way of life. It based its efforts on Stalin's famous definition of the new art: Socialist content in national form. And national form in music, dance, and poetry could come from nowhere if not folk art.

Our ensemble rode the exhilarating waves of that policy. It soon gained national fame. It took on singers and dancers and became a major cultural enterprise, performing on hundreds of stages and making annual tours abroad. And we didn't sing only the traditional lays about brigands slitting their beloveds' throats. We wrote new pieces all our own: a hymn to Stalin, mass songs about the breakup of individual farms and the success of collective agriculture. Our repertory did not merely look backwards. It was alive. It was part of the most contemporary history. It accompanied history.

The Communist Party gave us its enthusiastic support. Our political reservations quickly melted away. I myself joined the Party at the beginning of forty-nine. My friends from the ensemble soon followed suit.

7

But in those days Ludvik and I were still close. When did the first shadow fall between us?

As if I didn't know. It was at my wedding.

I'd been studying in Brno—violin at the Academy of Music and music theory at the university. During my third year there I started having problems. Papa's health began to fail. He had a stroke. He came out of it, but from then on he had to be very careful. I kept worrying about his being by himself. If anything happened to him, he couldn't even send me a telegram. Every Saturday I'd come home with my heart in my mouth, and every Monday morning I'd leave for Brno with new anxieties. There finally came a point when I couldn't take them any more. They tortured me on Monday, tortured me more on Tuesday, and on Wednesday I threw all my clothes into my bag, paid off my rent, and told the landlady not to expect me back.

I remember walking home from the station as if it were today. I had to cross a field to get from the town to our village. It was autumn, just before twilight. The wind was blowing, and some boys were flying paper kites on long, long strings. Papa had once made me a kite. He would take it out to the field with me, throw it up in the air, and run until the wind lifted it into the sky. I never enjoyed it much. Papa loved it. And I was touched by the memory of it that day and quickened my pace. The idea crossed my mind that Papa had sent those kites into the air after Mother.

From childhood on I've always pictured Mother in heaven. Oh, it's been years since I believed in God or life eternal or anything like that. I'm not talking about faith. I'm talking about fantasies. And I don't see why I should have to give them up. I'd feel orphaned without them. Vlasta calls me a dreamer. She says I don't see things as they are. Well, she's wrong. I do see things as they are, but in addition to the visible I see the invisible. Fantasies have their place in life. Fantasies are what makes homes of houses.

I didn't learn about my mother until long after she had died, so I never had a chance to mourn her. I've always taken pleasure in imagining her young and beautiful in heaven. None of the other children had mothers as young as mine.

I like to think of Saint Peter perched on a stool looking down on earth through a tiny window. My mother often visits him there. Peter will do anything for her because she is pretty. He lets her look out too. And Mother sees us. Papa and me both.

Mother's face was never sad. Quite the opposite. When she looked down on us through the window in Peter's booth, she often smiled. They who dwell in eternity know no sorrow. They know that life on earth lasts but an instant and reunion is imminent.

But when I went to live in Brno and left Papa alone, Mother's face began to look sad and reproachful. And I wanted to live in peace with her.

So I hurried home. The kites flew so high they seemed suspended from the heavens. I was happy. I had no regrets about what I'd left behind. Not that I didn't love both my violin and musicology. But I had no real ambition. And nothing, not even the most promising career, could have meant more to me than the joy of coming home.

When I told Papa I wouldn't be going back to Brno, he was terribly upset. He didn't want me to ruin my life for his sake. So I managed to make him believe I'd been expelled for poor marks. That made him even more upset. But I didn't let it bother me. I hadn't come home to sit around doing nothing. I went on playing first fiddle in our ensemble and found a job as violin teacher in the local music school. I could do the things I enjoyed.

Spending time with Vlasta was one of them. Vlasta lived in the neighboring village, which today, like my own village, has been incorporated into the town. She danced with our ensemble. I was studying in Brno when I met her, and I liked being able to see her on a daily basis now that I'd returned. But I didn't fall in love with her until somewhat later—unexpectedly, when during a rehearsal she took such a spill that it broke her leg. I carried her in my arms to the ambulance. I could feel her body, all slender and frail. And suddenly I realized to my astonishment that I was nearly six feet two and weighed well over two hundred pounds, that I could have been a lumberjack, and she was light and fragile.

It was a moment of revelation. In Vlasta's wounded frame I suddenly saw another, more familiar figure. How could I have failed to notice it before? Vlasta was "the poor man's daughter" of all the folk songs! The poor girl who had nothing on earth but her good name, the poor girl whom everyone humiliates, the poor girl in rags, the poor little orphan girl.

Literally, of course, that was hardly the case. She had both her parents, and they were anything but poor. But for that very reason—they had been well-to-do farmers—the new age was driving them to the wall. Vlasta would come to rehearsals in tears. They had been made to give up nearly all their produce to the authorities. Her father had been proclaimed a kulak. His tractor and tools had been requisitioned. He had been threatened with arrest. I felt sorry for her and thought of myself as her protector. I would protect the poor man's daughter.

From the time I saw her in the light of the folk song tradition, I felt as if I were reliving a love experienced a thousand times over. As if I were playing it from an ancient score. As if the songs were singing me. I gave myself up to the resonant stream of time and dreamed of my wedding to be.

Two days before the ceremony Ludvik appeared out of nowhere. I was delighted to see him. I immediately told him the news and said that as my best friend he was bound to be my witness. He gave me his word. And kept it.

My friends from the ensemble staged a real Moravian wedding for me. They came for us early in the morning, playing and singing and wearing folk costumes. A fifty-year-old cimbalom virtuoso had taken on the duty of "patriarch," the leader of the celebration. First Papa regaled them all with slivovitz, bread, and fatback. Then the patriarch signaled for silence and recited in a sonorous voice:

> Right honored guests, maidens and masters,
> Ladies and gentlemen!
> I have summoned you all to this abode
> Because the youth who here abideth hath made bold
> To ask that we with him might wend our way to the
> father of Vlasta Netahal,
> Which gentle maid he hath now chosen for his bride....

The patriarch is the heart and soul of the entire ceremony. That is how it has always been. That is how it has been for the last thousand years. The groom has never been the subject of the wedding. He is its object. He is not getting married. He is being married. Someone is using the marriage to take hold of him, and he sails along on it as on a giant wave. It is not his place to act or speak. The patriarch acts and speaks for him. No, not even the patriarch. It was age-old tradition passed on from one man to the next, sweeping him along towards its own sweet stream.

Led by the patriarch, we set off for the neighboring village. My friends played as we walked across the fields. A group of Vlasta's people, also in folk costume, was waiting for us in front of her house. The patriarch recited:

> We are weary travelers
> And do beseech you
> To grant us entry to this humble abode,
> For we are in sore need of food and drink.

An elderly man stepped forward from the group. "If ye be worthy, be ye welcome." And he invited us to enter. Silently we crowded in. We were only weary travelers, as the patriarch had called us, and did not at first disclose our true intent. But then the old man, who was spokesman for the bride's family, challenged us, saying, "If ye have a burden upon your hearts, speak ye now."

And the patriarch began to speak. First he spoke obliquely and in parables, and the old man answered him in kind. Only after much digression did the patriarch reveal why we had come.

Whereupon the old man asked him the following question:

> Pray tell, dear friend,
> Why doth this honest groom desire to take this honest
>   maid to wife?
> Is't for the flower or the fruit?

And the patriarch replied:

> Well knoweth every man that flowers bloom in beauty
>   and in grace, causing the heart much joy,
> But flowers fade
> And fruits do ripen.
> Thus do we take this bride not for the flower, but the
>   fruit, whence cometh great reward.

The responses continued until the bride's spokesman brought them to an end, saying, "Let us then call the bride to hear whether she give her consent." Then he went into the next room and returned leading a woman in folk costume. She was tall, thin, and bony, and her face was veiled by a scarf. "Here is thy bride."

But the patriarch shook his head, and we all protested vociferously. The old man tried to talk us into accepting her, but finally had to take the masked woman back. Only then did he bring out Vlasta. She was wearing black boots, a red apron, and a multicolored bolero. On her head was a garland of flowers. She looked beautiful. He placed her hand in mine.

Then he turned to the bride's mother and called out to her in a doleful voice, "Alas, the mother!"

At those words my bride withdrew her hand from mine, threw herself at her mother's feet, and bowed her head. The old man continued:

> Mother dear, forgive me all the wrongs which I have
> done thee!
> Mother dearest, I beg thee, forgive me all the wrongs
> which I have done thee!
> Mother most beloved, I beg thee by the five wounds of
> Christ, forgive me all the wrongs which I have done
> thee!

We were no more than mimes for an age-old text. And the text was beautiful and exciting, and every bit of it was true. Then the music started up again, and we proceeded to town. The official ceremony took place at the town hall, but the music didn't stop there either. Then came dinner. After dinner there was dancing.

Finally, late in the evening, the bridesmaids removed the garland of rosemary from Vlasta's head and ceremonially handed it to me. They made a pigtail of her loose hair and wound it round her head. Then they clapped a bonnet over it. This rite symbolized the transition from virginity to womanhood. Of course, Vlasta had long since lost her virginity. She wasn't strictly entitled to the symbol of the garland. But I didn't consider that important. At a higher and more binding level, she didn't lose it until the very moment when bridesmaids placed her wreath in my hands.

Good Lord, why is it the memory of that garland of rosemary affects me more than our first embrace or Vlasta's real virgin blood? I don't know why, but it does. The women sang songs about the garland floating off across the water and the waves weaving it into red ribbons. It made me want to weep. I was drunk. I could just see the flowers floating and the brook passing them on to the stream, the stream to the tributary, the tributary to the Danube, and the Danube to the sea. I saw the garland go, never to return. No return. That was what brought it home to me. The basic situations in life brook no return. Any man worth his salt must come to grips with the fact of no return. Drink it to the dregs. No cheating allowed. No making believe it's not there. Modern man cheats. He tries to avoid all milestones on the road from birth to death. Traditional man is more honest. He sings his way into the heart of every basic human situation. When Vlasta's blood stained the towel I'd placed beneath her, I had no idea I was dealing with the fact of no return. Now there was no way out. The women were singing songs of farewell. Stay, stay, my gallant swain, and grant me leave to part with my dear mother. Stay, stay, restrain thy whip, and grant me leave to part with my dear father. Stay, stay, rein in thy horse, for I have yet a sister dear and do not wish to leave her. Farewell, my maiden friends, for they are taking me from you, nor will they suffer my return.

Then it was night, and the procession accompanied us home.

I opened the gate. Vlasta paused on the threshold and turned again to the cluster of friends in front of the house. Suddenly one of them broke into a final song:

> On the threshold she stood,
> Budding fair maidenhood,
> The fairest rose of all.
> Then the threshold she crossed,
> All her beauty she lost,
> Lost her beauty beyond recall.

Then the door closed behind us, and we were alone. Vlasta was twenty, I a bit older. But I couldn't help thinking she'd crossed the threshold and from that magic moment onward her beauty would fade like flowers on the vine. I saw that future fading in her. I saw it begin. She's not just a flower, I thought to myself. She bears the fruit within her. I felt the inexorable order of it all. I accepted it and merged with it. I thought of Vladimir, whom I could not know then and could not begin to picture. And yet I did think of him and past him to his children. Then Vlasta and I climbed into the bed piled high with quilts, and it was as though all mankind in its never-ending wisdom had taken us into its gentle arms.

8

What did Ludvik do to me at the wedding? Nothing really. He was tight-lipped and strange. When the dancing began in the afternoon, the boys in the ensemble tried to give him a clarinet. They wanted him to play. He refused. Not long after that he left altogether. Luckily I was pretty far gone by then and didn't pay much attention to the matter. The next day, though, I realized his departure had left a blot on the proceedings. The alcohol diluting in my blood exaggerated it out of all proportion. Vlasta made it worse. She'd never liked Ludvik.

When I told her Ludvik would be my witness, she had been less than pleased. The morning after, she was quick to remind me of his behavior. She said he'd gone around all day looking as if we were putting him to great inconvenience. She'd never seen anyone so conceited.

That same day Ludvik came to see us. He brought Vlasta some gifts and made his apologies. Would we forgive him for acting as he had yesterday? He told us what had happened. He'd been kicked out of both the Party and the university. He didn't know what to expect next.

I couldn't believe my ears and hardly knew what to say. But Ludvik didn't want anybody's pity and quickly changed the subject. The ensemble was leaving in two weeks for a major foreign tour. Provincials that we were, we could hardly wait for it to begin. Ludvik understood and started asking me all about it. But I remembered right away that Ludvik had yearned to go abroad since he was a child and now his chances of getting out were very slim. At that time and for many years thereafter, people with political blemishes on their records were not allowed out of the country. I saw how different our lives had become, and now it was my turn to change the subject. If I discussed the tour, I would be throwing light on the gulf that had suddenly opened between our destinies. I wanted to shroud it in darkness and was wary of any word liable to throw the least bit of light on it. But I couldn't find a single one that didn't. Everything I said with the slightest bearing on our lives served to remind us that we'd taken separate paths. That we had different opportunities, different futures. That we were being borne off in opposite directions. I thought that by sticking to trivialities I could cover up our mutual estrangement. But that only made matters worse. My banter was so obviously forced that the conversation quickly ground to a halt.

Ludvik soon said good-bye and left. He had volunteered for a labor brigade somewhere, and I was off with the ensemble to see the world. Several years passed before I saw him again. I wrote him a few letters when he was in the army. Each time I sent one off I was left with the same sense of dissatisfaction I'd had after our last talk. I was unable to face up to the fact of Ludvik's fall. I was ashamed of the success I'd made of my life. I found it intolerable to dole out words of encouragement or sympathy to Ludvik from the heights of my complacency. Instead I made believe nothing had changed between us. I went on about what we were doing, what was new in the ensemble, our latest cimbalom player, our latest adventures. I tried to make it sound as though my world were still our common world.

Then one day my father received an announcement of the death of Ludvik's mother. None of us had even known she was ill. When Ludvik disappeared from my horizon, she had disappeared with him. Holding the announcement in my hand, I realized how indifferent I had become to people even slightly removed from the path my life had taken. My successful life. I felt guilty without actually having done anything wrong. And then I noticed something that gave me a shock. The announcement had been signed by the Kouteckys. There was no mention of Ludvik at all.

The day of the funeral arrived. From early morning I felt nervous at the prospect of seeing Ludvik again. But Ludvik never came. Only a handful of people followed the coffin to the grave. I asked the Kouteckys where Ludvik was. They shrugged their shoulders and said they didn't know. The procession stopped at a large tomb with a heavy marble stone and the white statue of an angel.

The property of the rich builder's family had been confiscated and they were living on a meager income. All they had left was the large family vault. What I couldn't understand was why the coffin was being laid in their vault.

Only later did I learn that Ludvik had been in prison at the time. His mother was the only one in town who'd known. When she died, the Kouteckys took over the body of the black sheep sister-in-law and proclaimed it their own. At last they were avenged on their ingrate of a nephew. They had robbed him of his mother. They had covered her up with a heavy marble stone guarded by a white angel with curly hair and a sprig of flowers. I'll never forget that angel, soaring above the ravaged life of a friend whose parents' corpses had been snatched from him along with everything else. It was an angel of devastation.

9

Vlasta is opposed to all forms of extravagance. For her, sitting out in the garden at night just because you feel like it is an extravagance. Suddenly I heard a vigorous tapping at the windowpane. On the other side of the window loomed the severe shadow of a woman's figure in a nightdress. I am obedient by nature. I can never say no to those weaker than myself. And because I am six feet two and can lift my own weight and more, I haven't yet found anyone I could resist.

So I went back inside and lay down next to Vlasta. To break the silence, I mentioned seeing Ludvik earlier in the day. "Is that so?" she said with a display of indifference. There's nothing I can do about it. She can't stomach him. All this time, and she can't stand him. Not that she has anything to complain about. Since our wedding she's seen him exactly once. In fifty-six. By then I could no longer gloss over the gulf dividing us, not even to myself.

Ludvik had been through military service, a prison sentence, and several years in the mines. He was making arrangements in Prague to resume his studies and had come to take care of a few legal formalities with the police. Again I was nervous about seeing him. But what I found was nothing like the broken malcontent I had expected. Far from it. Yet he was also different from the Ludvik I had known. He had a rough, flippant quality about him, and a kind of inner peace as well. Nothing calling for pity. It looked as though we'd have no trouble bridging the gap I had so feared. To renew old ties, I invited him to a rehearsal of our ensemble. I still thought of it as his ensemble too. What did it matter that the cimbalom, second violin, and clarinet had been taken over by different musicians and I was the only one left of the old crowd?

Ludvik sat next to the cimbalom player and followed the rehearsal from there. First we played our favorite songs, the ones we used to play at school. Then we ran through a few of the new ones we'd unearthed in remote mountain villages. Finally we did a set of those we consider most important. They are not genuine folk songs, but folk-like songs we ourselves have composed. We sang about plowing up the old border plots to make one immense collective field out of a multitude of private ones, about the poor who were now masters in their own country, about a tractor driver whose tractor station always saw to his needs. The music was indistinguishable from the music of authentic folk songs, but the words were more topical than the newspapers. Our favorite was the one about Julius Fucik, the Communist hero tortured by the Nazis during the occupation.

Ludvik sat and stared at the cimbalom mallets racing from string to string. Every once in a while he poured himself a small glass of wine. I watched him over the bridge of my violin. He was deep in thought and never once looked at me.

Wives began tiptoeing into the room, a sign that the rehearsal was coming to an end. I invited Ludvik home. Vlasta made us something to eat and then went to bed, leaving us alone. Ludvik talked about everything under the sun. But I could tell that the real reason he was so talkative was to avoid what I wanted to talk about. And how could I fail to talk to my best friend about our greatest shared possession? So I broke into his idle chatter. What did you think of our songs? He answered without hesitation that he liked them. But I wasn't going to let him get off with a polite word or two. I wanted to pin him down. What did he think of the new songs we'd composed ourselves.

Ludvik didn't want to get into an argument. But step by step I urged him on until finally he said what was on his mind. Those traditional songs we'd found he thought were truly beautiful. Otherwise he didn't care for our repertory. We were pandering to prevailing tastes. And no wonder. We performed for all different kinds of audiences and wanted to please them all. So we stripped our songs of everything that made them unique. We stripped them of their inimitable rhythms, imposing conventional rhythmic patterns in their place. We chose our songs from the most recent past because they were easier to listen to, more accessible.

I disagreed. We were barely getting started. We wanted folk music to be as popular as possible. That was why we had to make concessions to popular taste. The most important thing was that we'd created our own *contemporary* folklore, new folk songs with something to say about life as we live it now.

He disagreed again. The new songs offended his ears. They were pitiful imitations! Fakes!

To this day it pains me to think back on it. Who was it who warned us that if we kept looking backwards we'd end up like Lot's wife? Who was it who fantasized about folk music spawning the new style of the age? Who was it who urged us to give folk music the push it needed to bring it into step with history?

That was all a utopia, said Ludvik.

A utopia? But the songs are there! They exist!

He laughed in my face. You may sing them, you and your ensemble, but show me one other person who does. Show me one collective farmer who sings your collective farm songs for pleasure. He couldn't keep a straight face. They're so unnatural, so forced. The propaganda sticks out like a poorly sewn-on collar. A pseudo-Moravian pseudo-folk song about Fucik! How ridiculous can you get! A Prague Communist newspaperman! What did he have in common with Moravian farmers?

134

I objected that Fucik belonged to us all and that we had a right to sing about him in our own way.

In your own way? You don't sing the way we sing! You sing the way Agitprop tells you to sing! Look at the words. And why sing about Fucik in the first place? Was he the only one in the underground? The only one tortured?

But he's the one everybody knows!

Of course he is! The propaganda machine wants a nice neat gallery of martyrs with a chief martyr at its head.

Why do you have to be so sarcastic? Every age has its symbols.

True, but who becomes a symbol? That's the interesting part. Hundreds of people just as courageous are now completely forgotten. Famous people too. Politicians, writers, scientists, artists. None of them became symbols. You don't find their pictures hanging in schools and offices. And many had important achievements to their credit. In fact, that's what held them back. Achievements can't be touched up, cut down, or reshaped. That's what kept them from gaining entrance to the propaganda hall of fame.

But what about *Notes from the Gallows*? Only Fucik could have written that!

And what about the hero who keeps his mouth shut? The hero who doesn't need to turn his last moments into a spectacle. A public lecture. Fucik, though far from famous at the time, decided it was of the utmost importance to inform the world of what he thought, felt, and experienced in prison and to leave mankind some general words of wisdom. So he scribbled it all out on tiny scraps of paper, risking the lives of those who smuggled them out of prison and kept them safe. Think of the opinion he must have had of those thoughts and impressions! Think of the opinion he must have had of himself!

Now he was going too far. So Fucik was nothing more than a self-satisfied windbag?

But there was no stopping him. No, he replied, that wasn't the main thing that compelled him to write. The main thing was his weakness. Because being brave in private, without witnesses, without recognition, face to face with yourself—that took great dignity and strength. And Fucik needed an audience. In the privacy of his cell he created a fictitious audience for himself. He needed to be seen! To be nourished by applause. If not real, then fictitious. He needed to turn his cell into a stage and make his lot bearable by acting it, portraying it, rather than merely living it!

I was prepared to find Ludvik despondent. Even bitter. But I hadn't anticipated such venom or malicious irony. What had Fucik the martyr done to him? A man must remain true to his principles. I know Ludvik was punished unjustly, but that only makes it worse! In that case the motivation behind the change in principles is only too clear. Can a man abandon everything he's stood for just because he's been insulted?

I said as much to his face. But then something unexpected happened. He didn't respond at all. It was as though the fever of his fury had suddenly subsided. He gave me a quizzical look and then, quite calm and collected, told me not to be upset. He might well be wrong. But he said it in such a strange, cold voice I could tell he didn't mean it. I didn't want our talk to end on that false note. Irritated as I was, I refused to let go of my original plan. I still meant to come to terms with Ludvik and renew our old friendship. Even though we'd clashed head on, I hoped that eventually, once our quarrel had died down, we would be able to find our way back to the common ground of those wonderful times we'd had together. But all my attempts to keep the conversation going were in vain. Ludvik kept apologizing for overstating his case and letting himself go as usual. He asked me to forget everything he'd said.

Forget everything he'd said? Why forget a serious discussion? Why not keep it alive? It wasn't until the next day that I grasped the real meaning behind Ludvik's request. Ludvik stayed overnight and ate breakfast with us. After breakfast we had another half hour in which to talk. He told me what a hard time he'd been having getting permission to do his last two years at the university. How being expelled from the Party had marked him for life. How wherever he went he was distrusted. That it was only thanks to a few friends from before the February coup that he had any chance of going back to school. He talked about other friends in similar positions. He talked about how they were followed and had their every word taken down. How people in their circles were interrogated and how a zealous or malicious piece of testimony could blight their lives for yet a few more years. Then he abruptly changed the subject to something trivial, and when the time came to say good-bye, he told me he was glad to have seen me, and asked me again to forget what he'd said the day before.

The connection between the request and the reference to his friends' experiences was only too clear. I couldn't get over it. Ludvik had stopped speaking to me because he was afraid! Afraid our talk might not remain private! Afraid I would denounce him! Afraid of me! It was awful. And again, completely unexpected. The gulf between us was much deeper than I had thought. Deep enough to keep us from finishing our conversations.

10

Vlasta is asleep. Every now and then she snores a bit, poor thing. They're all asleep. And here I lie, a towering hulk, meditating on how powerless I am. That talk with Ludvik had really brought it home to me. Until then I'd been gullible enough to believe the situation was in my hands. Ludvik and I had never done anything to hurt each other. With a little good will I could patch things up whenever I pleased.

As it turned out, nothing was in my hands. Neither our falling out nor our reconciliation. So I began to hope that it was in the hands of time. Time has passed. Nine years since our last meeting. Ludvik has his degree with an excellent job in a field he enjoys. I follow his progress from afar. With affection. I can never regard Ludvik as an enemy or a stranger. He is my friend. But he is under a curse. Like the fairy tale prince's bride when she's changed into a snake or a toad. And in fairy tales the prince always saves the day by his loyalty and patience.

But time hasn't yet wakened my friend from his spell. More than once during those years I heard of visits he'd made here. But he never came to see me. And today when I saw him, he turned away. Damn that Ludvik.

It all began the last time we talked. Year by year I've felt a wasteland growing up around me and an anguish spreading within. More tedium, less joy, less success. The ensemble used to go on a foreign tour every year, but then the invitations began to dwindle, and now we're hardly invited anywhere. We work all the time. work harder than ever, but we're surrounded by silence. I'm standing in an empty hall. And I have the feeling it's Ludvik who has ordered me to be alone. Because it's not your enemies who condemn you to solitude, it's your friends.

Since that time I've started taking refuge on a road through the fields. I go there more and more often, to a lone wild rose bush on the verge. There I meet the last of the faithful. A deserter with his men. A wandering minstrel. Beyond the horizon a wooden cottage. And in the cottage—Vlasta, the poor man's daughter.

The deserter calls me his king and has promised me asylum whenever I need it. All I have to do is go to the rose bush, he says, and he will be there.

It would be so simple to find peace in the world of fantasy. But I've always tried to live in both worlds without giving up one for the other. I have no right to give up the real world even though I am losing everything in it. Perhaps it will be enough in the long run if I manage one thing. One last thing:

To make of my life a clear and unequivocal message and hand it down to the one person able to grasp it and carry it on. Until I have done so, I may not join the deserter on his ride to the Danube.

The person I have in mind, my only hope after all my defeats, lies asleep a wall away. The day after tomorrow he will mount his steed. His face will be hidden by ribbons. He will be called king. Come to me, my boy. I am falling asleep. You will be called by my name. I will sleep. I will dream of you on your steed.

PART FIVE

1

I had a good, long sleep. I didn't wake up until after eight, didn't remember any dreams, good or bad, didn't have a headache, but didn't want to get out of bed either; so I just lay there. Sleep had erected a wall between myself and my Friday-evening encounter, a windbreak that made me feel (for the moment at least) secure. It wasn't so much that Lucie had dropped out of my consciousness as that she had returned to her former abstract state.

Abstract state? Yes. When Lucie disappeared from Ostrava so mysteriously and cruelly, I had no practical way of going after her. And as time went on (and I was released from military service), I gradually lost all desire to do so. I told myself that however much I'd loved her, however *unique* she was, she was inextricably bound up with the *situation* in which we met and fell in love. I considered it a logical fallacy to isolate a loved one from the totality of circumstances in which the first encounter takes place and in which he or she lives, to expend great mental energy for the purpose of purging the loved one of everything but his or her *self,* that is, of the love story which the lovers experience together and which gives their love its shape.

After all, what I love in a woman is not what she is in and of herself, but what she offers me, what she is *for me.* I love her as a character in my love story. What would Hamlet be without the castle at Elsinore, without Ophelia, without concrete situations to go through, without *lines?* What would be left but a voiceless, vacuous, illusory essence? Thus, Lucie without the Ostrava landscape, without the roses proffered through the fence, without the shabby clothes, and without my own endless weeks of despair would cease to be the Lucie I'd once loved.

Yes, that was how I saw it, that was how I conceptualized it, and as the years went on, I grew almost afraid of running into her again: I knew that we'd meet in a place where Lucie was no longer Lucie and that I'd lack the ability to patch things up. Which doesn't mean, of course, that I'd stopped loving her, that I'd forgotten her, or that her image had paled; on the contrary; in the form of a quiet nostalgia she remained very much a part of me; I longed for her as one longs for something irrevocably lost.

And having become part of the irrevocable past (something that lives in the past, but is dead to the present), she gradually lost all corporeality, physicality in my mind and turned into a kind of legend or myth, inscribed on parchment and laid in a metal casket at the very foundation of my life.

Perhaps that was why, incredibly enough, I wasn't sure whether the woman in the barbershop was Lucie, why the next morning (duped by the interlude of sleep) I felt that the encounter had been less than *real* and that it had taken place on the level of legend, prophecy, or riddle. If on Friday evening I'd been bowled over by Lucie's real presence and suddenly transported to a far-off time when she held sway, on Saturday morning it was all I could do to look into my calm (and well-rested) heart and ask: *Why* did I meet her? Was the Lucie story in for a new installment? What did our encounter mean and what was it trying to *tell* me?

Do love stories, apart from happening, being, have something to say? For all my skepticism, I had clung to a few superstitions—the strange conviction, for example, that everything in life that happens to me has a sense beyond itself, *means* something, that life in its day-to-day events speaks to us about itself, that it gradually reveals a secret, that it takes the form of a rebus whose message must be deciphered, that the stories we live in life comprise the mythology of our lives and in that mythology lies the key to truth and mystery. Is it all an illusion? Possibly, even probably, but I can't seem to rid myself of the need to *decipher* my life continually.

I lay on the creaky hotel bed with thoughts of Lucie—by now a mere idea, a mere question—running through my mind. The bed began to creak, and as soon as the creaking entered my consciousness, my thoughts turned (abruptly, brutally) to Helena. The creaking bed was like a call to duty: I heaved a sigh, slipped my feet off the bed, sat up, stretched, gave my scalp a quick massage, looked out the window at the sky, and stood up. My Friday encounter with Lucie, insubstantial as it may have appeared in the clear light of morning, had nonetheless dulled and tempered my interest in Helena, an interest so intense only a few days before. All that was left of it now was an *awareness* of interest, a sense of obligation to a lost interest which my mind assured me would return in all its intensity.

I went over to the washbasin, threw off my pajama top, and turned the tap on full force; I cupped my hands under the stream of water and immediately started splashing my neck, shoulders, and body; I rubbed myself down with a towel; I wanted to send the blood coursing through my veins. Suddenly I felt alarmed, alarmed by my indifference to Helena's arrival, alarmed that my indifference (my temporary indifference) would spoil a once-in-a-lifetime opportunity. I decided to eat a hearty breakfast and wash it down with a shot of vodka.

I went downstairs to the coffee shop, but all I found was a host of mournfully stranded chairs, legs up, on bare tables, and an old woman in a dirty apron puttering around in their midst.

I walked over to the reception desk and asked the porter, ensconced behind the counter in a deep armchair and deep lethargy, whether I could get breakfast in the hotel. Without moving an inch, he told me that the coffee shop was closed on Saturdays. I went outside. It was a beautiful day, with clouds scudding across the sky and a gentle wind swirling the dust in the street. Hurrying to the square, I passed a crowd of women of all ages standing in front of the butcher's; they were holding shopping bags and nets, and patiently, lifelessly waiting their turn. A few of the people strolling or scurrying by caught my attention because of the red-hooded cones they held before them like miniature torches and licked with delight. Soon I came out into the square. Before me stood a sprawling one-story structure, a cafeteria.

I went in. It was a large room with a tile floor and tables on long legs where people stood eating sandwiches and drinking coffee or beer.

I didn't feel like eating breakfast there. From early morning I'd had my heart set on a good solid breakfast of eggs, bacon, and a shot of alcohol to restore my lost vitality. I remembered a restaurant a short walk away in another square, a square with a small park and a Baroque monument to victims of the plague. That restaurant was not particularly attractive either, but all I needed was a table, a chair, and a waiter, just one, to serve whatever was on hand.

I walked past the monument. There was a saint on the pedestal, a cloud on the saint, an angel on the cloud, and on that angel's cloud another angel, the last. I took a long look at the poignant pyramid of saints, clouds, and angels masquerading in stone as heaven, then at the real heaven—a pale (morning) blue hopelessly removed from that dusty stretch of earth.

I crossed the park with its neat lawns and benches (though bare enough to maintain the atmosphere of dusty emptiness) and tried the restaurant door. It was locked. I began to realize that my dream breakfast would remain a dream, an alarming thought, because with childlike obstinacy I'd made up my mind that a hearty breakfast was the key to success for the entire day. I realized that provincial towns made no special arrangements for eccentrics wishing to break their fasts sitting down and that their restaurants would not open until much later. So rather than set off in search of another place to eat, I turned and walked back through the park.

Again I passed people carrying little red-hooded cones, and again I thought they looked like torches, but this time I wondered whether there wasn't some ulterior meaning in their shape, because those torches were not torches, but *parodies of torches,* and the pink dot of delight they so solemnly displayed was not pleasure at all, but a *parody of pleasure,* which would seem to capture the inescapably parodical essence of all torches and pleasures in this dusty little backwater. Then it occurred to me that as long as I kept meeting lickerish torchbearers, I was going in the direction of a pastry shop where I could find that table and chair and perhaps some black coffee and a bite to eat.

Instead of a pastry shop I came to a milk bar. There was a long line of people waiting for cocoa or milk with rolls, the same high tables for eating and drinking, and in the back a few regular tables and chairs, all taken. So I joined the line, and after inching along for a few minutes I was able to buy a glass of cocoa and two rolls and find a table which, though encumbered by a half-dozen more or less empty glasses, offered a spot free of spilled liquid.

I wolfed it all down with depressing haste: in no more than three minutes I was back in the street; it was nine o'clock; I had two hours to go: Helena had taken the early flight from Prague and was due in on a bus from Brno just before eleven. I saw that those two hours were as good as lost, wasted.

Of course, I could have made the rounds of my childhood haunts, passing for a moment of sentimental meditation before the house where I was born and where my mother lived until she died. I often think about her, but here, in the town where her remains lie buried fraudulently under alien marble, my memories all seem contaminated: they might commingle with the feeling of powerlessness and bitterness I associate with that time, and I don't want that to happen.

So there was nothing for me to do but sit on a bench in the square, stand up after a while, go over to the shopwindows, glance at the titles of the books in the bookshop, buy a copy of *Rude Pravo* at a newsstand, go back to the bench, skim the dull headlines, read a couple of fairly interesting reports in the foreign affairs column, then get up again from the bench, fold the paper, and throw it away in mint condition; next, walk slowly up to the church, stop in front of it, peer up at its two towers, climb its broad steps and enter the vestibule, then the church proper, diffidently, so no one would be shocked when the newcomer failed to cross himself.

As more and more people came in, I started feeling like an intruder who doesn't know what to do with himself, how to bend his head or clasp his hands, so I went out again, looked at the clock, and saw that I still had plenty of time left. I tried to focus my mind on Helena and put the extra time to work; but the thoughts wouldn't come, wouldn't budge; the best I could do was conjure up a visual image of her. It's a well-known phenomenon, after all: when a man waits for a woman, he finds it extremely difficult to think of her and can do little else but pace up and down under her frozen effigy.

And pace I did. Across from the church I noticed a line of ten empty baby carriages standing outside the old town hall (today the building of the Municipal Council). While I wondered what they were doing there, a breathless young man pushed another carriage up to those already there, the woman accompanying him (who looked quite nervous) lifted a white lacy bundle (clearly containing a baby) from the carriage, and together they hurried into the hall. Mindful of the hour and a half I had left to kill, I went in after them.

The broad staircase was lined with eager onlookers, and walking up the stairs, I saw more and more of them, mostly in the second-floor corridor (the stairs leading to the third floor were empty). The event they had gathered for was apparently to take place on this floor, most probably in the room off the corridor whose open door was packed with people. I too went in and found myself in a modest-sized hall with seven or eight rows of chairs occupied by people who seemed to be waiting for a performance to begin. On a dais at the head of the room was a long table covered with red cloth, and on the table, a large bouquet in a vase; the artistically arranged folds of the national flag adorned the wall behind the dais; immediately in front of the dais (and about ten feet from the first row of the audience) stood eight chairs facing it in a semicircle; and at the other side of the hall, in the back, was a small harmonium with a bald old man wearing glasses hunched over its open keyboard.

There were still several free chairs in the hall; I took one. For a long time nothing happened, but the people, far from bored, were leaning over and whispering to one another in keen anticipation. Meanwhile the groups that had remained in the corridor filtered in, occupying the few remaining seats and lining the walls.

Finally the action got under way: a door behind the dais opened to reveal a woman wearing a brown suit and glasses; she looked out into the hall over her long thin nose and raised her right hand. The people around me fell silent. Then she turned back towards the room she'd just left, apparently to give a sign to someone there, but instantly she was facing us again, leaning against the wall and flashing a fixed, ceremonial smile. Everything seemed to be perfectly synchronized, for at the very moment her smile came on, the harmonium started wheezing behind my back.

A few seconds later a flaxen-haired red-faced young woman appeared in the door behind the dais, her elaborate hairdo and makeup contrasting with the terrified expression in her eyes and the white swaddling clothes in her arms. The woman in glasses pressed closer to the wall to let the woman with the baby past, beckoning her forward with her smile. The woman advanced slowly, unsure of herself, clutching the baby; then another woman with babe in arms emerged, and after her (in single file) a miniature detachment of them. I kept my eye on the leader: at first she stared up at the ceiling, then her eyes fell and met the glance of someone in the audience; the glance so ruffled her that she tore her eyes away and smiled, but the smile (there was no missing the *effort* it had cost her) quickly vanished, leaving only a rigid configuration of the lips. All this happened within a period of seconds (the time it took to cover the fifteen or twenty feet from the door); but because she was walking too straight a line and failed to turn when she came to the semicircle of chairs, the woman in glasses had to detach herself from the wall (frowning slightly), hurry over to her, tap her gently on the shoulder, and remind her which way to go. The mother quickly corrected her course and led the other mothers around in front of the chairs. There were eight of them in all. Their procession finally complete, they stood with their backs to the audience, each before a chair. The woman in brown pointed to the floor; the women gradually got the message and (their backs still to the audience) sat down (with their bundles) on the chairs.

The shadow of dissatisfaction left the face of the woman in brown, and she was smiling again as she walked over to the half-open door and into the back room. After standing there a few seconds, she stepped briskly back against the wall. A man of about twenty appeared in the doorway. He wore a black suit and a white shirt whose collar, stuffed with a patterned tie, was cutting into his neck. He kept his eyes on the floor and wavered slightly as he walked. He was followed by seven other men of varying ages, but all in dark suits and white shirts. They walked up behind the chairs where the women were perched with their babies, and stopped. Then, however, a few of them started looking around disconcertedly. The woman in brown (whose face shadowed instantly as before) ran up to them and, hearing out a whispered plea, nodded permission, whereupon the men sheepishly changed places.

Resuming her smile, the woman in brown went back to the door. This time she didn't have to nod or make a sign. The new pack trooping in knew exactly what it was doing and did it with unselfconscious discipline and all but professional elegance: it was composed entirely of ten-year-olds, arranged boy girl, boy girl. The boys wore dark-blue trousers, white shirts, and folded red kerchiefs with one point hanging down their backs and the other two tied in a knot around their necks; the girls wore dark-blue skirts, white blouses, and the same red kerchiefs at their necks; each child carried a small bouquet of roses. They moved, as I say, with supreme confidence, and instead of branching off towards the chairs, they spread out along the dais. Then they stopped, did a left face, and stood looking directly out at the mothers and the audience.

There was another short pause, and one final unaccompanied figure appeared at the door and advanced directly to the long table covered in red on the dais. He was a middle-aged man without a hair on his head. He walked with dignity, his back straight; he wore a black suit and carried a bright red portfolio. Halfway along the table, he stopped and turned to the audience, bowing to them slightly as he did so and revealing a bloated face and a broad red, white, and blue ribbon hanging from his neck, its ends bound by a large gold medal dangling in the vicinity of his stomach and bobbing up and down as he leaned forward.

All of a sudden (with no announcement whatsoever) one of the boys standing in front of the dais began to speak in a loud voice. He said spring had come and all mommies and daddies were full of joy and the whole earth was rejoicing. He went on in that vein until one of the girls broke in and said something along the same lines, that is, rather less than lucid, but full of the words "mommy," "daddy," and "spring." She also introduced the word "rose." Then she was cut short by another of the boys, who was in turn cut short by another of the girls, though there was no evidence they were quarreling; in fact, they were all saying more or less the same thing. One boy, for instance, proclaimed that children were peace. The girl who came after him said that children were flowers. Then the children concurred in unison, and stepping forward, they each stretched out the hand holding the bouquet. Because there were eight of them and eight women sitting in the semicircle, each woman received a bouquet. The children then went back to their places in front of the dais and didn't say another word.

Now it was the turn of the man standing above them on the dais, and opening his red portfolio, he began to read. He too spoke of spring, of flowers, of mommies and daddies, but he spoke of love as well, of how love bears fruit, and suddenly his vocabulary underwent a complete transformation and words like duty, responsibility, the State, and citizenship started cropping up and mommy and daddy became mother and father, and soon he was enumerating all the blessings the State offered them (the mothers and fathers) and reminding them that it was their duty in return to bring up their children to be model citizens of the State. He called on all parents present to confirm their intention to do so by signing their names in the parents book, and indicated a thick leather-bound volume lying at one end of the table.

At that point, the woman in brown went up to the mother sitting nearest the book and tapped her on the shoulder. The mother looked up and the woman took her baby. Then the mother stood and walked over to the table. The man with the ribbon around his neck opened the book and handed the mother a pen. The mother signed and returned to her seat, where the woman in brown gave her back her baby. Then the appropriate husband went over to the table and signed; then the woman in brown picked up the next mother's child and sent the mother over to the table; then her husband signed, then the next mother, the next husband, and so on until they were all done. Then the strains of the harmonium wafted through the hall again, and the people around me in the audience rushed up to the mothers and fathers to shake their hands. I too was on my way forward (as if wanting to shake someone's hand) when suddenly the man with the ribbon around his neck called me by name and asked me whether I recognized him.

I hadn't recognized him, of course, even though I'd watched him all through his speech. To avoid answering his vaguely unpleasant question in the negative, I asked him how he was. Not too bad, he said, and all at once I placed him: Kovalik, an old schoolmate of mine; it had just taken some time to reconstruct his features, which were blurred by his new fleshy face. In any case, Kovalik had been one of the less memorable students: neither goody-goody nor rowdy; not particularly friendly, but no lone wolf; no more than mediocre in his studies—in a word, inconspicuous. And since he'd lost the hair that used to hang down over his forehead, I had an easy excuse for not recognizing him right away.

He asked me what I was doing here, whether I had any relatives among the mothers. I said no, I hadn't, I'd come out of idle curiosity. He gave me a contented smile and launched into an explanation of how the Municipal Council had done a great deal to imbue civil ceremonies with dignity, adding with modest pride that as the official in charge of civil transactions he could take some of the credit and had even been commended at the district level. I asked him whether what I'd seen was a christening. He told me no, it wasn't a christening, it was a *welcoming of new citizens to life*. He was clearly glad to have a chance to expand on the subject. He said there were two great opposing camps involved: the Catholic Church with its traditional thousand-year-old rites and our civil institutions faced with the necessity of supplanting the thousand-year-old rites by their own, new ones. He said that people would not stop going to church to have their children christened or get married until our civil ceremonies matched church rites in dignity and beauty.

I told him it was obviously no easy matter. He agreed and said he was glad that civil-transactions officials like himself were finally getting a little support from our artists and it was about time artists saw their duty and gave our people real socialist burials, weddings, and christenings (here he immediately corrected himself to "welcomings of new citizens to life"). Take the poems the Pioneers had just recited, he said; they were really beautiful. I nodded and asked whether there might not be a more effective way of weaning people away from religious ceremonies, namely, giving them the option to reject all ceremony.

He said that people would never give up their weddings and funerals. And anyway, from our point of view (he emphasized the word "our" as if to make it clear to me that he too had joined the Communist Party several years after its victory) it would be a pity not to use them to bring people closer to our ideology and our State.

I asked my old classmate what he did with people who didn't want to take part in his ceremonies, whether there were any such people. He told me yes, of course there were, since not everybody had come round to the new way of thinking yet, but if they didn't attend, they kept receiving invitations, and most of them came in sooner or later, after a week or two. I asked him whether attendance at the ceremony was mandatory. No, it wasn't, he replied with a smile, but the Municipal Council used attendance as a touchstone for evaluating people's sense of citizenship and their attitude towards the State, and in the end people realized that and came.

In that case, I said, the Municipal Council was stricter with its believers than the Church. Kovalik smiled and said that was just the way it was. Then he asked me up to his office. I told him unfortunately I was a little pressed for time because I had to meet someone coming in on a bus. He asked me whether I'd seen any of the "gang" (meaning our classmates). I told him unfortunately I hadn't, but I was glad for the chance to see at least him, because as soon as I had a child to christen I'd know where to go. He laughed and gave me a friendly punch on the shoulder. We shook hands, and I went out into the square again, wondering what to do with the remaining fifteen minutes.

Fifteen minutes is not a long time. I crossed the square, walked past the barbershop, peered through the window (knowing full well that Lucie couldn't be there, wouldn't be in until later in the day), then stood in front of the bus station thinking of Helena: her face hidden under a layer of dark powder; her reddish, obviously dyed hair; her figure, far from slim, though retaining the basic proportions necessary to make a woman a woman. I thought of the traits that placed her on the titillating borderline between the repellent and the attractive: her voice, too loud to be pleasant; her outlandish gestures, betraying a pathetic desire to *continue* being attractive. . . .

I had seen Helena only three times in my life, too little to fix her image in my mind. Whenever I tried to conjure it up, one or another of her features stood out to such an extent that she would turn into a caricature of herself. But no matter how inaccurate my imagination was, it had—by its very distortions, I feel—managed to capture an essential feature of Helena's existence, something hidden beneath her outward form.

I was unable to rid myself of the image of Helena's flabbiness, flaccidity, which was characteristic not only of her motherhood and her age, but even more of her true calling: the erotic victim. Did it really derive from her essence, or was it more a symptom of my own attitude to her? Who can tell? The bus was due any minute, and I longed to see a Helena who conformed completely to the interpretation my fantasies had contrived. I ducked into the doorway of one of the buildings, hoping to observe her for a while, to watch her look around *helplessly* and wonder suddenly whether she'd made the trip in vain.

When the large express bus pulled into the square, Helena was one of the first to alight. She wore a slate-blue Italian plastic raincoat, the kind popular at the time in foreign-currency shops for giving those who wore it a young, sporty look. It did a lot (turned-up collar, belt pulled tight) for Helena as well. After surveying the square, she took a few steps forward to check the area obscured by the bus, then, far from standing and waiting helplessly, immediately turned and headed in the direction of the hotel where I was staying and she had a room booked for the night.

Once more I realized that my imagination offered me no more than a distorted image of her. Fortunately she was always more attractive in the flesh than in my mind, which observation I confirmed watching her from behind as she strutted to the hotel in her high heels. I set off after her.

When I entered the lobby, she was leaning against the reception desk, registering with the listless clerk. "Ze-man-ek," she was telling him. "Helena Zemanek." I stood behind her, listening to her give her particulars. As soon as the clerk was through, she asked, "Is there a Comrade Jahn staying here?" No, there wasn't, he mumbled. I stepped up to her and laid my hand on her shoulder from behind.

2

Everything that had gone on between Helena and myself was part of a precise and deliberate plan. True, Helena had not entered into the relationship without designs of her own, but they did not go far beyond that vague female desire to preserve the spontaneity and sentimental poetry of a romance, a desire that ipso facto restrains the woman from directing the course of events, orchestrating them in advance. I, on the other hand, had from the start been careful to orchestrate the love story I was about to experience, to leave nothing to the whims of inspiration, neither choice of words and suggestions nor choice of a room for our time together. I was wary of the slightest risk, afraid to bungle an opportunity that meant so much to me not because Helena was particularly young, particularly nice, or particularly attractive, but purely and simply because her name was Zemanek and her husband was a man I hated.

That day at the institute when they informed me that a woman named Zemanek was coming to interview me for the radio about our research, I did think of my former friend and wonder whether their shared name wasn't more than a coincidence, but I quickly dismissed the idea, and if I was unhappy about their sending her to me, it was for different reasons entirely.

I don't care for journalists. They are for the most part shallow, flip, and jargon-ridden. The fact that Helena worked for radio rather than a newspaper only fanned my aversion. In my view newspapers have one mitigating feature: they make no noise. They are tedious, but they are quiet about it; they can be put aside, thrown into the wastepaper basket. Radio is tedious, but lacks that mitigating feature; it persecutes us in cafés, restaurants, trains, even private dwellings, insofar as the inhabitants have grown incapable of living without continuous aural pap.

But I was equally irritated by the way Helena spoke. I could tell that before setting foot in the institute she'd thought her whole feature through and that all she needed from me was a few facts and figures, a few examples to prove her hackneyed points. I did my very best to make things tough for her; I deliberately spoke in complex and confusing sentences and tried to upset the preconceived notions she'd brought with her. When at one point she came dangerously close to understanding what I was saying, I put her off the track by becoming familiar; I told her how striking her red hair looked (though I thought the exact opposite) and asked her how she liked her work at the station and what she liked to read. And thinking to myself as I kept up my end of the conversation, I came to the conclusion that the coincidence in names was not necessarily a coincidence. There seemed to be a family resemblance between this phrase-mongering, loudmouthed, pushy woman and the man I remembered as a pushy, loudmouthed phrasemonger. So in the light, almost flirtatious tone the conversation had assumed, I started asking about her husband. The clues fitted neatly into place; after only a few questions I had identified him beyond a doubt. I can't quite say it occurred to me then and there to get to know her as well as I eventually did. Far from it. The revulsion I felt the moment she entered the room was only intensified by the discovery. My first reaction was to look for a pretext to cut the interview short and pass her on to another member of the institute; I even had a blissful image of throwing her out the door, smile and all, but unfortunately it was impossible.

Then, at the very moment I felt I couldn't stand it anymore, Helena, stirred by my more intimate questions and remarks (and unaware of their purely investigative function), threw me off guard with a few natural feminine gestures, and my hatred suddenly took on a new complexion: behind the veil of her radio reporter antics I saw a *woman*, a concrete woman capable of functioning as a woman. Just the kind of woman Zemanek deserved, I said to myself with a private little sneer, and quite adequate punishment; but then I changed my mind: the contempt I was so quick to heap on her was too subjective, too forced; in fact, she must have been rather pretty once, and there was no reason to assume that Pavel Zemanek no longer enjoyed using her as a woman. I kept up the bantering tone of the conversation without giving any indication of what was on my mind. Something told me to find out as much as I could about the *female* side of my interviewer, and that automatically set us off in a new direction.

Given the mediation of a woman, certain qualities characteristic of affection may be superimposed on hatred—characteristics like curiosity, the desire to be close to someone, the urge to cross the threshold of intimacy. I was in a state akin to bliss imagining Zemanek, Helena, and their world (their alien world) and sybaritically indulging my hatred (my attentive, almost tender hatred) for Helena's appearance, hatred for her red hair, hatred for her blue eyes, hatred for her short bristly lashes, hatred for her round face, hatred for her sensuous, flared nostrils, hatred for the gap between her two front teeth, hatred for the ripe fleshiness of her body. I observed her the way men observe the women they love; I observed her with the seeming intent of etching everything about her in my memory. And to disguise the rancor behind my sudden interest, I lightened my tone even more, which made her correspondingly more feminine. I kept thinking that her mouth, her breasts, her eyes, her hair, all belonged to Zemanek, and I mentally fingered them, held them, weighed them—testing whether they could be crushed in my fist or shattered against the wall—and then carefully reexamined them, first with Zemanek's eyes, then with my own.

Perhaps I did have a fleeting and utterly impractical Platonic fantasy of chasing her from the no-man's-land of our persiflage to the combat zone of the bedchamber. But it was only one of those fantasies that flash through the mind and leave no trace. Helena announced she was grateful for the information I'd given her and wouldn't take any more of my time. We said good-bye, and I was glad to see her go. The odd sense of elation had passed, leaving unadulterated antipathy in its wake, and I felt uncomfortable at having treated her with such intimate concern and cordiality (feigned though they were).

Nothing would have come of the meeting had not Helena herself phoned a few days later and asked whether she might see me. Perhaps she really did need me to go over what she'd written, but at the time I had the distinct impression it was an excuse and that her tone of voice invoked more the intimate, lighthearted side of our conversation than its professional aspect. I quickly adopted the tone myself, and stayed with it. We met at a café, and by way of provocation I skirted the issue of the interview entirely and ran down her professional interests at every opportunity; I watched her lose her composure, just what I needed to gain the upper hand. I invited her to go to the country with me. She protested, reminding me she was a married woman. Nothing could have given me greater pleasure. I lingered over her delightful objection, playing with it, joking about it, constantly coming back to it. The only way she could get me off the subject in the end was to accept the invitation. From then on everything went exactly according to plan. The plan I'd dreamed up had fifteen years of hatred behind it, and I was confident, without quite knowing why, that it would come off without a hitch.

Yes, things were going according to plan. I picked up Helena's small overnight case at the reception desk, and we went upstairs to her room, which was every bit as depressing as my own. Even Helena, who had a rare talent for describing things as better than they were, had to admit it was unattractive. I told her not to be upset, that we'd manage somehow. She gave me a glance dripping with meaning. Then she said she wanted to freshen up, and I said, Right, I'll wait for you in the lobby.

When she came downstairs (wearing a skirt and pink sweater under her unbuttoned raincoat), I was again struck by how elegant she could look. I told her we'd go and have lunch at the House of the People, that the food there was far from good, but the best there was. She said that since I was a native she would put herself entirely in my hands, offer no resistance. (She seemed to be choosing her words with their double entendre value in mind, a laughable and gratifying effort on her part.) We followed the route I'd taken that morning in my vain quest for a decent breakfast, and Helena kept making a point of how happy she was to get to know my hometown. But although she was in fact here for the first time, she never once looked around or asked what this or that building was, never gave the slightest indication she was visiting a strange city. I wondered whether her lack of interest stemmed from the kind of spiritual decay that causes normal curiosity towards the outer world to atrophy or from the fact that she'd concentrated all her attention on me and had none left for the outside world; I was inclined to favor the second hypothesis.

Again we walked past the memorial to the plague: saint holding cloud, cloud angel, angel second cloud, second cloud second angel; the sky was bluer than it had been earlier; Helena took off her raincoat, tossed it over her arm, and remarked how warm it was; the warmth intensified the sense of the pervasive dusty void; the monument jutted up above the square like a piece of broken-off sky that couldn't find its way back; I thought to myself that we too had fallen into this oddly deserted square with its park and restaurant, fallen irrevocably, that we too had been broken off from something, that we were wasting our time trying to scale the heights in thought and word when our every deed was as base as the earth itself.

Yes. I was struck by an acute awareness of my own *baseness;* it had taken me by surprise; but what surprised me even more was that it didn't horrify me, that I accepted it with a certain feeling of pleasure, no—joy, relief; and the pleasure I felt was heightened by the certainty that the woman walking by my side was letting herself in for a dubious afternoon adventure on the basis of motives scarcely nobler than my own.

The House of the People was open, and because it was only eleven forty-five, the restaurant was still empty. The tables were laid, and opposite every chair was a soup bowl containing a knife, fork, and spoon on a paper napkin. We sat down, picked up the utensils and napkins, set them next to our plates, and waited. Several minutes later a waiter appeared in the kitchen door. He surveyed the dining hall with a weary eye and turned to go back into the kitchen.

"Waiter!" I called.

He turned around and took a few steps in the direction of our table. "Did you want anything?" he asked, still fifteen or twenty feet away. "We'd like something to eat," I said. "No food until twelve," he replied, and turned again to go back to the kitchen. "Waiter!" I called again. He turned around. "Tell me," I had to shout because he was quite a distance away, "have you got any vodka?" "Vodka? No." "Well, then, what have you got?" "Rye," he called out over the distance, "or rum." "Is that all?" I shouted. "Then bring us two ryes."

"I haven't even asked you if you drink rye," I said to Helena.

Helena laughed. "I can't say I make a habit of it."

"That's all right," I said. "You'll get used to it. You're in Moravia now, and rye is the most popular drink among the people here."

"Well, that's different!" said Helena with delight. "There's nothing I like better than your average bar, the kind long-distance drivers and construction workers go to for good plain food and drink."

"So you like lacing your beer with rum."

"Well, not quite," she said.

"But you like being with the people."

"Oh, yes," she said. "I can't stand those chic places with a dozen waiters hovering over you and serving you one dish after another. . . ."

"That's right. There's nothing better than a hole in the wall where the waiter refuses to look at you and you can't breathe for the smoke and the stink. And rye—there's nothing like it. I never touched anything else when I was a student. Never could afford anything else."

"I like simple food too, like potato fritters and nice fat sausages fried in onions...."

I have become such an inveterate skeptic that whenever someone starts listing his likes and dislikes I am unable to take it seriously, or to put it more precisely, I can accept it only as an indication of the person's self-image. I didn't for a moment believe that Helena breathed more easily in filthy, badly ventilated dives than in clean, well-ventilated restaurants or that she preferred raw alcohol and cheap, greasy food to haute cuisine. If her words had any value at all, it was because they revealed her predilection for a special pose, a pose long since outdated, out of style, a pose going back to the years of revolutionary enthusiasm, when anything "common," "plebeian," "plain," or "coarse" was admired and anything "refined" or "elegant," anything connected with good manners, was vilified. Helena's pose brought me back to my youth; Helena's person—to Zemanek. My early-morning concerns quickly dissolved, and I began to concentrate.

The waiter brought us two jiggers of rye on a tray, placed them in front of us, and left behind a sheet of paper (the last carbon copy, no doubt) with an all but illegible blur of the day's dishes on it.

I raised my glass and said, "Here's to rye—good, plain rye!"

She laughed, touched her glass to mine, and said, "I've always yearned for someone simple and direct. Unaffected. Straightforward."

We each took a swig. "A rare breed," I said.

"But they do exist," said Helena. "You're one."

"I wouldn't say that," I said.

"But you are."

Once more I was amazed by the incredible human capacity for transforming reality into a likeness of desires or ideals, but I was quick to accept Helena's interpretation of my personality.

"Who knows? Perhaps," I said. "Plain and simple. But what does it mean? It means being what you are, wanting what you want and going after it without a sense of shame. People are slaves to rules. Someone tells them to be this or that, and they try so hard that to the day they die they have no idea of who they were and who they are. Which makes them nobody and nothing. First and foremost a man must have the courage to be himself. So let me tell you right away: I'm attracted to you, Helena, and I want you, married or not. I can't put it any other way, and I can't let it go unsaid."

It was an embarrassing thing to have to say, but I did have to say it. The conquest of a woman's mind follows its own inexorable laws, and all attempts at bringing her round with rational arguments are doomed to failure. The wise thing to do is to determine her basic self-image (her basic principles, ideals, convictions) and contrive (with the aid of sophistry, illogical rhetoric, and the like) to establish a harmonious relation between that self-image and the desired conduct on her part. For example, Helena dreamed of "simplicity," "candor," "openness"—ideals that clearly had their roots in the evolutionary puritanism of an earlier time and came together in her mind with the idea of a "pure," "unsullied," highly principled, and highly moral man. But because the world of Helena's principles was based not on careful considerations but (as with most people) on a logical suggestion, nothing was simpler than to apply a crude little bit of demagoguery and merge the idea of the "straightforward man" with behavior altogether unpuritanical, immoral, and adulterous, thereby preventing the desired behavior (that is, adultery) from entering into traumatic conflict with her inner ideals. A man may ask anything of a woman, but unless he wishes to appear a brute, he must make it possible for her to act in harmony with her deepest self-deceptions.

Meanwhile, people had been trickling into the restaurant, and soon most of the tables were occupied. The waiter now reappeared and was going from table to table taking orders. I handed Helena the menu. She said I knew more about Moravian food and handed it back.

There was of course absolutely no need to know anything about Moravian food since the menu was exactly the same as in all restaurants of its category and consisted of a narrow selection of standard dishes, all equally unalluring and therefore difficult to choose from. I was still dolefully contemplating the smeary page when the waiter came up and asked me impatiently for our order.

"Just a second," I said.

"You wanted to order fifteen minutes ago, and you still haven't made up your minds." When I looked up, he was gone.

Fortunately he came back fairly soon, and we ventured to order roulade of beef and another round of rye, this time with a soda chaser.

Helena (chewing energetically) remarked how marvelous it was ("marvelous" was her favorite word) to be sitting with me in a strange place, a place she'd dreamed of so often during her days in the ensemble when she sang the songs of the region. She knew it was wrong of her to feel so happy with me, she said, but she couldn't help it, she hadn't the will power, and that was that. I told her there was nothing more reprehensible than feeling ashamed of one's own feelings.

As we came outside, the monument to the plague victims confronted us again. It looked laughable. "Look, Helena," I said, pointing to it. "Look at those saints go. Scrambling up to heaven. And what does heaven care about them! Heaven doesn't know they exist, the winged clodhoppers!"

"How true," said Helena. The fresh air had reinforced the effect of the alcohol. "Why do they keep them anyway, those holy statues? Why don't they build something to celebrate life instead of all that mysticism?" Yet she still had enough self-control to add, "Or am I just full of hot air? Am I? Well, am I?"

"No, you're not, Helena. You're absolutely right. Life is beautiful, and we can never celebrate it enough."

"Right," said Helena. "No matter what people say, life is marvelous; if you want to know who gets my goat, it's those killjoy pessimists; I have plenty to complain about, and you don't hear a peep out of me; what for, I ask you, what for, when life can offer me a day like today; oh, how marvelous it all is: this strange new town, and being here with you. . . ."

I let her ramble on, inserting a word of encouragement whenever she paused. Before long we were standing in front of Kostka's building.

"Where are we?" asked Helena.

"There's no decent public place to get a drink in this town," I said. "But I know a small private one. Let's go up."

"Where are you taking me?" Helena protested, following me.

"It's a genuine Moravian tavern. Ever seen one?"

"No," said Helena.

I unlocked the door to his flat, and we went in.

3

Helena was not in the least taken aback to see that the "tavern" was in fact a borrowed flat, nor did she require any commentary. In fact, from the minute she crossed the threshold she seemed determined to switch from the game of flirtation to the act that has a single clear meaning and believes it is not a game but life itself. She stopped in the middle of Kostka's room and half turned towards me, and I could tell from the look in her eye that she was waiting for me to go up to her, kiss her, and take her in my arms. In that moment she was the Helena of my dreams, utterly defenseless and at my mercy.

I went up to her; she lifted her face to mine; but instead of kissing her, I smiled and rested my fingers on the shoulders of her blue raincoat. She understood and unbuttoned it. I took it out to the entrance hall and hung it up. No, now that everything was ready (my appetite and her surrender), I had no intention to rush and risk missing the slightest nuance of the *entire effect* I had in mind. I started a trivial conversation; I asked her to sit down; I pointed out all kinds of domestic details; I opened the cupboard containing the bottle of vodka Kostka had shown me, and pretended to be surprised; I twisted off the cap, put two small glasses on the coffee table, and poured some out.

"I'll be drunk," she said.

"We'll both be drunk," I said (knowing very well that I wouldn't get drunk, that I would be careful not to get drunk, because I wanted to keep my memory intact).

She didn't smile; she remained serious; she took a drink and said, "You know, Ludvik, I'd be terribly unhappy if you thought I was just another one of those bored matrons out for a fling. I'm no babe in the woods. I know you've had many women and they themselves have taught you not to take them seriously. But I'd be so unhappy..."

"I'd be unhappy too," I said, "if you were just another bored matron out for a fling to escape from her husband. If that's all you were, our meeting here like this would have no meaning for me whatsoever."

"Really?" said Helena.

"Really, Helena. You're right. I have had many women and they have taught me to think nothing of trading one for the next, but meeting you is something different."

"You're not just saying that?"

"No, I'm not. When I first met you, I knew right away that you were the one I'd been waiting for all these years."

"You wouldn't talk like that if you didn't mean it, would you?"

"Of course not. I'm not good at hiding what I really feel from women. That's the one thing they've never taught me. No, I'm not lying, Helena, no matter how incredible it may seem: the first time I laid eyes on you, I knew you were the one I'd been waiting for. Waiting without even knowing you. Knowing only that I would have you. That it was fate."

"God," said Helena, closing her eyes. Her face had broken out in red spots, perhaps from the alcohol, perhaps from the excitement; she was becoming more and more the Helena of my dreams: utterly defenseless and at my mercy.

"If only you knew, Ludvik. That's just what I felt too. Right from the start I knew this was no passing fancy. That's what frightened me so. I'm a married woman, and I knew what I felt for you was the truth, you were my truth, and there was nothing I could do about it."

"And you are *my* truth, Helena," I said.

Sitting alone on the couch, she trained her large unseeing eyes on me while I observed her greedily from my chair. I put my hands on her knees and inched up her skirt until her stocking tops and garters came into sight, and a sad, pitiful sight they were on those already fleshy thighs. Helena didn't react to my touch; she sat there motionless.

"If only you knew . . ."

"Knew what?"

"About me. The way I live. The way I have been living."

"And how have you been living?"

She smiled bitterly.

Suddenly I was afraid she would trot out the banal excuse of all unfaithful wives and, by denigrating her marriage, rob me of its value at the very moment it was about to become my prey. "For God's sake, don't start telling me about how unhappily married you are, how your husband doesn't understand you."

"That wasn't what I wanted to say," said Helena, flustered by my attack, "though . . ."

"Though that's just what you've been thinking. Every woman starts thinking along those lines when she's alone with a man. But that's where all the lying begins, and you want to stick to the truth, Helena, don't you? You must have loved your husband; you've not the type who gives herself without love."

"No," said Helena softly.

"What is your husband like, anyway?"

She shrugged her shoulders and smiled. "Just a husband."

"How long have you known each other?"

"Thirteen years as man and wife and a few years before that."

"You must have been a student then."

"Yes, it was my first year."

She tried to pull her skirt down, but I caught her hand and stopped her. "What about him?" I went on. "Where did you meet him?"

"In a folk ensemble."

"A folk ensemble? So your husband sang?"

"Yes, we all did."

"And you met in a folk ensemble. . . . A beautiful backdrop for young love."

"Yes."

"The whole period was beautiful."

"You have good memories of it too?"

"It was the most beautiful period in my life. Was your husband your first love?"

"I don't want to think of my husband just now," she said.

"I want to know you, Helena. I want to know everything about you. The more I know of you, the more you'll be mine. Did you have anyone before him?"

"Yes," she said, nodding.

I felt a kind of letdown at the thought that Helena had had another man. It seemed to undermine her attachment to Pavel Zemanek. "Was it serious?" I asked.

She shook her head. "Idle curiosity."

"So your husband was your first real love?"

She nodded. "But that was long ago."

"What did he look like?" I asked quietly.

"Why do you want to know?"

"I want you to be mine with all your heart and soul, with all your past." I stroked her hair.

If there is anything that prevents a woman from telling a lover about her husband, it is rarely tact or true propriety; it is simply the fear that what she says will wound him. Once the lover dispels that fear, she is grateful to him and feels a new freedom, but more important, she has something to talk about. For topics of conversation are not infinite, and husbands are the most gratifying topics for wives, the only topics in which they feel sure of themselves, the only topics in which they are *experts*, and people are always happy to have a chance to show off their expertise. So as soon as I assured Helena it wouldn't upset me, she completely opened up on the subject of Pavel Zemanek and got so carried away she didn't bother to paint in the dark areas and went on at great length and in great detail about how she'd fallen in love with him (the straight-backed fair-haired youth), how she'd looked up to him when he became the ensemble's political officer, how she and all the girls she knew admired him (he had a marvelous way with words!), and how their love story had merged harmoniously with the spirit of the time, in defense of which she also had several things to say (how in the world were we to know that Stalin had ordered loyal Communists to be shot?), oh, not because she wished to *veer off* into politics, but because she felt herself personally involved. The way she defended the period of her youth and the way she identified herself with it (as if it had been her *home*, a home she'd since lost) seemed almost like a challenge; it was as if she were saying, Take me, but with one proviso: that you let me remain as I am and accept my *convictions* as part of me. Making so much of convictions in a situation where body, not mind, was the real issue is abnormal enough to demonstrate that the woman in question was to some extent traumatized by her convictions: either she feared being suspected of having no convictions whatsoever, or (as is more likely in Helena's case) she harbored secret doubts about them and hoped to regain her certainty by staking something of indisputable value in her eyes: the act of love (perhaps in the cowardly unconscious confidence that her lover would be more concerned with making love than discussing convictions). But I did not find Helena's challenge disagreeable; it brought me closer to the crux of my passion.

"Do you see this?" she asked, pointing to a small silver pendant attached to her watch by a short chain. I leaned over to have a look, and Helena explained that the carving was meant to represent the Kremlin. "It's a gift from Pavel." And she told me the whole story of how many, many years ago a lovesick Russian girl had given it to a Russian boy named Sasha, who had gone off to fight in the big war, and how the end of the war had found him in Prague, which he protected from destruction, but which brought destruction down on him. The Red Army had set up a small hospital on the top floor of the spacious house where Pavel lived with his parents, and there the mortally wounded Lieutenant Sasha spent the last days of his life. Pavel became friends with him and stayed by his side for days on end. Just before he died, Sasha gave Pavel the Kremlin ornament, which he had worn on a string around his neck throughout the war. Pavel looked on it as his most treasured keepsake. Once, when they were still engaged, Helena and Pavel had quarreled and were thinking of breaking up, but then Pavel had come over and given her that trinket (and treasured keepsake) as a peace offering, and from then on Helena had never taken it off, seeing in it a kind of message (I asked her what kind of message, and she answered, "a message of joy"), a baton to be carried all the way to the finish line.

She sat facing me (I could see where the garters snapped on to the fashionable black Lastex panties), her face still flushed (with alcohol and, perhaps, the excitement of the moment), but her features had temporarily faded behind the image of someone different: Helena's tale of the thrice-tendered ornament had suddenly (at one fell swoop) revived in me the presence of Pavel Zemanek.

Not for a second did I believe in the existence of Sasha, the Red Army man; and even if he had existed, his real life would have vanished into thin air behind the grand gesture by which Pavel Zemanek had transformed him into a character in his own personal legend, a sacred figure, an instrument of sentiment, a sentimental argument, a religious artifact which his wife (clearly more constant than he) would venerate (zealously, defiantly) as long as she lived. I had the feeling that Pavel Zemanek's spirit (his flagrantly exhibitionistic spirit) was with us, in the room; and all at once I was in the midst of that scene of fifteen years past: the main auditorium of the Division of Natural Sciences; Zemanek is sitting at a long table on a dais in the front of the hall, flanked on one side by a fat, round-faced, pigtailed girl in an ugly sweater and on the other by the young man representing the District Council. Behind the dais hangs a large blackboard, on its left a framed portrait of Julius Fucik. I am sitting in one of the seats that rise in tiers opposite the table, the same person who, fifteen years later, is looking at Zemanek through the eyes of that time, watching him as he announces that "the case of Comrade Jahn" is open for discussion and says, "I shall read to you from the letters of two Communists." Whereupon he pauses, picks up a slim volume, runs his fingers through his long, wavy hair, and begins to read in an ingratiating, almost tender voice.

"'Death, you have been long in coming. And yet it was my hope to postpone our meeting until many years hence. To go on living the life of a free man, to live more, love more, sing more, and wander the world over . . .'" I recognized Fucik's *Notes from the Gallows.* "'I loved life, and for the sake of its beauty I went to war. I loved you, good people, rejoicing when you returned my love, suffering when you failed to understand me. . . .'" That text, written clandestinely in prison, then published after the war in a million copies, broadcast over the radio, studied in schools as required reading, was the scripture of the age. Zemanek read out the most famous passages, the ones everyone knew by heart. "'May melancholy never taint my name. That is my testament to you, Father, Mother, and sisters, to you, my Gustina, to you, Comrades, to everyone I have loved. . . .'" The drawing of Fucik on the wall was the work of Max Svabinsky, the wonderful old virtuoso art nouveau painter of allegories, plump women, butterflies, and everything delightful; after the war, or so the story goes, Svabinsky had a visit from the Comrades, who asked him to do a portrait of Fucik from a photograph, and Svabinsky had drawn him (in profile) with infinite grace of line and inimitable taste in such a way as to make him seem almost virginal—fervent, yet pure—and so striking that people who had known him personally preferred Svabinsky's noble drawing to their memories of the living face. Meanwhile Zemanek read on, and everyone in the hall was silent and attentive. The fat girl at the table couldn't tear her eyes away from him. Then suddenly his voice grew firm, almost menacing; he had come to the passage about Mirek the traitor: "'And to think that he was no coward, a man who did not take flight when bullets rained down on him at the Spanish front, who did not knuckle under when he ran the gauntlet of cruelties in a concentration camp in France. Now he pales under the cane of a Gestapo agent and turns informer to save his skin. How superficial was his bravery if so few blows could shake it. As superficial as his convictions . . . He lost everything the moment he began to think of himself. To save his own life, he sacrificed the lives of his friends. He succumbed to cowardice and through cowardice betrayed them. . . .'" Fucik's face hung on the wall as it hung in a thousand other public places in our country, and its expression was so striking, the radiant expression of a young girl in love, that it made me feel inferior for my appearance as well as my crime.

And Zemanek read on: "'They can take our lives, can't they, Gustina, but they cannot take our honor and love. Can you imagine, good people, the life we might have led if we had met again after all this suffering, met again in a free life, a life made beautiful by freedom and creativity? The life we shall lead when we finally achieve everything we've longed for and fought for and I now die for?'" After the pathos of these last sentences Zemanek paused for a moment.

Then he said, "That was a letter written by a Communist in the shadow of the gallows. Now I shall read you another letter." And he read out the three brief, laughable, horrible lines from my postcard. When he broke off again, there was a general hush, and I knew I was doomed. The silence went on and on. Zemanek, inspired showman that he was, deliberately allowed it to last. Finally, he called on me to give my side of the story. I knew I was past defense: if none of my arguments had had any effect up to now, how could they possibly have any today, when Zemanek had measured my postcard against the absolute standard of Fucik's torments. Of course, I had no option but to stand up and say my piece. Once more I explained that the message was meant to be a joke, and condemned it as totally inappropriate and crude, spoke of my individualism and intellectualism, of my isolation from the people, even uncovered traces of complacency, skepticism, and cynicism in myself. The only thing I could say in my favor was that despite it all I was still devoted to the Party and in no way its enemy. A discussion followed. The Comrades accused me of contradicting myself; they asked me how a man who admitted to being a cynic could be devoted to the Party: a fellow student, a woman, reminded me of certain obscene expressions I had used and asked me whether that was the way a Communist spoke; others made abstract remarks on the petty bourgeois mentality and then cited me as a concrete example; and they all seemed to agree that my self-criticism had been superficial and insincere. Then the girl sitting next to Zemanek, the girl with the pigtail, said, "Tell me, how do you think the Comrades tortured by the Gestapo, tortured to death, would have reacted to your words?" (I thought of my father and realized they were all pretending not to know how he'd died.) I said nothing. She repeated the question, forcing me to answer. "I don't know," I said. "Think a little harder," she insisted. "You know the answer." What she wanted was for me to pass a harsh sentence on myself through the dead Comrades' imaginary lips, but instead I felt a wave of fury rush through me, a wave of unforeseen and unprecedented fury, and rebelling against the many weeks of self-criticism, I answered, "They faced death without flinching. They weren't petty. If they had read my postcard, they might well have laughed."

The girl with the pigtail had offered me a chance to salvage at least something. It was my last opportunity to understand the extent of the Comrades' criticism, identify with it, accept it, and thereby gain a measure of understanding from them. But my unexpected reply had abruptly excluded me from their sphere of thought; I had refused to play the role played at hundreds of meetings, hundreds of disciplinary proceedings, and, before long, at hundreds of court cases: the role of the accused who accuses himself and by the very ardor of his self-accusation (his complete identification with the accusers) begs for mercy.

A new hush came over the hall. Then Zemanek spoke. He said he was unable to find anything the least bit humorous in my anti-Party pronouncements. He referred again to Fucik's words and said that in critical situations indecision and skepticism inevitably turned into treachery and the Party was a stronghold which tolerated no traitors within its walls. He said that my response clearly proved I had failed to understand a thing and that not only did I not belong in the Party, but I did not deserve the funds which the working class had laid out for my education. He proposed that I be excluded from the Party and expelled from the university. The people in the room raised their hands, and Zemanek told me I was to surrender my Party card and leave.

I stood up and placed my card on the table in front of Zemanek. Zemanek didn't look at me; he no longer saw me. But now I see his wife sitting in front of me, drunk, her face on fire and her skirt pushed up to her waistline. The black of her Lastex panties marks the beginning of her heavy legs, the very legs whose opening and closing have provided the rhythm, the pulsations for a decade of Zemanek's life. Placing my hands on those legs, I seem to have that life in my grasp. I peer into Helena's face, into her eyes, half closed at my touch.

4

"Take off your clothes, Helena," I said quietly.

As she stood up from the couch, the hem of her skirt slipped back down to her knees. She gazed fixedly into my eyes, and without saying a word (or taking her eyes off me), she began to unbutton her skirt along the side. Thus freed, it slid down her legs onto the floor; she stepped out of it with her left foot, used her right foot to raise it up to her hand, and laid it on the chair. She stood there for a moment in sweater and slip, then pulled the sweater over her head and tossed it over onto the skirt.

"Don't watch," she said.

"I want to see you," I said.

"I don't want you to see me while I undress."

I went up to her. I clutched her from either side under the armpits and let my hands run down to her hips; under the silk of her slip, slightly damp with sweat, I could feel the soft curves of her body. She leaned upward, her lips half open from habit (bad habit) for a kiss. But I didn't want to kiss her; I wanted to look at her and go on looking as long as possible.

"Take your clothes off, Helena," I said again, and moved away myself to take off my jacket.

"There's too much light," she said.

"The light's just fine," I said, and hung my jacket over the back of the chair.

She pulled the slip up over her head and threw it on top of the sweater and skirt; she unfastened the stockings and slid them down off her legs one after the other; instead of throwing them onto the chair, she stepped over to it and carefully laid them out; then she thrust out her chest and reached behind her back, and after a few seconds her tightly braced shoulders relaxed and fell forward, causing the bra to fall with them; it slid down her breasts, which, pressed together by her arms, were large, full, pale, and, naturally, quite heavy and pendulous.

"Take off your clothes, Helena," I repeated for the last time. Looking me straight in the eyes, she pulled off the black Lastex panties hugging her thighs with their flexible cloth and tossed them on top of the pile. She was naked.

I took careful note of every detail of the scene. I had no interest in finding instant pleasure with a woman (that is, *any* woman); what I wanted was to take possession of one *particular* alien, private universe and to do so within the course of a single afternoon, a single act of love in which I was to be more than a man in the throes of physical passion, in which I was to be a man guarding his fugitive prey with total vigilance.

Until then I had possessed Helena with my eyes alone. While she yearned for the warm caresses to start and conceal her body from my cold stare, I kept my distance. I could almost feel the moisture of her lips, the sensual impatience of her tongue. Another second, then one more, and I went up to her. Standing in the middle of the room between two chairs piled high with our clothes, we put our arms around each other.

"Ludvik, Ludvik, Ludvik . . ." she cooed. I led her over to the couch. "Come," she said. "Come to me, come to me."

Physical love only rarely merges with spiritual love. What does the spirit actually do when the body unites (in its age-old, universal, immutable motion) with another body? Think of the wonderful ideas it comes up with during those times, proving as they inevitably do its superiority over the never-ending monotony of the life of the body! Think of the scorn it has for the body, which (together with its partner) provides it with the raw material for fantasies a thousand times more carnal than the bodies themselves! Or conversely: think of the joy it takes in disparaging the body by leaving it to its push-pull game and giving free rein to its own wide-ranging thoughts: a particularly challenging chess problem, an unforgettable meal, a new book. . . .

There is nothing particularly rare about the union of two

strange bodies. Even the union of spirits may occasionally take place. What is a thousand times more rare is the union of the body with its own spirit in shared passion.

What then was my spirit doing while my body was making love to Helena?

My spirit had registered a female body. It was indifferent to the body. It knew that the body had meaning for it only as a body which had been seen and loved in just such a way by a third party not now present; that was why it tried to look at the body through the eyes of the third, absent party; that was why it did its best to become the third party's medium; the naked body, the bent knee, the curve of belly and breast—it all took on meaning only when my eyes were transformed into the eyes of the third party; not until then did my spirit enter his *alien* gaze and merge with him; not only did it take possession of the bent knee and the curve of belly and breast, it took possession of them in the way they were seen by the third party.

And not only did my spirit become the medium of the absent third party; it ordered my body to become the medium of his body, and then stood back and watched the struggle of two writhing bodies, two connubial bodies, until all at once it commanded my body to be itself again, to intervene in the connubial coitus and destroy it brutally.

A blue vein bulged on Helena's neck, a convulsion ran through her body; she turned her head to one side, her teeth bit into the pillow.

Then she whispered my name, and her eyes pleaded for a few moments' respite.

But my spirit commanded me to persevere; to drive her from delight to delight; to force her into a multitude of positions and leave no glance of the absent third party hidden or concealed; to grant her no respite, no, and repeat the convulsion again and again, the convulsion in which she is real and authentic, in which she feigns nothing, by which she is engraved in the memory of the absent third party like a stamp, seal, cipher, sign. And thus to steal the secret cipher, the royal seal! To rob Pavel Zemanek's sacred chamber; to ransack it, make a shambles of it!

I watched Helena's face flushed and disfigured by a grimace; I laid my hand on it: I laid my hand on it as if it were something to be turned one way or the other, pummeled or kneaded, and I felt her face welcoming my hand on precisely those terms: like a thing eager to be turned and pummeled. I turned her head to one side; then to the other; I turned it back and forth several times, and suddenly the motion became a slap; and a second; and a third. Helena began to sob and moan, but with excitement, not pain; her chin strained up to find me, and I beat her and beat her and beat her; then I saw her breasts straining upward as well and (arching up over her) beat her all over her arms and sides and breasts. . . .

Everything comes to an end, my beautiful act of despoliation included. She lay diagonally over the couch on her stomach, tired, exhausted. I could see the brown birthmark on her back and beneath it, on her buttocks, the red dappling from my blows.

I stood up and staggered across the room; I opened the door to the bathroom and went in; I turned on the cold water and washed my face, hands, and body. I raised my head and looked at myself in the mirror; my face was smiling; and the minute the smile registered, it turned into a laugh, a burst of laughter. Then I dried myself off with a towel and sat on the edge of the bath. I wanted to be alone for a few seconds, savor the rare delight of sudden privacy, rejoice in my joy.

Yes, I was satisfied, perhaps even perfectly content; basking in my victory, I had no use for the minutes and hours to come.

Then I went back into the room.

Helena was no longer lying on her belly; she had turned onto her side and was looking up at me. "Come to me, darling," she said. Ignoring her invitation, I went over to the chair where my clothes were lying and picked up my shirt.

"Don't put your clothes on," begged Helena, and stretching an arm out in my direction, she repeated, "Come to me."

I had only one desire: to be spared these trying moments or, barring that, to render them totally anodyne, insignificant, light and airy, weightless; I wanted to avoid touching her body again; I was horrified she'd make a show of tenderness; but I was just as horrified she'd resort to histrionics, make a scene; so I gave up my shirt and sat down next to her on the couch. It was awful: she snuggled up to me and laid her head on my leg; she kissed me and kissed me; soon my leg was soaked; it turned out not to be her kisses, though: when she raised her head, I saw her face was wet with tears. Wiping them away, she said, "Don't be upset, darling. Don't be upset if I cry." And she nestled even closer, put her arms around me, and burst into sobs.

"What's the matter?" I said.

She shook her head, saying, "Nothing, silly, nothing at all," and began covering my face and whole body with ardent kisses. "I'm in love," she said, and when I failed to respond, she went on talking herself. "Laugh at me if you like, I don't care. I'm in love. In love!" When I still said nothing, she added, "And happy." Then she pointed to the unfinished bottle on the table. "How about a little vodka?"

I didn't feel like a drink or like giving Helena one; I was afraid that any further consumption of alcohol would lead to a dangerous prolongation of the afternoon's activities (whose success was contingent upon their being over and done with).

"Please, darling." She was still pointing at the table. "Don't be cross," she added apologetically. "I'm just happy. I want to be happy...."

"You don't need vodka for that," I said.

"Don't be cross. I just feel like it."

What could I do? I poured her a glass of vodka. "Sure you don't want any more?" she asked. I shook my head. She tossed it down and said, "Leave it there." I set the bottle and glass down on the floor by the couch.

She was quick to recover from her momentary fatigue; suddenly she was a little girl wanting to be happy and gay and to let everybody know about it. She evidently felt completely free and easy in her nakedness (all she had on was her wristwatch with the Kremlin miniature dangling from it on its chain) and tried out a number of positions for comfort, crossing her legs under her and sitting Turkish style, then straightening them out again and leaning on an elbow, and finally rolling over onto her belly and pressing her face into my lap. She told me in every way she could muster how happy she was, kissing me all the while. I showed considerable self-restraint, I thought, because her wet mouth refused to be satisfied with my shoulders and face and seemed determined to get at my mouth as well (and unless blinded by desire, I loathe wet kisses).

Then she told me she'd never known anything like this before; I said (just to say something) she was exaggerating. She swore by all she held dear that she never lied in love, that I had no reason to doubt her. She'd been certain, she said by way of proof, certain from the start; the body has a foolproof instinct; oh, naturally I'd impressed her with my intelligence and my *élan* (yes, *élan;* I wonder how she discovered that in me), but she'd also known (though she would never have dared bring it up until now) that our two bodies had instantly signed that secret pact the human body signs only once in a lifetime. "And that's why I'm so happy. Now do you see?" She swung her legs down from the couch, leaned over for the bottle, and poured herself another glass. "What can I do?" she said with a smile after drinking it down. "If you won't join me, I'll have to drink by myself!"

Although I considered the incident closed, I won't deny the pleasure I took in Helena's words; they confirmed the success of my venture and the basis for my contentment. And mostly because I didn't quite know how to react and didn't want to appear too removed, I suggested she was exaggerating when she talked about a once-in-a-lifetime experience; hadn't she herself told me her husband had been the great love of her life?

Helena immediately sank into deep thought (she was sitting on the couch, her feet resting on the floor, her legs spread slightly apart, her elbows propped on her legs, and her right hand holding the empty glass) and said quietly, "True."

Perhaps she supposed that the intensity of the emotional experience she'd just enjoyed bound her to an equally intense sincerity. "True," she repeated, adding that it was probably wrong of her to denigrate something that once had been in the name of today's miracle (the word she chose to describe our lovemaking). She drank another glass and launched into a monologue about how the most powerful experiences in life were impossible to compare; for a woman love at twenty and love at thirty were completely different; she hoped I understood what she meant: physically as well as psychologically.

And then (making a rather illogical jump) she announced that actually there was a certain resemblance between me and her husband! She couldn't quite put her finger on it; I didn't look a thing like him, but she couldn't be wrong; she had a foolproof instinct enabling her to look deep into people, behind their exteriors.

"I'd be extremely interested to know what it is that makes me resemble your husband," I said.

She told me not to be cross; I was the one who brought up the subject in the first place; I had asked her to tell me about him; that was the only reason she'd dared to mention him. But if I wanted to know the whole truth, she would tell me: only twice in her life had she been attracted to anyone so strongly, so completely and utterly—to her husband and to me. The thing we had in common, she said, was a mysterious *élan vital,* a certain joy that emanated from us, the joy of youth eternal, its strength.

Helena may have used a rather vague vocabulary in her attempt to clarify my resemblance to Pavel Zemanek, but there was no denying that she saw and felt the resemblance and clung to it tenaciously. I can't say she shocked or offended me, but I was amazed at how ridiculous her position was. I went over to the chair and started dressing.

"Have I said something wrong, darling?" she asked, sensing my displeasure. She got up and came over to me; she began stroking my face and begging me not to be angry with her; she tried to stop me from dressing (for some strange reason she looked on my trousers and shirt as her enemies). Then she went to great lengths to convince me she really loved me and wasn't using the word in vain; she would find a way to prove it; she knew right away when I'd asked about her husband that it didn't make sense to talk about him; she didn't want any man, any stranger, coming between us; yes, stranger, because her husband had long been a stranger to her. "I haven't been living with him for three years now, silly. The only reason we don't get a divorce is little Zdena. He has his life, I have mine. We're strangers actually. He is no more than my past, the ancient past."

"Is that true?" I asked.

"Nothing could be truer," she said.

"You're lying. I don't believe you," I said.

"I'm not lying. We live in the same flat, but not as man and wife. It's been years since we've really lived together."

She had the pitiful look of a mistress in distress. Again and again she assured me she was telling the truth; she wasn't trying to deceive me; I had no cause to be jealous of her husband; it was all in the past; she hadn't even been unfaithful today, because she didn't have anyone to be unfaithful to; and I didn't need to worry: our lovemaking had been not only beautiful, but *pure*.

Suddenly I realized with terrifying clarity that there was no reason for me not to believe her. When she saw that, she relaxed a bit and immediately pestered me to tell her I believed her, tell her out loud; then she poured herself a glass of vodka and tried to get me to do the same (I refused); she kissed me; it made my flesh creep, but I couldn't turn away from her; I was fascinated by the idiotic blue of her eyes and the nudity of her body (still animated, full of go).

But now I saw her nudity in a new light; it was nudity *denuded*, denuded of the allure that until now had accompanied all the faults of age in which I thought I saw a condensation of Helena's marriage, past and present, and which I therefore found attractive. Now that she stood before me bare, without a husband or conjugal bonds, utterly *herself*, her lack of physical charm lost all its ability to excite me; it too became itself—a simple lack of charm.

Helena no longer had any idea of how I saw her; she was getting more and more drunk, more and more contented; she was glad that I believed her declaration of love, but didn't quite know how to show it. With no warning she squatted down in front of the radio (with her back to me), turned it on, and started playing with the dial; she found some jazz; she stood up, her eyes gleaming; she made a clumsy imitation of the undulating movements of the

twist (I stared with horror at her breasts flying from side to side).
"Is that right?" She laughed. "Do you realize I've never tried
these new dances?" She laughed again, very loudly, and came
towards me with arms outstretched; she asked me to dance with
her; she was angry with me for refusing; she said she didn't know
the dances, but was willing to learn, and it was my job to teach
them to her; she wanted to be young again with me. She asked me
to assure her she was still young (and I did). She noticed that I
was dressed and she was naked; she laughed; it struck her as inexplicably odd; she asked whether the man who lived here had a
full-length mirror so she could see what we looked like. There was
no mirror, only a glass-fronted bookcase; she tried to make us out
in the glass, but the image wasn't sharp enough; she went up close
to the bookcase and burst out laughing again over the titles of the
books: the Bible, Calvin's *Institutes*, Pascal's *Provincial Letters
Against the Jesuits*, the works of Hus; she took out the Bible,
struck a solemn pose, opened the book at random, and began to
read in a clerical voice. She asked me whether she would have
made a good priest. I said that reading from the Bible became her,
but it was time to put her clothes on, because Mr. Kostka would
be back any moment. "What time is it?" she asked. "Half past
six," I said. "Liar!" she shouted, grabbing my left wrist and looking at my watch. "It's only a quarter to six! You're trying to get
rid of me!"

I longed for her to be gone, for her all too material body to
dematerialize, melt, turn into a stream and flow away, or evapo-
rate, fly out the window—but there it was, a body I'd stolen from
no one, in which I'd revenged no one, destroyed no one, a body
abandoned, deserted by its partner, a body I'd intended to use but
which had used me instead and was now rejoicing brazenly in its
triumph, rollicking, reveling.

It proved beyond my powers to cut short my bizarre torment;
she didn't start dressing until nearly half past six. Putting on her
bra, she noticed a red mark on her arm where I'd hit her; she
patted it, saying she'd wear it as a memento until she saw me
again; she quickly corrected herself: she would certainly see me
long before the memento on her body had disappeared! Standing

there facing me just as she was (with one stocking on and the other in hand), she made me promise we'd see each other before then; I nodded; that wasn't good enough: I had to promise we'd see each other *many times* before then.

She took a long time getting dressed. She left a few minutes before seven.

5

I opened the window: I yearned for a breeze to waft away all memory of my ill-starred afternoon, every trace of odor and emotion. Then I quickly put the bottle away, straightened up the cushions on the couch, and when I felt all traces of her had disappeared, I sank into the armchair near the window to wait (almost imploringly) for Kostka: for his masculine voice (I craved the sound of a deep male voice), his long, scrawny frame and *flat* chest, his peaceful way of talking, both eccentric and wise, for whatever he could tell me about Lucie, who in contrast to Helena was so delectably incorporeal, abstract, so far removed from all conflicts, tensions, and dramas, and yet not without influence on my life: the thought crossed my mind that she'd influenced it much in the way astrologists think the movements of the stars influence human life; and as I sat there snugly in the armchair (under the open window still exterminating Helena's odor), I suddenly thought I knew why Lucie had flashed on the scene during these two days: it was to demolish my vengeance, to turn to mist everything I'd come here for; because Lucie, whom I'd loved so much and who had inexplicably run from me at the last moment, was the goddess of escape, the goddess of vain pursuit, the goddess of mists; and she still held my head in her hands.

PART SIX

<hr>

1

We hadn't seen each other in many years, and actually we'd met
only a few times in our lives. Yet oddly enough in my imagination
I meet Ludvik Jahn very frequently indeed, and I regard him in
my soliloquies as my prime adversary. I've grown so accustomed
to his incorporeal presence that coming across him yesterday in
flesh and blood caught me off my guard.

I call Ludvik my adversary. Have I the right to do so? Each
time I meet him I seem by coincidence to be in a helpless situation, and each time he is the one who helps me out of it. Yet
beneath our external alliance lies an abyss of internal discord. I
don't know whether he is as intensely aware of it as I am. He has
clearly attached greater significance to our external sympathies
than to our internal conflicts. He has been merciless to external
adversaries and tolerant to internal misunderstandings. Not I. I
am the complete opposite. Which is not to say I dislike Ludvik. I
love him, as we love our adversaries.

2

I first met him in 1947 at one of those stormy meetings that racked all institutions of higher learning in those days. The fate of the nation was at stake. We all sensed it, myself included, and in all the discussions, debates, and balloting I stood with the Communist minority.

Many Christians—Catholics and Protestants alike—held it against me. They considered me a traitor for throwing in my lot with a movement that inscribed atheism on its shield. When I run into these people today, they assume that the intervening fifteen years have sufficed to show me the error of my ways. But I am forced to disappoint them. To this day I haven't altered my position one iota.

Of course Communism is atheistic. Though only those Christians who refuse to cast out the beam in their own eye can blame Communism itself for that. I say "Christians." Yet who are they really? Looking around me, I see nothing but pseudo-Christians living exactly like unbelievers. And being a Christian means living differently. It means taking the path Christ took, *imitating* Christ. It means giving up private interests, comforts, and power, and coming face to face with the poor, the downtrodden, and the suffering. And is that what the churches are doing? My father was a working man. Though chronically unemployed, he never lost his humble faith in God. He constantly turned his pious face to God, but the Church never turned its face to him. And so he remained forsaken amidst his near and dear ones, forsaken within the church, alone with his God until he fell ill and died.

The churches failed to realize that the working-class movement was the movement of the downtrodden and oppressed supplicating for justice. They did not choose to work with and for them to create the kingdom of God on earth. By siding with the oppressors, they deprived the working-class movement of God. And now they reproach it for being godless. The Pharisees! Yes, the socialist movement is atheistic, but is that not a sign of divine judgment directed at every Christian? A condemnation of our lack of sympathy for the poor and suffering?

And what am I to do in this situation? Should I be shocked at the drop in church membership? Should I be shocked at the anti-religious propaganda taught in the schools? How silly! True religion does not need the approval of secular power. Secular disapproval only strengthens faith.

Or should I fight socialism because we made it atheistic? Sillier still! I can only lament the tragic error that led socialism away from God. And I can try to elucidate the error and work to rectify it.

But why all the alarm, fellow Christians? Everything that happens happens according to God's will, and I often wonder whether God isn't purposefully giving mankind a sign that mortals cannot sit on His throne with impunity and that without His participation even the most equitable order of worldly affairs is doomed to failure and corruption.

I remember the years when people here thought they were but a few steps from paradise. How proud they were that it was their paradise and that they would need no help from heaven to reach it. And suddenly it vanished before their eyes.

3

In any case, until the February coup my being a Christian played into the Communists' hands. They enjoyed hearing me expound on the social content of the Gospel, inveigh against the corruption of the old world with its private property and public wars, and argue the affinity between Christianity and Communism. Their main concern, after all, was to attract the broadest possible support, and they therefore tried to win over believers as well. Soon after the coup, however, things began to change. As a lecturer at the university I took the side of several students due to be expelled for the political stance of their parents. By protesting, I came into conflict with the administration. And suddenly doubts began to be raised about whether a man of such firm Christian convictions was capable of educating socialist youth. It looked as though I'd have to fight for my survival. Then I heard that a student by the name of Ludvik Jahn had stood up for me at a plenary meeting of the Party. He'd claimed it would have been base ingratitude to forget what I'd meant to the Party before the coup. And when they brought up my Christian beliefs, he said they were surely just a phase I was going through, a phase I was still young enough to outgrow.

I went to see him and thank him for coming to my defense. Not wishing to deceive him, however, I made it quite clear that I was older than he thought and there was no hope at all of my "outgrowing" my faith. Soon we were debating the existence of God, the finite and the infinite, Descartes's position on religion, Spinoza's status as a materialist, and many other things. We didn't agree about anything. I finally asked Ludvik whether he didn't regret standing up for me now that he saw how incorrigible I was. He answered that religious faith was a private affair and of no concern to anyone but the individual.

I never saw him at the university again. As it turned out, our lives took similar paths. Three or four months after our talk Jahn was expelled from the Party and the university, and six months after that I too left the university. Was I thrown out? Driven out? I can't quite say. All I can say for certain is that doubts about me and my convictions started up again. And that some of my colleagues hinted I would do well to make a public statement along atheistic lines. And that I had some unpleasant scenes in class when aggressive Communist students tried to insult my faith. My imminent departure was most definitely in the air. But I must also say that I had a number of friends among the Communists on the faculty and that they still respected me for my pre-February stance. It would probably have taken very little—a gesture of self-defense on my part—to bring them to my aid. But I refused to make that gesture.

4

"Follow me," said Jesus to His disciples, and without demur they left their nets, their boats, their homes and families, and followed him. "No man having put his hand to the plow and looking back is fit for the kingdom of God."

182

If we hear Christ's appeal, we must follow it unconditionally. Familiar though these words from the Gospel may be, in modern times they have a mythical ring to them. What is left to appeal to in our prosaic lives? And where shall we go, whom shall we follow once we do leave our nets?

And yet the voice uttering the appeal can reach us even in today's world if we listen hard for it. It does not come through the mail like a registered letter. It comes disguised. And rarely does it disguise itself in something all pink and enticing. "Not the deed which thou choosest, but that which befalls thee against thy will, thy mind, and thy desire; that is the path thou must tread, thither do I call thee, there be thou His disciple, that is thy time, that is the path thy Master trod," wrote Luther.

I had many reasons for being attached to my position at the university. It was relatively comfortable, it left me plenty of time for my own research, and it promised a lifetime career and an eventual professorship. At the same time, I was alarmed at my attachment to it. I was alarmed all the more at seeing large numbers of valuable people, teachers and students, forced to leave the universities. I was alarmed at my attachment to a comfortable life, whose calm security distanced me more and more from the turbulent fates of my fellow men. I realized that the voices raised against me at the university were an *appeal*. I heard someone calling to me, someone warning me against a comfortable career that would tie down my mind, my faith, and my conscience.

Of course, my wife, with whom I had a five-year-old child, did everything in her power to get me to defend myself and stand up for my position at the university. She had our son and the future of our family in mind. Nothing else existed for her. When I looked into her already aging face, I was alarmed at her constant anxieties about tomorrow and the coming year, her woeful anxieties about all tomorrows and all the coming years ad infinitum. I was alarmed at the burden they implied, and in my mind I heard Jesus' words: "Take therefore no thought for the morrow; for the morrow shall take thought for the things of itself. Sufficient unto the day is the evil thereof."

My enemies expected me to be tormented with remorse, while in fact I felt an unexpected resilience. They thought I would find my freedom restrained, while in fact I had discovered the real meaning of freedom. I realized that man had nothing to lose, that his place was everywhere, everywhere that Jesus once had been; in other words, everywhere among men.

After my initial surprise and regret I decided to meet the malice of my enemies head-on. I accepted the wrong they inflicted on me as a coded appeal.

5

Communists assume, in a manner eminently religious, that a man who is guilty in the face of the Party may gain absolution by doing a stint with the working class in agriculture or industry. During the years after the February coup many intellectuals found their way to the mines, to factories, to building sites and state farms, whence after a mysterious period of purification—sometimes long, sometimes not quite so long—they might be returned to offices, schools, and other branches of public service.

When I tendered my resignation to the university administration without applying for a research position, when indeed I requested to be placed on a state farm as a technical adviser, my Communist colleagues, friends and foes alike, interpreted the move in terms of their faith, not mine, that is, as an unprecedented example of self-criticism. They all applauded it and helped me to find a good job on a state farm in western Bohemia, a job under a decent director and in a beautiful setting. They sent me on my way with an unusually favorable letter of recommendation.

I was truly happy in the new atmosphere. I felt reborn. The state farm had been set up in a derelict and scantily populated border village from which the Germans had been expelled after the war. It was surrounded by hills, most of them treeless pastureland. Cottages of other long, straggly villages dotted the valleys at widespread intervals. The frequent mists swirling across the countryside served as a screen between me and the settled land, and the world was as on the fifth day of creation, when God still seemed undecided about whether to hand it over to man.

The people were closer to that primeval state as well. They confronted nature face to face—endless pastures, herds of cows, flocks of sheep. I felt at ease among them. I soon had a number of ideas about how to put the vegetation in the hilly countryside to better use, how to introduce fertilizers, new ways of storing hay, experimental fields for medicinal herbs, a greenhouse. The director was grateful to me for my ideas, I to him for enabling me to earn my bread by useful work.

6

It was 1951. September was cool, but in the middle of October the weather suddenly warmed up, and we had a wonderful autumn lasting well into November. The haystacks drying along the hillsides spread their perfume far over the land. Delicate meadow saffrons shimmered in the grass. It was then that word of the runaway girl began to go round.

One day a group of boys from a neighboring village had gone out into the freshly mown fields, and in the midst of their boisterous talk they noticed a girl crawl out of a stack, all tousled and full of hay, a girl none of them had ever seen before. Terrified, she looked this way and that, then darted off into the woods, disappearing before they could gather their wits and run after her.

A peasant woman from the same village told a similar story. One afternoon, when she was busy with something in the yard, a girl of about twenty in a threadbare coat had suddenly appeared out of nowhere and asked, eyes on the ground, for a crust of bread. "Where are you going, girl?" the woman asked her. The girl replied she had a long way ahead of her. "On foot?" "I've lost my money," she replied. The woman asked no more and gave her bread and milk.

And finally our shepherd reported that one day up in the hills he'd left a piece of bread and butter and a jug of milk next to a tree stump and gone off after his flock, and when he returned, the bread and jug had mysteriously vanished.

The children immediately seized on the stories, their eager imaginations inventing more and more of them. Whenever anyone lost anything, they were quick to take it as proof of her existence.

They claimed to have seen her bathing one evening in the pond just outside the village, though it was early November and the water was quite cold by then. Another time they heard a woman's voice singing somewhere off in the distance. The adults said that one of the cottages on the hill had its radio turned up full blast, but the children knew who it was. It was the runaway, wandering along the hilltops, her hair flowing free, singing.

One evening the children made a fire of potato tops near the wood and threw potatoes into the glowing ash. As they stared into the woods, one of the girls called out that she saw the runaway peering back at them from the shadows. A boy picked up a lump of earth and hurled it in the direction the girl had indicated. Oddly enough, no cry rang out. Something completely different happened. The children started shouting at the boy and nearly came to blows with him.

Whatever it was, the lump of earth had kindled a feeling of love for the girl in the children. That very day they left a small pile of baked potatoes near the remains of the fire, covering them with ashes to keep them warm and sticking a broken fir branch on top. They even found a name for the girl. On a piece of paper torn from a notebook they penciled out in large letters: *Wandering Fairy, This Is for You.* They laid the paper near the pile of potatoes and weighted it down with a lump of earth. Then they went and hid in the surrounding bushes, waiting for the timid figure to appear. Evening darkened into night, and still no one came. Finally the children had to leave their hiding places and go home. But at the crack of dawn they were back at their posts. Just as they had thought. The potatoes were gone and, with them, the note and the branch.

The children enjoyed pampering their fairy. They left her jugs of milk, bread, potatoes, and messages. But they never put their gifts in the same place twice. They avoided setting out food in a *fixed* spot, as if it were meant for beggars. They were playing a game with her. A game of hidden treasure. They started from the spot where they had left the first pile of potatoes and moved farther and farther from the village into the countryside. They left their treasures against stumps, at the foot of a large rock, near a wayside cross, by a wild rose bush. They never betrayed the whereabouts of the hidden gifts to anyone. They never violated the delicate web of the game, never lay in wait for the girl nor tried to surprise her. They allowed her to maintain her invisibility.

7

But the fairy tale soon came to an end. One day the director of our farm went deep into the countryside with the chairman of the Local Council to look over some abandoned cottages and decide whether they could be used as overnight accommodations for farm laborers working a long way from the village. On their way they were overtaken by rain, which quickly became torrential. Nearby they spotted a low-lying cluster of firs with a gray hut at its edge: a barn. They ran up, opened the door—it was secured only by a wooden stake—and crawled inside. Light filtered through the open door and cracks in the roof. Their eyes lit on a smooth patch of hay. Having stretched out on it, they listened to the raindrops falling on the roof, breathed in the intoxicating scent, and talked about this and that. Suddenly, running his hand through the wall of hay behind him, the chairman felt something hard among the dry wisps. It was a suitcase. An ugly old cheap suitcase made of vulcanite. How long the two men brooded over the mystery I don't know. What I do know is that they opened the suitcase and found four girl's dresses in it, all of them new and attractive. The glamour of the contents, I am told, contrasted oddly with the provincial lackluster of the case, and they immediately suspected robbery. Under the dresses they found a few articles of lingerie and in the lingerie a bundle of letters tied with a blue ribbon. That was all. To this day I know nothing of the letters. I don't even know whether the director and the chairman read them. All I know is that from the letters they learned the name of the case's owner: Lucie Sebetka.

While they were contemplating their unexpected find, the chairman discovered something else in the hay: an old, chipped jug. The blue enamel jug of milk whose mysterious loss the shep-

herd had been retelling in the tavern every night for the past two
weeks.

After this, the affair simply ran its course. The chairman hid in
the trees to wait for her, while the director went down to the village and sent the local policeman back up after the director. At
dusk the girl returned to her fragrant bower. They let her go in,
let her close the door behind her, waited half a minute, and then
went in after her.

8

Both the men who trapped Lucie in the barn were the salt of the
earth. The chairman, formerly a poor farmhand, was an honest
father of six. The policeman was a naïve, coarse, good-natured fellow with an immense mustache. Neither of them would have hurt
a fly.

Yet I felt something strangely akin to anguish when I heard how
they caught her. Even now I can't suppress a twinge in my heart
when I think of the director and the chairman rummaging
through her suitcase, fingering the most intimate articles of her
private life, the tender secrets of her dirty linen, prying where
they had no business to pry.

I have the same agonizing feeling whenever I picture her hay-
lined lair with no means of escape, with a single door blocked by
two hefty men.

Later, when I learned more about Lucie, I realized to my astonishment that both these agonizing situations gave me the insight I
needed to grasp the very essence of her fate. They were both *images of defilement*.

9

Lucie did not sleep in the barn that night. She slept on an iron
bed in a former shop the police had set up as an office. The next

day her case was heard before the Council. They learned that she had previously worked and lived in Ostrava. She'd run away because she couldn't stand it there anymore. When they tried to pry anything more specific out of her, they were met with stubborn silence.

Why had she chosen to come here, to western Bohemia? Her parents lived in Cheb, she said. And why hadn't she gone back to them? She'd left the train long before Cheb because on the way she began to be afraid. Her father had done nothing but beat her.

The chairman of the Local Council informed her they would have to send her back to Ostrava since she'd left without the proper discharge papers. Lucie told them she would get off the train at the first stop. They shouted at her for a while, but when they saw it wasn't helping matters, they asked her whether they should send her home, to Cheb. She shook her head vehemently. They tried being strict with her again, but finally the chairman gave in to his own lenient nature. "What do you want, then?" She asked whether she might not be allowed to stay on and work. They shrugged and said they'd ask at the state farm.

The director was fighting a constant battle with the labor shortage. He approved the Council's proposal on the spot. Then he informed me I'd be getting the help in the greenhouse I'd requested for so long. The same day the chairman of the Council came to introduce me to Lucie.

I remember it well. It was late November, and after weeks of sun autumn had begun to show its dark side. It was drizzling. She stood there in a brown overcoat, suitcase in hand, head bowed, a vacant look in her eyes. The chairman, standing next to her and holding the blue jug, announced ceremoniously, "If you've done anything wrong, we forgive you. We have faith in you. We could have sent you back to Ostrava, but we've let you stay. The working class needs honest men and women everywhere. Don't let it down."

He then went to the office to hand over the shepherd's jug, and I took Lucie to the greenhouse, introduced her to the two girls she'd be working with, and explained to her what her job entailed.

10

When I think back on those days, Lucie overshadows everything, though I can still make out the figure of the chairman of the Council quite clearly. When you were sitting across from me yesterday, Ludvik, I didn't want to offend you. Now that you are opposite me again in the form in which I know you best, as an image and a shadow, I can say it straight out: That former farmhand who hoped to create a paradise for his companions in misery, that honest naïve enthusiast saying his high-flown piece about forgiveness, faith, and the working class, was much closer to my heart and mind than you, even though he never once did anything special for me.

You used to say that socialism sprouted from the soil of European rationalism and skepticism, a soil both nonreligious and antireligious, and that it is otherwise inconceivable. But can you seriously maintain that it is impossible to build a socialist society without faith in the supremacy of matter? Do you really think that people who believe in God are incapable of nationalizing factories?

I am altogether certain that the strain of thought stemming from the teachings of Jesus leads far more naturally to social equality and socialism. And when I think of the most passionate Communists from the first period of socialism in my country—the Council chairman who put Lucie in my care, for example—they seem a good deal more like religious zealots than Voltairean skeptics. The revolutionary era from 1948 to 1956 had little in common with skepticism and rationalism. It was an era of great collective faith. A man who kept in step with the era experienced feelings that were all but religious: he renounced his ego, his person, his private life in favor of something higher, something suprapersonal. True, the basic doctrines of Marxism are purely secular in origin, but the significance now assigned them is similar to that of the Gospel and the Biblical commandments. They have grown into a body of thought which is inviolable and therefore, in our terminology, inviolate.

The era now passing or already passed had something of the spirit of the great religious movements. What a shame it was incapable of carrying religious self-revelation through to its ultimate conclusion. It had religious gestures and feelings, but remained empty and godless within. At that time I still believed that God would have mercy, that He would make Himself known, that at last He would sanctify this great secular faith. I waited in vain.

For in the end the era turned coat and betrayed its religious spirit, and it has paid dearly for its rationalist heritage, swearing allegiance to it only because it failed to understand itself. Rationalist skepticism has been eating away at Christianity for two millennia now. Eating away at it without destroying it. But Communist theory, its own creation, it will destroy within a few decades. It has already done so in you, Ludvik. And well you know it.

11

As long as people can escape to the realm of fairy tales, they are full of nobility, compassion, and poetry. In the realm of everyday existence they are, alas, more likely to be full of caution, mistrust, and suspicion. That was how they treated Lucie. No sooner did she leave the children's fairyland and resume the form of a real girl—a fellow worker, a roommate—than she became the object of a curiosity not without the malice people reserve for angels banished from heaven and fairies banished from tales.

The fact that she was so quiet didn't help either. After about a month, her file from Ostrava arrived at the farm. It told us she'd started off in Cheb as an apprentice hairdresser. As the result of a morals charge she'd spent a year at a reformatory, and it was from there she'd gone to Ostrava. In Ostrava she was known as a good worker. Her behavior in the dormitory was exemplary. The only complaint against her, oddly enough, was that shortly before running away she had been caught stealing flowers in a cemetery.

The information was quite sparse, and instead of shedding light on Lucie's mystery, it made it that much more puzzling.

I promised the director I'd look after her. I found her intriguing.

She worked without fussing and concentrated well. Hers was the calm sort of shyness. She displayed none of the eccentricities that might be expected in a girl who had lived several weeks alone in the woods. She told me over and over that she was happy on the farm and didn't want to leave. Since she was placid and always willing to give way, she gradually won over the girls who worked with her. Yet there was always something in her silence that betrayed a life of pain and a wounded soul. What I hoped was that she would confide in me, but I also knew she'd been through enough quizzings and questionings in her life to make any approach I might take sound like a cross-examination. So instead of putting her on the spot, I began talking myself. I talked to her every day. I told her of my plans to cultivate medicinal herbs on the farm. I told her how in the old days country people used decoctions and solutions of various herbs to cure themselves. I told her about burnet, with which they treated cholera and the plague, and about saxifrage or breakstone, which actually does break up kidney stones and gallstones. Lucie listened attentively. She liked herbs. But what saintlike simplicity! She knew nothing about them and would have been hard put to name more than one or two.

Winter was nearly upon us, and Lucie had nothing to wear but her pretty summer things. I helped her to budget her salary. I prevailed upon her to buy a raincoat and sweater and, as time went on, things like boots, pajamas, stockings, a new overcoat...

One day I asked her whether she believed in God. She responded in a way I considered peculiar. She said neither yes nor no. She shrugged her shoulders and said, "I don't know." I asked her whether she knew who Jesus Christ was. She said she did. But she didn't know a thing about Him. Only that He was somehow connected with the idea of Christmas. It was all a haze, a few chance images that made no sense together. Until that time Lucie had known neither faith nor doubt. I suddenly felt a moment of vertigo, something akin to what a lover must feel when he discovers no male body has preceded his in his beloved. "Do you want me to tell you about Him?" I asked, and she nodded. By then the hills and pastures lay under snow. I talked. Lucie listened....

12

She'd had too much to bear on her slender shoulders. She needed someone to help her, but there was no one. The help religion offers is so simple, Lucie: Yield thyself up. Give yourself, give the burden bearing down on you. There is such relief in the gift of yourself. I know you've never had anyone to give yourself to. You've been afraid of everybody. But there is God. Give yourself to Him. You will feel lighter.

To yield yourself up means to lay aside your past life. To root it out of your soul. To confess. Tell me, Lucie, why did you run away from Ostrava? Was it because of those flowers in the cemetery?

Partly.

Why did you take them, anyway?

She'd been depressed, so she'd put them in a vase in her room at the dormitory. She also picked flowers in nature, but Ostrava was a black place with hardly any nature left—all dumps, fences, empty lots, and here and there a scraggly clump of bushes coated with soot. The only pretty flowers were in the cemetery. Lofty flowers, majestic flowers. Gladioli, roses, and lilies. Chrysanthemums too, with their voluminous blossoms and fragile petals. . . .

And how did they catch you?

She enjoyed going to the cemetery and went there often. Not only for the flowers she took away with her, but for the beauty and the calm of it as well. The calm was comforting to her. Every tomb was like a private little garden, and she liked to spend some time in front of one or another of them, examining the gravestones with their sad inscriptions. So as not to be disturbed, she would imitate the visitors, the elderly ones in particular, and kneel before a stone. Once she took a fancy to a grave nearly fresh. The coffin had been buried there only a few days before. The earth on the grave was loose and still strewn with wreaths, and in front, in a vase, stood a magnificent spray of roses. Kneeling down under the celestial canopy of a friendly weeping willow, Lucie was suffused with a feeling of ineffable bliss. Just then an elderly gentleman and his wife came up to the grave. Perhaps it was the grave of a son or brother, who knows. They saw an unfamiliar girl kneeling by the tomb. They stood there thunderstruck. Who could she be? They must have felt something ominous in her presence, a family secret perhaps, an unknown relative or abandoned lover of the deceased. . . . They were afraid to disturb her, and looked on from a distance. They watched as she stood up, took the beautiful spray of roses they had placed there a few days before, turned, and left. Then they ran after her. Who are you? they asked. She was mortified and barely able to stammer out a few words. Finally they realized the girl hadn't known the deceased at all. They called over an attendant. They demanded to see her identification papers. They shouted at her, told her there was nothing more abominable than robbing the dead. The attendant confirmed it wasn't the first flower theft in her cemetery. They called a policeman and questioned her all over again. She confessed everything.

13

"Let the dead bury their dead," said Jesus. Flowers on graves belong to the living. You didn't know God, Lucie, but you longed for Him. You glimpsed a revelation of the unearthly in the beauty of earthly flowers. You didn't need those flowers for anyone but yourself. For the void in your soul. And they caught and humiliated you. But was that the only reason you ran away from the black city?

She was silent for a while. Then she shook her head.

Someone hurt you.

She nodded.

Tell me about it, Lucie.

It was a very small room. A bare light bulb hung crooked, naked, obscene from the ceiling. There was a bed against the wall with a picture over it, a picture of a handsome man kneeling in a blue robe. It was the Garden of Gethsemane, but Lucie didn't know it. That was where he had gone with her, and she had fought and screamed. He tried to rape her, ripped off her clothes, but she tore away from him and ran.

Who was he, Lucie?

A soldier.

Did you love him?

No, she didn't love him.

Then why did you follow him into that room with nothing but a bare bulb and a bed?

It was the void in her soul that drew her to him. And all the poor girl could find was a buck private still wet behind the ears.

But there's one thing I still don't understand, Lucie. Since you did go into that room with him, the room with the bare bed, why did you run away afterwards?

Because he was nasty and vicious like the rest of them.

The rest of them, Lucie? Who do you mean?

She was silent.

Who did you know before the soldier? Tell me, Lucie! Tell the truth!

14

There were six of them and one of her. Six of them between the ages of sixteen and twenty. She was sixteen herself. They called themselves a gang and spoke of it with awe, as if it were a pagan sect. On that day the key word was initiation. They had brought a few bottles of cheap wine with them. She took part in their drinking bouts with blind obedience. It provided an outlet for the unrequited love she felt for her father and mother. She drank when they drank, laughed when they laughed. Then they ordered her to strip. She had never undressed in their presence. But since, when she hesitated, the leader of the gang took his own clothes off, she realized the command was not directed at her alone, and complied docilely. She trusted them, trusted even their roughness. They were her shelter and shield. She couldn't imagine what it would be like to lose them. They were her father, they were her mother. They drank, laughed, and gave her more commands. She spread her legs. She was afraid—she knew what it meant—but did as she was told. Then she screamed, and the blood gushed out of her. The boys roared, raising their glasses, pouring the sparkling rotgut down their leader's back, all over her body, between their legs, and bawling vague phrases about Christening and Initiation, and then the leader stood up from her and the next member of the gang went over and took his place, and so it went in order of seniority until it came time for the youngest of all, who was sixteen like Lucie, and Lucie couldn't take any more, she couldn't stand the pain, all she wanted to do was to rest, be by herself, and because he was the youngest she dared to push him away. But just because he was the youngest he refused to be humiliated. He was a member of the gang after all, a full-fledged member! And to prove it he slapped her hard across the face, and no one in the gang stood up for her. As far as they were concerned, he was fully justified and merely claiming his due. The tears streamed down her cheeks, but she lacked the courage to put up any more resistance, so she spread her legs for the sixth time. . . .

Where did it happen, Lucie?

At the flat of one of the boys, while his parents were on night shift. They had a kitchen and one room, and the room had a table, a couch, and a bed, over the door hung a framed "God Grant Us a Happy Home" needlepoint and over the bed a print of a beautiful lady in a blue gown holding a child to her breast.

The Virgin Mary?

She didn't know.

And afterward, what happened then?

Oh, then it happened over and over, either in the same flat or in other ones, out in the fields too. It got to be kind of a habit with them.

Did you enjoy it, Lucie?

No, she didn't. From that time on they treated her worse, they were even rougher with her, but there was no way out, nowhere to go.

And how did it end, Lucie?

One night the police barged into one of those empty flats and took them all away. The gang had some thefts on its conscience.

196

And though Lucie hadn't known, it was common knowledge that she hung around with the gang, common knowledge too that she gave its members everything a young girl could give. She was the disgrace of all Cheb, and at home they beat her black and blue. The boys got varying sentences, and she was sent to a reformatory. She spent a year there—until she was seventeen. She wouldn't have returned home for anything on earth. That is how she ended up in the black city.

15

I was surprised and somewhat taken aback when Ludvik revealed to me on the phone the day before yesterday that he knew Lucie. Fortunately, he hadn't known her for very long. He'd apparently had a superficial friendship with a girl who lived in the dormitory with her. When he asked me about her again yesterday, I told him the whole story. I'd long felt the need to shed the burden, but had never found anyone I could trust with it. Ludvik has some feeling for me and is at the same time sufficiently removed from my life, to say nothing of Lucie's. I therefore had no need to fear for Lucie's privacy.

No, I've never repeated a word of what Lucie confided in me to anyone but Ludvik. Though of course everyone on the farm knew from her file that she'd been to a reformatory and stolen flowers from a cemetery. They were nice enough to her, but they never stopped reminding her of her past. The director called her "the little grave robber," and while he meant it in jest, it kept her past sins constantly alive. Lucie was ceaselessly, continuously guilty. And what she needed more than anything was total absolution. Yes, Ludvik, she needed absolution, she needed to go through that mysterious rite of purification so unfamiliar and incomprehensible to you.

For people don't know how to offer absolution by themselves, nor do they have the power to do so. They lack the power to annihilate a sin once it has taken place. They need outside assistance. Divesting a sin of its validity, voiding it, rubbing it out of time, in other words making something into nothing, requires a mysterious and supernatural act. Only God—because He is exempt from earthly laws, because He is free, because He can work miracles—may wash away sin, transform it into nothing, and absolve the sinner. Man can hold out absolution to his fellow man only insofar as he founds it on divine absolution.

You cannot grant absolution, Ludvik. You cannot forgive, because you do not believe. You are obsessed by the plenary session when all those hands went up against you, destroying your life in unison. You've never forgiven those people. And not only as individuals. You seem to think of them as a miniature model of mankind. You've never forgiven mankind. Ever since then you've mistrusted it, despised it. Oh, I can understand why. But that doesn't alter the fact that the general scorn you have for your fellow man is terrifying and sinful. It has become your curse. *Because to live in a world in which no one is forgiven and all redemption is impossible is to live in hell.* You are living in hell, Ludvik, and I pity you.

16

Everything terrestrial which belongs to God may also belong to the devil. Even the motions of lovers in the act of love. For Lucie they described a province of corruption and vice. She associated them with the bestial adolescent faces of the gang and the insistent soldier. I can see him so clearly I feel I know him. He mixes the most banal, cloying words of love with the brutal actions of a male cut off from women by the camp fence. And Lucie suddenly discovers that the tender words are nothing but a false mantle over a brutal, bestial body. The whole universe of love collapses before her eyes into a pit of loathing and disgust.

Here was the source of the disease. Here was where I had to begin. A man who walks along the seashore brandishing a lantern in his outstretched hand may well be a lunatic. But on a night when the waves have led a ship astray, the same man is a savior. The planet we inhabit is a no-man's-land between heaven and hell. No act is of itself either good or bad. Only its place in the order of things makes it good or bad. Even the physical act of love, Lucie, is not in itself either good or bad. If your love is in harmony with the order created by God, if it is a true love, then your loving will be good and make you happy. For God has decreed that "a man shall leave his father and his mother and shall cleave unto his wife; and the two shall be one flesh."

I spoke to Lucie every day. Day after day I reassured her that she was forgiven, that she had no cause to torture herself, that the time had come for her to undo the straitjacket of her soul and yield herself up to God's order, where everything, the love of the flesh included, would find its place.

And so the weeks went by. . . .

Then came the first days of spring. The apple trees on the slopes had begun to blossom, and their crowns looked like swinging bells in the gentle wind. I closed my eyes to hear their velvet tones. And when I opened them, I saw Lucie wearing her blue smock, hoe in hand. She was looking down into the valley and smiling.

I watched her smile, studied it eagerly. Was it possible? Until then her soul had been in eternal flight from both past and future. She had been afraid of everything. Past and future were treacherous maelstroms. She clung desperately to the leaky lifeboat of the present, a precarious refuge at best.

And suddenly she'd smiled. For no apparent reason. A bolt from the blue. A smile that told me she'd begun looking to the future with confidence. I felt like a mariner sighting land after many long months at sea. And I was happy. Leaning against the gnarled trunk of an apple tree, I closed my eyes again for a moment. I heard the breeze and velvet bells in the white treetops, I heard the birds trilling, and before my closed eyes I heard their song transformed into thousands of lanterns carried by invisible hands to a great ceremony. And though I could not see the hands, I could hear high-pitched voices, and I knew they were children, a happy procession of children. . . . And all at once I felt a hand on my cheek. And a voice saying, "You're so kind, Mr. Kostka. . . ." I didn't open my eyes. I didn't move the hand. I still saw the birds' voices as a host of lights, I still heard the ringing of the apple trees. And then I heard the voice, fainter now, add, "I love you."

Perhaps I should have let things go no further and left, knowing I had done my duty. But before I could take hold of myself, I let a giddy weakness take hold of me. We were completely alone in the wide open country among the pitiful little apple trees, and as I folded Lucie in my arms, we sank together into the bower of nature.

17

What shouldn't have happened happened. When I saw Lucie's newly tranquil soul shining through her smile, I knew I'd reached my goal. I should have left, but I didn't. It could only end badly. We continued to live on the same farm. Lucie was happy, glowing. She was like the spring gradually turning into summer all around us. But I was far from happy. I was terrified by the great female springtime at my side. Now that I had awakened it, it was turning all its blossoms to me, blossoms not mine to take. I had a wife and son in Prague, patiently awaiting my rare visits home.

I did not wish to break off my intimacies with Lucie for fear of wounding her, yet I did not dare go on with them, knowing I was beyond my rights. Though I desired her, I was afraid of her love, unsure of what to do with it. Only with the greatest effort was I able to maintain the natural tone of our former talks. My doubts had come between us. I felt that the spiritual assistance I'd given Lucie had been shown up for what it was. That I'd desired her physically from the moment I'd seen her. That I'd been a seducer in priest's robes. That all my talk of Jesus and God was no more than a cover for the most carnal of desires. I felt that the moment I yielded to my sexuality I'd violated the purity of my original intention and been stripped of all merit before God.

Yet no sooner did I arrive at that conclusion than I made a complete about face. What vanity! What presumption! Wishing to be worthy! Trying to please Him! What are man's merits to God? Nothing! Nothing at all! Lucie loves me and her health depends on my love! If I fling her back into despair to save my own purity, will God not despise me all the more? And what if my love *is* sinful! Which is more important: Lucie's life or my chastity? It will be *my* sin, will it not? *I* will be the one to bear it, to suffer for it!

Then one day the outside world intervened and cut short my reflections. The central authorities decided to press trumped-up political charges against my director. When it became clear he would defend himself tooth and nail, they tried to strengthen their case by claiming he was surrounded by suspicious elements. I was supposedly one of them: a man said to have been expelled from the university for views hostile to the State and a cleric to boot. The director did his best to prove I wasn't a cleric and hadn't been expelled from the university, but the more he protested the more he revealed of our friendship and the more he harmed himself. My situation was well nigh hopeless.

Is that injustice, Ludvik? Yes, that's the word you use whenever you hear about such an incident. But I don't know what injustice is. If there were nothing standing over human affairs and if actions had only the significance ascribed to them by those who perform them, then the concept of "injustice" would be warranted and I could cite the injustice of being more or less thrown off the state farm where I'd worked with such devotion. It might even have been logical for me to stand up against the injustice of it all, to wage an all-out campaign for my puny human rights.

But it is often the case that events have a meaning quite different from the one their blind authors ascribe to them; they are frequently disguised instructions from above, and the people through whom they occur are merely the unwitting messengers of a higher will whose existence they do not even suspect.

I was certain that was the case here too. So I accepted the developments on the farm. I even felt relieved. I saw in them a clear directive: Leave Lucie before it is too late. You have accomplished your task. The fruits of your labors do not belong to you. Your path leads elsewhere.

As a result, I did the same thing I'd done two years earlier at the Division of Natural Sciences. I said good-bye to a tearfully disconsolate Lucie and confronted the impending disaster head-on. I offered to leave the farm of my own accord. The director did protest a bit, but I could tell he was doing it only out of decency and at bottom was glad to see me go.

The difference was that this time the voluntary nature of my departure made no impression whatever. I had no pre-February Communist friends to strew my path with good advice and flattering recommendations. I left the farm a man resigned to the idea he was unfit to do anything significant in this State. And so I became a construction worker.

18

It was an autumn day in 1956. In the dining car of the Prague–Bratislava express I saw Ludvik for the first time in five years. I was on my way to a factory construction site in eastern Moravia. Ludvik had just finished his stint in the Ostrava mines and had gone to Prague for permission to resume his studies. Now he was returning home to Moravia. We scarcely recognized each other. And when we did, we were amazed, each of us, at the way the other's life had turned out.

I still remember the sympathy in your eyes, Ludvik, as you listened to my tale about leaving the university and about the state farm intrigues that led to my becoming a bricklayer. I am grateful for your sympathy. You were furious. You spoke of injustice, of wrongs perpetrated, of lack of respect for intellectuals. You blew up at me too: why hadn't I stood up for myself, why had I surrendered without a fight? We should never leave anywhere voluntarily, you said. Let our opponents do the dirty work themselves! What's the point in easing their consciences for them?

You a miner, I a bricklayer. Our stories so similar, and the two of us so different. I forgiving, you implacable; I humble, you proud. So outwardly similar and inwardly remote!

You knew much less about our internal split than I. When you gave me the full details of why you'd been expelled from the Party, you took it for granted that I was on your side and equally indignant at the bigotry of the Comrades who punished you for making fun of their sacred cow. What made them so upset? you asked, utterly sincere.

Let me tell you a story. In Geneva, at the time when Calvin's word was law, there lived a boy not too different from yourself, an intelligent boy always game for a laugh. One day they found a notebook of his filled with satirical gibes at Jesus Christ and the Gospel. What made them so upset? he must have thought, that boy not so different from yourself. He'd done nothing wrong. It was all just a joke. He had no hate in him. Disrespect, apathy, yes, but no hate. They put him to death.

Please don't think I approve of their cruelty. All I'm trying to say is that no great movement designed to change the world can bear to be laughed at or belittled. Mockery is a rust that corrodes all it touches.

Take your own example, Ludvik. They expelled you from the Party, from the university, put you in among the politicals for your military service, then kept you down in the mines for another two or three years. And you? You gnashed your teeth in resentment, convinced of the great injustice done you. That sense of injustice still determines every step you take. I don't understand you! How can you speak of injustice? They sent you to a penal battalion for enemies of Communism. Granted. But was that an injustice? Wasn't it more like a great opportunity? Think of what you could have accomplished among the enemy! Is there any greater mission? Didn't Jesus send His disciples "as sheep in the midst of wolves"? "They that be whole need not a physician, but they that are sick," as Jesus said. "For I am not come to call the righteous, but sinners to repentance. . . ." And you had no desire to go among the sinful and the infirm!

You will argue that my comparison is invalid, that Jesus sent His disciples "in the midst of wolves" but with His blessing, whereas you were first excommunicated and damned and only then sent among the enemies as an enemy, as a wolf among wolves, as a sinner among the sinful.

You mean you deny you were a sinner? You mean you don't feel the slightest bit guilty in the eyes of your fellow men? Where do you get your pride? A man devoted to his faith is humble and must humbly bear the most unjust of punishments. The humiliated shall be raised up. The repentant shall be purified. They who are wronged are thereby given the chance to test their fidelity. If the only reason you turned bitter towards your fellow men was that they placed too great a burden on your shoulders, then your faith was weak and you failed the test.

I cannot take your side in your quarrel with the Party, Ludvik, because I know that great deeds on this earth can be accomplished only by a band of infinitely devoted men who humbly yield up their lives to a higher cause. Your devotion, Ludvik, is far from infinite. Your faith is fragile. How can it be otherwise, when you refuse all other points of reference but yourself and your own miserable reason?

I am no ingrate, Ludvik. I know what you've done for me and for many others who have been hurt in one way or another by the current regime. I know you use your pre-February connections with high-ranking Communists and your present position to intervene, intercede, intermediate. I like you all the more for it. But let me tell you for the last time: Look deep into your soul! The deepest motive for your good deeds isn't love. It's hatred! Hatred of those who once hurt you, who raised their hands against you in that hall! Since your soul knows no God, it knows no forgiveness. You long for retribution. You identify those who hurt you then with those who hurt others now, and you take your revenge accordingly. Yes, revenge! I can feel it in your every work. But what are the fruits of hatred if not more hatred, a chain of hatred? You are living in hell, Ludvik, I repeat, in hell, and I pity you.

19

Had Ludvik heard my soliloquy, he might well have called me an ingrate. I realize he's helped me a great deal. That time in fifty-six when we met on the train he was terribly distressed at the life I was leading and immediately set to thinking of ways to find me work I would enjoy and derive satisfaction from. I was amazed by his speed and efficiency. He lost no time looking up a childhood friend who he hoped could find me a job teaching science at a local secondary school. It was quite daring of him. Antireligious propaganda was still going strong, and it was all but impossible to hire a Christian as a secondary school teacher. That is what Ludvik's friend felt too, but he did come up with another idea: the virological department of the local hospital, where for the last eight years I've been breeding viruses and bacteria on mice and rabbits.

That's how it is. If it weren't for Ludvik, I wouldn't be living here. Neither I nor Lucie.

Several years after I left the farm she got married. She couldn't stay on the farm because her husband wanted to work in a city, though they didn't quite know where they wanted to settle. In the end she prevailed on him to move here, to the town where I was living.

I've never received a greater gift, a greater reward. My little lamb, my little dove, the child I'd healed and nurtured with my soul had come home to me. She wanted nothing of me, wants nothing of me. She has a husband, but she still wants to be near me. She needs me. She needs to hear my voice now and then. To see me at Sunday services. To meet me in the street. I was happy when she moved here. It made me realize that I was no longer young, that I was older than I thought, and that Lucie was perhaps the only accomplishment of my life.

Is that too little, Ludvik? Not at all. It's enough for me, and I'm happy. I'm happy. I'm happy....

20

Oh, how I delude myself! How hard I try to convince myself I've taken the right path! How I parade my faith before the infidel!

Yes, I did bring Lucie into the fold. I calmed and healed her. I cured her of her disgust for the things of the flesh. And disappeared from her life. Yes, but what good did I do her?

Her marriage hasn't turned out well. Her husband is a brute.

He's openly unfaithful to her, and rumor has it he beats her as well. Lucie has never said a word about it to me. She knows the pain it would cause me. She's made her life out to be a model of happiness. But we live in a small town where nothing remains secret for long.

Oh, how I delude myself! I interpreted the political intrigues aimed at the director of the state farm as a sign from God. But how can I be sure of recognizing God's voice among all the others? What if the voice I heard was only the voice of my own cowardice?

I had a wife and child in Prague, didn't I? True, I wasn't much devoted to them, but I couldn't part with them either. I was afraid of getting into a situation I couldn't get out of. I was afraid of Lucie's love and didn't know how to handle it. I was afraid of the complications involved.

I set myself up as the angel of salvation, when in fact I was merely another of her seducers. I loved her once, a single time, then turned away. I acted as though I were offering her forgiveness, when she actually should have forgiven me. She wept in despair when I left, and several years later she came and settled in my town. She spoke to me. Turned to me as to a friend. She has forgiven me. One thing is clear: It hasn't happened often in my life, but that girl loved me. I held her life in my hands. Her happiness was within my power. And I ran away. No one has ever wronged her as I did.

Wasn't what I tried to pass off as a divine appeal really just an excuse to shirk my human obligations? I am afraid of women. Afraid of their warmth. Afraid of their constant presence. I was terrified of a life with Lucie just as I am terrified at the thought of moving permanently into the teacher's two-room flat in the neighboring town.

And what was the real reason behind my voluntary resignation from the university fifteen years ago? I didn't love my wife. She was six years older than I. I couldn't stand her voice anymore or her face or the monotonous tick-tock of the family clock. I couldn't live with her, but neither could I inflict a divorce on her, because she was a fine woman who had never done anything to hurt me. And suddenly I heard the saving voice of an appeal from on high. I heard Jesus calling me to forsake my nets.

Tell me, God, is it true? Am I truly so wretched and laughable? Tell me it isn't true! Reassure me! Speak to me, God! Louder! In this jumble of voices I can't seem to hear You!

PART SEVEN

1

When late that evening I got back to the hotel from Kostka's place, I was determined to leave for Prague first thing in the morning: there was nothing to keep me in my hometown now that my ill-fated mission was over. Unfortunately, my thoughts were in such a whirl that I spent half the night tossing and turning on my bed (my creaky bed) without closing my eyes; when I finally did drop off, I still kept waking up, and it wasn't until early morning that I fell into a deep sleep. As a result, I didn't get out of bed until nine, by which time the morning buses and trains had all left. When I realized I'd have to wait till two in the afternoon for the next connection to Prague, I was terribly depressed: I felt like a man who has been shipwrecked. Suddenly I had a great hunger for Prague, for my work, for the desk in my flat, for my books, and there was nothing I could do but grit my teeth and go down to the dining room for breakfast.

Afraid of meeting Helena, I walked in cautiously. She wasn't there (which meant she was out scurrying round the neighboring village with a tape recorder over her shoulder, pestering the passersby with a microphone and silly questions), though the room was packed with people generating a lot of noise and a lot of smoke as they sat at their beers, black coffees, and cognacs. I saw, to my chagrin, that once again my hometown would begrudge me a decent breakfast.

I went out into the street; the blue sky, the ragged little clouds, the gathering humidity, the slightly rising dust, the street running into the broad, flat square, the spire (that's right, the one that looks like a soldier in an ancient helmet)—they all exuded a kind of empty melancholy. In the distance I could hear the drunken drone of a Moravian lament (a curse on homesickness, the steppe, the Uhlan raids), and suddenly I seemed to see Lucie before me, Lucie and the whole ancient incident, which so resembled the drawn-out rhythm of the song and spoke so directly to my heart, a heart hordes of women had crossed (like a steppe) without leaving a trace, just as the dust rising over the broad, flat square leaves no trace and settles between the cobblestones, until, rising again, it flies off in a gust of wind.

I strode across those dusty cobblestones under the oppressive weightlessness of the void lying over my life: Lucie, the goddess of smoke, had first deprived me of herself, then yesterday nullified my carefully calculated attempt at revenge, and now transformed even the memory of herself into something utterly laughable, a grotesque illusion: Kostka's story has made it clear that all these years I've had a different woman in mind and never really known who Lucie is.

I'd always taken comfort in seeing Lucie as something abstract, a legend and a myth, but now I realized that behind the poetry of my vision hid a starkly unpoetic reality; that I didn't know her; that I didn't know her as she actually was, in and of herself. All I'd been able to perceive (in my youthful egocentricity) was those aspects of her being touching directly on me (my loneliness, my captivity, my desire for tenderness and affection); she had never been anything more to me than a *function of my situation;* everything beyond that concrete situation, everything she was in her own right, had escaped me entirely. And since she was merely the function of a situation, it stands to reason that when that situation changed (when another situation took over, when I myself grew older and changed), *my* Lucie vanished with it, and all that was left of her was what had escaped me, what didn't concern me what was beyond me. Consequently, it also stands to reason that after fifteen years I failed to recognize her. In my eyes (and I'd never thought to consider her except insofar as I was concerned) she had long been a different person, a stranger.

For fifteen years the message of my defeat had been trailing me; now it had caught up with me. That eccentric Kostka (whom I'd never taken more than half seriously) had meant more to her, done more for her, known more about her, and loved her *better* (I say *better* and not *more* because the power of my love could scarcely have been greater): she'd told him everything—she told me nothing; he'd made her happy—I made her unhappy; he'd known her physically—I lost my chance. And all I needed to do in order to possess the body I so desperately desired was simply to understand her, get to know her, love her not only for what she was to me but for everything about her that did not touch me directly, that was hers and hers alone. But I was unable to do it and thereby hurt both myself and her. A wave of anger washed over me; I was angry with myself and about my age at the time, that ludicrous *lyrical* age, when a man is too great a riddle to himself to tackle riddles outside himself and when other people (no matter how he loves them) are mere walking mirrors in which he is amazed to find the images of his own feelings, his own emotions, his own values. Yes, for fifteen years I'd thought of Lucie as the mirror that preserved my image of those days!

I recalled the bleak room and its lonely bed and the streetlamp shining in through the dirty glass; I recalled Lucie's ferocious resistance. It was all a bad joke: I thought she was a virgin, and she put up a fight because she wasn't a virgin and feared the moment of truth. But there was another explanation as well (one which corresponds to Kostka's view of her): her initial sexual experiences were so cruel they imbued her with a repugnance for the act of love, deprived it of the meanings other people give it, emptied it entirely of affection and love; half-child, half-whore, she thought the body ugly and love incorporeal; soul engaged body in silent, stubborn combat.

This interpretation (so melodramatic, yet so plausible) reminded me of the deplorable discord (I knew it well and in many of its forms) between body and soul and summoned up (for the pathetic is in constant competition with the ludicrous) a story that once gave me a good laugh. A good friend of mine, a woman of rather flexible morals (of which I had taken ample advantage), became engaged to a physicist and firmly resolved to make him her first *love*, but to make certain it was *true* love (as opposed to the scores of love affairs she'd been through), she refused him all physical intimacy until the wedding night, and on their evening walks in the park would do no more than squeeze his hand and kiss him under the streetlamps, thereby enabling her soul (unhampered by a body) to soar into the clouds and give in to the vertigo it found there. A week after they were married she filed for divorce, complaining bitterly that he had ruined the love of her life by proving to be a rotten, all but impotent lover.

The drone of the Moravian song in the distance now mingled with the grotesque aftertaste of the story, the dusty emptiness of the square, and my depression, the latter reinforced by the hunger rumbling through my entrails. I happened to have ended up in the vicinity of the milk bar, but when I tried to push the door open, it wouldn't budge. "They're all at the festival today," a passerby told me. "The Ride of the Kings?" "Right. They've got a stand there."

I let out a curse, but there was nothing I could do about it; I set off in the direction of the song, my hunger pangs guiding me to the folklore festival I'd hoped to avoid.

2

Exhaustion. Exhaustion from early morning. As if I'd been out carousing all night. And I slept all night. If that watered-down version deserves the name sleep. It was all I could do to keep from yawning over breakfast. Soon people started dribbling by. Vladimir's friends and some nosy onlookers. Then a boy from the cooperative brought over the horse for Vladimir. And in the midst of it all who should show up but Kalasek, the District Council adviser for cultural affairs. For two years now we've been at loggerheads.

He was wearing a black suit and looking very serious. He had an elegant woman with him. A Prague radio reporter. I was going to be their guide, he said. The woman wanted to tape some interviews for a program about the Ride.

No, thank you! Not me! Not me! I'm not going to play the fool. The reporter went on about how thrilled she was to meet me in person, and of course Kalasek started in too: it was my political duty to go with them. The fool. I almost had my way. I told them my son was today's king and I wanted to be on hand while he got ready. But then Vlasta stabbed me in the back. Getting him ready was her job, she said. Why didn't I run along and help them to do the taping.

So in the end I did as I was told. The radio woman had set up headquarters in a room at the District Council. Besides her tape recorder she had brought along a young man to run errands for her. She didn't stop talking for a minute, except to laugh, that is. Finally she put the microphone to her lips and asked Kalasek the first question.

Kalasek gave a little cough and was off. The cultivation of folk art was an integral part of Communist education. The District Council was fully aware. That was why it fully supported. He wished them every success and fully shared. He thanked everyone who had taken part, the enthusiastic organizers and the enthusiastic schoolchildren, whom he fully.

Exhaustion, exhaustion. The same old words. Fifteen years of the same old words. And now from the mouth of Kalasek, who didn't give a damn about folk art. Folk art was a mere gimmick to him. Another way of showing how active he'd been. Of following guidelines. Of tooting his own horn. He hadn't lifted a finger for the Ride, he'd cut our budget down to the bone, yet he was the one who'd get the credit. The lord and master of local culture. A former delivery boy who couldn't tell a violin from a guitar.

The reporter had put the microphone back to her lips. Was I satisfied with this year's Ride of the Kings? I felt like laughing in her face. The Ride hadn't even started yet! But she laughed at me instead. I had so much experience with folklore, she said. Surely I knew how it would turn out. That's the way they are. They know everything ahead of time. They know the future from A to Z. The future has already happened and is simply rerunning itself for them.

I had half a mind to tell her exactly what I thought. That the Ride would be worse than in past years. That folk art was losing supporters year by year. That the authorities had lost interest as well. That it was all but dead. The folk music blaring out of radios all the time had nothing to do with the case. What all those folk instrument orchestras and folk song ensembles played was more opera or operetta or hit tunes than folk music. Folk instruments with a conductor, score, and music stands! Symphonic orchestrations! What blasphemy! The music you so revel in, my dear lady, is nothing but good old romanticism with a thin veneer of folk melody. Real folk art is dead, yes, dead and buried.

That is what I would have liked to spit into the microphone. In the end I said something different. The Ride of the Kings was splendid. The power of folk art. A blaze of color. I fully shared. I thank everyone who has taken part, the enthusiastic organizers and the enthusiastic schoolchildren, whom I fully.

I felt ashamed for saying the things they wanted me to say. Was I that much of a coward? That well trained? That exhausted?

I was glad to be done with it and made a hasty exit. I was anxious to get home. There were a lot of people in the yard, some just hanging about, others decorating the horse with bows and ribbons. I wanted to see how Vladimir was doing. I went inside, but the door to the living room where they were dressing him was locked. I knocked and called out. You have no business in here, Vlasta answered from inside. It's the robing of the king. Let me in, damn it! I said. Why won't you let me in? It's against tradition, she replied from inside. I didn't know of any tradition preventing a father from being present while the king dressed, but I didn't want to contradict her. I'd detected a note of interest in her voice, and it made me feel good. It made me feel good to know they were taking an interest in my world. My poor orphaned world.

So I went back into the yard and chatted with the people decorating the horse. It was a heavy draft horse. Patient and calm.

Then I heard the sound of voices coming through the gate from the street. It was followed by some shouts and a drum roll. My time had come. I was all excited. I opened the gate and went out. The Ride of the Kings was marshaled in front of the house. Horses adorned with ribbons and streamers. Young riders in colorful folk costumes. Just like twenty years ago. Twenty years ago when they came here for me. When they asked my father to give them his son to be king.

Up near the gate sat the two pages, disguised as women, but holding sabers. They were waiting for Vladimir, whom they would accompany and guard all day. A young man rode out from the band, and halting his mount right in front of me, he recited the following lines:

> Hear ye, hear ye, one and all!
> Kind father, we have come our greetings for to bring
> And ask you for your leave to make your son our king!

Then he promised that they would keep good watch over the king. That they would conduct him safely through the enemies' hosts. That they would not deliver him up into their hands. That they were eager for the fray. Hear ye, hear ye!

I looked back. In the shadow of our house sat a figure astride a finely bedecked horse. He wore a woman's costume with puckered sleeves, and his face was covered with brightly colored ribbons. The king. Vladimir. Suddenly I forgot my exhaustion and depression and felt completely at ease. The old king was sending the young one out into the world. I went over to him, and standing on tiptoe to be as near as possible to his hidden face, I whispered, "Good luck, Vladimir!" He didn't respond. Didn't move. He's not supposed to, Vlasta said to me with a smile. He's not allowed to say a word until evening.

3

It took me no more than a quarter of an hour to reach the village (in my youth it was cut off from the town by a belt of fields, but now the two had all but merged); the singing I'd heard back in town (it had sounded so distant and sad there) now blared out in full force from loudspeakers attached to houses and telephone poles (eternal fool that I am, I let myself go bleary-eyed over the supposedly drunken nostalgia of the voice, and it turned out to be nothing more than a reproduction, compliments of District Council's technical resources and a pair of scratchy seventy-eights!). Just outside the center of the village a kind of triumphal arch topped by an enormous WELCOME sign in red ornamental lettering had been erected for the occasion; the crowd was quite dense, and while most of the people wore everyday clothes, a few old codgers had taken out their folk costumes: high boots, white linen trousers, and embroidered shirts. Here the street widened into a village green: a broad patch of grass between the road and the nearest row of houses; among the trees dotting the grass a few stands had been set up (also for the occasion) to sell beer, soft drinks, peanuts, chocolate, gingerbread, sausages with mustard, and cream-filled wafers; one of the stands belonged to the milk bar and was offering milk, cheese, butter, yogurt, and sour cream; none of the stands served hard alcohol, but nearly everyone looked drunk to me; people kept crowding round the stands, getting in one another's way, gawking; now and then someone would break into song, but it was always a false start (accompanied by a drunken flourish of the arm): two or three bars of a song immediately drowned out by the din of the crowds and the invincible blast of the recorded folk song from the speakers. The place was littered (though it was still early and the Ride had yet to start) with paper beer cups and paper plates smeared with mustard.

The aura of temperance surrounding the stand of milk and yogurt was bad for business; I bought a cup of milk and a roll without having to wait, and moved off to a less crowded spot to sip my milk in peace. Just then I heard a commotion coming from the other end of the green: the Ride of the Kings had arrived.

Small black hats with cockerel feathers, white shirts with full pleated sleeves, blue vests with tufts of red wool, and colored paper ribbons fluttering from the horses' harnesses filled every inch of the green; soon now the loudspeaker music and buzzing voices were joined by new sounds: whinnying horses, and horsemen chanting:

> Here ye, hear ye, one and all,
> From hill and dale, from near and far,
> And learn what came to pass this Whitsunday!
> We have a needy king, and yet right virtuous,
> And that day thieves did rob his empty lands
> Of full one thousand head of cattle. . . .

Pandemonium assaulted ear and eye alike; everything clashed: the folklore from the speakers and the folklore on horseback, the vivid colors of the costumes and horses and the ugly browns and grays of the spectators' poorly cut clothes, the forced spontaneity of the costumed riders and the forced officiousness of the organizers running around in their red armbands among the horses and people and trying to keep the chaos within bounds, by no means a simple task, not because the spectators were unruly (luckily they were not very great in number) but because the road hadn't been closed to traffic; and though there were organizers posted at either end of the procession signaling vehicles to slow down, cars and trucks and roaring motorcycles still wove their way through the Ride, spooking both horses and riders.

To be frank, my reasons for steering clear of this (or any other) folklore event had nothing to do with what I actually witnessed: I was prepared for the lack of taste, I was prepared for the unholy alliance of true folk art with kitsch, I was prepared for overblown speeches by idiot orators, yes, I was prepared for the worst in bombast and hypocrisy, but what I wasn't prepared for was the sad and almost touching *shabbiness* of it all; it pervaded everything: the pitiful stands, the small but unruly and inattentive crowd, the battle between daily traffic and anachronistic ritual, the jibbing horses, the raucous speakers bellowing their two unchanging folk songs with mechanical insistency and completely overpowering (along with the roar of the motorcycles) the young horsemen as they screamed their lines and the veins stood out on their necks.

217

I threw my cup away. Now that the Ride had completed its show for the audience on the green, it started out on its several-hour-long peregrination through the village. I knew it all by heart: during the last year of the war I myself had ridden as a page (dressed in ceremonial woman's garb and armed with a saber) beside Jaroslav, who was king. I had no desire to indulge in sentimental reminiscences, but (won over, perhaps, by the shabbiness of the Ride) I saw no reason to turn my back on its pageantry; I set off slowly behind the procession, which had spread out and now covered the road. In the center of the group was a cluster of three riders: the king, flanked on either side by a page wearing woman's clothes and carrying a saber; they were surrounded in more or less free form by the royal escort or *ministers*. The rest of the procession was split into two independent wings riding on either side of the street; here too the riders' roles were precisely defined: there were the *standard-bearers* (sporting flags whose shafts they had stuck into their boots in such a way that the red embroidered banner fluttered alongside the horses' flanks), and *heralds* (reciting before each house their versified message about the needy and yet right virtuous king who had been robbed of *three thousand pieces of silver* from his *empty coffer* and *one thousand head of cattle* from his *empty lands*), and finally the *collectors* (whose only function was to call for contributions "For the king, my good woman, for the king!" and hold out a cane basket to receive them).

4

Thank you, Ludvik, I've known you just eight days now, and I love you as I've never loved before, I love you and trust you, I don't have to think, I just trust you, because even if my mind deceived me or my emotions or my soul, the body can't pretend, the body is more honest than the soul, and my body knows it has never experienced anything like yesterday, lust, affection, cruelty, pleasure, pain, my body has never dreamed of anything like it, our bodies made our vows yesterday, now our heads have only to follow, I've known you just eight days now, Ludvik, and I thank you.

I thank you too for coming at just the right moment, for saving me. It's been beautiful all day today, the sky is radiant, I'm radiant, everything went so well this morning, we went to the house where the king and his parents live and recorded the summoning ritual, and there he was, he scared the living daylights out of me, I didn't know he'd arrived, I didn't expect him here so soon from Bratislava, and I didn't expect him to be so cruel, imagine, Ludvik, bringing her with him, the cad!

Fool that I am, I thought to the last that my marriage wasn't completely ruined, I thought it could still be saved, fool that I am, I nearly sacrificed you for that rotten marriage, I nearly called off our rendezvous here, fool that I am, I nearly let myself be taken in by that sugary voice of his telling me he would stop off for me here on his way from Bratislava, he had a lot he wanted to talk over with me, just the two of us, and now he brings that child, that babe in arms, that twenty-two-year-old, thirteen years younger than me, it's so degrading to lose out on account of being born too early, I felt so helpless I could have screamed, but I couldn't scream, I had to smile and shake hands with her politely, oh, how grateful I am to you, Ludvik, for giving me that strength.

When we were alone for a moment, he said now we'd have a chance to talk things over, just the three of us, that would be the most honorable way, honor, honor, I know what he means when he starts talking about honor, for two years now he's been angling for a divorce, and he knows he won't get anywhere with me alone, he's counting on the shock of a face-to-face confrontation, he thinks I'll be ashamed to look like a shrew and I'll break down and give in on my own. How I hate the man, calmly slipping a knife between my ribs when I'm working, on an assignment, when I need to be calm and collected, the least he could do is show some respect for my work, some consideration, but no, that's the way it's been for years, I'm the one who's always bullied, humiliated, I'm the one who always loses, well, not this time, not when I have you behind me, you and your love, when I still feel you in me and on me and those handsome young horsemen all around me cheering and shouting, I almost feel they're calling out that I have you and life and the future ahead of me, and suddenly, it flooded over me, a pride I'd almost lost, and I managed to give him a sweet smile and say, There isn't any need for me to go to Prague with you, I'd hate to intrude, and anyway I have the station's car, as for the agreement you wanted to talk over, we can settle it all very quickly, I'll just introduce you to the man I'm planning to live with, I'm sure we'll come to an amicable arrangement.

Maybe it was a wild thing to do, well, and what if it was, it was worth it for that moment of sweet pride, it was worth it, suddenly he turned on the charm, he was obviously relieved, but scared too, scared I didn't mean it, he made me say it again, and this time I told him your full name, Ludvik Jahn, I made it absolutely clear to him, don't worry, believe me, I promise not to stand in the way of our divorce, don't worry, I don't want you anymore, wouldn't want you even if you wanted me. But we'll still be good friends, he said, and I smiled and said I didn't doubt it.

5

Years ago, when I was still playing the clarinet in the ensemble, we used to rack our brains for an explanation of what the Ride of the Kings really meant. Legend had it that when the Hungarian King Matthias was fleeing Bohemia in defeat, he and his cavalry were forced to hide here in the Moravian countryside from their Czech pursuers and beg their daily bread. The Ride of the Kings was said to be a reminder of that historic event, but all it took was a brief perusal of source documents to show that the tradition of the Ride antedates by far the misadventures of the Hungarian king. Where did it come from and what does it mean? Does it perhaps date back to pagan times, a survival of the rites of passage by which boys became accepted as men? And why are the king and his pages dressed as women? Is it meant to reflect how an armed band (be it Matthias' or a much earlier one) led its leader through enemy country in disguise, or is it a survival of an ancient pagan superstition according to which transvestism offers protection from evil spirits? And why is the king forbidden to utter a word throughout the Ride? Why is it called the Ride of the Kings when there is only one king involved? What does it all mean? No one knows. There are a number of hypotheses—none of them proved. The Ride of the Kings is a mysterious rite; no one knows what it signifies, what its message is, but just as Egyptian hieroglyphs are most beautiful to people who cannot read them (and perceive them as mere fanciful sketches), so perhaps the Ride of the Kings is beautiful to us at least partly because the message it was meant to communicate has long been lost, leaving the gestures, colors, and words to stand out all the more clearly.

And so, much to my surprise, the initial mistrust with which I followed the straggly departure of the Ride soon fell away, and I found myself enthralled by the colorful cavalcade slowly advancing from house to house; not only that, the loudspeakers, which a few minutes before had been monopolizing the airwaves with a strident female voice, had now fallen silent, and the only sound to be heard (apart from the occasional rumble of the traffic, which I've long since learned to turn off) was the strange music of the heralds.

I felt like standing in place, closing my eyes, and listening: here, in the midst of a Moravian village, I had the sensation of hearing *verse* in the most primitive sense of the word, the kind of verse I could never hear on the radio or on television, or even on the stage, verse as a rhythmic and ritualistic heralding, a construct on the border of speech and song, verse whose meter alone exuded an incantatory spirit, the very spirit emanating from the amphitheaters of ancient Greece. It was a sublime and *polyphonic* music: each of the heralds declaimed his verse in a monotone, but each on his own individual note, so the voices combined willy-nilly into chords; then too, the boys did not all declaim simultaneously; each began declaiming at a different place, a different house, so the voices came from various directions at various times and the result was reminiscent of a richly variegated canon; one voice finished, another sang on, and a third was about to enter in its own key.

The Ride of the Kings moved down the main street (constantly interrupted by traffic) until it came to a predetermined corner and split up, the right wing continuing straight ahead, the left wing turning off into a side street. The first house was a little yellow cottage with a fence and a garden of colorful flowers. The herald's improvisations were inspired: the cottage had a handsome *pump* and the mistress of the cottage had a *lump* of a son; there was in fact a green pump in front of the cottage, and its mistress, a roly-poly forty-year-old, was happy enough with the description of her son to laugh and give the rider calling out "For the king, my good woman, for the king!" (the collector) a contribution. No sooner had the collector dropped it in the basket fastened to his saddle than another herald called out to the woman that she had a figure quite *divine* but he much preferred her *wine*, and making a cup out of one hand, he threw back his head and pretended to take a swig from it. Everyone watching began to laugh, and the woman, both embarrassed and pleased, ran into the house, returning almost immediately (she must have had everything ready) with a bottle and glass and gave each of the horsemen a drink.

While the king's retinue was drinking and joking, the king himself stood motionless and grave a short way off with his two pages, and perhaps it is a king's duty to maintain his dignity and exclusivity in the presence of his clamorous troops. Both pages' mounts stood close by the king's, so close that their boots touched (on their breasts the horses wore large gingerbread hearts studded with tiny mirrors and trimmed with colored sugar; their foreheads were decked with paper roses and their manes interwoven with colored crepe paper ribbons). All three mute horsemen were dressed in wide skirts and starched puckered sleeves; the pages wore richly ornamented bonnets on their heads, the king a glittering silver tiara hung with three long, wide ribbons, blue on each side and red down the middle, which completely hid his face and made him look both mysterious and inspired.

I was enchanted by the ceremonious trinity; twenty years ago I had sat astride a garlanded horse just like them, but because I'd seen the Ride *from within*, I hadn't seen a thing; only now could I really see it, and I couldn't tear my eyes away: the king (a few feet away) sat so straight he could have been a statue under guard; and maybe, it suddenly occurred to me, maybe he wasn't a king at all, maybe he was a she; maybe he was Queen Lucie come to show me her true form, for her *true* form was actually her *hidden* form.

At the same time it occurred to me that Kostka with his strange combination of meditation and frenzy was quite a crank, and while the things he'd told me could conceivably be true, there was room for doubt; he did know Lucie, of course, he might even know a lot about her, but he didn't know one vital fact: the soldier who tried to have his way with her in the miner's borrowed flat—Lucie really loved him; how can I possibly believe that Lucie picked those flowers out of some vague religious longing when I remember she picked them for me; and if she hid it from Kostka, that and the whole six sweet months of our love, then she merely wanted to keep it private and not even he knew her; nor was it entirely clear she'd moved here because of him; it may have been mere coincidence, but it may also have been because of me; she did know it was my hometown, after all. The story of the first rape was true, I felt, but I now doubted certain details: parts of it were colored by the blood-and-thunder mentality of a man stimulated by the thought of sin, parts by a blue so blue that they could derive only from a man addicted to gazing up at the heavens; it was perfectly clear: Kostka's tale mixed truth with fiction and produced a new legend (closer to the truth, perhaps, more beautiful, more profound) to superimpose on the old.

Looking at the veiled king, I saw Lucie riding (unknown and unknowable) majestically (and mockingly) through my life. Then (in reaction to some external stimulus) my glance moved slightly to the side and met the glance of a man who had evidently been watching me for some time and smiling. "Hello," he said and, unfortunately, came up to me. "Hello," I said. He held out his hand; I shook it. Then he turned and called to a girl I hadn't noticed until then. "What are you waiting for? Come on, I want to introduce you." The girl (a bit too tall, but pretty, with dark hair and dark eyes) came up and introduced herself as Miss Broz. She gave me her hand, and I introduced myself, adding "Pleased to meet you." "It's been years, man," the man said jovially. It was Zemanek.

6

Exhaustion, exhaustion. I couldn't seem to get over it. The Ride set off for the village green with its king, and I plodded along behind them, taking deep breaths to overcome my fatigue. I stopped several times to chat with neighbors who'd come out to have a look. Suddenly I felt I was just another one of them. That my days of travel and adventure were over. That I was hopelessly bound to the two or three streets where I lived.

By the time I reached the green, the Ride had started down the long main street. I was just about to drag after it again when I saw Ludvik. He was standing by himself on the grass near the road looking thoughtfully at the riders. Damn that Ludvik! I wish he'd go to hell and get the hell out of my life! Avoiding me all this time. Well, today I was going to avoid him. And I turned away and decided to rest on a bench under an apple tree and listen to the voices of the heralds.

So there I sat, listening and watching. The Ride gradually drifted away. It clung pitifully to either side of the road, letting the constant stream of cars and motorcycles pass. A bunch of people were trailing behind. A pathetically small bunch. Fewer people come to the Ride every year. Though this year Ludvik had come. What was he doing here anyway? Go to hell, will you, Ludvik! It's too late now. Too late for everything. You're a bad omen. A foreboding of evil. Now of all times. When my Vladimir is king.

I looked away. There was only a handful of people left on the green: at the stands and at the tavern door. Most of them were drunk. Drunkards are the most loyal supporters of folk festivals. The only ones left. Folklore gives them an occasional noble pretext for a drink.

Then old man Pechacek came and sat beside me on the bench. It wasn't like in the old times, he said. I agreed. It wasn't. How beautiful the Rides must have been a few decades back, a few centuries back! Nowhere near as fancy as they are today, though. Nowadays they're half kitsch, half masked ball. Gingerbread hearts on the horses' chests! Reels of paper ribbons bought in department stores! The costumes have always been colorful, but they used to be plainer. Horses had nothing but a scarlet sash round their necks and over their breasts. The king too wore a simple veil, not a mask of patterned ribbons. Though he did have a rose between his teeth. To keep him from talking.

You're right, old fellow, it was better back then. No one had to run after the young people and beg them to take part. No one had to sit through meeting after meeting and argue over who would take care of the organizing and who receive the proceeds. The Ride of the Kings used to gush forth like a fountainhead from the heart of village life. It would gallop from village to village gathering alms for the king. Sometimes it met up with another Ride, and there would be a battle. Both sides defended their kings with great verve. Knives and sabers would flash, blood flow. When the members of one Ride captured the king of another, they would drink themselves into a stupor at the expense of the king's father.

You're so right, old fellow, so right. Even back when I was king, during the occupation, it was different from today. Yes, even after the war it was still worth something. We thought that we could build a completely new world. That people would return to folk ways. That the Ride of the Kings would once again gush forth from the depths of their lives. We wanted to help it all to happen. We organized one folk festival after the next. But a fountainhead can't be organized. And if it doesn't gush, it doesn't exist. Look how we have to squeeze out our songs, our Rides, everything. They're the last drops, the very last drops.

Ah, well. The Ride was no longer in sight. It had probably turned down some side street. But we could still hear the heralds. Their invocations were magnificent. I closed my eyes and imagined myself living in another age. Another century. Long ago. And then I opened them and told myself how good it was that Vladimir was king. King of a realm nearly extinct, but a realm most magnificent. A realm that could count on my loyalty to the end.

I stood up from the bench. Someone had called out a greeting. It was Koutecky. I hadn't seen him for ages. He had trouble walking and used a cane. I'd never liked him, but today I felt sorry for him in his old age. "Where are you off to?" I asked. He said he took a constitutional every Sunday. "How did you like the Ride?" I asked him. "Didn't even watch it," he said with a wave of the hand. "Why not?" I asked. Once more he dismissed it with a wave of the hand, and suddenly it dawned on me why he hadn't watched it: Ludvik was there among the spectators. Koutecky didn't want to run into him any more than I did.

"Can't say that I blame you," I said. "My son's taking part, and even I don't feel like trailing along." "Your son? You mean Vladimir?" "Yes," I said, "he's king." "That's interesting," said Koutecky. "What do you mean?" I asked. "Very interesting," he said, his eyes lighting up. "Why is that?" I asked again. "Because Vladimir is with Milos," said Koutecky. I had no idea who Milos was. Milos was his grandson, he told me, his daughter's son. "But that's impossible," I said. "I just saw him, a moment ago, saw him riding off on his mount!" "Well, I saw him too," said Koutecky. "Milos drove him over to our place on his motorcycle." "Ridiculous," I said, though I couldn't stop myself from asking, "Where were they going?" "If you don't know," he said, "I'm not going to be the one to tell you." And off he went.

7

I certainly hadn't expected to meet Zemanek (Helena had told me he wouldn't be picking her up until the afternoon), and found the whole thing highly disagreeable. But what could I do? There he was, standing in front of me, looking just the way he used to look: his blond hair was as blond as ever, even if instead of combing it back in long curls he had it cut short and wore it drooping stylishly over his forehead; he still stood erect and arched his neck back; he was still jovial, complacent, invulnerable, still enjoyed the favor of the angels and was obviously now enjoying the favors of a young girl whose beauty immediately put me in mind of the painful imperfection of the body I had been with yesterday afternoon.

Hoping our encounter would be brief, I tried to answer his barrage of banal questions with equally banal responses: he reiterated the fact that we hadn't seen each other for years, adding how surprising it was that after so long an interval we should meet "in this godforsaken hole"; I told him I was born here, whereupon he apologized and said that in that case he was sure God hadn't quite forsaken it; Miss Broz laughed; I failed to react altogether, saying instead that I wasn't surprised to meet him here, because, if I remembered correctly, he'd always loved folklore; Miss Broz laughed again and said they hadn't come for the Ride of the Kings; I asked her whether she had anything against the Ride of the Kings; she said it didn't appeal to her; I asked her why; she shrugged, and Zemanek said, "Come now, Ludvik, times have changed."

Meanwhile, the Ride had moved one house farther, and two riders were struggling with their mounts, which had grown restless. One shouted at the other, accusing him of failing to control his horse; the cries of "idiot" and "moron" mingled rather drolly with the ritual of the festival. "Wouldn't it be great if the horse bolted!" said Miss Broz. Zemanek laughed heartily at the thought, but before long the horsemen had managed to calm the horses down, and hear ye, hear ye resounded again, calm and majestic, through the village.

As we trooped along after the sonorous voices down a side street lined with gardens full of flowers I hunted for a natural, spontaneous excuse to say good-bye to Zemanek; meanwhile, I had to walk dutifully alongside his pretty companion and keep up my part of the conversation; I learned that in Bratislava, where they had been this morning, the weather was as nice as it was here; I learned that they had driven here in Zemanek's car and that just outside Bratislava they'd had to change the spark plugs; I also learned that Miss Broz was Zemanek's student. I knew from Helena that he taught Marxism-Leninism at the university, but even so I asked him what his field was. *Philosophy* was his answer (I found the nomenclature highly indicative; a few years ago he would have called it *Marxism,* but in recent years it had so declined in popularity, especially among the young, that Zemanek, for whom popularity had always been the main criterion, discreetly concealed his Marxism behind the more general term). But if I remember correctly, I said, surprised, your field was biology; my remark was a thinly veiled allusion to the fact that many university teachers of Marxism were more or less amateurs who had come to the field more as propagandists than as scholars. At this point Miss Broz intervened to announce that while most teachers of Marxism had political pamphlets in their heads instead of brains, Pavel was different. Pavel couldn't have put it better himself; he protested mildly, thereby simultaneously demonstrating his modesty and inciting the young lady to further praise. And so I learned that Zemanek was one of the most popular teachers, that his students worshiped him for the same reasons he got on the administration's nerves: namely, he always said what he thought, he was courageous, and he stuck up for the young. And since Zemanek kept proffering mild protestations, I learned the details of various battles Zemanek had fought in the past few years: how they'd even tried to fire him for refusing to stick to the rigid, outdated curriculum and wanting to introduce students to everything going on in modern philosophy (they claimed he had attempted to smuggle in "hostile ideology"); how he'd saved a boy they were about to expel for some boyish prank (an altercation with a policeman) that the chancellor (Zemanek's enemy) had wished to present as a *political* misdemeanor; how afterwards the female students had held a secret poll to determine their favorite teacher and he'd won hands down. By now Zemanek had halted all attempts to stem the flood of praise, and I said to Miss Broz (with an irony, alas, too elusive for her to understand) that I knew what she meant because, as I remembered it, Zemanek had been well-liked and highly popular back in my student days as well. Miss Broz nodded enthusiastically: she wasn't in the least surprised, since Pavel was such a fabulous speaker and could cut any opponent to ribbons. "Well, and what of it?" Zemanek laughed. "Even if I cut them to ribbons in a debate, they can cut me up in more efficient ways."

The cocksure complacency of this last remark convinced me that Zemanek hadn't changed a bit; its *content,* however, sent a chill up my spine: Zemanek seemed to have made a clean break with his former views, and if a conflict of a political nature were to arise, I would find myself on his side, like it or not. That was what was so horrible; that was what I least expected; though there was nothing miraculous about his about face; on the contrary, it was quite usual; great numbers of individuals had done it, and the whole country was actually doing it gradually. The point was that I hadn't counted on it in Zemanek: he was petrified in my memory in the form in which I'd last seen him, and I was damned if I'd grant him the right to change in the least detail.

There are people who claim to love humanity, while others object that we can love only in the singular, that is, one or another individual. I agree with the latter view and would add that what goes for love goes for hate as well. Man is a being that aspires to equilibrium; he balances the weight of the evil piled on his back with the weight of his hatred. But try concentrating your hatred on mere abstractions—injustice, fanaticism, cruelty—or, if you've gone so far as to find the human principle itself worthy of your hatred, try hating humanity! Hatred on that scale is beyond human capacity, and consequently the only way man can ease his anger (conscious as he is of his limited power) is to concentrate it on an individual.

That is what sent the chill up my spine. Suddenly it occurred to me that from one minute to the next he could point to his metamorphosis (which, it seemed to me, he was suspiciously eager to flaunt) and ask my forgiveness in its name. That was what struck me as so horrible. What would I tell him? How would I respond? How would I explain I couldn't make peace with him? How would I explain it would mean the end of my precarious inner balance? How would I explain it would send one side of my inner scales flying into the air? How would I explain I used my hatred to balance out the weight of the evil I bore as a youth? How would I explain I considered him the embodiment of all the evil I had known? How would I explain I *needed* to hate him?

8

Horses crammed their way into the narrow street. I could see the king, but only at a distance. He was sitting on his horse apart from the others, but with his pages on either side. I was confused. True, he had Vladimir's slightly curved back. I could see that

229

clearly as he sat there motionless, almost indifferent. But was he
really Vladimir? He might just as easily have been someone else.

I worked my way closer to him. I simply had to recognize him.
Didn't I know by heart the way he held himself, the way he
moved? Didn't I love him? And didn't love have its instincts?

Now I was right beside him. I could have called to him. It was
all so simple. But it would have been no use. The king must not
speak.

Then the Ride moved on to the next house. Now I would recognize him! The horse's first step would force him to move, and that
motion would betray him. As the horse stepped forward, the
king's back did in fact arch slightly, but the motion gave me no
hint as to who was behind the veil. The garish ribbons across his
face remained frustratingly opaque.

9

As the Ride moved past several more houses (with us and a handful of other onlookers still hovering about), we moved on to other
topics: Miss Broz had shifted from Zemanek to herself and was
holding forth on how she loved hitchhiking. She spoke about it
with such (though not entirely spontaneous) enthusiasm that I
could tell at once I was in for the *manifesto of her generation*.
The very thought of a generation mentality (the pride of the herd)
has always repelled me. After Miss Broz had developed her provocative claim (which I've heard a good fifty times now from people her age) that all mankind can be divided into those who give
hitchhikers lifts (the freethinkers, the adventurers, and the hu-
manists) and those who don't (the self-centered Socialist bourgeoisie), I jokingly called her a "dogmatist of the road." She answered curtly that she was neither dogmatist nor revisionist nor
sectarian nor deviationist, that those were all words we had
dreamed up, that they belonged to us and were completely alien
to *them*.

"You see?" said Zemanek. "They're different. *Fortunately*,
they're different. Even their vocabulary is different. They don't

care about our successes, they don't care about our failures. You won't believe this, but on entrance exams when we ask them about the purges, they don't know what we're talking about. Stalin is just a name to them. And most of them have no idea there were political trials in Prague!"

"I don't think that's fortunate; I think it's terrible," I said.

"True, it doesn't say much for the education they're getting. But think how liberating it is for them. They've simply closed their minds to our world. Rejected it and all it stands for."

"And blindness has given way to blindness."

"I wouldn't put it that way. I find them quite impressive. They love their bodies. We neglected ours. They love to travel. We stayed put. They love adventure. We spent all our time at meetings. They love jazz. We were satisfied with pale imitations of folk music. They're interested in themselves. We wanted to save the world and with our messianic vision nearly destroyed it. Maybe they with their egotism will be the ones to save it."

10

Can it be? The king! That upright figure veiled in bright colors! How many times have I seen him thus, pictured him thus? My most intimate fantasy! And now that it's come true, all the intimacy is gone. Suddenly it's just a painted larva, and I don't know what's inside. What intimacy is there in the real world if not in my king?

My son. The person nearest me. Here I stand in front of him, and I don't even know if he's my son or not. What do I know if I don't know even that? What certainties remain to me here below if not even that is certain?

11

While Zemanek eulogized the younger generation, I contemplated Miss Broz; attractive and agreeable, I concluded sadly and with a mixture of envy and regret at the thought she wasn't mine. She was walking alongside Zemanek, talking away, taking his arm every other second, giving him confidential looks, and I was reminded once more (as I am reminded with greater frequency every year) that since Lucie I'd had no girl I could love and respect. Life was having a good laugh at my expense, sending me a reminder of my failure in the form of the mistress of a man whom only the day before I thought I'd defeated in grotesque sexual combat.

The more I liked Miss Broz, the more I realized how much she shared the views of her contemporaries, for whom my contemporaries and I merged into a single amorphous mass, corrupted by the same incomprehensible jargon, the same overpoliticized thought, the same anxieties (which they considered cowardice or fear), the same bizarre experiences from a dark and distant age.

It was then I began to see that the similarity between myself and Zemanek was not limited to the fact that Zemanek had changed his views, brought them more in line with my own; it went much deeper, encompassing our destinies *as a whole:* in the eyes of Miss Broz and her contemporaries we were alike even when we were at each other's throats. I suddenly felt that if I were forced (and I would have to be forced!) to tell Miss Broz the story of my expulsion from the Party, she would find it remote and too *literary* (a theme treated many times in many bad novels), the two of us would come off equally badly; my ideas and his, my position and his—to her they were equally perverse. I saw our quarrel, which I had deemed so immediate and alive, sinking into the healing waters of time, which, as we all know, can smooth over the differences between entire epochs, let alone two puny individuals. But I fought tooth and nail against time's peace offerings; I do not live in eternity, I am anchored to my meager thirty-seven years and have no desire to sever the chain (as Zemanek has done by rushing to embrace the mentality of the young); no, I do not wish to reject my fate, renounce my thirty-seven years, even if they represent so insignificant and fleeting a snatch of time that it is even now being forgotten, has already been forgotten.

And were Zemanek to lean over confidentially, start talking about the past, and ask for a reconcilation, I would refuse; yes, I would refuse even if Miss Broz interceded, and all her contemporaries, and time itself.

12

Exhaustion. Suddenly I was tempted to wash my hands of the whole business. To walk away and stop worrying about it. I'm tired of this world of material things. I don't understand them. They play tricks on me. I have another world. A world where I feel at home, where I am at home. The road, the rose bush, the deserter, the wandering minstrel, Mother.

But in the end I took hold of myself. I had to. I have to bring my quarrel with the world of material things to its proper conclusion. I have to get to the bottom of all the lies and deceptions.

Who is there to ask? The riders? And make myself a laughingstock? I thought back to morning. The robing of the king. And at once I knew where to go.

13

We have a needy king, and yet right virtuous, the horsemen intoned a few houses farther on, and we trailed along dutifully, the horses' richly beribboned rumps bobbing blue, pink, green, and violet before us. Suddenly Zemanek pointed in their direction and said, "Look there's Helena!" I looked over to where he was pointing, but saw only the colorful bodies of the horses. Zemanek pointed again. "There!" Then I did see her—she was half hidden behind a horse—and I felt myself blush: the way Zemanek had pointed her out to me (not as "my wife," but as "Helena") showed he knew we were acquainted.

Helena was standing on the edge of the sidewalk holding a microphone in her outstretched hand; a wire ran from the microphone to a tape recorder that hung over the shoulder of a boy wearing jeans, a leather jacket, and earphones. We stopped a short way off. Zemanek said (both abruptly and casually) that Helena was a wonderful woman: not only did she still look fantastic, she had a good head on her shoulders; he wasn't the least surprised we'd hit it off so well.

I felt my cheeks burn: Zemanek hadn't meant his remarks as an attack; he was only trying to be affable. The same held for Miss Broz and her significant glances brimming with awareness, sympathy, even complicity. I could have no doubt where I stood.

Zemanek kept up the banter about his wife, making it plain (with various hints and innuendos) that he was in the know but didn't object, because he was perfectly liberal when it came to Helena's private life; to make it all sound that much more free and easy, he pointed to the sound technician and said that the boy there ("Doesn't he look like a gigantic beetle with those earphones?") had been dangerously in love with Helena for two years and I'd better keep an eye on him. Miss Broz laughed and asked how old he was two years ago. Seventeen, said Zemanek, old enough to fall in love. Then he added jokingly that Helena wasn't a cradle-robber by any means, she had her standards, but a boy like that—the more frustrated he got, the more his temper would rise, and he was sure to have a fast uppercut. To which Miss Broz replied (in the spirit of our little talk) that I looked as though I could handle him.

"I'm not so sure about that," said Zemanek with a smile.

"Don't forget I worked in the mines. I still have some of those muscles left." All I'd meant to do was to keep the ball rolling; I had no idea I'd overstepped the bounds of banter.

"You worked in the mines?" asked Miss Broz.

"These twenty-year-olds," Zemanek went on pertinaciously, "when they roam the street in gangs, they're dangerous as hell. If they don't like the way you look, you're in for it."

"How long?" asked Miss Broz.

"Five years," I said.

"When?"

"Nine years ago."

"Oh, that's ancient history," she said. "I'll bet your muscles are all flabby by now." She wanted to put her own little joke in too. As it happened, I had just been thinking that my muscles were not the least bit flabby, that in fact I was in excellent shape and could easily beat my towheaded companion to a pulp, and that—most important and most depressing—I had nothing but my muscles to rely on if I decided to pay my old debt.

Again I pictured Zemanek turning to me with a big smile and asking me to let bygones be bygones. I realized I'd been double-crossed: Zemanek's plea for forgiveness rested not only on his change of views, not only on time, not only on Miss Broz and her contemporaries, but on Helena (yes, by now they were all on his side!), because forgiving me my adultery was merely a bribe for me to forgive him.

Scrutinizing (in my imagination) his face, the face of a black-mailer cocksure of his connections, I felt so much like punching him in the nose that I could actually see it: the riders were still swarming about, shouting; the sun was a glorious gold; Miss Broz was going on about something; and what did my wild eyes behold but the blood pouring down his face.

Yes, I could see it all plainly; but what would I really do if he asked me to forgive him?

I realized with a shock that I'd do absolutely nothing.

Meanwhile we'd made our way over to Helena and her technician, who was just removing his earphones. "Have you met?" she asked, surprised to find me with Zemanek.

"Oh, we've known each other for years," said Zemanek.

"What do you mean?" Now she was more surprised.

"We've known each other since the university," said Zemanek. "We were students together." We had reached, or so I thought, one of the last bridges leading to that place of infamy (of execution) where he would ask me for forgiveness.

"Heavens, what a coincidence!" said Helena.

"Happens all the time," said the technician, to remind them of his existence.

"Oh, yes, I haven't introduced you two," Helena said to me. "This is Jindra."

I shook hands with Jindra (a singularly unattractive boy) and Zemanek said to Helena, "Miss Broz and I, we originally planned to take you back with us, but now I see you'd rather go back with Ludvik, so . . ."

"You're coming with us?" asked the boy in jeans, sounding less than inviting.

"Have you got your car here?" Zemanek asked me.

"I haven't got a car," I answered.

"Then you can go with them," he said.

"But I go eighty," said the boy in jeans, "so if that bothers you . . ."

"Jindra!" said Helena sharply.

"You could come with us," said Zemanek, "but I suspect your new friend takes priority over your old one." He was so casual about calling me his *friend* that I was certain the dishonorable truce was imminent; to make matters worse, he stopped talking altogether and seemed to be hesitating about whether to take me off to the side for a private chat (I hung my head, ready to lay it on the block), but I was mistaken. Zemanek looked at his watch. "We're rather short on time, actually. We planned to be back in Prague by five. We'll just have to say good-bye, I suppose. Ciao, Helena." He shook her hand. "Ciao," he said to the sound technician and me and shook our hands too. And as soon as Miss Broz had shaken hands with us all, off they went, arm in arm.

Off they went. I couldn't take my eyes off them: Zemanek— back straight, blond head high (victorious), brunette at his side; she—beautiful from the back too, light of step, likable; I liked her almost painfully, because her departing beauty was so icily *indifferent* to me, just like Zemanek, just like my entire past, which I had come here to avenge, but which had slipped by me unseeing, treated me like a stranger.

I was stifling in the humiliation and shame of it all. I wanted nothing more than to disappear, go off by myself, blot out the whole sordid incident, the stupid joke, blot out Helena and Zemanek, blot out the day before yesterday, yesterday, and today, blot it out so thoroughly that not a trace remained. "Would you mind if I had a word with Comrade Zemanek in private?" I asked the sound technician.

I took Helena aside, but she had something to tell me first, something about Zemanek and his girl, a confused apology for having told him everything; but I was past caring; I was consumed by a single desire: to get away, away from her and the whole incident; to leave it all behind me. I had no right to deceive Helena any longer; she was quite innocent with respect to me, and I'd acted despicably: I'd turned her into a mere object, a rock I'd tried (and failed) to throw at somebody else. I was stifling in the ridiculous failure of my revenge, and I was determined—late as it was, before it was more than late—to put an end to it. There was no point in trying to explain: not only would I have wounded her with the truth, she would have been incapable of understanding it. All I could do was to stick to the bare facts and repeat several times over that this was our last time together, I wouldn't be seeing her again, I didn't love her, and she'd have to understand.

It turned out far worse than I'd imagined: she went pale, began to quake, wouldn't believe me, refused to let me go; I suffered a minor martyrdom before I could shake her off and beat my retreat.

14

Horses and streamers everywhere, and I just stood there, stood and stood, and then Jindra came up and took my hand and squeezed it and asked me what the matter was, what was wrong, and I let him hold my hand and said, nothing, Jindra, nothing at all, and my voice sounded like somebody else's, shrill and unnatural, and then I started talking very fast about what we still needed to tape, and we've got the invocations, we've got two interviews, I still have the commentary to do, strange how I went on and on about things I couldn't possibly care about, and he stood silent beside me, crushing my fingers.

He'd never actually touched me before, he was too shy, but everyone knew he was in love with me, and now he was standing beside me, crushing my fingers, and I was rambling on about the program, which I didn't care about, and thinking only of Ludvik, though, oddly enough, I found myself wondering what I looked like to Jindra, I probably looked a fright after the shock of it, or maybe not, I wasn't crying, after all, just a bit upset....

Listen, Jindra, give me a minute to myself, and I'll go and write the commentary and then we can tape it right away, he wouldn't let go and kept asking what was wrong, but I pulled free and went straight to the District Council, where we'd borrowed a room, and at last I was alone, in an empty room, I collapsed on a chair, laid my head on the table, and didn't move. I had a terrible headache. I opened my bag to see if there was anything I could take for it, though I don't really know why I bothered, I knew I had no pills, but then I remembered that Jindra always carried a whole pharmacy with him, his coat was hanging on the hook, I rummaged through his pockets, and sure enough I came up with a small bottle of analgesics, something for headaches, toothaches, neuralgia, and neuritis, it didn't say anything about afflictions of the soul, but at least it would take care of my head.

I found a tap in a corner of the room next door, I filled an old mustard jar with water and took two tablets. Two is enough, that will take care of it, though it won't help my other problems, not unless I swallow a whole bottle's worth, it's poisonous in massive doses, and Jindra's bottle is nearly full, it might be enough.

It was only an idea, a sudden flash, but it kept coming back, forcing me to think about why I was alive, what sense there was in my going on, but that's not true really, I didn't think anything of the sort, I hardly thought at all, I just tried to imagine myself no longer alive, and suddenly I felt so blissful, so oddly blissful that I almost burst out laughing, I actually may have laughed a bit.

I put another tablet on my tongue, I really had no intention of poisoning myself, I merely held the bottle tightly and said to myself, "My death is in my own hands," I couldn't get over how simple it all was, it was like gradually going up to an abyss, not to jump, just to look down. I filled the glass with water, took the tablet, and went back to our room, the window was open, and the sound of hear ye, hear ye, from hill and dale, from near and far, was still floating somewhere in the distance, though it blended together with the racket of the cars, the trucks, and those awful motorcycles, they drown out everything beautiful, everything I've always believed in, lived for, the racket was unbearable, the feeble voices unbearable, I closed the window, and again I felt that long, lingering pain in my soul.

Through all our life together, Pavel never once hurt me as you did, Ludvik, in a single minute, I forgive Pavel, I understand him, his flame burns fast, he's in constant need of fresh pastures, new audiences, he hurt me all right, but now through this pain I see him without malice, as a mother might, yes, he's a show-off, a clown, and I can laugh at his attempts through the years to wriggle out of my embrace, well, good-bye and good riddance, Pavel, but Ludvik, I don't understand you at all, you came to me wearing a mask, first to resurrect me, then to throw me back down, you're the one I can't forgive, the one I curse, the one I beg to return, come back, and have mercy.

God, maybe it's just a terrible misunderstanding, maybe Pavel told you something when you were alone together, I don't know, I asked you, I begged you to explain why you didn't love me anymore, I wouldn't let you go, four times I held you back, but you wouldn't listen, it was all over, that was all you would say, over, finished, once and for all, irrevocably, all right, then, it's over, I finally agreed, and my voice went shrill and weak, somebody else seemed to be speaking, a pre-adolescent girl, *I hope you have a good trip*, I said in that shrill voice, that's funny, I wonder why I wanted you to have a good trip, it just kept coming out, I hope you have a good trip. . . .

Maybe you don't know how much I love you, surely you don't know how much I love you, maybe you think I'm just another matron out for an adventure, why can't you see: you're my destiny, my life, my everything. . . . Maybe you'll find me here laid out under a white sheet and then you'll understand you've killed the most precious thing you ever had in life. . . . Or else you'll come and oh, my God, I'll still be alive, and you'll still be able to save me, and you'll kneel down by my side, and I'll stroke your hands, your hair, and I'll forgive you, forgive you everything. . . .

15

There was really nothing else I could have done: I had to put an end to the whole sorry episode, the bad joke which, not content to remain itself, had monstrously multiplied into more and more stupid jokes; I wanted to erase not only the entire day, which was in fact a pure accident resulting from a late start and the lack of train connections, but also everything leading up to it, the whole stupid sexual conquest of Helena, which—it too, as I now saw— was based on error.

I was in as much of a hurry as if I heard Helena's footsteps right behind me, and I wondered, even if it were possible, even if I could erase these few wasted days from my life, what good would it do when the *whole* story of my life was conceived by error: the accident, the absurdity of the bad joke on the postcard? And to my horror I realized that things conceived by error were every bit as real as things conceived by reason and necessity.

How happy I would be to revoke the whole story of my life! But what power have I to do so when the errors it stemmed from were not wholly *my own? Who*, in fact, made the error of taking my stupid joke seriously? Who made the error of arresting and sentencing Alexej's father (long since rehabilitated, but nonetheless dead)? So frequent, so common were those errors that they cannot be considered mere exceptions, "aberrations" in the order of things; they *were* the order of things. And who made them? History itself? History the divine, the rational? And why call them history's *errors? What* if history plays jokes? And all at once I realized how powerless I was to revoke my own joke: I myself and my life as a whole had been involved in a joke much more vast (all-embracing) and absolutely irrevocable.

Looking out over the village green (now silent—the Ride was making its rounds at the other end of the village), I noticed a large sign propped up next to the tavern door, announcing in red letters that today at four in the afternoon a cimbalom ensemble would be giving a concert in the open-air restaurant. Since I had almost two hours left before my bus was due to leave and since it was time to eat, I went in.

16

It was so tempting to inch my way up to the abyss, lean out over the railing, peer down into it, I only wish it could bring me solace and reconciliation, I only wish that down there, down there if nowhere else, down there at the bottom of the abyss we could find each other and be together, free of misunderstandings, malicious tongues, old age, sorrow, together forever. I went back to the other room with only four tablets inside me, that was nothing, I was still a good way off from the abyss, hadn't even reached the railing. I poured the rest of the tablets into my palm. Then I heard a door opening in the corridor, I was scared, I stuffed the tablets into my mouth and swallowed them as best I could, but they were too much all at once and grated painfully in my throat even when I tried forcing them down with water.

It was Jindra, he asked me how the commentary was coming along, and suddenly I was another person, no more helplessness, no more shrill, metallic voice, I knew just what to do and how to go about it. Oh, Jindra, I'm so glad you're here. Would you do me a favor? He blushed and said he'd do anything for me and he was happy to see me looking better. Yes, I'm fine now, can you wait just a minute, I have to dash off a note, and I sat down, found a piece of paper, and wrote: Dearest Ludvik, I loved you body and soul, and now my body and soul have nothing left to live for. Farewell, I love you, Helena. I didn't even reread what I'd written, Jindra was sitting across from me, following my every move, but unaware of what I was doing, I quickly folded the paper, but couldn't find an envelope to put it in, Jindra, you don't happen to have an envelope, do you?

Without thinking twice Jindra went over to the cabinet by the table, opened it up, and started rummaging in it, at any other time I'd have told him off for going through other people's things, but at that moment I needed an envelope, and quickly, the one he gave me had the District Council letterhead on it, I slipped the letter in, sealed it, and wrote Ludvik Jahn on the front, Jindra, do you remember the man standing with my husband and that girl and me, yes, the dark one, I have to stay here, and I want you to locate him and give him this.

Again he took my hand, the poor boy, I wonder what he was thinking, how he interpreted my excitement, he couldn't have a clue about what was actually involved, he could only sense I was in some kind of trouble, he held my hand tightly again, and suddenly he bent down and took me in his arms and pressed his lips to mine, I tried to stop him, but he held me close, and then it flashed through my mind he was the last man I'd ever kiss, this was my last kiss, and suddenly I felt reckless, and I returned his embrace and held him close and opened my lips and felt his tongue on mine, his hands on my body, and I was overcome by a giddy sense of absolute freedom, a sense that nothing mattered anymore, because I'd been abandoned by everyone and my world had crumbled, I was free to do exactly as I pleased, as free as the girl we threw out of the radio station, she and I were in the same position, my world was in pieces, I could never put it together again, I no longer had any reason to be faithful or anybody to be faithful to, I was completely free, just like that girl from the station, that whore who slept in a different bed every night, if I went on living, I'd do the same, I felt Jindra's tongue in my mouth, I was free, I knew I could make love to him, I wanted to make love to him, anywhere at all, here on the table or on the bare floor, but now, right away, make love one last time, before the end. Then suddenly Jindra scrambled to his feet and, beaming proudly, said he was off and would be right back.

17

Racing through the small, smoke-and-people-filled room, the waiter used one arm to balance a large tray piled with a mound of dishes, on which I barely had time to recognize portions of wiener schnitzel and potato salad (apparently the single Sunday dish), and the other to make a passageway for himself through the people and the five or six tables out into the corridor. Following in his wake, I found an open door at the end of the corridor and stepped into a garden, where people were also eating. At the very back, under a linden tree, I spied an empty table; I went over to it and sat down.

The touching hear ye, hear ye still floated across the roofs of the village, but it came from so far that by the time it penetrated the tavern garden it sounded almost illusory. And its imaginary illusion gave me the feeling that nothing around me belonged to the present, that it was all part of the past, a past fifteen or twenty years old, a past of which hear ye, hear ye, Lucie, and Zemanek were all part; and Helena was merely a rock I wanted to throw at that past. These last three days had been nothing but a shadow dance.

What? These last three days alone? My whole life seems to have swarmed with shadows, with the present occupying less than the place of honor. I see a moving walkway (which represents time) and a man (who represents me) running in the direction opposite to the direction the walkway takes; but the walkway moves faster than I and therefore gradually bears me away from the goal I am running to reach; that goal (odd goal, situated in the *wrong direction!*) is a past of political trials, of auditoriums where hands go up, of fear, of penal battalions and Lucie, a past which still has me under its spell, which I am still trying to decipher, unravel, and which still prevents me from living as a man should live, facing forward.

And then there's the bond I tried to use as a link with the past that hypnotizes me, the bond of vengeance; unfortunately, vengeance, as I have discovered for myself these past few days, is as vain as my backward race. Yes, the day when Zemanek did his recitation from Fucik's *Notes from the Gallows* in the lecture hall—that was the time for me to go up to him and punch him in the nose, then and only then. When vengeance is tabled, it turns into an illusion, a personal religion, a myth which recedes day by day from its cast of characters, who remain the same in the myth of vengeance, while in reality (the walkway never stops moving) they have changed radically: today another Jahn stands before another Zemanek, and the blow I still owe him is beyond resurrection or reconstruction, is lost once and for all.

As I cut into the large piece of wiener schnitzel on my plate, I heard the strains of hear ye, hear ye floating faintly and mournfully over the village roofs; I pictured the veiled king and his retinue and thought how sad it was that human gestures were so mutually unintelligible.

For many centuries young men have been riding forth from Moravian villages like this one today with strange messages whose incomprehensible words they spell out with touching fidelity. At some point far in the past a group of people had something important to say, and they come alive again today in their descendants like deaf-and-dumb orators holding forth by means of beautiful and incomprehensible gestures. Their message will never be deciphered not only because there is no key, but because people lack the patience to listen in an age when the accumulation of messages old and new is such that their voices cancel one another out. By now history is nothing more than the thin thread of what is remembered stretched out over the ocean of what has been forgotten; but time moves on, and new eras will arise, eras the limited memory of the individual will be unable to grasp; centuries, millennia, will therefore fall away, centuries of paintings and music, centuries of discoveries, battles, books, and the consequences will be dire: man will lose all insight into himself, and his history— unfathomable, inscrutable—will shrink into a handful of senseless schematic signs. Thousands of deaf-and-dumb Rides will set out to deliver their messages to those far-off descendants of ours, and none of them will have time to listen.

Sitting in my corner of the garden restaurant over an empty plate with no consciousness of having taken a bite, I contemplated how I too (at this very moment) was caught up in that vast and inevitable forgetting. The waiter came and took my plate, stopping only to brush a few crumbs off the tablecloth with a napkin. A wave of depression came over me, not so much because the day

244

had been futile as because not even its futility would remain; it would be forgotten with this table and the fly buzzing round my head and the yellow pollen scattered over the tablecloth by the flowering linden and the sluggish service so characteristic of the present state of the society I live in; and the society itself would be forgotten and all the errors and injustices that obsessed me, consumed me, that I'd vainly attempted to fix, right, rectify—vainly, because whatever happened happened and could not be reversed.

Yes, suddenly I saw it all clearly: most people willingly deceive themselves with a doubly false faith; they believe in *eternal memory* (of men, things, deeds, peoples) and in *rectification* (of deeds, errors, sins, injustice). Both are sham. The truth lies at the opposite end of the scale: everything will be forgotten and nothing will be rectified. All rectification (both vengeance and forgiveness) will be taken over by oblivion. No one will rectify wrongs; all wrongs will be forgotten.

I took another careful glance around me, because I knew it would all be forgotten: the linden tree, the people at the tables, and the tavern, which (uninviting from the street) was quite attractively overgrown with climbing vines here in the garden. My glance reached the door to the corridor just in time to register the disappearance of the waiter (the overtaxed heart of the now all but deserted and once more peaceful hideaway) and (as soon as the darkness had swallowed him up) the appearance of a boy in leather jacket and jeans. He stepped into the garden and looked around; the moment his eyes lit on me, he headed in my direction; it was several seconds before I realized he was Helena's sound technician.

I always find it painful when a loving and unloved woman threatens to make a comeback, so when the boy handed me the envelope ("From Mrs. Zemanek"), my first impulse was to postpone reading it. I told him to have a seat; he did (leaning on one elbow and squinting contentedly at the sun-drenched linden). I laid the envelope before me on the table and said, "How about a drink?"

He shrugged his shoulders; I suggested vodka, but he said no, he had to drive and drinking before driving was strictly prohibited; he wouldn't mind watching, though, if I felt like it. I didn't feel like it at all, but since the envelope was lying there in front of me and I wasn't looking forward to opening it, any alternative seemed welcome. I asked the waiter, who happened to be passing, to bring me a vodka.

"Tell me, what does Helena want?" I said.

"How should I know?" he replied. "Read the letter."

"Anything urgent?" I asked.

"Do you think she made me memorize it in case I was attacked?" he said.

I picked up the envelope (it had the official letterhead of the District Council on it), then put it back down on the tablecloth, and, for want of anything better to say, remarked, "A pity you're not joining me."

"It's for your own safety," he said. The hint was clear: he wanted to take advantage of our tête-à-tête to clarify the status of the journey and his chances of being alone with Helena. He was a perfectly nice boy; his face (small, pale, and freckled, with a short, turned-up nose) mirrored everything going on inside him; perhaps what made it so transparent was its hopeless childishness (I say hopeless because its abnormally tiny features were not the type that age makes any more virile; in other words, his face as an old man would be an old man's version of a child's face). His childish look must have been a terrible bane to him, and the only thing he could do about it was to disguise it in every way possible (just like—oh, that eternal shadow dance!—the boy commander): by his dress (his leather jacket was broad-shouldered, well-fitted, and well-sewn) and his behavior (he was self-assured, slightly coarse, and, whenever possible, cool and indifferent). Unfortunately, he constantly gave himself away: he blushed and his voice cracked when he was the least bit excited (I noticed that as soon as we met), and in general he lacked control of his facial and body expression (clearly he meant to show me how little he cared whether I went to Prague with them or not, but when I assured him I'd be staying behind, his eyes unmistakably lit up).

When the waiter placed two vodkas on the table, the boy held up his hand and said, no, it was all right, he would have one. "I wouldn't want you to drink alone," he said. "Your health," he added, raising his glass.

"And yours!" I said. We clinked glasses.

During the ensuing conversation I learned that the boy was expecting to leave in about two hours, since Helena wanted to go over the material they'd taped and add her commentary where necessary. That would mean it could go on the air tomorrow. I asked him what it was like working with her. He blushed and said that Helena knew what she was doing but was a bit too tough on her staff; she was always willing to work overtime and didn't seem to care that some people were in a hurry to get home. I asked him whether he was in a hurry to get home. No, he said, he was having a fine time. Then, taking advantage of the fact that I brought up the subject of Helena, he asked casually, "Where do you know her from?" When I told him, he pressed on. "She's really great, isn't she."

As soon as I mentioned Helena, he tried even harder to look self-satisfied, which I again put down to his desire to keep up a front; since his desperate adoration of Helena was doubtless common knowledge, he was obliged to do everything in his power to avoid being branded with the unfortunate stigma of unrequited lover. So although I didn't take his confidence altogether seriously, it did lighten the load of the letter in front of me, and finally I picked it up and opened it: "Body and soul ... nothing left to live for. Farewell ..."

Looking up, I saw the waiter at the other end of the garden and called out, "Waiter!" The waiter nodded, but refusing to be deflected from his orbit, vanished into the corridor.

"Come on. There's no time to lose," I told the boy. I stood up and hurried across the garden; the boy followed. We had gone down the corridor and were nearly across the dining room by the time the waiter ran up to us.

"Schnitzel, soup, two vodkas," I dictated.

"What's the matter?" asked the boy in a timid voice.

I paid the waiter and told the boy to take me to Helena, quickly. We set out at a brisk pace.

"What's going on?" he asked.

"How far is it?" I asked back.

He pointed some distance ahead of us, and I broke into a run; he followed suit, and we soon reached the District Council building. It was a single-story structure, whitewashed, with a gate and two windows on the street. We went straight in and came to a dreary office furnished with two desks, back to back, under a window; the tape recorder lay open on one of them; it was flanked by a pad and a handbag (yes, Helena's); there were chairs at both the desks and a metal hatstand in a corner. Two coats were hanging on it: Helen's blue raincoat and a man's dirty trench coat.

"This is it," said the boy.

"This is where she gave you the letter?"

"Yes."

For the moment, at least, the office was hopelessly empty; "Helena," I shouted; I was alarmed to hear how anxious and apprehensive my voice sounded. There was no response. "Helena," I shouted again.

"Do you think she's . . ."

"Looks like it," I said.

"Is that what the letter was about?"

"Yes," I said. "Did they give you any other room?"

"No," he said.

"What about the hotel?"

"We checked out this morning."

"Then she's got to be here," I said, whereupon he himself started calling "Helena!" in an anxious, constantly cracking voice.

I opened the door to the adjacent room, another office: desk, wastepaper basket, three chairs, cabinet, and hatstand (the hatstand was the same as the one in the first office: a metal rod perched on three legs and spreading out up above into three metal branches; because there were no coats hanging on it, it looked almost human, orphan-like; its metallic nudity and ludicrously raised arms filled me with anxiety); except for a window over the desk the walls were bare; there was no other door leading out; the two offices were evidently the only rooms in the building.

We went back to the first one; I picked up the pad and

thumbed through it; all I could find was some hastily scribbled notes for (judging by the few phrases I could make out) a description of the Ride of the Kings; no message, no further parting words. I opened the handbag: handkerchief, wallet, lipstick, compact, two loose cigarettes, cigarette lighter; no bottles for pills or potions. I tried feverishly to think what Helena would do, and the only thing I could come up with was poison; but if poison was the answer, then there should have been a bottle somewhere. I went over to the hatstand and rummaged through the pockets of her raincoat: they were empty.

"What about the attic?" the boy said impatiently, having apparently concluded that my search of the room, though scarcely begun, was getting us nowhere. We ran out into the hallway, where we saw two doors: one had a glass pane that gave a murky view of the back courtyard; when we opened the other one, we found an ominous staircase; the stone steps were covered with a layer of dust and soot. We ran up them and were immediately engulfed in darkness: the only light, dull and gray, came from a skylight (whose glass was filthy). All we could make out was the outlines of various odds and ends (boxes, garden tools, hoes, spades, rakes, huge stacks of files, and an old dismantled chair); we tripped at every step.

I wanted to call out "Helena!" but was overcome with fear, fear of the silence that would follow. The boy didn't call either. We turned the place upside down, went into every nook and cranny without saying a word, but I could feel how agitated we both were. In fact, our silence was what made it all so horrible; it represented the tacit recognition that we no longer expected a response, that we were merely looking for a body, hanging or prostrate.

Our mission still unaccomplished, we went back down to the office. Once more I went through everything in the room: desk, chairs, and the hatstand flourishing Helena's raincoat; then I went next door: desk, chairs, cabinet, and the other hatstand, its arms outstretched in despair. The boy shouted (for no reason) "Helena!" and I (for no reason) opened the cabinet, revealing shelves of files, stationery supplies, gummed paper, and rulers.

"There's got to be something else!" I said. "A toilet! Or a cellar!" We went out into the hallway again; the boy opened the door leading to the courtyard. The courtyard was very small; there was a rabbit hutch in one corner; on the other side of the courtyard was a garden with a number of fruit trees spotting the uncut grass (in the far reaches of my mind I noticed how beautiful the garden was: splashes of blue sky hanging among the green branches, tree trunks rough and crooked, with bright yellow sunflowers shining around them); then at the far end of the garden in the idyllic shade of an apple tree I saw a wooden country outhouse. I immediately ran up to it.

The revolving wooden latch, attached to the narrow frame by a large nail (placing the latch in a horizontal position enabled the door to be closed from the outside), was standing upright. I inserted my fingers in the crack between the frame and the door and, applying gentle pressure, determined it was locked from within; that could mean only one thing: Helena was inside. "Helena, Helena," I called softly. There was no reply but the rustling of apple-tree branches against the wooden wall of the shack.

The silence in the locked latrine led me to expect the worst; the only thing to do was to rip the door off, and I was the only one to do it. I inserted my fingers in the crack between the frame and the door and pulled with all my might. The door (fastened not by a hook but, as is often the case in the country, by a mere bit of string) gave at once and swung wide open. There before my eyes, on the wooden seat, in the stench of the latrine, sat Helena. Pale, but alive, she looked up at me in terror and instinctively tugged at her skirt, but despite her best efforts she couldn't even bring it down to the mid-thigh region, and holding on to the hem with both hands, she squeezed her legs tightly together. "For God's sake, get out of here!" she cried in anguish.

"What's the matter?" I shouted at her. "What have you taken?"

"Get out of here! Leave me alone!"

At this point the boy appeared behind my back and Helena cried out, "Get away, Jindra! Get away!" She lifted herself up and reached out for the door, but I stepped in between her and the door, causing her to totter backward and fall back down on the round opening of the seat.

In no time she bounced up again and hurled herself at me in desperation (it could only have been *desperation* that gave her the strength, because she had precious little left to draw on after what she had just been through). She grabbed the lapels of my jacket with both hands and shoved me with all her might; we both ended up barely over the threshold. "You beast, you! You beast!" she screamed (if the frantic squawks of her enfeebled voice could be called a scream), and tried her best to shake me; then all at once she let go and started off across the grass in the direction of the courtyard. Her plan was to run away, but it didn't work: her confused exit from the outhouse had left her no time to adjust her clothes, and her panties (the ones I knew from the day before, the Lastex ones that did double duty as a garter belt) were still wound round her knees and kept her from advancing (her dress was also down, but her silk stockings had bunched up along her calves and their dark top border and the garters attached to them were visible under the skirt); she took a few short steps or rather jumps (she was wearing high heels), but before she had gone even ten feet she fell (fell onto the sunny grass, under the branches of a tree, near a tall, gaudy sunflower); I took her arm and tried to help her up; she tore away from me, and when I bent down over her again, she started flailing wildly and managed to land several blows before I could seize her, pull her up, and using my arms as a straitjacket, pin her to me. "Beast, beast, beast, beast!" she hissed venomously, pummeling me on the back with her free hand; when I said (as delicately as possible), "Calm down, Helena," she spat in my face.

Without relaxing my grip, I said, "I'm not letting you go until you tell me what you took."

"Get away, get away, get away!" she repeated frantically, until suddenly she went quiet, ceased all resistance, and said "Let me go" in so completely different a voice (weak and weary) that I loosened my hold; what I witnessed, to my great horror, was her face convulsed in excruciating exertion, her jaws clamped shut, her eyes staring out into space, and her body bent slightly forward.

"What's wrong?" I asked; she turned without a word and headed back to the outhouse; I'll never forget the way she walked, the slow, jerky steps of her fettered feet; she had only a few yards to cover, but more than once she was forced to stop, and in those intervals I gained some sense (from the way her body cramped) of the battle she was waging with her outraged entrails; finally she reached the outhouse, grabbed hold of the door (which had remained wide open), and pulled it shut behind her.

For a while, I stood rooted to the spot where I had gathered her from the ground, but when a loud plaintive moan arose from the outhouse, I recoiled a step or two. It was then I realized the boy was still there. "You stay where you are," I told him. "I'll go and find a doctor."

I ran into the office; I spotted the phone right away; it was sitting on the nearest desk. I had a harder time finding a phone book; there was none in sight; I tried pulling open the middle drawer of the desk that had the phone on it, but it was locked, as were all the smaller side drawers; the other desk was locked as well. I went next door; the desk there had only one drawer, and though it wasn't locked, there was nothing in it but a few photographs and a paper knife. I didn't know what to do, and I had begun (now that I knew Helena was alive and free from mortal danger) to feel weary myself; after standing a few seconds in the middle of the room staring dumbly at the hatstand (the scrawny metal hatstand with its hands up like a soldier ready to surrender), I opened the cabinet (for want of anything better to do); there on a stack of files was the blue-green telephone directory for Brno and surrounding areas; I took it over to the telephone and looked up the number of the hospital. I had dialed the number and heard the first few rings when the boy burst into the room.

"Don't bother with the phone! It's all over!" he called to me.

I didn't understand.

He came up and tore the receiver from my hand and put it back on the hook. "It's all over, I tell you!"

I asked him to explain what he meant.

"It wasn't poison at all!" he said, going over to the hatstand; he stuck his hand into the pocket of the man's trench coat and came out with a small bottle, which he opened and turned upside down; it was empty.

"You mean that's what she took?" I asked.

He nodded.

"How do you know?"

"She told me."

"Is it yours?"

He nodded. I took it from him. It had "Analgen" written on the label.

"Don't you realize that analgesics can be harmful in large doses like that?" I shouted at him.

"There were no analgesics in it," he said.

"Then what was in it?"

"A laxative," he snapped.

I gave him hell: how dare he make fun of me at a time like this; I had to know what had happened; I wouldn't stand for any more of his insolence; I wanted a straight answer right then and there.

Since I raised my voice, he raised his: "Look, I've told you they were laxatives. Does everybody have to know my guts are fucked up?" And I realized that what I'd taken for a stupid joke was in fact the truth.

Looking at him, at his bright red face, his snub nose (just large enough to accommodate the flock of freckles), I understood exactly what had happened: the aspirin bottle was meant to disguise his ludicrous ailment as much as the jeans and leather jacket were meant to disguise his ludicrous little-boy face; he was ashamed of himself and the endless adolescence he dragged along behind him; I loved him just then: his sense of shame (that adolescent noblesse) had saved Helena's life and spared me years of sleepless nights. I gazed upon his protruding ears with a kind of dazed gratitude. Yes, he had saved Helena's life; but at the price of all but unbearable humiliation; that much was obvious, as obvious as the fact that the humiliation would serve no purpose, have no meaning, prove completely and utterly unjust; it was yet another unrectifiable link in the chain of unrectifiable links; I knew I was guilty and felt an urgent (though vague) need to run to her, run and raise her up out of her humiliation, humble myself, abase myself before her, assume all blame and responsibility for the senselessly cruel incident.

"Why are you staring at me like that?" barked the boy. I walked past him and into the hallway without responding, and turned in the direction of the back door.

"What are you going out there for?" he asked me, grabbing me from behind by the shoulder of my jacket and trying to jerk me back towards him; for a second we looked each other in the eye; then I gripped his wrist and removed his hand from my shoulder. He walked past me and stood in front of the door. I went up to him and was about to push him out of the way when he swung and punched me in the chest.

It was a feeble blow, but he jumped away and then back again in a naïve imitation of a boxer's stance. His features wore a mixture of apprehension and rash courage.

"She doesn't need you for anything!" he yelled at me. I stood my ground. It occurred to me he might be right: there was nothing I could do to rectify the unrectifiable. Seeing me standing there doing nothing to defend myself, he went one step further and yelled, "She can't stand your guts! She doesn't give a shit what happens to you! She told me! She doesn't give a shit!"

Nervous tension lowers a person's resistance not only to tears, but to laughter as well; the literal sense of the boy's last words made the corners of my mouth start twitching. That infuriated him; this time he got me in the teeth, and I just managed to dodge the follow-up. Then once more he jumped away and put up his fists like a boxer, but this time they so covered his face that only his oversized pink ears were visible behind them.

"That's enough," I said. "I'm going now."

"Coward!" he called after me. "Chicken! I know you had a hand in this! I'll get you yet, you bastard!"

I went out into the street. It was empty as only a street can be after a parade or festival; a gentle breeze picked up the dust and whisked it along the flat ground, as devoid of people as my mind was devoid of thoughts. . . .

Not until later did I realize that I still had the empty bottle in my hand; I looked at it; it was all scratched and worn: clearly it had seen long service as camouflage for the boy's laxatives.

The bottle brought to mind two others, the ones containing

Alexej's barbiturates; and they made me realize that the boy had not in fact saved Helena's life: even if there had been analgesics in the bottle, they couldn't have given her more than an upset stomach, especially with the boy and myself so nearby; Helena's despair had settled its accounts with life at a nice safe distance from the threshold of death.

18

She was standing in the kitchen over the stove. Standing with her back to me. As if nothing had happened. "Vladimir?" she replied without turning. "You saw him yourself. Why ask?" "You're lying," I said. "Vladimir went off this morning on the back of young Koutecky's motorcycle. I've just come to tell you I know. I know why you made so much of that silly radio woman. I know why I wasn't allowed to see the robing of the king. I know why the king kept silent even before the Ride began. You planned it all very carefully."

My confidence threw her for a while, but she soon regained her presence of mind and tried to defend herself by launching an offensive. It was an odd attack. Odd because the opponents didn't stand face to face. She had her back to me and her nose in the gurgling soup. She didn't raise her voice. It was almost indifferent. As if to say that the things she told me were things everyone else had known for ages and it was only because I was so thick and had such funny ideas that she had to put it into words for me. If that was what I wanted, fine. Vladimir had never wanted to be king, not from the very start. And Vlasta wasn't a bit surprised. There was a time when the boys put together the whole Ride by themselves. Now umpteen different organizations had a say in the matter, even the Party District Council. People couldn't move a finger on their own anymore. Everything was run from above. The boys used to choose their own king. Vladimir had been recommended to them from above to gratify his father, and they'd all been obliged to go along with it. Vladimir was ashamed of being singled out for his father's sake. Nobody liked people who relied on pull.

"You mean Vladimir is ashamed of me?" "He doesn't want to rely on your pull," she repeated. "Is that why he's so close with the Kouteckys? Those morons? Those petty bourgeois?" I asked. "Exactly," said Vlasta. "Milos isn't allowed to go to the university because of his grandfather. Just because his grandfather owned a construction company. Vladimir can do anything he pleases. And just because you're his father. It's hard on him, can't you see?"

For the first time in my life I lost my temper with her. They'd tricked me. All this time they'd been coolly observing my excitement grow. Watching me make a sentimental fool out of myself. First they tricked me coolly, then they watched me coolly. "Did you really have to trick me like that?"

Vlasta salted her noodles and said I always made things difficult. I lived in another world. I was a dreamer. They didn't want to deprive me of my ideals, but Vladimir was different. He didn't care about my singing and whooping. It bored him, bored him to tears. I'd just have to accept it. Vladimir had a modern outlook. He took after her father. Now, there was a man who knew what progress was. The first in the village to have a tractor. Before the war. Then they took everything away from him. Ever since the fields had gone over to the cooperative they'd yielded only half as much.

"I'm not interested in your fields. What I want to know is where Vladimir went. He went to the motorcycle races in Brno. Admit it."

She stood with her back to me, stirring the noodles as she talked. Vladimir looked just like his grandfather. He had his chin and his eyes. Anyway, Vladimir didn't care about the Ride of the Kings. Yes, if I really wanted to know, he had gone to the races. He was watching the races. What of it? He was more interested in motorcycles than old nags with ribbons over their eyes. Why not? Vladimir was modern, up-to-date.

Motorcycles, guitars, motorcycles, guitars. A stupid, alien world. "And what does it mean to be modern and up-to-date?" I asked.

She stood with her back to me, stirring the noodles, and answered that I wouldn't even let her modernize our flat. The fuss I'd made over a single contemporary floor lamp! I didn't like the modern lamp fixtures either. Everybody thought that floor lamp was beautiful. That was the kind of lamp people were buying nowadays.

"Enough," I told her. But there was no stopping her. She was all wound up. With her back to me. Her small, spiteful, skinny back. That was what got to me the most. That back. That back without eyes. That smug, complacent brick wall of a back. I wanted to shut her up. Turn her around to face me. But I found her so repulsive then I didn't even want to touch her. I decided to make her turn another way. I opened the cabinet and took out a plate. I dropped it. She stopped talking in midsentence. But she didn't turn. Another plate, other plates. She still had her back to me. Hunched forward into herself. I could tell by her back that she was afraid. Yes, she was afraid, but she was even more stubborn. She wouldn't give in. She stopped stirring and stood motionless, gripping the wooden spoon in her hand, hanging on to it as if it could somehow save her. I hated her, and she hated me. She didn't move, and I didn't take my eyes off her. I just kept dropping item after item from the shelves of the cabinet. I hated her, and I hated her whole kitchen. Her modern model kitchen with its modern cabinets, modern plates, and modern glasses.

I didn't feel troubled. I just looked calmly, sadly, almost wearily at the floor full of broken china, of the scattered pots and pans. I had thrown my whole home on the floor. The home I'd loved and looked on as a refuge. The home where I'd borne the tender yoke of the poor man's daughter. The home I'd peopled with folktales, songs, and good spirits. On these very chairs we'd sat and eaten our dinners. Oh, those peaceful family dinners that saw the gullible breadwinner hoodwinked and bamboozled day after day. I picked up one chair after another and broke their legs off. I set them down on the floor next to the pots and the broken china. Then I turned the kitchen table upside down on them. Vlasta was still standing motionless by the stove, her back to me.

I went out of the kitchen and into my room. It had a red globe on the ceiling, a contemporary floor lamp, and an ugly modern couch. My violin lay in its black case on the harmonium. I picked it up. At four o'clock we had a concert in the outdoor restaurant. It was only one. Where could I go?

I heard sobs in the kitchen. Vlasta was crying. Her sobs were heartrending, and somewhere deep inside me I felt a tinge of regret. Why hadn't she started crying ten minutes earlier? Perhaps I could really have brought myself to believe the old poor-man's-daughter illusion again. But it was too late now.

I left the house. The invocations were still floating over the village roofs. We have a needy king, and yet right virtuous. Where could I go? The streets belonged to the Ride of the Kings, the house to Vlasta, the taverns to the drunks. Where did I belong? An abandoned king past his prime. A poor but honest king. A king with no heir. The last king.

Fortunately, there are some fields out beyond the village. A road. And the Morava River ten minutes away. I lay down on the bank. I tucked my violin case under my head. I lay there for a long time. An hour, maybe two. Thinking of how I'd come to the end of the road. From one day to the next, all of a sudden. And here it was. I had no idea what would happen next. I had always lived in two worlds at once. I believed in their mutual harmony. It was a delusion. Now I've been ousted from one of them. The real one. Only the world of make-believe is left to me now. But I can't live in a world that is all make-believe. Even though they're expecting me there. Even though the deserter is calling for me and has a horse ready and a red veil for my face. Yes, now I knew. Now I saw why he forbade me to take off my veil and insisted on telling me everything himself! Finally I understood why the king's face had to be veiled! Not to prevent him from being seen, but to prevent him from seeing!

I couldn't imagine myself getting to my feet and walking. I couldn't imagine myself taking a single step. They were expecting me at four. But I wouldn't have the strength to pick myself up and go there. I liked it here. Here by the river. Where the water flowed serene and from time immemorial. The water flowed serene, and I would lie there serene, lie there for a long, long time.

Then someone called my name. It was Ludvik. I expected another blow. Not that I was afraid. Nothing could have shaken me now.

He sat down beside me and asked whether I was going to the afternoon performance. "Don't tell me you're planning to go," I said. "I am," he said. "Is that what you came for?" "No," he said, "that's not what I came for. But things turn out differently from the way we expect." "Yes," I said, "very differently." "I've been wandering through the fields for an hour now. I had no idea I'd find you here." "I had no idea I'd find *you* here." "I have a favor to ask you," he said, not looking me in the eye. Just like Vlasta. He couldn't look me in the eye. But I didn't mind it in his case. In his case I found it rather comforting. It seemed to me a kind of reserve. A reserve that warmed and consoled me. "I have a favor to ask you," he said. "I was wondering whether you'd let me sit in with the ensemble this afternoon."

19

I still had a few hours before the next bus was due to leave, and driven by the ferment within me, I slipped away from the village and into the fields, trying my best to ban all thoughts of the day from my mind. It wasn't easy: I could feel my lip swelling at the point where the boy's fist had connected with it, and again the shadow of Lucie emerged to remind me that all my attempts to right the wrongs done me had led to my wronging others. I tried to put it all out of my mind: I'd been through it all so many times before I knew it backwards; I tried to make my mind blank, admit only the calls of the riders (now scarcely audible), and let them carry me out of myself, out of my awkward life story, and provide some relief.

Taking the paths that encircle the village, I finally reached the banks of the Morava and set off downstream; on the opposite bank were a few geese in the foreground, a stretch of wooded land in the background, and nothing but fields in between. Then I saw a figure lying in the grass some distance ahead. Moving closer, I realized who it was: he was lying on his back gazing up at the sky, using his violin case for a pillow (the fields were everywhere, flat and distant, as they'd been for centuries, with only the new steel pylons and high-tension wires breaking the pattern). Nothing would have been easier than to pass him by: he was so taken with the sky he didn't notice me. But this time I didn't want to pass him by; it was myself I was trying to avoid, myself and my persistent thoughts; and so I went up to him and called his name. He looked up with eyes that struck me as timid and apprehensive, and I noticed (it was the first time I'd seen him at close range for a number of years) that of the thick hair which had once added an inch or two to his already lofty stature only a sparse fringe remained: the crown of his head was bare under a few pitiful strands; the missing hair reminded me of the long years since I'd seen him, and suddenly I was sorry I had gone so long without making contact, keeping out of his way (from the distance, scarcely audible, came the calls of the riders), and I felt a rush of guilty love for him. Lying there before me, resting on one elbow, he was big and clumsy, while his violin case was small and black, like a baby's coffin. I knew that his ensemble (once *my* ensemble too) would be performing later in the afternoon, and I asked if I might join them.

I made the request before thinking it through (words seemed to precede thought); but as rash as it was, it was in complete accord with the way I felt; I was, at the moment, suffused with a sorrowful feeling of love for a world left behind years before, a distant, ancient world where riders circle the village with their masked king, where people wear pleated white skirts and sing in the streets, a world that merges for me with images of my home, my mother (my kidnapped mother), and my youth; all day that love had been silently growing in me, and now it had burst out, almost in tears; I loved that lost world and begged it to offer me sanctuary.

But how and by what right? Hadn't I turned away from Jaroslav only the day before yesterday because in my mind he incarnated that hateful brand of folk music? Hadn't I that very morning approached the folk festival with distaste? What suddenly tumbled the barriers that for fifteen years had kept me from enjoying the memories of my youth in the cimbalom ensemble, from making frequent and happy trips home? Could it be the fact that several hours earlier Zemanek had sneered at the Ride of the Kings? Could *he* have been the one who instilled in me a distaste for the folk song and now cleansed me of it? Was I really just the needle of a compass, and he the arrow? Was I really so ignominiously dependent on him? No, it was not only Zemanek's mockery that enabled me to regain my love for the world of folk costumes, songs, and cimbalom ensembles; the main reason I could love it again was that that morning I had (unexpectedly) found it in ruins; and not only in ruins, but *abandoned;* abandoned by bombast and hullabaloo, abandoned by political propaganda and social utopias, abandoned by the swarms of cultural officials and the feigned enthusiasm of my contemporaries, abandoned (even) by Zemanek; that state of abandonment had purified it; it had cleansed it as a body about to expire is cleansed; it had luminated it with an irresistible *final beauty;* that state of abandonment had given it back to me.

The performance was scheduled to take place in the same open-air restaurant where not long before I'd had lunch and read Helena's note; by the time Jaroslav and I arrived, there were a few elderly people seated at tables (patiently waiting for the music to begin) and a more or less equal number of drunks staggering from table to table; several chairs had been set out under the spreading linden tree at the back, and a bass still shrouded in gray canvas rested against its trunk; a man in a white pleated shirt was quietly running the mallets over the strings of the open cimbalom; the other musicians stood nearby, and Jaroslav introduced them all to me: the second fiddle was a doctor at the local hospital; the bass was an inspector of cultural affairs for the District Council; the clarinet (who agreed to lend me his instrument and alternate with me) was a schoolteacher; the cimbalom was an economic planner at the factory. He was the only one I remembered: apart from him and Jaroslav, it was an entirely new group. Jaroslav introduced me to the audience with great ceremony as an old veteran of the ensemble, one of its founding members, and today's clarinet of honor, whereupon we took our seats under the tree and began to play.

Many years had passed since I'd held a clarinet in my hands, but the song we started out with was an old favorite of mine, and I soon got over my initial stage fright, especially after the others voiced their approval and refused to believe I hadn't played in so long; then the waiter (the same one I'd paid in such a rush a few hours before) pulled up a small table, set it under the branches of our tree, and put a demijohn of wine and six glasses out for us; every now and then we would have a sip. After a few songs I nodded to the teacher, who took back his clarinet and told me again how well he thought I played; I was delighted; leaning up against the trunk of the tree and watching the ensemble carry on, I felt a long-forgotten sensation of companionship come over me, and I was grateful for its soothing presence at the end of this grim day. And suddenly Lucie appeared before my eyes, and I decided I finally knew why she'd turned up first at the barbershop and then in Kostka's story, his amalgam of truth and legend: it was because she wanted to tell me that her fate (the fate of a rape victim) was very much like mine; that even though we'd failed to understand each other and were lost for each other, our life stories were twinned, intertwined, ran parallel, because they were both *stories of devastation;* much as Lucie was devastated by physical love and therefore deprived of life's most elemental value, so I was robbed of values I had originally meant to live by, values pure and innocent in origin; yes, innocent: physical love, devastating though it may have been in Lucie's case, is still innocent, just as the songs of my region and the ensemble playing them are innocent, and the region itself, much as I'd grown to hate it, and Fucik, whose portrait I couldn't stomach, and the word "comrade," though I always heard a threat in it, and the word "future," and many other words. The blame lay elsewhere and was so great that its shadow had fallen over a vast area, over the world of innocent things (and words) and was devastating them. We lived, Lucie and I, in a world of devastation; and because we lacked the ability to commiserate with the things thus devastated, we turned our backs on them, offending both them and ourselves in the process. Lucie, my Lucie, so much and poorly loved, is that what you have come for after all these years? To plead on behalf of a devastated world?

When the song came to an end, the teacher handed me his clarinet, saying that he was done for the day, that I played better than he did and I deserved to play as much as possible anyway, since who knew when I'd be back. Catching Jaroslav's eye, I said I'd be very glad for a chance to come back and see them soon. Jaroslav asked me whether I really meant it. Absolutely, I said, and we struck up the next song. Jaroslav had long since abandoned his chair and, poised with his head back and his violin—against all the rules—leaning far down on his chest, walked up and down as he played; the second fiddle and I also stood up from time to time, particularly when we needed more space for our flights of improvisation. During those moments of high adventure, when our inventiveness, precision, and feeling for the group were put to the test, Jaroslav became the heart and soul of us all, and I was filled with admiration for the dazzling musician concealed within his giant-like exterior. Jaroslav too (more than anyone, actually) represented the devastated values of my life; he had been taken from me, and I (to my great detriment and disgrace) had let him go, my most faithful, most guileless, most innocent friend.

Meanwhile, the audience had undergone a gradual metamorphosis: the half-empty tables of people following our performance with enthusiasm from the start had been taken over in large part by a crowd of young people (perhaps from the village, more likely from the town) who ordered beer and wine (at the top of their voices) and were soon (as soon as the alcohol had time to take effect) indulging their uncontrollable need to be seen, heard, recognized. As a result, the atmosphere had changed completely, grown noisier and more nervous (the boys staggered from table to table, yelling to one another and to their girls); I suddenly realized that instead of concentrating on the music I was keeping one eye on the tables and observing those adolescent faces with open hostility. Watching those long-haired small fry spitting out saliva and words indiscriminately and with great ostentation, I felt a sudden resurgence of my old hatred for that last stronghold of immaturity, and I saw myself surrounded by a company of third-rate actors wearing masks of mindless virility and arrogant brutishness; I found little comfort in the thought that the masks hid other (more human) faces, since the real horror of it all lay in the fact that the masked faces were so fiercely devoted to the inhumanity and vulgarity of the masks.

Evidently Jaroslav shared my sentiments, because suddenly he lowered his violin and said he had no desire to play for the new audience. He suggested we leave, take a path through the fields, the way we used to do long ago; it was a nice day, the sun would be setting soon, but the evening would be warm and the stars out, we could head for a wild rose bush somewhere and play just for ourselves, for our own enjoyment, the way we used to do; we'd fallen into the habit (the stupid habit) of playing exclusively on prearranged occasions, and he'd had about all of that he was going to take.

At first everyone agreed and seemed almost relieved: they too felt that their passion for folk music deserved a more intimate atmosphere. But then the bass (the inspector of cultural affairs) pointed out that we had promised to play until nine; the Comrades from the District Council were counting on us, the manager of the restaurant too; that was how things had been planned; we had to fulfill our obligation; otherwise, the whole organization of the festival would fall apart; we could play out in the fields some other time.

Just then the lights, attached to long wires stretching from tree to tree, all came on at once; since it was not yet dark and barely even dusk, they spread no light and simply hung there in the graying arena like large frozen teardrops, whitish teardrops that refused to be brushed away, yet did not fall; they brought with them a sudden inexplicable melancholy that no one seemed able to withstand. Again Jaroslav asked us (almost begged us) not to go on, to wander off into the fields to a wild rose bush and play for the joy of it, but suddenly he made a gesture of resignation, pressed the violin back to his chest, and started playing.

This time we didn't let ourselves be distracted by the audience and played with much greater concentration: the more apathetic and rude the surroundings became, the more we felt like an abandoned island, the more we turned in towards one another, until in the end we managed to forget what was going on around us and create a magic circle of music; it was like being walled off from the drunks in a glass cabin at the bottom of the sea.

"If mountains were paper and water ink, if stars were scribes and the whole world helped them to think, they could not draft my love's true testament," sang Jaroslav without removing the violin from his chest, and I felt happy inside the songs (inside the glass cabin of the songs), where sorrow wasn't playful, laughter wasn't mocking, love wasn't laughable, and hate wasn't shy, where people love with all their body and soul (yes, Lucie, body and soul), where people dance for joy and leap into the Danube in despair, where love is still love, pain pain, and values free from devastation; I felt *at home* within these songs, I felt I derived from them, their world had marked me for good, it was my home, and if I had betrayed it, I had only made it *all the more* my own thereby (because what voice is more plaintive than the voice of the home we have wronged?); yet I was equally aware that my home was not of this world (though what kind of home was it if it wasn't of this world?), that everything we sang and played was only a memory, a monument, a re-creation in images of something that no longer was, and I felt the firm ground of my homeland sinking under my feet, felt myself falling, clarinet in hand, falling into the depths of years and centuries past, fathomless depths (where love is love and pain pain), and I said to myself in amazement that my only real home was this descent, this searching, eager fall, and I gave myself up to it, savoring the sensuous vertigo.

When I looked over at Jaroslav to see whether I was alone in my exaltation, I noticed (his face was lit by a lantern hanging from the linden tree) that he was very pale; I noticed he'd stopped singing along with himself and his lips were tightly clenched; his anxious eyes had taken on a look of fear; he had started playing wrong notes; his violin hand was slowly slipping downward. Suddenly he stopped playing and fell back in his chair. "What's the matter?" I asked, kneeling down beside him; the sweat streamed down his face, and he clutched his left arm up near the shoulder. "The pain is terrible," he said. The others were still caught up in the spell of the music, and the cimbalom instinctively took advantage of the fact that the clarinet and first fiddle had dropped out to take off on his own, accompanied only by second fiddle and bass. But I immediately went up to the second fiddle (remembering that Jaroslav had introduced him to me as a doctor) and called him over to Jaroslav. While the cimbalom and bass played on, the second fiddle took Jaroslav's left wrist and held it for what seemed like an eternity; then he raised his eyelids and looked into his eyes; finally he touched his beaded forehead. "Is it your heart?" he asked. "Arm and heart both," said Jaroslav; he was green. By this time the bass had looked over, propped his bass against the tree, and come up to us, so the cimbalom was completely on his own now, entirely unaware of what was going on, and thoroughly enjoying his solo. "I'm going to phone the hospital," said the second fiddle. "What is it?" I asked quietly. "Pulse practically nonexistent, sweat ice-cold. A coronary if there ever was one." "Oh, my God!" I said. "Don't worry, he'll get over it," he said, and hurried off into the building, pushing his way through the people too drunk to notice that the music had stopped, people too intent on themselves, their beer, their blather, and their abuse, which in the far corner of the garden had ended in a brawl.

Finally the cimbalom stopped playing, and we all stood in a circle around Jaroslav, who looked up at me and said it had all happened because we'd stayed, he hadn't wanted to stay, he'd wanted to go out in the fields, especially now that I'd come, especially now that I'd come back, how beautiful it would have sounded under the stars. "Quiet now," I told him. "What you need now is peace and quiet." And what I said to myself was that although he would probably get over it, as the second fiddle had predicted, he would lead a very different life, a life without passionate devotion, without jam sessions, a life under the watchful eye of death, and I was struck by the thought that a person's destiny often ends before his death and Jaroslav's destiny had come to an end. Overwhelmed with grief, I stroked his bald head and the long strands of hair mournfully trying to cover it, and I realized with a shock that my journey home, undertaken to wreak vengeance on my enemy Zemanek, was ending with my stricken friend Jaroslav (yes, at that moment I could picture myself holding him in my arms, holding him and carrying him, carrying him, big and heavy as he was, carrying my own obscure guilt; I could picture myself carrying him through the indifferent mob, weeping as I went).

We had stood there with him for about ten minutes when the

second fiddle reappeared and signaled us to help him to his feet, and supporting him under the arms, we led him through the din of the drunken adolescents and out into the street, where a shiny white ambulance with its headlights on stood waiting.

Completed December 5, 1965

FOR THE BEST IN PAPERBACKS, LOOK FOR THE

In every corner of the world, on every subject under the sun, Penguin represents quality and variety – the very best in publishing today.

For complete information about books available from Penguin – including Pelicans, Puffins, Peregrines and Penguin Classics – and how to order them, write to us at the appropriate address below. Please note that for copyright reasons the selection of books varies from country to country.

In the United Kingdom: Please write to *Dept E.P., Penguin Books Ltd, Harmondsworth, Middlesex, UB7 0DA*

If you have any difficulty in obtaining a title, please send your order with the correct money, plus ten per cent for postage and packaging, to *PO Box No 11, West Drayton, Middlesex*

In the United States: Please write to *Dept BA, Penguin, 299 Murray Hill Parkway, East Rutherford, New Jersey 07073*

In Canada: Please write to *Penguin Books Canada Ltd, 2801 John Street, Markham, Ontario L3R 1B4*

In Australia: Please write to the *Marketing Department, Penguin Books Australia Ltd, P.O. Box 257, Ringwood, Victoria 3134*

In New Zealand: Please write to the *Marketing Department, Penguin Books (NZ) Ltd, Private Bag, Takapuna, Auckland 9*

In India: Please write to *Penguin Overseas Ltd, 706 Eros Apartments, 56 Nehru Place, New Delhi, 110019*

In Holland: Please write to *Penguin Books Nederland B.V., Postbus 195, NL–1380AD Weesp, Netherlands*

In Germany: Please write to *Penguin Books Ltd, Friedrichstrasse 10–12, D–6000 Frankfurt Main 1, Federal Republic of Germany*

In Spain: Please write to *Longman Penguin España, Calle San Nicolas 15, E–28013 Madrid, Spain*

In France: Please write to *Penguin Books Ltd, 39 Rue de Montmorency, F-75003, Paris, France*

In Japan: Please write to *Longman Penguin Japan Co Ltd, Yamaguchi Building, 2–12–9 Kanda Jimbocho, Chiyoda-Ku, Tokyo 101, Japan*

Cat's Grin François Maspero

'Reflects in some measure the experience of every French person . . . evacuees, peasants, Resistance fighters, *collabos* . . . Maspero's painfully truthful book helps to ensure that it never seems commonplace' – *Literary Review*

The Moronic Inferno Martin Amis

'This is really good reading and sharp, crackling writing. Amis has a beguiling mixture of confidence and courtesy, and most of his literary judgements – often twinned with interviews – seem sturdy, even when caustic, without being bitchy for the hell of it' – *Guardian*

In Custody Anita Desai

Deven, a lecturer in a small town in Northern India, is resigned to a life of mediocrity and empty dreams. When asked to interview the greatest poet of Delhi, Deven discovers a new kind of dignity, both for himself and his dreams.

Parallel Lives Phyllis Rose

In this study of five famous Victorian marriages, including that of John Ruskin and Effie Gray, Phyllis Rose probes our inherited myths and assumptions to make us look again at what we expect from our marriages.

Lamb Bernard MacLaverty

In the Borstal run by Brother Benedict, boys are taught a little of God and a lot of fear. Michael Lamb, one of the brothers, runs away and takes a small boy with him. As the outside world closes in around them, Michael is forced to an uncompromising solution.

FOR THE BEST IN PAPERBACKS, LOOK FOR THE 🐧

A SELECTION OF FICTION AND NON-FICTION

Social Disease   Paul Rudnick

Take a trip (preferably by cab) to Manhattan's most exclusive nightclub – the fabulous Club de. Here are the darlings of the ultra-*outré* New York – a snorting, 'snow'-gilded world of outrage, sex and sleepless nights. 'The satirical richness of *Social Disease* has the snap of a bullwhip' – *Washington Post*

Book of Laughter and Forgetting   Milan Kundera

'A whirling dance of a book . . . a masterpiece full of angels, terror, ostriches and love . . . No question about it. The most important novel published in Britain this year' – Salman Rushdie in the *Sunday Times*

Something I've Been Meaning to Tell You   Alice Munro

Thirteen brilliant and moving stories about women, men and love in its many disguises – pleasure, overwhelming gratitude, pain, jealousy and betrayal. The comedy is deft, agonizing and utterly delightful.

A Voice Through a Cloud   Denton Welch

After sustaining a severe injury in an accident, Denton Welch wrote this moving account of his passage through a nightmare world. He vividly recreates the pain and desolation of illness and tells of his growing desire to live. 'It is, without doubt, a work of genius' – John Betjeman

In the Heart of the Country   J. M. Coetzee

In a web of reciprocal oppression in colonial South Africa, a white sheep farmer makes a bid for salvation in the arms of a black concubine, while his embittered daughter dreams of and executes a bloody revenge. Or does she?

Hugging the Shore   John Updike

A collection of criticism, taken from eight years of reviewing, where John Updike also indulges his imagination in imaginary interviews, short fiction, humorous pieces and essays.

The Rebel Angels   Robertson Davies

A glittering extravaganza of wit, scatology, saturnalia, mysticism and erudite vaudeville. 'He's the kind of writer who makes you want to nag your friends until they read him so that they can share the pleasure' – *Observer*. 'His novels will be recognized with the very best works of this century' – J. K. Galbraith in *The New York Times Book Review*

Still Life   A. S. Byatt

In this sequel to her much praised *The Virgin in the Garden*, A. S. Byatt illuminates the inevitable conflicts between ambition and domesticity, confinement and self-fulfilment while providing an incisive observation of cultural life in England during the 1950s. 'Affords enormous and continuous pleasure' – Anita Brookner in the *Standard*

Heartbreak Hotel   Gabrielle Burton

'If *Heartbreak Hotel* doesn't make you laugh, perhaps you are no longer breathing. Check all vital signs of life, and read this book!' – Rita Mae Brown. 'A novel to take us into the next century, heads high and flags flying' – Fay Weldon

August in July   Carlo Gébler

On the eve of the Royal Wedding, as the nation prepares for celebration, August Slemic's world prepares to fall apart. 'There is no question but that he must now be considered a novelist of major importance' – *Daily Telegraph*. 'A meticulous study, done with great sympathy . . . a thoroughly honest and loving book' – *Financial Times*

The News from Ireland   William Trevor

'An ability to enchant as much as chill has made Trevor unquestionably one of our greatest short-story writers' – *The Times*. 'A masterly collection' – *Daily Telegraph*. 'Extremely impressive . . . of his stature as a writer there can be no question' – *New Statesman*

The Book of Laughter and Forgetting

'His marvellous novel mingles a hedonist's love of eroticism, fantasy and fun with knife-sharp political satire (it recounts, for example, the case of a Communist leader who is so thoroughly erased from history that nothing is left of him but his hat). A masterpiece, full of angels, terror, ostriches and love' – Salman Rushdie

Laughable Loves

These are stories about the sport of love – Don Juanism, ageing, male and female power, and seductions undertaken for all kinds of intriguing motives. Master of fiction's most graceful illusions and surprises, Milan Kundera has been acclaimed by figures as diverse as Jean-Paul Sartre and Philip Roth and these stories have been described thus, 'Kundera's stories are dances ... experienced by Chekhov ... X-rayed by Freud.'

The Farewell Party

A telephone call announcing an unwanted pregnancy sends Klima, jazz trumpeter from Prague, back to the fertility spa where he had spent a night with a pretty nurse named Ruzena. Kundera's novel opens up a brilliant exposé of the illusions and ambiguities by which we live.

Life is Elsewhere

Winner of the Medicis Award in France for best foreign novel of the year.

A brilliant, unsparing and highly comic novel that is a portrait of the self-deluded artist defining himself.